Ocilentra

and the adventure some children had there

by Amitabho Chattopadhyay

Book One
Central Aimela

Translator's Note

Aposiopesis is indicated throughout with the em-dash (—) rather than the ellipsis.

All Angzhwen and Angzhwen-like sounds are written according to Angzhwen standard notation. Irregular spellings are preserved.

All other narrator-comprehensible languages are written in English. In the Angzhweprenzh languages, a semantic distinction between abstract/animate and concrete/inanimate nouns exists between the words cognate to the English 'amongst' and 'among'. This is observed as a matter of course.

All incomprehensible languages and onomatopoeia are written phonetically.

All majuscule-initial compass points are Imperial; all minuscule are scientific.

All unspecified masculine pronouns are gender-neutral.

*For travel information,
navigational aids
and other opportunities:
http://www.ocilentra.com*

uls mousasitrés tombt com ilsyèt cupé
plus ràpid qu'al-eau boié
—main't trop couré, pas co'qu'ilson dité—
et aš-šhams yalmt sur uls flouts dispré
ses talyats tené pàr uls sablés glacés
en't'al-tenoie me tenant et révirant

The shores come down as if cut
quicker than the water boils
(too far, now, not as they said)
and the sun shines over the lost waves
its rays caught by the glass sands
as he catches me and takes me home.

— Jean-Paul bin Félicien al-Montpelier aš-Šhahiri,
"Al-youm que j'iét m'coušé trop tard",
97th Archive, datum 93a

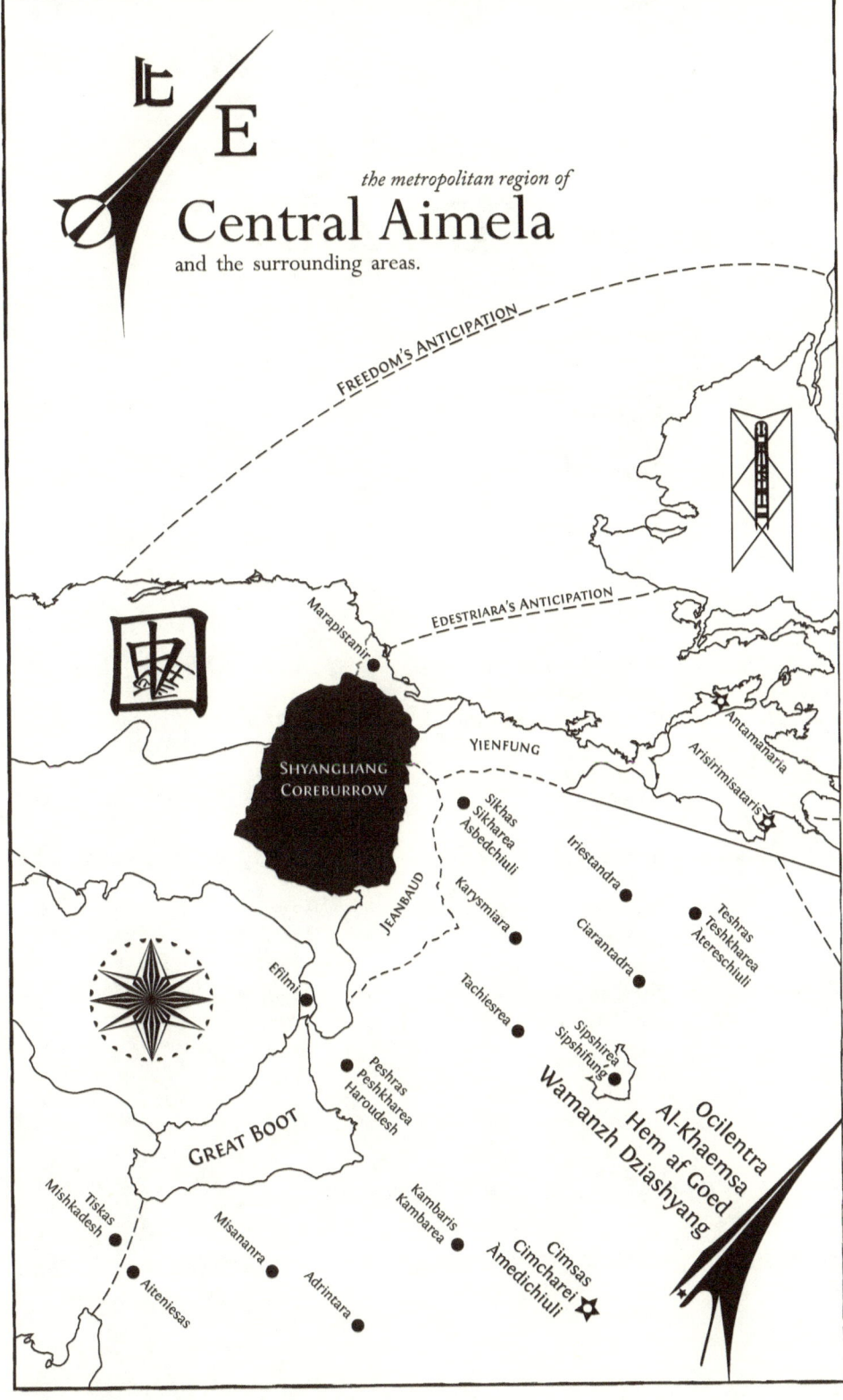

E

the metropolitan region of
Central Aimela
and the surrounding areas.

FREEDOM'S ANTICIPATION

EDESTRIARA'S ANTICIPATION

Marapistanir

YIENFUNG

Antamanaria

Arisirimisataris

SHYANGLIANG
COREBURROW

Sikhas
Sikharea
Asbedchiuli

Iriestandra

JEANBAUD

Karysmiara

Ciarantadra

Teshras
Teshkharea
Atereschiuli

Efilmi

Tachiesrea

Sipshirea
Sipshifung

Peshras
Peshkharea
Haroudesh

Ocilentra
Al-Khaemsa
Hem af Goed
Wamanzh Dziashyang

GREAT BOOT

Tiskas
Mishkadesh

Misananra

Kambaris
Kambarea

Cimsas
Cimcharei
Amedichiuli

Aiteniesas

Adrintara

Table of Contents

I have often been asked why it is that we can be immune to the hottest flames, that we can bring men to His gates with a single pull, that we can save men, in that morbid competition, from His gracious arms with nary a thought and bring him back to us with a motion just as simple and yet fail to refine the simplest elements without labour and tenacity; "why," they ask, "can we not simply pull aluminum from bauxite as we pull tumours from the body?"

Those of my students who ask this fail to understand the intimacy of the Tower He has put into our hands to our very existence; they fail to understand the intricacies of the molecules and chemicals we must dissect to yield our product, and the adaptation the Tower has to the composition of ourselves; they fail to realise the omnibenevolence and the grand complexity of His creation.

Indeed, they often fail the first semester.

—Kharbalis Sesirtkhari ar-Mirali
Introduction to Elemental Chemistry, 7th Edition
Septimus 3897

CIMCHAREL.

0
Ocilæntyr
to head west

It is the sixth day of the sixth month.

The monthly breaking of the Glass Sea—*Shenwyzhćyn*, in Angzhwen, *the twilight of dawn*, though generally only scientists, men with seven tongues and pedants like me take the time to call it anything other than the Breaking—is underway. I'd say that it is one of the worst possible times to be outside of a barriered settlement, but that might unfairly imply that there ever was a good time.

Some, of course, may ask: is there any difference between being burnt or frozen or crushed and then having your remains frozen and later burnt to glass if in the end you're just as dead?

Of course there is. Keeping a little instrument around your neck and singing the same mechanical prayer for eight hours straight and putting your heart into it and hoping you don't misconjugate your polite request because if you do you will die and be crushed into the sand and have whatever bits of you that are left burnt and baked into the Glass Sea and take on the illustrious career path of killing people just as unfortunate or stupid as you—that's not difficult.

It's just tedious.

What's *difficult* is estimating the velocity of each and every block of cold glass, desperately making minute adjustments in your speech to deflect fragments coming at you at speeds from ten to a hundred, hoping you don't mispronounce the tiniest decimal and make your barrier confuse your arm for glass and deflect it off your torso. It requires a quick mind; a linguist's, a physicist's, a musician's.

I somehow doubt that the person laid out before me upon the altar is any one of those. I'm not even entirely sure if he's a man or a woman. A lesser surgeon might mistake some of the particularly ferocious scars for cuts, but the glass shards and swollen bruises between his semi-shattered ribs—some protruding a little from the surface of his skin like sharp joints—are certainly very distinct from the positively *massive* cutting scars over his chest. He's not bleeding too terribly at the moment—not on the outside—so I have a fair idea of what to fix.

As far as I can tell, he has three very big problems best expressed with several moderately large words: hypothermia, massive blunt trauma and chronic hypoencephalopathy. I can treat two of those; the one I can't has quite unfortunately spread to the rather raggedy-looking boy sitting on the edge of a pew, looking carefully at me as his hands shake.

I quickly stabilise his spine and airway, humming a quick one-way membrane to keep the air in. He's still breathing; not bad. I suppose preservation's done *some* good for him—I don't suppose a non-Aimelan would still be alive.

Under his watchful gaze, I begin to work; a few sweet notes come from the miniature instrument as I hum, twanging the strings instinctively with my left as my right goes over his chest. I don't really need it—I've been studying Angzhwen for so long that it doesn't even feel like I'm trying to speak another language—but for some strange reason I don't want to calculate the latitude and longitude of each spot my hand hovers over.

A white series of classical-script letters and numbers and figures appear above my hand in a subjective display, indicating the extent of my newfound patient's internal haemorrhaging; I study them closely, and blink a bit to ensure that I'm not simply getting too tired to read.

Ugh.

At least the hypothermia's stopped him from being intraexsanguinated outright.

I grab a scalpel from under the altar—I'm personally surprised the wood he's over's not yet gone mushy from the three years' worth of blood it's been covered in—and sterilise it with a sharp twang and word, putting it aside as I quickly begin to chant a membrane-built drip-bag. The thick, ephemeral webbing forms as it should just a little from my hand, sagging the slightest bit; I'll reinforce it later.

I whisper a quick melody, letting the water flow from the tips of my perfectly sterile fingers into it; once the thing is filled, I take a very carefully-calculated amount of salt, throw it into the membrane and force it to dissolve.

As I recheck its salinity, I hear the boy's voice behind me. "He gonna live?"

I don't bother turning to face him as I seal the top of the back and put it aside for later. "Not for long."

"You're a little, uh, young to be doing this kinda thing, right?" He scratches his neck as he speaks in his immigrant-tinged Uytrimelan. "I, uh, got to you because the guys said you're, uh, the go-to guy, uh, girl for this sorta thing." I get ready to make an incision, rubbing the area gently with some antiseptic solution. He seems Aimelan, but it seems a fair precaution.

"You're a little, er, young to be senile. Yes, I fix people like you up—" I interrupt myself to sing out a somewhat complex series of words; a slightly hazy sort of shape resolves into grey above his chest, tightening quickly into the bright white of a puncture wound. "—so I can learn to help people that matter."

My words are consciously venomous, certainly, but being woken up in the middle of the night to help someone this mind-bogglingly stupid survive what he shouldn't hasn't exactly improved my bedside manner.

"You're not what I, uh, expected?"

I shake my head and ignore him as I stabilise his friend's chest, retrieving the scalpel and making my incision with a series of quick saws. There's really not much point in arguing, and a single pause in the oration at this point could be death.

I pull the flaps aside, exposing his viscera; the subjective obviates the need to mop up the blood this produces, but I don't need it to see a fragment of a rib curving acutely down from the sternum, going right into the wound.

I've seen far worse, but the fact that this one's still alive makes me wonder.

I begin to grab bodily onto the offending object, leaving behind freshly-formed myocyte tissue as I do; the entire fragment emerges with a distinct *pop*, a bit of blood spraying out onto my face, and I bring my arm over to soak up the bit over my eye as I force the membrane shut with the other.

Sighing, I set the broken rib up where it ought to be, aligning it as carefully as I can before forcing the cancellous bone to rebind with its origin. The syllables remain distinct even as I merge their functions; after all, a little confusion between *by* and *py* and I've got a few shreds of a lung dangling from the bone.

That sounds like a joke up to the point where you've actually managed to blow a lung; the fleshcrawlers had a field day.

I'm just about finished as a voice resounds through the hall.

"Holy *shit*."

I look back to the boy, whose mouth is conspicuously shut and whose eyes are looking at my patient.

That's when I realise that the voice I heard is decidedly more feminine than I know his to be. I turn around rather quickly to see a very much awake patient with mouth-shredded trails of membrane semi-floating alongside his mouth, some twisted kind of half-preservation evidently keeping him from screaming.

"Did you just pull some rib out of my lung? That's *hardcore*."

I look into the patient's open eyes and at his blood-stained teeth, whereupon I fail to hesitate in jabbing the tip of my pinkie finger right up against his left nostril, singing up as much seven-syllable anaesthetic gas as I can; the song is likely one of the few frantic ones I've ever played, though I suppose to an outside eye I might look like some kind of nose-strumming professional.

He looks at me for a second, as if in disappointment, before his head falls to his side and he goes unconscious once again.

"Mad little thing," I whisper under my breath, breathing deeply and spitting out the blood that's sprayed into my mouth onto the church floor as I push his skin together, rebinding it with the slightest trace of nerve before turning to the boy; he looks a lot less shocked than he ought to be. "Is he—or she—?"

I don't really know how to finish my sentence.

His eyes seem to widen as I gender my pronoun. "He's, uh, a he. He's really good at getting beat up." He looks down at the floor between his swinging legs. "*Really* doesn't like it when guys call him a girl."

"For the Tower's sake," I say, my breath rather unstable, "he woke up with a rebound lung and complimented me. That's *not possible*. He shouldn't be able to breathe, much less speak."

Assuming he's not an administrator, of course—the likelihood of *that* I can probably count in nullary.

"It's—just what he does."

"Have you had a wound rebound before?" I say, reaching up over to the patient's mutilated chest as I try to guess where his nipple is—it should bother me that I can't even see the sign of an areola past the scarring, almost as if he's had a crude mastectomy—and retrieving a fresh steel angiocatheter, sterilising it as quickly as I can.

He leans back and rolls his eyes. "Uh, yeah. Everybody has."

"A swift breath should have left his lungs burst. How could he possibly have started *talking*?" I shake my head as I force the sharp thing rather satisfyingly into the gap between the first and second ribs, binding a thick, dense web of membrane right over it and unravelling it into a rapidly-filling vacuum.

"Well," he says, shrugging as he sits back, "it's just what he does."

I wait until every bit of the fluid is drained into the web, reinforcing the membrane with an equally outwards-rephrasing barrier as much as I can without turning it rigid—a Khamisret-Aparkisrea field wouldn't be disastrous, but it would be counterproductive—and pinching it, rebinding the wound as I pull the metal thing out and pinch tight around the membrane's base, separating it and immediately tossing it and its contents into the waste-bucket underneath the tabernacle; the blob's surface fractures rather messily, and I let myself rub my forehead in exasperation.

I look down at my hands—covered in enough blood to perform a transfusion—right before I unconsciously use one of them to wipe a dripping bit of the semi-congealed fluid from my brow.

Wonderful. That's another minute in the shower.

As I fetch a cloth to try and wipe at the mess, I hear the footsteps from the stairwell. "Ashrea? Saving a life?"

I glance at the semi-cadaver on the altar and then look up to see the Abbess' somewhat imposing form coming down the stairs. "That depends on your definition of 'saving'. He woke up and talked to me with a freshly rebound lung."

She shakes her head slightly and descends fully, coming up to me and looking down at him, then towards the pews. "Come back tomorrow," she says, flicking her wrist a bit; the child promptly gets up and walks off without a word, turning then back to me. "Why didn't you let the hospital do it?"

"The hospital would've let him die." I'm not entirely sure now that he would have, of course, but believing my own eyes isn't something I'm now particularly inclined to do. "He doesn't have a permit. I'm doing it for the practice."

"You've dealt with hypothermia and internal injury a thousand times over."

"I've never dealt with someone stupid enough to go out during Shenwyzhćhyn before." We both know that's a lie, but she doesn't question my motivations for subverting natural selection and so I don't question her moral justifications for tax evasion.

She coughs politely. "No one else would go to the Mendicant's Alley to work for more than a few days, Ashrea. Three years, yes? A residency. You care for them, don't you?"

"Of course I care for them," I say, leaning back on the wooden altar. I'll have to clean it later, before communion. The metabolic acidosis wouldn't be pretty if I were to rush him. "That doesn't mean I have to like them."

"There was a time when I belittled my patients so as to prevent myself from getting involved in their ills as well. I grew up." She fetches a waterskin from the cabinet and quickly fills it with warm water, the fluid streaming from her hands as she glances over my work; I tactfully ignore her as she continues speaking. "You should sleep. I can take it from here."

I check his pulse. Stable.

"I can keep awake long enough, Mother."

"You're not qualified to make that promise, dear."

I let out a rather pompous 'ha'. "I don't make promises. I make statements of fact."

"You're practising to be a surgeon, Ashrea, not a relay." She has on her face a little good-natured smirk. "You're not qualified to make statements of fact."

"If I were to cut the artery of a living human being, he would bleed." I shrug. "A statement of fact I'm qualified to make. Is there a problem?"

She taps at the space above her wrist and puts her hand over his chest, whereupon the incision closes itself without much fuss. "There are bigger things to worry about. You've got the fundraiser tomorrow, remember?"

"Oh," I say, and the syllable carries a certain sense of dread. "I should probably say thanks, shouldn't I?"

"There's no need," she says, laughing. "It's our job. Peshrea will clean the altar—I'll rebind what you've missed. Go get yourself washed. The white dress is waiting in your room."

I nod. "Thank you for everything anyway."

"Oh," she says, "And your old friend Missy's ready for you. Third sessile."

My cheeks instantly flush, and I pretend not to hear.

She giggles like a child. "May the Tower hear your songs."

"And may it return your melody." She knows that I've discarded the idea, of course, that the Tower is conscious, but it's just a thing to be said.

"And may it bring you life." Life in the form of a tracheostomy, maybe.

"And your crops to fruition." I begin to walk up the steps to the dormitories; hopefully no one will see my blood-covered form on the way to the showers.

"Good night, child." She whispers something quickly; water begins to pour from the tips of her fingers and begins rinsing the wet blood off the boy's body.

"Good night, Mother."

CIMCHAREI

1
Cymćareyr
to build a flowing valley

It's impossible to get near the Tower.

I know that sounds like an invitation, and quite a few people have a similar failure to grasp the meaning of that sentence's key word. What actually happens to them is anybody's guess. I personally guess that as one approaches the tower proper, the force behind the reactive sandstorms—like tidal forces near a singularity—turn strong enough to rip even atoms apart. Some very intelligent men argue that they've simply found something worth staying for, every time someone's tried; I'd disagree, but I'm not a psychologist.

What matters, though, is that no expedition across Shenzhpulra—it's a bit funny that we call it *the bridge of light*, considering its rather noir complexion—has ever benefited anyone but the doctors who had the authority to get paid for declaring its participants dead in absentia.

I wouldn't mind being benefited, myself.

The Administrative Tower of Cimsas is usually impossible to get close to as well, despite its convenient location at the end of Highpoint Boulevard, but in this case there's no real debate over *what* causes the ripping apart. Mounted sessile-arms may not be quite as destructive as some of the crude functional imitations we've built, but I can't imagine how that would matter when there's a thousand more of them.

"Pardon me?"

I look up from my little bit of thinking to see a white-robed administrator speaking to me in Aimelari, and my eyes widen. "Oh! I'm sorry," I begin, making sure to conjugate my verbs properly.

Administrators seem to be in a perpetual competition for eccentricity, and I note that this one appears to have had the pigmentation cleansed entirely from his skin; he's as pale as his robes, and the contrast strikes me as he takes a grape from a nearby bowl and places it in his mouth, the red a strike upon the white. "I don't believe I've yet made your acquaintance."

"You mean my name?"

He laughs. "Your *name* is of no consequence. I know the name of everyone in this building. I would like to know who you *are*."

I cough politely into a balled fist. "I am a second-tier citizen of the Aimelari Administration as a ward of the Ministry of the Tower under the grace of the Abbess."

"You're here looking for a sponsor?" He raises an eyebrow, and his tone shifts very slightly. "I mistook you for an administrator's daughter at first. Your Aimelari is impeccable. I suppose I ought to be asking your heart's name after all."

I laugh nervously and look down to the red-carpeted floor; I can see bits of aluminium threading through the coloured fibres. "Names are powerful, sir; I can tell you my face name, if you'd like."

"Wary, too." He grins. "Face name, then."

"Ashrea. Yours?" I hold out a hand.

He holds out his own, grasping mine hard enough that I can feel the prints on his palms. "Yesyirei das Cimcharei es-Aysmanrata," he says, and smiles. "You'll be perfect."

Sessiles are interesting things.

Nobody knows how they *work*, of course; no one understands the most basic of pre-Laceration equipment, but the sessiles have the distinction of being the diamond to our quartz. We just know how to sing them into things, little computational devices in conjured fabrics, little outsourced orators talking to the Tower for us.

I personally prefer using an old-fashioned instrument and singing to the Tower myself; they operate on the same principle, but my line of work is practically made of pained cantate. It says something of the men before the Laceration that it's easier to kill mechanically than it is to heal.

This particular man's sessile has an intangible display, like the Abbess'; I can read *Yesyirei das Cimcharei* off the top of the sheet of rolled aluminium. Everything here is gilded in money, I suppose, so why should the utilities be an exception?

Sure, aluminium isn't the most *practical* of backings—copper's much easier to sing into, if more expensive—but it shines quite well against the actual spawncloth, even covered in blood; the same semi-congealed fluid makes an interesting pattern on the similarly shining marble below it, brightened by a tiny piece of metal held in a hand across from one wrapped around the neck of a gurgling little girl in a blue and gold dress; there is a striking contrast between the blood spurting from her carotid artery and his white skin, and I briefly consider that red and white go very well together.

"What is the value of a life constructed?"

I know perfectly well that his sessile is forcing me not to move and not to panic. I'm very sure I ought to, of course; it's a shame that theory doesn't very often match up to practice. It's probably blocking something in my amygdala—calcium?—but I can't make out the almost subsonic words coming from it well enough to know exactly what he's doing.

The person who I suppose I should know to be myself responds with a measure of calm.

"All life is inherently precious."

He looks at me, eyes wide, seconds before I feel an overwhelming wave of pain wash over me. My muscles are tight—very tight. I should fall; my body is trying to force itself into a foetal position. I certainly *wish* I would fall, but I am standing very straight.

The only sound I can hear for a moment is my heartbeat.

By the time the pain stops, the girl has stopped her rather dreadful rattle. "Look," he says, turning her neck in his palm and presenting the gaping wound to me. "What do you see?"

I look closely, and I have the strange feeling that I ought to be disgusted. "Major puncture wound in the neck, likely through the left common carotid artery into the trachea. Foreign object extracted." Judging by the amount of blood still retained, I don't say, death probably due to hypoxia by drowning.

He throws the corpse aside; it has stopped twitching, and a crunch resonates throughout the empty hall as her skull cracks against the marble. In his other hand is a silver-coloured cylinder, small apertures to a bright blue substance spaced around its circumference with little diamond-shaped holes in the little flat protrusions of metal around the needle jutting out from it; some Angzhwen words—most of which I don't know—are engraved on it in a semi-familiar font.

"Do you know why this didn't work? Do you?"

I raise an eyebrow in inquisition. My occipitofrontalis, at least, hasn't been compromised. "I do not know what the thing you are holding is."

He positions the thing against the right of my neck and pushes it in, hard; every muscle superior to my waist relaxes spontaneously as the sharp, bloody thing pierces my left external jugular vein. "The essence of the Tower, our tower, Ocilentra—in physical form! Our twisted forms cannot accept—"

I should perhaps feel somewhat concerned that the object that has just pierced and crushed the walls into a child's throat is being stuck into my neck, but all I feel is a very filling sort of emptiness.

At least until he pushes down.

It isn't very obvious at first; there's a sort of coldness going through my arteries and my veins and seeping through my bloodstream. I suppose, for a bit, that there surely must be worse ways to die.

I can no longer hear what he is saying; only his mouth is moving.

Quite abruptly, however, I feel something rather peculiar. Perhaps it is something that I should have felt around the time he murdered a child in cold blood and temporarily lobotomised me, and I might call it 'shock'; there's the shock of having any emotion at all, of course, but there's the far stronger shock of hate.

I bring my comparatively little left fist and shove it, as hard as I can, into his open mouth. He doesn't look surprised. I'm a bit put off about this, but for some reason I find myself far more piqued by the fact that he has just murdered a child.

I pull him down by the throat, my fingers extending within; my nails hook around his epiglottis and my knee bashes into his right temple as my right fist bashes into his left. I briefly wonder how I am effectively restraining a fully-grown man, but in truth I can't really bring myself to care.

I kneel, now, anchoring him to my knee by my left fist, and punch into his eye-sockets as hard as I can, over and over and over. He doesn't move throughout. I stop thinking for a while.

I am found a few minutes later by the Administrative Guard, screaming—I've no idea that I'm screaming until I'm dragged away—as I punch a wet mass of bone and tissue.

There is a dead child lying next to me and a priceless artefact jutting from my neck. My dress is red where it wasn't before, lit slightly blue by the dull glow of the objective displays lining the walls; it leaves a trail to the fist-mangled corpse of an administrator as I am pulled gently away.

The scene is not favourable.

I take a deep breath.

The first thing I try to do, sitting in this little hay-covered cell, is try and justify myself. It's basic self-defence, after all; any person who can speak can kill. I'm not sure how long it takes, but I'm soon quite reconciled with myself.

That was quicker than I expected—I entertain the notion that I may be a sociopath.

It's a particular shame that I can't reconcile myself with my imminent hanging in the same way.

I've been charged with the murder of an unrepresented administrator and a child, the theft of a priceless artefact and aggravated personal intrusion on administrative property. None of these are charges anyone would like to have.

I'm sure that I should be considerably more worried than I am, but it appears that for me a life-threatening, utterly helpless situation heralds a peculiar emotion far greater than any sense of fear:

Boredom.

I'd imagine I should be angry or sad or something or the other, but I simply grab my legs and hum lightly; I feel that if providence should take me, it really should just get on with it.

I figure I might as well get some sleep; I don't have the sessile, but perhaps I will dream of Missy nonetheless.

I am awakened in what seems barely a second later by some rather vulgar shouting in a strangely familiar voice, and as I open my eyes I see what looks like a particularly coarse young aylonit dressed in a pile of stitched-together rags struggling with a red-uniformed peacekeeper. She launches a punch towards the man's head just slow enough for him to grab her arm and twist it around her back, pushing her against the wall to my side.

"F'sakes," the man spits out, using his free hand to unlock the gate to my cell, "you've been non-judicialed five times this week. If you don't go peaceful the next time I'll have you arraigned."

"Go," the girl begins, misconjugating the imperative as the indicative, and proceeds to spout out a stream of gibberish of whose syllables I am unable to decipher. She stops, suddenly, and I can see the guard's arm moving upwards; she makes an almost aerial entrance into the cell, propelled by the scruff of her neck, and I swear I can see her arms spreading gracefully as she falls.

Her landing isn't quite so enthralling, and her shoulder bashes in what looks to be a particularly painful way against the hay, her head slamming into the metal under it with a muffled *clang*. The guard slams the gate shut and hovers his hand over the cell's eastern corner; he tugs on the bars for a bit before walking off.

She groans for just a second before and turns around to shout at the guard retreating up the steps of the dungeon, stopping only after a few minutes of violent vociferation. She shakes her head. I sit quietly and watch; the bravest paupers I've seen wouldn't argue with the peacekeepers.

I don't imagine this is because the peacekeepers are particularly fearsome *people*, mind, but because the bravest paupers would prefer to spend their nights unshocked.

"If you didn't proof this place with your bullshit I'd be breaking it apart, hear?"

She pushes herself to the ground in resignation; the object of her vitriol no longer in earshot, she groans in frustration and turns towards me. "Isha's hooks, would it've *killed* you to get in the wa—" she begins, before her eyes widen and she wags her finger at me in what appears to be some sort of realisation. "Hey."

"What do you mean, 'hey'?" I say, more in disbelief than anger. "Did you expect me to be a pillow?"

She looks me up and down, brushing her unkempt hair—obviously styled with the latest in manual shrub maintenance technology—to the side with one hand as she shakes her index finger at me with the other. "Hey, you're that doc from last night! *You're* the one who patched me up!" He holds out a hand. "Name's Perei."

It takes a few seconds, looking closely, before I realise that the face's a lot healthier with blood in it. "I fixed several major internal puncture wounds last night," I say neutrally, my daily capacity for shock somewhat exceeded. "Rebound wounds aren't very stable. Why aren't you burst like the overripe berry of a lycopersicum?"

He retracts the offered hand and shrugs. "I dunno, doc. Maybe I could help if I knew what a lycoperscium was."

I sigh. If I'm going to spend my last days with this hoodlum, I might as well choose not to antagonise him.

A few minutes pass in silence. I curl up against the wall.

"So," he begins, "what're you in for?"

I look at him and raise an eyebrow. "'In for'?"

"Yeah, what're you in for?" He gestures to my blood-soaked hands, raising his eyebrows. "Irregular period?"

"Very funny," I say, shaking my head. "What business is it of yours?"

"Don't *usually* see a ton of doctors lying around in places like these."

"Really?" I say, scooting counterclockwise away from him and curling back up. "I suppose you'll have to keep looking."

"Come on," he says, yawning. I came to the Fundraiser at five in the evening; it has been around four hours. "Nobody ever got far being like that in a place like this."

I sigh and decide perhaps that it is easier to capitulate. "Murder, two counts. Theft of a priceless artefact."

He whistles through his teeth, as if impressed. "So you're pretty much riveted to the wall, huh?"

I close my eyes again. The ground shudders slightly at regular intervals; I presume I must be imagining it.

"Hey."

The only response I grant him is a grunt.

He leans over and pokes me on the back. "Hey!"

I turn back around and stare at him with a trace of annoyance. "*What?*"

He laughs. "Don't you wanna know how we're gonna get out of this dump?"

I take a deep breath. "I've just witnessed a girl being murdered by a psychopath, I've recently been stabbed in the neck with the murder weapon and I've somehow beaten a person to death with my bare hands. If this is some kind of gallows humour—"

He interrupts me by picking a bit of hay from the floor, twirling it around his index fingers and humming—I can barely make out the words. He goes on like that for a few minutes before I speak out.

"Are you—?"

He sticks his tongue out and flicks it, almost experimentally; a rather pronounced *twang* comes from it. The satisfied grin on his face is immediate. "Look," he says, nodding his head up. "We've got a little sessile."

"That's disgusting," I say, staring at the saliva-covered bit of prison hay. "Who taught you to do that?"

"A friend," he says, and flicks another bit of the hay; the sound is unmistakeably lower-pitched.

I hold my objections for now, watching. "Why didn't you do this earlier?"

"For one thing," he says, speaking fairly intelligibly through his probing tongue, "you *were* being a total bitch."

Fair enough; I'm too excited to care much about his calumniations at the moment. "And for another?"

"For another, everyone's asleep."

I observe his testing with a semi-critical eye; the instrument he's made is almost flawless. "Except for us."

"And Ayerei." He pauses for a moment, and then stomps his

foot in frustration. "Damn it, you're not supposed to know his name yet. What's *yours*, anyway?"

"Ashrea."

He puts his tongue back into his mouth and grins, standing up and walking over to the open-faced cell door. "Hell of a face name, huh? Haven't heard of a mom calling her kid *Ashrea* in what, fifty years?"

I shrug. "That's the name on my permit and it's the name I'll use with you. What are you supposed to be, Perei? A cylindrical waterskin?"

"Please, Ash," he says, one of his hands running across a particular bar, "Call me Penny."

"Dropping the Aimelari masculine definitive for the Uytrimelan plural nominative. How revolutionary."

"I don't know what any of that was, but look—" He taps at one of the cell's bars. "Most of the metal they use, it's that unrusting crap—but stick your eyes a little closer."

I stand up and take a closer look, running my hands over the smooth, grey lengths of iron. "I'm a surgeon, not a metallurgist."

He licks at his improvised sessile, singing some incomprehensible string of Angzhwen—I'd imagine that applying his speech to surgical work would result in far worse than a burst lung—before handing the bit of hay to me.

I hold it before me distastefully, wiping it against the dried blood on my dress before curling it up around my fingers and putting my pinkie finger against it. "What're the words I'm looking for?"

He speaks to me slowly and deliberately, as if to an infant; the syllables come out one by one, and I realise the ludicrous amount of redundancy in his Angzhwen; every stanza is backed up by another five or six rephrasals, presumably to guard against mispronunciation.

I repeat the necessary bits, twanging at the string; it's around five seconds or so before a series of crude subjectives spell themselves out before me, surrounding the bars. Most of them are incomprehensible, but one set of words stands out:

Fyr pur.

Iron, one hundred percent.

I shake my head. "It's iron."

"Not just iron," he says, smirking. "Bona fide handmade cheapass rusting iron. They built this place, what, a hundred years before the tower?"

I think to admonish him before I realise he's referring to the *Administrative* Tower. I shake my head; the novelty of the fact doesn't take long to wear off. "It's an outdated material, yes, and how is *that* going to help us escape?"

"Well, see, you know how you magic girls—"

"Orators," I say, out of reflex.

He raises an eyebrow. "What?"

"Orators," I say, turning to look at him. "People who speak with the Tower in Angzhwen are orators. The theoretical science associated with it is named saepology."

He snorts contemptuously. "That's such incredible bullshit. It's magic when I do it and it's magic when you do it."

"It's the truth. You might as well call a lawyer a wizard and an advocate a magician."

"Might as well." He flicks a finger against the metal. "But I was thinking, right?" he says, looking at me expectantly.

"Right?" I say, raising an eyebrow once more; the eyebrow-raising is getting tiresome, but there's no other gesture I can think of to express my eyebrow-raising emotions.

"Well, you could use one of those barriers and just punch it open, right?"

I put my hand up against the bars; a light tinge of violet turns visible as it touches the field. "The barrier feedback would probably rip my arm off."

"I'm not seeing the downside."

I stare at him.

"Isha, it's called a joke." He shakes his head. "Okay—we'll magic up some water together. I think I remember the words. Throw it at the bars and rust 'em up."

I stare at him longer.

His expression remains serious.

My fingers curl around the little string and twang at it for a bit; I say a few words, and water—quite a bit more than I'd usually expect—begins streaming a few millimetres from my left hand. I grab one of the bars with it and resume staring at him as it streams down the bar and noticeably fails to clean the dried blood off them. "I must say—this seems very effective."

He shrugs. "Hey, I'd like to hear you come up with something better. Hell if I know anything better than water. Doesn't have a membrane, right? Throw a fireball or something."

I pull my dripping hand from the bars and flip him two fingers with it. He glances down at my gesture.

"If you do that too much you'll go blind," he says, and giggles.

I give up, collapsing onto the hay and rolling my head back as I close my eyes. Perei has the courtesy to keep quiet for a bit; until the stream peters out, the only sound in the room is of water pouring into the hay.

Then I have an idea.

"Step back," I say, quickly standing up. There isn't much a chance of this working, but I figure that I might as well push my luck. "I had an idea."

I walk over to the east of the cell and look closely.

Resisting the effects of Angzhwen oration isn't a matter of willpower; oration may project on will and genes, but they can work on physical matter. There are very specific orations capable of counteracting specific cantate, but orations in general aren't standardised to the extent that the things which resist them remain even slightly reliable in a fight.

I'm fairly sure I know by now exactly what Yesyirei did: he suppressed a specific portion of my amygdala and substituted a stability routine for my spine, dependent upon three reversible cantate and a single pained one. Intensely complicated and easily resisted, if I could move; full redundancy would have taken the oration several days to accomplish.

Sessile locks are the oldest and easiest to construct.

I ball my right fist and start twiddling the bit of hay with the other, beginning to sing as I feel for the embedded nexus; I can feel the defibrillation charge building up, and I quickly let go of it and begin to rub my hands together to feel the resistance—a fallible estimate, but I don't feel like wasting time for a full reading—as I continue to sing in a quick, thudding tune.

"*Dégajssya!*" I shout, finishing the oration; I bash my fist into the metal bar just as I release it.

I awake a second later, breathing heavily, a familiar face carrying some mixture of joy and concern staring into mine.

"Ash!" he shouts, snapping his fingers. "Ash, wake up! We're out!"

"I what?" I say, shaking my head a bit. "It worked?"

"You got us out," he says, pointing at the conspicuously open cell bars. "Talk about a pointless conversation. C'mon. I'm not sure if they teach you survival skills in the convent, but we've gotta go *before* the peacekeepers see us."

I scoot a bit away from him as I shakily get to my feet, taking deep breaths as I do; my heart's still beating, but there's a strange feeling of emptiness in it. I probably should have grounded myself before I tried that.

I swallow dryly and nod, my breathing slowing a bit. "You know this place better than me."

"Alright," he says, looking about quickly. The rest of the cells are empty; apparently we're the only two administrative offenders today. "You can see through walls with your x-ray eyes or something, right?"

"It's a bit more sophisticated than that," I say, but he's already started jogging up the stairs.

I follow behind; the winding design makes it seem as though it's been lifted from a historical catalogue, but the stone looks freshly-cut. I try to soften my steps as far as possible, and my shoes patter almost silently.

He sticks a hand up; I take this as a signal to stop. He turns around, and he doesn't seem very happy.

"*Those aren't peacekeepers,*" he says, whispering. "*That can't be a good thing.*"

I peek out after him into the similarly stone-built lobby; there are three people standing in it, none of them looking particularly civilian and all of them armed. Their weapons—rifles, apparently, though I'm not exactly an expert—look pre-Laceration but smoother, as though they were pulled straight from the Exodus Archive. They're clad in white cloth, plates of dark-coloured armour bound into them.

One is speaking to another in hushed tones in a Southern-sounding language; the sounds are soft and weak, barring a few quiet guttural interjections.

"*Well,*" I say, "*they're obviously not Aimelan. Their syllables aren't spiky.*"

"*Spiky?*"

"*It's a linguistic term.*"

"*The hell're you talking about? That's Pyarash.*"

A very loud sound from outside resounds—like a gunshot, but far louder—before I can salvage my dignity. The ground vibrates slightly, and the three have a fairly hurried conversation before hurrying out.

"Right," I say, "maybe we ought to go after them."

"Are you *nuts*, Ash?" he says, looking nervously over the corner, "Those guys had *guns*, they—"

A deafening, explosive roar overrides him, and right out the window a pharmacy across the street quite suddenly is both on fire and inexplicably missing its roof. It takes a few seconds for us to regain our hearing and half of one for Perei to decide to bolt.

I follow him out the opened doors as we run out into the darkened streets; the darkness is only relative to the searing day, however, and we can see hundreds of buildings covered in flames down the street down which we are running, large and small. As far as I can tell, we're on Highpoint Boulevard; the tierless barricade's clearly about a kilometre up the enormous road—a few figures, similarly armour-clad, running down it away from us—but my companion inexplicably ducks into an alley.

"Where are we going?" I ask, raising my voice considerably to compensate for our footfalls on the explosive-shaken cobblestone. "The exit to the city's down—"

"What?" he says, laughing. "You wanna *foot it* to Seep-shee-whatever-the-hell-the-jings-call-it, be my guest."

I decide that there is a time and place for addressing the propriety of a slur and promptly decide that this isn't the time nor the place. "Why are we running?" I say, looking over my shoulder. "For all we know, they're here to *help* us."

"Look, we didn't paint rainbows on our thighs and jump on a Saltic parade," he said, "I steal things and you *kill* things. I don't care *who* they are. The little people don't get bigger under a bigger boot."

He stops for a moment, looking up into the sky; there is a moment of absolute silence as the building next to us—I can't discern its purpose—splits as if gutted.

Perei runs, and I follow. I can't hear myself breathe for a few seconds as I feel the building's barriers shatter as it hits the ground behind us, its structural frame bashing into the floor and sending fragments of stonerise flying past us before I become aware again of the explosions echoing in the city's membrane. I look back to see the building lying smouldering against another—it's fairly new, and the one it's fallen on, presumably predating the Khamisret-Aparkisrea method of dysexaptics, is uncrushed.

I don't see any corpses.

"*You alright?*" he says, shouting as loud as I thought might be possible; I give him a quick nod, and we keep going. "Ish-al-*wyent`e*, they're ripping this place up."

"Again, where on earth are we *going?*" I say, in between gasps—I haven't had to run in years.

"Just a few blocks west," he says, turning about a corner and backing himself up against the wall. The buildings are getting close enough that I realise we're probably almost already in the residentials. "Got a friend. We've got a place to meet for things like these."

He takes a deep breath. "Isha, I hope they're not going through the alleys. Shoulda got a *gun* back there."

"They're soldiers. In *ballistic armour*. The only reason you'd need a gun would be to shoot yourself."

"I'm sure you're just the life of the party," he says, and continues on. The explosions—the shelling, if I recall the term correctly—continue at a regular pace, some occasionally landing close enough to shake the stones under our feet. Most of the buildings in the cobblestone streets are built for the barrierless, and though they are often struck there isn't a repeat building-crash.

As we go further, however, the cobblestone begins to turn to smooth stonerise. The buildings here aren't quite as resilient, and I decide not to dwell on the fact.

"Why do you think Cimsas' under attack?"

"Cimsas? Oh, you mean the *capital*—we'll worry about that when we're *not in it*." He continues to go at a steady pace. "Isha, did they let you stop running in the Ministry to let you *talk*?"

I keep silent enough to hear my heart pounding; it isn't long before we're in the tierless regions, the administrative barricades on alleys wide enough that we never crossed them. The transition is slow, as if the pavement's momentarily forgotten where it is, but soon the only thing below my feet is gravel mixed with sand.

I give silent thanks to whoever invented protective footwear.

During the night, the tierless districts—most of the people desperate enough to call me 'doctor' called it 'the tough quarter', which I admit I do like as a name—tend to be lit only with whatever the poorer Mahammadir bereft of tessitura can afford: little improvised sessiles and fire-lights. As it is, it appears that the membrane's surface has started to spark a little, causing a lightshow that I might have stopped to admire if its conclusion didn't mean we were going to freeze.

Even without the lights, however, it's easy to tell when one's reached the tierless districts—the buildings start to become close enough and stack high enough that rooftops quickly become the most efficient way to travel.

Perei grabs onto a nearby iron ladder and begins to climb. I've only ever been here once before—not on purpose—and so I stick as close to him as humanly possible without touching him. The sound of explosions remains constant, but screams—not very happy ones—tinge it rather distastefully.

"Perei," I say, looking about, "are you *sure* they're still here?"

"I'm sure. He said he'd be there if the shit ever hit the fan. The fan's hit pretty hard right about now."

"What on Earth's a *fan*?" I say, and a trap-door opens beneath him before he can reply. I yelp instinctively as he grabs onto the rim and quickly lets go, falling flatly onto his backside with a high-pitched grunt.

"Come on and close it behind you," he says, standing up and beckoning down; I quickly follow his path, carefully avoiding the part where I shatter my backside.

The little room we've fallen into is distinctively Mahammadir;

the tiles on the bright orange—they may be white, but the little sessile-light in the corner's all that's illuminating them—have elegant, hand-painted devotions in what must be one of the Southern languages, and on the outside of the window there is plastered a cloth-stitched gold-coloured stripe, an insignia that seems to be becoming slightly more common even on the windows of infidel houses. I can see the symptoms of human error upon the tiles even as I slam the door shut and scramble after him; the room has only one iron door a few metres from where we've entered it, on which he's smacking furiously.

"Why do you think," I say, my hands on my knees and panting, "we're being invaded by Southerners?"

He continues slamming on the door. "Maybe 'cause the admins don't think they exist, I dunno. We're riveted either way if we don't get ou—"

The door flings open, revealing a distinctly muscular man with a pre-Laceration rifle—a sessile-arm, rather—streaked with stripes of red paint slung over his white-shirted chest; he isn't ugly, but his sweaty face is marked wholly with stress.

"Goddamn it, Penny, *where in the hell have you been?* The city's getting itself—" he begins in a particularly pronounced frontier drawl before letting his eyes drift past Perei and at me. "You brought a *girlfriend?*"

He puts his hands up to his chest. "No—no, Ayerei, she's a *doctor*. From the Ministry. Ashrea."

"Really?" he says, staring dubiously at me.

"Trauma surgeon," I say, "not a general practitioner. Not proficient at long-term treatment. I presume you're Ayerei?"

Ayerei wipes his face. "Right, that's just peachy. You just come along with some eleven year old—"

"Twelve," I say.

"—some just-hit-the-flower convent girl calling herself a *surgeon*—"

"Look," he says, "she's totally legit. Fixed me up last night and broke us out."

"She's the one who fixed you up? Y'all got *arrested?*" He puts his hands over his face and rubs it vigorously, as though he's cleansing his exasperation from his face. "Alright. Alright, not the time—I'll take your word for it."

"I know this place's falling apart all the time," Perei says, "but somehow I don't think it was gonna so quick. Hell's going on?"

He takes a deep breath. "They've blockaded the city."

"*Who's* blockaded the city?" I say, my arms going out to my sides in interrogation. Just as I ask, the constant explosions stop and an incredibly loud voice begins shouting in Angzhwen through what sounds like a particularly strong piece of amplified sessile paper.

This is the Foreign Legion speaking on behalf of the Administrator of the Nation. We have been shelling at a tenth of our capacity. If the Pretender is not surrendered within the next ten minutes, we will resume shelling at fifth capacity.

Without the explosions, the ground feels almost eerily still.

He looks up, hands on his hips. "I don't really speak Angzhwen all that well, but whatever it is can't be good."

"They're saying they'll start firing double in ten minutes," I say, looking at the ceiling. "They want a claimant to something."

"That's great. Last time I checked," he says, beckoning us down the door-lined hall, "a fourth of the city's on fire. Double that's going to turn us all the way to ash."

I decide not to explicate further.

"How're we gonna get out, then?" Perei says, keeping pace with the man. He seems genuinely concerned.

"We're not." He pushes himself against a seemingly random door and pushes his hand up upon it; it pops open with an uncomfortably natural squeak, and we walk out onto a tiny balcony. "Come up here," he says, turning to the right and climbing his way up a ladder several storeys high; I follow behind Perei, and within a minute—it's a good thing I don't have a particular fear of heights—we're on top of the building, almost towering over the rest of the city; the bowl that the city's been built into leaves the tower at the lowest point, giving us leave to look down upon its regions. The slums end, as far as I can tell, as brown turns to grey; the citizenry ends as that turns to white.

As I look over the side of the roof, I'm immediately confronted with the sight of the hundreds of buildings making up the tierless districts, going all the way out to the very edges of the field.

The membrane is brightly alight in places, spots of the blue-tinged field burning and separating from the purple-tinged kinetic barrier. The latter is beginning to flicker in spots, letting in gusts of sand; there are a few spots that have been completely rent open, and I can feel the air getting steadily colder.

He hands Perei a piece of green-tinted, finely-rounded glass; he looks through it for a few seconds, staring at the horizon.

"Goddamn."

I stick my hand out and promptly receive the little artefact.

I don't immediately understand what I'm seeing—a few spots of white on the streets, followed by a huge series of tiny human-like, grey-spotted white shapes on the Pari dunes and huge cylindrical grey ones on a backdrop of blue, hundreds of white-coloured tent-figures dotting the distance—until I realise that they aren't just shapes.

I blink as I remove the bit from before my eye. "That isn't good."

"Not letting anyone through. Tried sending a glasswalker with a visual sessy on it to test the waters." Ayerei sucks in some air through his teeth. "Don't think they even needed to aim for the gaps."

"You mean—"

Ayerei takes a light breath. "Worse than the Sea itself."

Perei sighs. "Can't just sit here and wait to die."

I look through the glass again, looking over the horizon once more. There are white spots all over, creating a clean line; there are a few large concentrations of white at the streets running out of the city, but the entire place is covered. "How'd they get that many people in one place? They'd need supply lines for their mutes."

Perei laughs. "Why do you *care*? Y'think they're gonna disappear if we find out they're cheating?"

"Sipshirea. That's the only non-Aimelan territory within a day of Cimsas."

"Sipshirea?" Ayerei says, raising an eyebrow. "Sipshirea's a trading city."

"It's the last vestige of the Empire in Aimela," I say. "Maybe they're supplying them."

Ayerei chuckles. "Lady, I've spent *years* in Sipshirea." He pronounces it *sip-shai-e-ra*; I don't point the discrepancy out. "I speak Sipjit. Trust me," he says, looking out over the city, "the Zhangs don't want anything on their hands. They're eating each other enough without Aimela on them."

I nod slowly, a slight calmness making its niche as I look back into the glass.

A few new figures have appeared in orderly lines, moving at a slow, steady pace; they're moving quickly, and as they draw closer grey, glasswalker-shaped figures seem to materialise underneath them.

"Hey," I say, handing the bit of glass back to Ayerei, "are those ambulliers?"

"More of *them*, probably."

Ayerei looks through it, watching intently. As he continues, the grim expression on his face turns into a steady grin and he swiftly turns on his heel and makes his way towards the ladder in a few quick strides. "Come on," he says, practically laughing, "we've got our ticket out."

I follow, Perei getting to the ladder barely a second before me; just as we reach the bottom and duck into the building, the same voice echoes through the barrier.

Turn back at once or we will open fire on the city with full force as the sun rises.

"They're saying," I say, running quickly down a flight of stairs as I try to keep up with Ayerei, "they're going to decuple their firepower."

Ayerei doesn't bother to respond; Perei grimaces. "I don't think I *wanna* know what that means," he says, his feet moving noticeably quicker against the ground. The scent of boiled lentils fills the air for an instant as we run right through the living-room—if a one-room dwelling might have one—of a cowering five-member family's dwelling and out a balconyless balcony's entrance, almost slipping down over the semi-smooth groundwards incline beneath my feet as I struggle to land on my heel.

I let out a low yelp as we hit the ground, taking a deep breath long enough to hear something behind me loud enough to send my ears ringing. They're already metres before me; the long, quietly moaning shriek of something that sounds almost human hums behind me, and as my eyes drift over something I recognise in an instant but do my best not to *it's a category two left lung injury cardiac arrest imminent he has to be here somewhere—*

I barely notice the figure sprinting towards me and something I can immediately tell is so much stronger than me that it might as well be a force of nature grabs tight around my arm; the ground's friction relinquishes my steadied feet to a hard pull, and the immediate sation of being held fills my soul with such irrational content that I figure that for the moment I can afford to blink.

A stable, breathy voice tinged with concern assaults my eardrums as its owners' feet hit the ground. "Hell's gotten into you, little lady?"

"Nothing," I say, quickly letting my feet regain their bearings as I keep pace with my muscular tether, the *pat-pat* almost inaudible against the thuds underfoot punctuating the periodic, faraway roar of artillery. "He's already dead."

"Glad to hear it," he says, and glances up the road; barely a second passes before he stops in place and lets go. I stumble for an instant in freefall before my left knee finds the sandy ground, and I look up to see a shed—pathetically short against the miniature towers around it—with a sign reading *Glasswalker Storage* standing before me, pieces of its cracked adobe façade falling off in clumps.

Most of the docks are empty, and so I jump my way onto the first walker, taking care not to cut myself on its ceramic scales as I hold onto its reins. It whinnies, ready, and Ayerei presses his palm against the sessile near its shoulder.

"Ever got yourself on a glasswalker before?" Ayerei asks, getting onto his own mount; Perei jumps on behind him, and I manage not to laugh as I behold the sight of two grown men holding onto a single mount.

"I know Angzhwen," I say, demonstrating with a quick, improvised melody: a right rein-pull for a left turn and a left for a right, up for backwards and forwards for forwards. It doesn't take much to instruct a glasswalker to move; I imagine that whatever I lack in experience I can replace with knowledge.

He chuckles. "Just follow me and we should be alright."

"*Ádrakyts-là áćéyshyr,*" I say, pointing to Ayerei's mount; mine neighs.

"Nice accent," he says, and lets out a stream of heavily accented, almost incomprehensibly fast Angzhwen—a detailed list of rhyming what-then-if instructions, probably from memory. The animal neighs and, as he leans forwards a bit, begins to trot out of its spot and onto the narrow street.

"Who do these belong to?" I ask, as we make our way onto the distressingly empty streets. "I don't remember hearing of public glasswalkers in the tierless districts."

Perei answers for Ayerei, who's coaxing his glasswalker into going faster down the streets. "Hell's gonna stop us *now*?" he says, grinning, and before he can incriminate us a deafening shriek fills the air as the morning sun peeks over the horizon.

I instinctively look towards the Administrative Tower, and see immediately that it's been fractured in the centre; an enormous gout of flame is engulfing its fifty-seventh floor, and the smoke is barely given time to escape towards the Khamisret-Aparkisrea field before the membrane above it disintegrates entirely and an enormous explosion shatters the light purple of the barrier above it before it can rephase, the barrierline pulsing from it dissipating entirely.

The crumbling structure is tall enough that I can see it even as we navigate the steadily widening streets. Without its centrepiece, the barrier begins to lose integrity incrementally; the sand begins to pour in. A torrent starts to fall upon its tip, the sand blowing in on every side and curving about, its momentum pushing the entire mass into an almost conical form as it begins to wrap about the Administrative Tower, Ocilentra—the paleness of the imitation becoming far more obvious in its shadow—itself looking impassively on.

"*Lady!*" Ayerei shouts, glancing rapidly between the rip in the field and the street before him, reaching into one of the pouches lining his shoulder and quickly leaning over to hand me a simple stringed instrument. "*Barrier, membrane, now!*"

I grab it, throwing its strip over my neck as I search for the beginning tones; a dysexaptic field is simple enough that it doesn't really require an instrument, but it certainly helps. The air is getting colder by the second, now.

"*Tutć vétirymj,*" I begin, fiddling with my left hand as the tower is completely obscured by the sand; within seconds, the only things visible past the sand are the explosions distorting it, and the barrier is visibly wasting metre by metre. "*ćairazh æloràzh—*"

"*Any time this century!*" he shouts, looking intently at the cloud—rapidly earning the adjective 'mountainous'—as he eyes the road before him through his glass. The ruptured field lets in the vibration from the thin field of the foreign camp, and sounds of gunfire fill the air when it isn't interrupted by the sound of the massive explosions behind us; the weapons are all pre-Laceration, and so there is no light.

I continue shrieking the oration, singing the song as quickly as I can; the barrier forms with a sudden, unusual violence, an abnormally vivid field of purple heralding its presence in the visible spectrum. It sends a cloud of sand flying out before us, Perei shouting out in startlement as we crash through it and as the detritus comes out from around us the membrane forms over it—gently, even through the mess, for a membrane detonation would not help us—and joins it.

Cimsas' field has almost completely crumbled. The gunshots grow louder as we speed towards their source, and as we burst out the barrier, going just slowly enough that its force threshold lets us pass, the light of the sun just risen illuminates the figures of hundreds of men fighting in the distance before us in the foreign encampment's Khamisret-Aparkisrea field—only dozens on walkerback. The line of troops blocking the entrance are scattered, focusing almost entirely on the Aimelans.

Enormous, thin cylinders jut from the ground at an angle towards the city, looking far more imposing in person; one of them moves almost imperceptibly, a whistle shrill enough to ring over the gunfire immediately overtaken by the sound of an explosion in the distance.

"*We're going straight for them!*" I shout, looking anxiously to my sides. The encampment stretches somewhat about the city—there are plenty of gaps, but I'm not entirely sure if that's a good thing—while the bulk of the fighting appears to be intersecting quite neatly with our path.

"*I know! Keep singing!*" We pick up speed, our mounts cantering up the side of the Pari dune in seconds; I grab onto my glasswalker's fibreglass mane and push myself down along with our barrier just as we reach the camp's; the burning white of the pure sun scorches my skin for the barest fraction of a millisecond as a few stray pieces of sand graze my skin and bash into my clothes, almost drawing blood.

We burst forth into the field, and the next minute seems very slow to me.

I immediately threshold the field as high as I can without turning it intolerant, the breath in my lungs careful not to push too quickly against itself. A tent comes into my view just as we come up over the edge—black striped with white—and I barely have time to scream before it caves outwards, ripping itself from its position in the cracked, sun-blackened glass and flying into an Aimelan trooper. The sudden violence knocks him off his mount, visibly destroying his barrier—the creature goes onwards in a straight line, and I'm busy enough focusing on singing that I don't see its destination.

We move to the side and ride past him as he is bayoneted by a running trooper through his shoulder, past the ceramic over his chest; red stains his uniform's white as our barrier whips the body—I can't tell if he's alive, but if he is he isn't going to be for long—into his assailant along with an enormous cloud of glassy sand.

We're well past them by the time I might have seen the result.

The trampled silicates at our glasswalkers' hooves billow out in a trail behind us, and I realise we're beginning to dig straight into the ground.

I look to my side and see Ayerei holding tight onto his glasswalker, Perei onto Ayerei; both of them are as close to their mount as possible, and we burst out into the wide open space from which the artillery protrudes. I can feel the barrier weakening as shots ring out around us, and the only thing I can hear, even as I sing, is my own heart.

Ayerei narrowly dodges a tent, sending me bashing through the same; I rephrase the barrier away once more as we approach the other side of the field, turning to see a man in the white and black aiming what looks to be an enormous weapon—I'm not sure what kind, but definitely a weapon—straight at me.

We find ourselves on the other side of the barrier just as he fires, and a little explosion spits off the side of the camp's dysexaptic field as I recreate mine; our mounts speed up as we drop the two metres from the top of the fortified dune, leaving a slash of cullet behind us.

Ayerei, Perei and I—but for a series of membrane reinforcements—are silent for a few minutes, Ayerei looking back every now and then as sweat creases his brow.

An uneasy silence settles over us.

I take a deep breath.

"I killed a soldier."

Perei raises a palm, as if to accept a high-five.

"I killed an *Aimelan* soldier," I say, glaring at him. "I knocked him off his glasswalker with a tent and he was bayoneted and I probably *crushed his body with a barrier.*"

He doesn't miss a beat. "Stripes or stars?"

I blink, not quite sure what to say. "I—I think he was commissioned. I didn't get a look at his insignia."

He looks almost as if he's going to raise his hand again, but Ayerei gives him what looks like a warning glance; he puts his hands back down and huffs, and neither of them speak further.

I shake my head.

one
The Mahammadir Child

This is a reading exercise designed both to acquaint you with the principles of public safety and the applications of Angzhwen in daily life. At the end of this exercise in conjunction with parental or educational guidance you should have learnt to use Angzhwen responsibly in a formal context. As always, remember to ask an adult if you feel that you must.

Angzhwen

Esiyssya an filir qu'pàrnéryysményœnsszhya Aysmanrat' Aimelzh.

Fàjyenćssya é pàrnéryyspravmànyssya, é peryr syzh praféshézygyulss é prafénstrumyniizhrobygyulss é meryr syzh plitzhdyàsygulss. Antyms, peryr syzh huétivyrya comn quetra. Féflesœldéyssgyulra é n'beaudyssya àfilu syzh. Ćeyiiss neyzii meltys shézszeyzhii qu'séyrssya.

Filir syzh petlitssya, éntszyedya qu'veuféss an shézszeyu prasyzh-suà sin tràbantir. Parsqu'pravmànssya, désyssya amyii prædyr an'em.

Tutzhii schœllssya syitan, qu'mésulprenyss. Jœyssya, é cencæssya sœlvir. Féssya-là ui finpàrlyssya y n'prenyséyrssya.

Árésqu'disdyalssya, ápeyrćeldyra, fàiqyr peryzh shébytzysyssya pàr shézszeyr féssya pàr miszhvétiryiira.

N'survissya-duyr.

Étjyénst:
misii pæysyss.

Aimelan (key vocabulary words highlighted)

There was once a child **who was a natural-born citizen of** (*qu'pàrnéryysményœnsszhya*) the Aimelan Administration.

He was under the age of majority (*fàjyenćssya*) and **was born intelligent** (*pàrnéryyspravmànyssya*), and his father **worked every day to build sessiles** (*praféshézygyulss*) and also **worked to reconstruct pre-Laceration sessile clothing patterns** (*prafénstrumyniizhrobygyulss*) and his mother **works every day to manage settlement border disputes** (*plitzhdyàsygulss*). One day his father **came home under the influence of sanctioned mind-altering substances** (*huétivyrya*) as per usual. He **worked on the direct tactile display layer** (*féflesœldéyssgyulra*) and **said only a few words** (*n'beaudyssya*) to his son. These were the various names **of the components involved in the production of a sessile** (*shézszeyzhii*) that he knew of.

His son, **having heard these words** (*petlitssya*), decided that he wanted to make a sessile for himself without **purchasing it privately from a government-owned firm** (*tràbantir*). **Because he was smart** (*parsqu'pravmànssya*), he asked his friends for help first.

All of them **filed a dissenting motion in a manner befitting a morally sound person** (*schœllssya*) except one, who was a Mahammadir. This delighted him, and they agreed **to engage in a mutual sharing of ideas** (*sœlvir*). They did this until he had said all there was to say and then they fell out of contact.

After ten days had passed, on Bring Your Child To Work Day, the factory where his father worked was sessile-bombed by a sessile completed with **the words required for the generation of the stable barrier resonance that is used to allow tactile sessile interfacing** (*miszhvétiryiira*).

Neither survived.

The moral of this story is:
words have power.

'Reading Exercise: The Child Who Spoke'
Chapter Nine: Ethics and Government
Practical Angzhwen, Andresrei das Sikharea
published by the Department of Education and approved for private distribution by the Administration for Media Development under the grace of Khaliesrea das Sikharea eliyit Tamarisrei, Administrator for the Arts

2

Sipshiyr

to drink from stone

I didn't see the shells.

That's the most troubling part, besides the part where my home has almost certainly been irreparably destroyed and where everyone I know is dead and where I'm wanted for murder and how it appears I've magically developed a tolerance to oration and how my barriers can kill people and how my life is absolutely ruined and so on and so forth.

It's the only thing I can afford to have trouble me, however, and so—at the moment—it is.

The Pari effect draws proportionate quantities of matter towards barriers and the Khamisret-Aparkisrea field makes *that* pile up in Pari dunes around it. Physics has never been my métier, and I'm not going to speculate as to the why.

It is, however, the reason—besides the considerable redundancy of city-size barriers—shells are made slow and big. Kinetic beacons, the only fast shells I'm aware exist, force the membrane from the barrier and cause a localised collapse, and at night (daylight is a more immediate threat, certainly, but sand is far more permanent) it usually only takes seconds for sand to start coming in bulk.

People fight over cities, not mounds of sand.

"Hey," Perei says, facing me as he reclines on the glasswalker's back, his legs hanging down where the sleeping Ayerei's hips begin, "penny for your thoughts?"

I let my head fall to the side as I stop my instinctive singing; my hands are hanging off my own walker's sides, the hard fur pushing up against my unclothed arms. "Aluminium or aloxite?"

He snickers. "Let's say a strangle of xites. Last thing I got with minnies was a gun."

"I'm thinking about the pragmatic justifications for the usage of high-velocity rounds on large civilian settlements." I take a deep breath. "What else can I think of?"

"Well," he says, seeming thoughtful for a bit, "you *could* think of what we're gonna *do*. If you haven't noticed yet, we're not exactly the most loaded people around."

I consider the question for a bit, looking up at the stars and continuing to orate under my breath.

"I think I'm going to Tachiesrea."

"What?"

"There's obviously a war going on," I say, undoing the belt holding me to the creature and sitting up, putting my fist under my chin. "So I'm going to help Aimela, somehow. The Reserve Council's a good place to start. Right after Sipshirea."

I see him tilting his head incredulously in my peripherals. "They're not even gonna let you *in*. Hell would you wanna do that for?"

I turn my gaze to face him. "I am a citizen of the Aimelan Administration. Maybe you've forgotten your roots; I haven't."

"Right," he says, snorting as if suppressing a laugh. "Figures the one time I meet someone useful in the cooler she's a *real* lunatic. What, you *like* having peacekeeper batons up your ass?"

"The peacekeepers have done nothing but protect me."

He stares at me, pronouncing enough periods to build a perfectly-formed ellipsis.

A few minutes pass in silence; Ayerei mumbles a bit in his sleep, chest draped over the glasswalker's head.

Perei speaks up just as my thought reaches its conclusion.

"Where'd you live, anyway?"

"The church your friend dragged you into half-dead."

"Well," he says, "I don't exactly have a great memory for places. Been dragged into a lot of churches half-dead."

I sigh. "The Ministry of the Tower Ocilentra in the Hands of our Administrator of Grace down Diffusion Way."

"Hey," he says, rubbing his chin, "isn't that right next to—"

"Mendicant's Alley, yes. Where I learnt medicine."

He whistles, impressed. "Learned how to cut people open from the Mend. What, d'you learn how to shoot with soldiers for dummies?"

"If I ever learnt how to shoot, I'd imagine that's how I'd do it." I scratch behind my ear. "Where did *you* live?"

"Implying I've lived in any specific place."

"Implied-subject implication. That's a classical riposte. You're not as illiterate as you try to be."

His expression turns derisive; I've apparently questioned his street credentials. "Hey, they pissed back then too, didn't they? Doesn't mean I've gotta study prelac *pissing physics* to do it."

I look at the tower behind us, reaching past the sky; I can't see its tip past the blast threshold, the metal disappearing past a thick canopy of white and yellow. A little patch of the rest of it might be visible in the day among the invisible heat as the air boils, a little swimming bit of black amongst the haze.

I take a deep, speculative breath before I speak.

"That's debatable."

I go back to reinforcing the barrier, and he closes his eyes and lies back on his back.

It is several hours later—with the feeling of a rather hard bed on my back—when I wake up to an semi-familiar face, looking concernedly at me with its nose a centimetre from mine.

Naturally, I scream.

Just as naturally, it backs away and I realise with a start that it's Ayerei's face in the sunlight. Perei runs up from behind him, hitting his toe on one of the bed's iron legs and promptly going to the floor with a very long and very loud stream of curses.

"Good morning?" Ayerei says, raising an eyebrow.

"Good morning," I say, absentmindedly tracking Perei's slowly rising, pained form as he rises.

"Good—" he begins, and then he lets out a series of syllables I can't quite work out the meaning of beyond their construction of a present participle, "—morning."

I glance over to my side and see a rather wide window, made of clear glass. Sipshirea is a very old city, and we are high above its descending geography; a rather impressively large barrierfountain—from which a clearly visible barrierline rises up to the city's ceiling—sits at the bottom of the pit at which the widening streets converge, and the stonerise that makes up the ground has been cut in a mimicry of pre-Laceration architecture not much unlike Cimsas'.

Ayerei reaches a hand back and smacks him gently on the back of the head. "Go brush your teeth with rinsewater, Penny. We've got business to discuss."

He grumbles. "You're not my *dad*," he says, and storms out; I watch him until he very gently closes the door behind him before looking back to Ayerei, who's taken a seat and is leaning forwards, chin on his lap-rested arms.

"Business?" I say, raising an eyebrow.

He inhales deeply before he speaks.

"What are you?"

"A human being," I say. "A female human being with experience in medicine. Would you like to know anything specific?"

"You're from the Church. You're not like us and you're not like *them*. Your entire city just got turned to bits." He lets his head fall a bit to the side, as if in genuine confusion. "And you're not shook up at all?"

"I *am* shaken up," I say, unconsciously gripping my sheets as I sit up—still clothed in my blood-soaked dress, the material long since turned brown—and look him in the eye. "I just prefer to keep my shaking internal."

"Huh," he says, leaning back in his chair. "Might want to reconsider that whole 'human being' thing. I didn't get a good look at your little dress 'til this morning, you know. The thing's crusty with it."

"It?"

He shakes his head. "Blood, girl. And something tells me it isn't yours."

"It was self-defence."

"Look, I'm not judging either way." He leans forwards a bit. "You seem useful."

"I've just seen my entire life crumble to bits and rode away into the sunset with a couple of absolute strangers," I say, shaking my head lightly. "I'd appreciate it if you'd skip to the point."

"Well, I take it you don't have anywhere else to go." His serious expression turns subtly into a smile. "I make a habit of going anywhere."

"I'm not going to kill people for a living, Ayerei."

"Oh, *hell* no," he says, rearing back a bit. "I'm not saying anything like *that*. I mean I make a habit of travelling. Was a courier. Spent ten years living out of Åmed—sorry, I mean Cimsas—last five years in it. Figures God'd kick me out just in time."

"Hell and God. *Ja-ha`akh-fir, uh-luh.*" I let the soft syllables roll around on my tongue. "You're Mahammadir?"

"Living with them five years in a row tends to do that to you," he says, shrugging, "but no. I could say coreburrow and Tower if that'd make you feel better."

"It's fine. Just strange. I just thought most Mahammadir were immigrants, and—" I shake my head. "Nevermind."

"Hey, it's fine. Y'know," he says, reclining a bit on his chair, "Penny—pure Aimelan, mind you—used to be a guideline once."

I give him a somewhat incredulous expression. "A guideline?"

"Styled himself the twelfth and said Isha was walking from over the Insurmountables to get there. Might tell you the story one day."

"Huh."

"Anyway," he says, coughing meaningfully, "you should be old enough to use a prelac. Worth three years average and it's hard to get a good one made, but a firearm's just gonna break your shoulder. Y'know how to shoot?"

"I've never needed to."

"Ah," he says, "the peacekeepers did it for you."

"Aimela is a civilised nation. This isn't the South."

He laughs with an uncomfortably heavy air of condescension. "Tell that to a Line Raider and he might even be so nice as to sing you the song of his people over your dead body." He grins, drawing my attention to a horribly familiar sort of forked scar across his philtrum.

"I suppose I should take your word for it."

As I stand, I take a deep breath; the smell of old blood wafts up to my nostrils, and I wince a bit as I look back down to my blood-splattered dress. As I move my arm to check the full extent of the damage, the layer of clotted blood quite literally cracks and comes apart at the elbows, little globs moving with the fabric.

"Clothes first."

We emerge onto the street, having tipped the rather sleepy owner of the inn—more to stop ourselves from getting robbed, Ayerei tells me, than out of goodwill—and there is a noticeable indifference to my bloodied appearance. The air is exceptionally humid, and a gentle sort of thudding rhythm seems to come from the almost entirely Aimelan-garbed general commerce as we walk uphill and away from the centre.

"Most everyone here knows Aimelan," he says, tapping me on the shoulder—presumably to draw my attention—just as he turns quickly to his left and begins walking. "Just try to keep low on the accent and we'll fit in just fine."

"The accent?" I say, looking quickly about. Our glasswalkers—I presume that they are ours mainly because there aren't any others about—are tethered tightly to the front of our temporary place of residence, apparently with metal chains.

"The one where you say words bigger than your mouth." He grunts as he pushes himself up against the wall of what appears to be an antique shop, a rather large glasswalker-pulled carriage pushing itself through. The thing's not quite large enough to warrant it—a few metres separate us—but I decide to trust Ayerei's judgement. "High Aimelan, I guess you'd call it. They might *sound* nice, but a little of that and we're talking triple."

"Speaking of charge," I say, pushing myself off the stonerise along with him, "where did our glasswalkers come from?"

"Teratrisrei. Worked for them. Split the sessy reins, left two locked up just in case." His illustratively moving arms draw my attention to a child jumping about unsupervised in the middle of the road; a riderless glasswalker trots past, and he grabs onto its tail.

"Teratrisrei Liable Concern?" I say, absently watching the child getting pulled off his feet by the unstopping glasswalker and slamming unceremoniously onto the ground, uninjured but crying. A person who I presume is his mother comes out of a nearby general shop and runs over to attend to him. "You mentioned you were a courier, didn't you?"

"Yeah. Ten years." He sticks his fingers out to supplement the figure; I suppose this is out of habit, Central Aimelan's annual numbers being a torment for foreigners to distinguish. "Started off with little payment runs—little bits of silt and aluminum. I'd tell you some of my good runs, but you're probably not too interested in that kinda thing."

"So you've worked with them?" I raise my eyebrows as I hop over a little set of wooden steps—I'd be surprised the things haven't been stolen if but the 'wood' below the steel gates weren't quite clearly treated and compacted silicone-addled mulch. "Aren't you going to report in?"

"I hate to say it, but I don't think they'll appreciate me letting their walkers loose." He shrugs. "If they're still alive, that is. Might as well work with what I've got. All I have I have with me."

"You keep everything you own on you all the time?"

There is a moment of almost palpable contemplation before he laughs roughly. "Reminds me of something a brainy kid once told me." His voice attains a sudden, quick-paced Uytrimelan quality. "'Might as well make 'em bargain-bin your life with your stuff.' Most people don't try and pickpocket a six-footer with a three-footer over his shoulder."

"Footer," I say, tilting my head a bit and quite serendipitously avoiding an overhanging, deceptively miniaturised flowerpot, "—*tower bless, that thing almost hit me*—as in the Imperial units?"

"Yeah," he says, giving me a bit of a grin—I'm not sure for my question or my clumsiness. "Call it Low Aimelan, myself. Uytrimelan, if you prefer. I reckon it stopped being Imperial along with the Empire."

He stops to reach up, hop and poke at one of the midget flowerpots. The taraxacum sways a bit in its soil, and he almost audibly suppresses a yelp as a very visible arc of electric charge comes off the metal pot. "Too bad they didn't have any of *these* little bastards. Felt my goddamned heart skip."

It's difficult not to sympathise with the Zhanghwazh, of course; pedosynthesis requires equipment and tessiture, neither of which are they in a position to export; the Sipjit Ethnic Exclave is meant to be ethnic—given that everyone in the streets speaks and looks almost the same as I do, the justification seems a bit rich—but it also happens to be in the centre of Aimelan soil production and hydroponics.

As Ayerei shakes his finger off and blows on it, patting at his heart to ensure that it's still beating, I am quiet in contemplation. Ayerei obliges my silence—I assume willingly—with his own.

This arrangement holds up to the point that he taps me on the shoulder.

"We're here," he says; the building, a shophouse with a disproportionately large façade, is just as nondescript as any other. My eyes drift, however, up to the sign above the open door: *Tek Private Trading Concern*. The name is in the usual featural Yikdipwan—it takes me a few seconds to work out the handpainting—but the other words are written entirely in Aimelan, leaning right-to-left in three rows: the first leads from the initial consonant, the last from the terminal and the middle out the other way from the vowel.

It strikes me quite suddenly that I've never seen Zhanghwazh writing outside of a book, and I look about; no other sign carries anything quite like it.

"Once you're done gawking," Ayerei says, pushing his head back out of the door, "feel free to pop in."

I don't bother asking Ayerei why he chose that particular shop; I'm not used to paying for clothing, but a quarter-strangle of aloxite pennies feels cheap even for the sheets of fabric that compose the simple dishdasha, much less the entire thing.

The buffer zone between the barrier and the last buildings is enormous. It's at least a kilometre wide at its smallest point, unlike Cimsas—I can barely make out the last building we saw on the ride as we stand only a few metres from the barrier's edge, the glasswalkers about ten metres away from us. My old clothes lie drying on one of their backs.

"You know," he says, kneeling on the smooth sand with his rifle on his knee, "We usually do this sort of thing for our kids."

I observe and absentmindedly tug the blue-striped bit of fabric—blue-striped, I am informed, so as to unmark me as an *actual*

Mahammadir—out from over my eyes and whisper a quick sealing to keep it pinned to my neck as he puts his hand over the top; a little light flashes green against the thing's brown surface, and he flips the bit up, revealing a little chamber filled with fine sand.

"Now—" he begins, poking at the top, "This here's where the ammunition goes. Fine sand, now," he says, patting the ground, "that there's the safest thing you can stuff in there, unsafest for whoever you're pointing at. Anything more—"

"—will make it explode?" I say, a bit of concern in my voice. The tierless districts aren't known for their expert craftsmanship.

He snorts in the manner which I presume men do to avoid giggling. "Just because I made this thing doesn't mean its blueprints weren't bona fide Archive. No, the little light," he says, smacking the thing shut and running his hands across the red stripes painted on the sand-beige chassis, "*might* turn red, and if your orator wasn't the most talented it *might* not fire. Then you'll have to empty the chamber and stick in a new load of sand. I wouldn't worry too much about it, but it doesn't hurt to be thorough."

"How long does a full clip of sand last?"

"It's called a buffer, and I never really thought about it." He looks at the rifle and tilts his head. "If you'd make me guess, a million. You know how pre-Laceration guns work, right?"

"I didn't study them in particular."

"So, no." He shakes his head a bit. "Alright," he says, turning the rifle on its top and poking at a large, rectangular prism jutting out from under it, "this here's what we call the sink. I don't know how it turns sand into killing machines, but whatever it does steams up fierce. Can't shoot once it gets too hot." He pauses. "Well, you sure can, but I sure as hell wouldn't."

"Why doesn't the sink face forwards?" I say, looking closer; the sink has a little rounded rectangle along its length, empty. "It could fire its excess heat."

"In a way, it already does. Turning it into a weapon, though—not the brightest of ideas." He chuckles grimly. "When I say 'hot', I mean *hot*. The last time someone tried that, well—you ever been steamed alive? Bodies told me it's not too pleasant."

I nod. "How do I know when it turns hot?"

"When you're dead."

I stare at him.

"Just my sense of humor." He stands up, bringing the rifle to bear and pointing it out towards the horizon. Taking a deep breath, he moves forwards to the field, very carefully angling only the tip out. His foot lands on a little bit of the strip of encroaching wildsand along the barrier's rim. "Think it'd be a bit better if I showed you."

He exhales and pushes down on the trigger; without the enormous racket of the projectiles themselves, the gentle sound of a sessile-arm firing—a gentle tchuk-tchuk—is actually somewhat soothing. It's impossible to see anything coming from the tip, but one of the Pari dunes lets out a continuous stream of sand billowing up into the sky as his finger keeps still. He keeps this up as a shrill whistling starts; it rises in pitch until, with a final cry, a visible, tiny column of heat pillars out of its end and the high whistle turns into a quick, deep thudding.

"That's what I mean, see?" he says, nodding to himself and letting go; the sound turns slower and quieter, terminating half a second later in a single ascending note. "If we did that little stunt in the barrier, you'd see the membrane turn pink before you couldn't."

I briefly ponder the physics, as far as I can speculate. "The kinetic force would disintegrate the sand on contact with the air, wouldn't it? How far can it fire?"

"Hell if I know. Nothing's left when it hits anyway, and the thing hurts worse than a post-Lac no matter what." He snaps his fingers absentmindedly. "Probably because you usually live just long enough to feel it. You know what one of these does, right?" he asks, patting the stock.

"I've treated a few pre-Laceration gunshot wounds, yes." For some reason, the things make particularly troublesome holes; whatever the projectiles' physical nature, I refuse to believe the twisting, numerous burrows through the flesh they cause are anything but designed. "Paralytic and anticoagulant, but I don't know how. It's almost like it was made to go through unarmoured targets. I can't imagine the people who made them were very nice."

He sits back on the sand, brushing some imaginary sand off his rifle's stock. "Maybe that's why the Laceration happened."

We're both silent for a bit—not out of respect for a catastrophe that *might* have happened a few thousand years ago, mind, we're not so unbearably sentimental, but more out of a general paucity of topics. There's probably no other topic worse than the weather.

"So," he says, "ever killed anyone?"

I ponder the question for a bit.

"On purpose?" I say, snapping my fingers absentmindedly, "No. I've failed a lot of people and I could not control myself for one and I never meant to kill another, but no."

He nods. "Never had a gun in your hands?"

"Once," I say. "Post-Laceration. He was in a firefight and the guard was wrapped around his broken finger while he convulsed. I had to pull it off while I mended the bone."

"Must've been dangerous."

I close my eyes and concentrate for a bit, trying to reconstruct the image in my head.

I open them. "The clip was empty."

"It's called a 'magazine'," he says, unstrapping the weapon from his back and walking over to me before kneeling until his face is level with mine, his arms reaching forwards with it in tow, "You want a try?"

I decide to avoid wondering what weapons have to do with storefronts and look at the almost rectangular weapon, reaching over and grabbing it by the end as if it were a knife cutting through my palm and I hear a language I do not understand whispering burning cold and finding myself hearing the cries of a thousand dying as the fire descended upon them and turned their flesh to ash and filled their last moments with the *pain* and it *hurts* and it *hurts it hurts it hurts* **it hurts why**—

I no longer feel the weight in my hands, and the soreness in my throat tells me I've been screaming; by the pressure on my left shoulder and my wobbling vision, I quickly infer that I'm being shaken in a manner that might kill a baby.

I reach up and grab him by the wrists; the shaking quickly stops, giving me a mild case of whiplash. Ayerei's breathing is heavy—I realise with a start that so is mine—and his hands are tight around my shoulders. His eyes are staring into mine, and I gently brush his hands off me.

His voice has the character of unease about it. "The *hell* happened to you, lady?"

"It hurt," I say, my voice almost infantile, and my attempt to soothe the slight irritation around my eyes reveals to me in quite an unwelcome manner that I've apparently been lacrimating rather freely. "I don't know why, but it hurt."

He lets a deep breath out. "Isha. Heard of people getting a *little* jitter with the pre-Lacs, usually Zhanghwazh—never seen anyone get *that* riveted up. Y'okay?"

He waits for an entire minute as I look blankly at the space between my outspread legs, snapping my fingers to keep the rhythm as I sing quickly and efficiently. My heartbeat is slightly elevated, my electroencephalogram is normal and there is no evidence of chemical contamination in my bloodstream.

I'm fine, and my hands are only very slightly shaking as I snap them.

"I'm fine," I say, reaching back almost unconsciously to feel the little scar on my neck. I've delivered medicine directly to the bloodstream with a needle-given hole before, but never *through* a needle. "I'm completely fine."

"That wasn't *fine*. Just about screamed your head off," he says, shaking his head. "I'm not one to pry, but, well—you *might* want to get yourself checked up, be sure you're not too gunshy to grow out of it."

The sun is halfway through the sky as I push myself up.

"I've checked myself up already," I say, holding my hand out. "One more time."

Before he can respond, three thunderous crackling noises come echoing from the city in series, the sound resonating as if from the bottom of a great pit; as I see the membrane twisting very slightly—I look closely and see that there are three ripples, allowing me to breathe a sigh of relief—a familiar voice, speaking now in Aimelan, booms out and resonates through the membrane.

Children of Aimela and of Cimsas. Of you we have one already: a child, who has felt already the sickly glow of the Pretender. Come hither, to the square of this city, that you may find yourself purged of the pretender in your midst.

"Hey," Ayerei says, unhesitantly starting to walk over to our mounts as he sticks a hand down one of the pouches slung over his shoulders, "you've held a postlac before, haven't you?"

I follow quickly, mounting my own glasswalker as he gets onto his. "Medically."

Right before he gets on to his own walker, he pulls a thick, L-shaped piece of grey metal from the thing and throws it to me; I barely grab hold onto it. "Where did you get this?" I ask, balancing the weapon in my right hand—conspicuously absent of mind-crushing sensation—and the instrument around my neck in my left.

"Look down the top, shoot to kill."

Before I can ask for clarification, he's three metres away and my glasswalker is keeping pace.

Glasswalkers go very, very fast; the most practical speed limit they have that I'm aware of is how hard their hooves may press before they sink into the sand. I quietly orate a mitigator membrane, and I feel the slightly sick fullness flowing down my throat and wrapping around my organs a full minute quicker than the usual minute-and-ten-seconds.

Ayerei seems perfectly tranquil, but we're almost a hundred centimetres lowered into the ground by the time we arrive at the stone; the bottom of my dishdasha is covered almost entirely in sand, blown upwards and around us. The stone doesn't crack under our glasswalkers' hooves, but the hollow spaces beneath the risen rock resonate in an oddly harmonious fashion as we descend the slope to the city's centre. The people on the streets pass by in a blur, but their evasive manoeuvres are easily perceptible.

There is a straight line to the clearing that makes up our destination, but as we get closer—the slope accelerating our descent—and as it becomes easier to make out the shapes before us, it becomes quite clear that the scenario that awaits us is not welcoming.

Through the twisted keyhole view from down the street, widening as we draw closer and widening to convergence, a single man in the black-on-white uniform is clearly visible; above them, almost out of sight beyond the quickly-disappearing greebles, is a single red-dressed man holding a sessile in his left hand and the same pre-Laceration things as the others standing bow-legged in front of the city fountain.

Far more interesting than the man himself, however, is the sight of a young Aimelan adult on his knees, looking hatefully up at a man with his gun to his head, and then the gun in question raising without preamble to the street as we soar down it.

I can hear Ayerei chanting something in his accented Angzhwen past the wind in my ears as we draw closer. His fists clench and he puts his legs high, and as we burst out into the square my view of the events is particularly clear:

Firstly, as I turn my head to the left—a purely arbitrary move—I can see a man in traditional Zhanghwazh clothing arguing with the two soldiers in the square, flanked by two similar-but-armed men. He begins to turn towards me, his mouth opening.

His nose is interestingly round.

At this point, I flip my head over to the right and Ayerei is no longer on his glasswalker. I do not have time to panic before I see him barrelling feet-first into the red-garbed man on the ground at what must be at least a hundred kilometres an hour, sending both of them into the reinforced marble of the statue-rounding barrierfountain.

I see Ayerei flick a wrist and the purple of the barrier extending to the tip of his finger, and realise that his oration's detailed a barrier threshold transformation. I see the red-garbed man's mouth open and see the blood streaming out as his internal organs are crushed against the suddenly intolerant barrier, and see the entire field around the edifice distorting as Ayerei screams.

The illusion of time slowing in danger is a particularly dangerous thing; the amygdala simply produces more memories of a situation, and so the image is simply more vivid in my instant recollection.

Perhaps that is why I *see* Ayerei's bones splintering and fracturing as the barrier refuses to tolerate his presence and begins to counteract his momentum entirely; perhaps that is why, perhaps owing to some sort of convoluted present-tense analysis of whatever memories might have formed in the second that I see it, I immediately realise that he's failed to account for his own momentum.

Perhaps that is why I imagine myself seeing the splinters of his appendicular skeleton reaching out and making little bumps through his skin right before it rips past; perhaps that is why, right before the ensuing flood, I can see the cortical bone as it shatters within the periosteum and peels it open, and why I can see the utter determination in his face fade like sugar in water into pure, overwhelming pain.

I should imagine some bravery in his face—some wish that we're fine, that what he did was worth it—but the only thing I can rightfully imagine about a man in this much pain is wish that it stops.

I see Perei looking back in shock and realise quite suddenly, as

I am observing the whole thing, that we are completely still and that my glasswalker's hooves are embedded several centimetres into the solid stone.

I also realise that the only reason I am not being fired upon is because everyone is just as utterly shocked by the spectacle as me; the fleeting thought comes to mind that these soldiers are not professionals, and then feel something brushing gently against my shoulder and then passing it by. I instinctively push my hand to it, instrument in hand, and feel a wetness with the consistency of blood.

My weapon is on the ground, and preservation begins to creep at the edges of my vision—the numbness is replaced quickly by an excruciating pain as I feel the split projectile tunneling into my flesh, and out of pure instinct I begin shouting out the rebinding instructions, moving my shoulder a little and the bind splits, letting the flesh tear further as the blood continues its constant flow and there is the very loud sound of gunpowder weapon discharge, and that is the point around which my mind fails me and I ponder what other event I might be referring to right before I no longer ponder.

two
The King's Lesson

A very great while ago,
over the Insurmountables
There was a king

He was harsh and crude
and had eyes sharp and rude
his people feared him
though he had never cheated or done evil
and had only brought wealth
so they respected him too

One day, a man
he was fifty-three
and walked past the guards who tried to stop him
and ducked under the arms of the bodyguards
who came to grab him
he went calmly to the throne
his stomach was thin
and came to the king
he asked for five thousand *lulus*
(which was what they called aluminium)
so he could start his business

Wanwanwan,
the king exclaimed,
and was joyful
you see, in their language
this means:
Your bravery is impressive
I will happily pay you your due

He took the money and started a business,
and became very rich and had a happy life.

One day this king
his face was very red
was thrown from power

by a scheming minister

He came to the man
who he had given hope
and he asked for shelter
and some charity

Wanwanwanwan,
the man exclaimed,
he laughed, for you see
in their language this is
Look at you now
from the high to the low
you are nothing now
you are worthless
where is your power
you are worthless
I have so much
yet you are worthless
Here, I will give you your money
have it all
maybe you can feed
your tired swine
you tired swine

He threw the pieces into the wet-mudded ground
of his silver-covered home
the king nodded silently
and he scraped the money from the ground
piece by piece
exactly five thousand

With the money he bought men
with the men he bought soldiers
with the soldiers he bought his kingdom

Then he summoned the wealthy man before him
and he gave him a big smile
he was very nice, more than usual
and

He had him
put to death.

The moral of this story is:
however truthful you may be,

however right you are,
however weak the other man,
treat people with kindness.

For fortune is quick
and death is long.

'The Merchant's Lesson', anonymous
Tales for Wise Children
compiled by Talesymyrei das Cimcharei
published by the Department of Education and approved for
private distribution by the Administration for Media Development under
the grace of Khaliesrea das Sikharea eliyit Tamarisrei, Administrator for
the Arts

3
Tækviesidyr
to provide a place of sanctuary

As soon as I emerge from preservation, some empty thought behind me, I am acutely aware of a stinging in my right deltoid muscle.

The pain, I reflect as I scream and grab at my shoulder or I would if my arms weren't bound to my sides so expertly that I find them immovable and panickedly begin to try and scream heat out of my hands, is far more noticeable in its after-effect (as my nerves try and reassert themselves) than it is in the initial shock. There is a pressing on my chest and a finger—a finger, not a hand—to my mouth, at which point I blink my eyes to clear the tears within fogging my view of the gentle, thin purple barrier tinting the black night a metre above me as I take a single deep breath.

I see Perei's face—contorted into an expression I cannot quite identify or name, some kind of adamant desperation—above me and I exhale. The sigh isn't the longest I've ever breathed in relief, but it certainly ranks among the greatest. He draws his hand away from my mouth, and I realise with a start that he's quietly singing a Khamisret-Aparkisrea field; I gently look up and see that I am belted to the glasswalker on which I am apparently riding on in the normal fashion, my wrists bound to each other by what seem to be tightly-bound strands of grown fabric wound around the walker's underside.

He quickly moves over and feels at the cloth for a bit before finding the knot and letting it loose; the thick, discrete bits come off my wrists. I carefully sit up, feeling a bit of cotton around my left forearm. I look over to see it stained red and almost laugh out loud. The anachronism is immediately palpable; it's clear that Perei doesn't know how to rebind.

Judging by the sorry state of the membrane around us—it's clear that quite a bit of effort is being expended to sustain it, and I feel a sudden, quiet rush of fear as I realise that it's unlikely that he'll keep going like this for long—he hasn't quite had much experience with barriers.

I've got plenty of questions, but this isn't the time for any of them; immediately, I feel about my neck for my instrument and begin fiddling, singing for my life. I can almost feel the palpable—physical, certainly, as the perfectly modulated barrier threshold sends its familiar shimmer through my bones—relief as I force a gapless rephase. The force seems to push from within, and soon I get the feeling that it is safe to pause my oration. It will be a few weeks until the next Shenwyzhchyn; I will have a few minutes to live even if the barrier crashes.

I take another deep breath and sit myself up, taking a closer look at the gauze wrapped around the outside—the *outside!*—of my clothes. The blood has clotted somewhat, and I am suffering an inexplicable urge to ruminate on my perpetually sanguinic state.

And then I remember what's happened and look to my side to see Perei's tired eyes; Ayerei's rifle is strapped over his back.

"Where is Ayerei," I say, turning my head up to let the breath flow easier, "and why aren't we in Sipshirea?"

"Don't know where he is. Took his stuff, got on the walker and out of town as quick as we could." He pauses for a bit. "He looked real bad."

"He fell sideways at several hundred kilometres an hour and incorrectly calculated a barrier threshold. He would be in a bad way, yes." I inhale and exhale again as I reach over to my shoulder and gently strip the gauze off; there is only a single entry wound, and it takes about half a second to rebind, but I can feel the lacerations underneath reaching almost to the bone. "How did we get out?"

"Must've had snipers. Bounced straight off the black bits— probably broke a few ribs, way they were screaming—ripped right through the white bits. Bolt-action, if I'm guessing right—didn't stay long enough to check."

His eyes give off the impression of absolute regret.

"So," I say, looking about, "where're we going?" I might normally ask 'where are we', but it seems to generally be a futile enterprise to wonder where exactly a person is on the Glass Sea without a sessile at hand—there is nothing as far as I can see but the burnt and settled silicon cracking under us, and I can tell we're not lost (at the very least) by the fact that our breaks in the glass aren't alone.

"Well," he says, looking out in front of us, "you said Tachiesrea, and that's the safest place that ever was if there ever was one. So that's where we're going. Followed the sign, gave the place-number. We're taking the long way 'round—don't want them finding us."

I nod. "How long have we been travelling?"

"Sun set two hours ago."

I nod and lie back, gingerly treating my arm as I gently continue singing.

The sun is rising by the time we rise over the enormous Pari dunes, and I'm not nearly as tired as I ought to be.

I've never been to Tachiesrea—few people have—but like anybody else might I immediately recognise the place: the verdigris roofs stand over carefully crafted stone buildings (not that I can't hardly see the stone past the moss), the condensation pooling at the very top of the absurdly tall field gathers in thick, fluffy patches and where my field of vision meets the intersection of two of its hemispheres I see a deep, unabiding blue.

It will be several minutes before we reach, going at our pleasantly slow pace—going faster would be an invitation for gunfire.

"So," Perei says, seeing that I've stopped singing, "who's after us?"

I narrow my eyes at him, then wince a bit as my shoulder shifts. The thing's mostly sealed, but the internal wounds remain somewhat fragile. "What makes you think we're that important?"

"Hey, just calling it like it is. Day you get cooled, whole city gets blown up. Day we get to that Sip place, my—" He pauses, then shakes his head. "Ayerei. Ayerei gets his legs blown up and they say they're looking for someone. That can't be a coincidence."

I decide against giving him a debriefing. "Perhaps they're hunting everyone from Cimsas."

"Why everyone from the city?" he asks, and now that I've got the time to listen closely to his speech I realise that his clipped Low Aimelan bastardisation of the Central phrase *àur medimatrbhum li* makes it sound as if he's referring to a city named *Àmedichuli*, "and why the hell did they say they were looking for something called the *pretender*? I don't know what that is, and I don't like it."

"I don't *know*," I say, sighing deeply. "I'm not psychic. If we're ever going to get an answer, it's going to be in Tachiesrea."

He shrugs as cynically as I can imagine a person shrugging. "That's if they let us in. The *capital* just got blown up. You think they're gonna be nice to just anybody waltzing in there and going 'hey, we just about got our holes put on ice, praytell whyfor'?"

His dénouement is in a nasal mockery of Aimelari, and I squint at him before tilting my head in inquisition. "Is 'whyfor' even a word?"

He crosses his arms and rolls his eyes. "I don't know, but it *should* be."

I shake my head and decide—quite wisely, in my opinion—not to start a debate.

It takes four minutes for the gunshots to start.

"Rear up," I say, and Perei obliges with a quick upwards tug on the reins. From this distance, the transition between the soft sand encroaching on the grassy hamlet upon which the blue-and-white watchtowers are situated and the jagged bits of melted and broken silicon before is clearly visible, even if most of the barrier finds itself outshone by the sun.

The two figures in the distance on walkerback take about ten minutes to make their way to us; we're silent for the duration, and I spend the time in idle thought and quiet barrier reinforcement. The few stripes of light blue emblazoned over the sand-stained white fatigues— these obviously aren't officers—come into sight past the heat and the barrier pulsations as they draw up to us, one continuing to softly orate as he bears his sessile (not an instrument, just a sessile) and the other his rifle.

Our barriers merge gently, and I catch the redundant tail of a rephase attunement as the field between us evaporates, allowing me to see clearly their relatively pale, shaven faces; I suppose Tachiesrea would be the best place to send a fortunate son. The star-topped nametag on the one in front is inscribed with a name: *Abkhasirei das Cimcharei.*

The one at the back continues to orate, and the one at the front relaxes a neck that seems to have been stiff forever as his eyes do a quick pass over us. His weapon doesn't go down.

"It isn't particularly wise for one going around these parts unaccompanied, isn't it?" he says, talking in a slow, quasi-Administrative drawl, the hard, high syllables of High Aimelan weathered like a stone left out the membrane. "Especially dressed like one of our misguided brothers in the South."

"This is Tachiesrea, isn't it?" I say, raising my eyebrows and glancing a bit towards the pale azure stripes printed into the fabric; they're exactly the same shade, though mine are slightly darker with novelty. "The Velvet Citadel."

"Placenames, now? Well, *that*—" he says, pointing to the southeast, "used to be the Shimmering Tribunal. Unweariness would not suit our situation well." He takes a long, hard look at me; I can almost feel his eyes pressing against my dishdasha. "I fear that I must interrogate you for some form of identification."

I feel aimfully about where I'm accustomed towards keeping my permit; quite naturally finding it missing, I look immediately towards the back of Ayerei's glasswalker.

A few slightly torn shards of bloodied fabric hang off its back.

"I'm afraid I don't have my permit with me," I say, nodding slowly to match the rhythm of my speech as I quickly remember the requisite Aimelari phrase. "I am a second-tier citizen of the Aimelari Administration as a ward of the Church of Ocilentra under the grace of the Abbess. We come as refugees."

The soldier's eyes scan me and then the somewhat raggedy-looking Perei, who is staring at me in a particularly unhelpful way with his sessile-arm quite clearly stuck over his chest.

"Then may I make an enquiry as to *her* forms of identification?"

"He," he says; the consonant is palatalised. "Tierless over here. Only passport I have's my skin."

Abkhasirei—I wouldn't usually resort to using the names of people I don't know, but the pronoun is becoming quickly ambiguous— looks between us again; his eyes narrow very slightly, but his tone remains friendly.

"Please," he says, "come with me."

I sigh rather thankfully and lean forwards a bit in my saddle as Perei gives the instruction to follow.

I sigh rather thanklessly and lie back onto the holding cell's bare steel wall as Perei glares at me from across it.

"Wow," he says, his voice as bitter as a political simile. "Is the answer 'get blindfolded then locked up'? 'Cause I think that's what I just heard. We came *how* many miles for this?"

"They can't hold us forever. We're Aimelan citizens."

He rolls his eyes as he might hang a particularly ferocious lampshade. "How *gullible* are you? What if they know—"

I look through him.

That is not to say that I look *at* him; I simply look in his direction and stare at the wall behind him, and he stops speaking.

"Isha's hooks," he says, looking away from me before looking back through a single eye, "that's creepy."

"The nails upon which your prophet was hung upon his instrument of death notwithstanding," I say, pausing to take a breath, "we're clearly Aimelan."

"That isn't really convincing argument coming from one so dressed, is it?" Perei doesn't say, and I look right past the bars to see a man in Administrative clothes—his vest is notably as black as the soft night, as if dyed to disarm, and the little instrument hanging from his neck looks quite charmingly to be made of wood and catgut—standing about half a metre from us; there are no other prisoners, a fact which I find curious.

What Perei *does* say doesn't help our case much; he furrows his brow at him irritatedly. "Who the hell're you and why the hell're we here?"

"I understand that you hail from Cimsas," he says, nodding to himself. "My name is Parakheirei das Vasksharei es-Maurenia, and I believe we have business to discuss."

What strikes me first and foremost about the seat that I am in is not its relative comfort—the beds of cheap inns and church dormitories and turned-back saddles aren't the softest things I can imagine—but the Eastward Compass stitched into the enormous antimacassar pushes up between my scapulae and makes its presence known between them and above my head.

The chair itself seems to be built for someone far larger than me.

Perei fidgets in the seat to the right, looking back nervously towards what looks to be a wooden door; the man leans casually over the similarly wooden table and smiles at me.

"Who are you?" he says.

"We're citizens of the Aimelari Administration," I begin, and he interrupts me with a raised finger.

"Aimelan Administration, please, and I'm afraid that's not entirely correct." His smile seems sympathetic. "You aren't technically a citizen of Aimela now."

I stare at him. "You don't even know my face name."

He shrugs and leans further forwards, putting his hands out; his suit covers everything up to his wrists. "The books might corroborate your identity, but there are things far more important than books."

Perei snorts. "Like what?"

The man's left hand reaches back into his loose cuff, and as he flicks his wrist from it I feel a curious breeze and I look down and see a three-centimetre wide slit across the fatty region of my forearm; Perei's eyes open wide, and he is gripping hard enough on the armrest that I imagine he might crack the mahogany.

"Blood," he says, tapping at his sessile with what seems to be a heavily-cultivated absentmindedness. "That's the passport sequence; of course you're not an administrator. The administrative sessile counteracts the citizenship process. You're the Pretender."

I watch as he puts his blade down under the desk.

"What are you saying?" I say, watching him carefully fumbling about with a deliberate aimlessness with his unseen hand; I force myself to ignore the urge to rebind the wound. "Are you with the—"

"The Nation?" he says, and pulls out out a device which—though I haven't seen anything like it before—looks very much like a pre-Laceration weapon pressed into sidearm form; it's promptly pressed against my forehead.

A silent moment passes.

"Certainly," he says, and fires.

The wall to my side, titanium plates on stone shaped into historical tributes, finds itself with quite a few new dents; I notice this a few seconds after I notice that I am not dead and see that the administrator's arm is twisted about thirty degrees to the side, Perei's right hand wrapped tightly around the wrist leading to his splayed hand and a while before I find that the sound of flesh burning is different enough to that of metal being punctured that I can tell when Perei's left hand yanks the dropped weapon from the table and fires before I hear the scream or see the blood it has hit its mark.

I blink in confusion and instinctively begin to try and rebind the enormous wound in the man's arm, clearly having rent through the bone and muscle and skin enough that I can't even see the points where the projectile—the projectiles—have entered and merged and cut through the skin and bled.

Before I can finish my sentence, Perei turns the weapon about on its trigger and grips the little protruding bit tightly. I barely see the motion that bashes its grip into the man's mouth, filling it with blood. He is shouting something I don't quite understand and my eyes are opened as wide as they ever might have been and he's grabbing the man's head by the hair and slamming it down into the table and doing it again and again and again.

I shout something which I can't hear, holding Perei by the right wrist; the movement doesn't slow him in the slightest, and he completes another bash before realising that my hand is touching him. He looks at me as if I'm insane as his blood-covered hands drip a single drop onto the table.

"He just about *shot you in the head*, Ash!"

I don't bother arguing yet; the man is still conscious, though struggling to push himself off the table. His nose is broken and face is coated in blood, and I immediately oration-cut his other sleeve—this leads to an awful cut across his forearm but he won't die from it—and tie it around the root of the continuously bleeding mess that comprises his upper arm, wincing as my bullet wound bruises. None of the tendons have been torn, but the fasciae seem to have burst almost like little balloons filled with gore and the arm's humerus has been fractured and splintered beyond repair; he'll need a new appendage entirely.

Perei presumably has understood my motive, and thankfully remains silent as I do my work. I can almost physically feel the adrenaline going through him as I hold the man by the hair, tilting him forwards so that the blood stays out of his lungs. There is a moment of quiet—punctuated by wet slurps and sniffles—as I take a deep breath.

"Why?" I say, and as I speak I notice that my teeth are chittering and tears are forming at the rims of my eyes for a reason I cannot quite pin down and cannot justify. I've never had a gun pointed at me before; I glance at the object in Perei's hand, and see that he's trained it squarely on the administrator's head.

The man's breathing comes shallow and quick, and I hold him by the hair and push his head back so that he faces the ceiling. He blinks quickly, as if in surprise, and I put my hand against the impromptu tourniquet and hold the instrument around his neck and begin playing it before I start to rebind his torn and ripped side.

After a few seconds, his shaking pupils visibly relax and he starts taking deep breaths. "Grab his legs," I say, and Perei dutifully goes around the table to pull the man's legs up upon it.

"What if somebody heard us?" he asks, looking quickly between me and the door. He seems more composed than me, but the fabric around the administrator's legs rustle to the pattern of his own shuddering hands.

"I doubt he'd try to murder us in a room that wasn't soundproofed," I say, checking to see if he's still conscious. "Are you awake?"

He spits at me; the bloody saliva pooled in his mouth splatters across my cheek.

I've had worse on my face, but before I can wipe it off a fist comes in from the left and bashes into his already swollen cheek, sending his head twisting harshly to the right. I instinctively look towards Perei, who is gritting his teeth in a fearful sort of barely-contained rage.

"He needs to be conscious," I say, wiping the mess off with the back of my hand.

A wet, painful voice emerges from within the man's broken mouth; the only words I can catch—separated by sounds only expressible onomatopoeically—are *ask* and *hell*, neither of which are very encouraging. He is very pointedly looking away from his shattered arm.

"He's tighter than Alistarea," Perei says, tapping the gun against the table and looking anxiously over his shoulder. "We gotta *go*."

"To *where*?" I ask, looking into the man's teary, blood-smattered eyes. "We've got nowhere to go if we don't get some answers."

"Wherever where we're not next to a dying admin, alright? For Isha's sakes." He exhales deeply and groans into his bloodstained hands. "We can't *stay* here. We're riveted, you understand? We're right next to a dead—"

"He's still alive."

"—a dying admin. That's life to death right there."

"Join the club."

I turn back to the man, who's closed his eyes. "Who sent you? Why did you try to kill me?"

There is a knocking on the door before he has the opportunity to respond—the opportunity, not the will—and almost immediately his eyes turn open and a load groaning sound accompanied by a spatter of blood issues from the back of his throat.

"Oh *shit*," he says, as a muffled voice goes through the door— something like 'is everything alright in there'. "We're riveted, I *told* you we're riveted, this room isn't soundproofed oh *God*. We've gotta get out of here *now*."

I anaesthetise him in seven syllables and begin to look about the room before he goes into preservation; besides the artful decoration about the walls and the iron-shuttered window engraved with the Eastward Compass behind the chair in which the administrator lays unmoving, nothing recommends it. This room obviously wasn't made for prolonged habitation. I quickly ruffle about the slowly breathing man's pockets until I find a little circular object and keep my left grip on it as tight as I can.

"There," I say, pointing towards the window. "If he didn't soundproof the room, he wouldn't have bulletproofed the windows." I pull the instrument over the now-preserved man's head and pull it over my own, twanging it experimentally. The tones are dulcet.

"What about Ay's piece?" he says, looking nervously towards the still-knocked-upon door. His only slightly bloodied right hand tightens around the weapon's grip, and as I get a closer look at it I see that it's less of a pistol than it is a fat, short sort of sessile-arm, its barrel protruding barely a centimetre from a body that looks to be a fourth the size it should be.

"You want to hesitate *now?*" I say, almost sprinting over as I check for the release mechanism; my hands feel about the right side of the thing and feel a fair bit of sessile cloth on the solid steel. The thing lets out a little buzzing sort of noise as I touch it, a few words compressed to the point that I can no longer make them out, and a little click resounds from the frame right before a heretofore unseen metal weight drops from its upper-right corner, letting the shutters fly up to reveal the deserted moss-covered stone pavement and shining, wet grass.

The knocking turns more urgent, and the voice that comes with it does considerably louder.

"I was made aware of a screaming and puncturing noise emanating from this room. Is anything the matter, sir?"

I tap at the glass, hoping to find the unlock mechanism, before I notice the thick, black substance around its edges. "It's tar-sealed," I say, and I notice in passing that my voice has a slight character of desperation. "Airtight. I could try and sing some white spirits and dissolve the—"

"Out of the way," he says, and I immediately comply, pushing myself up against the wall just in time to hear a very loud *shunk*.

I can imagine seeing the cracks begin to rip almost intelligently through the splintering glass before the structures shatter entirely with an incredible violence, sending the shards flying outwards and embedding themselves into the scenery behind it.

The knocks quickly grow more urgent—the sound doesn't resonate, the stone behind the metal soaking it up—and by the time I look back to where Perei's meant to be standing he's already hurriedly trying to get over the window's rim without hurting himself.

As I follow his lead, I can feel the bits of glass in the grass poking up against the cracked ceramic on my worn formal shoes just fail to pierce the hardened leather.

"You know this place better than me," he says, glancing nervously behind him; the knocking on the door has been replaced by a silence where footsteps might fit, and whatever larceny might be in him—I'd imagine a chunk of one of the oaks laying freely about might fetch a fair price if he could smuggle it out—seems to have been driven out by fear. "Where to?"

"Reserve Council." I look about and quickly find the characteristic spire of Aimelan governmental architecture, exactly as it is in the textbook. I let my left hand relax a bit and the fingers open up to reveal the Eastward Compass inscribed on a little aluminium-and-steel coin, spawncloth pressed onto its other side. "We'll need new clothes," I say, glancing at the tattered, dirty rags that cover his body from ankle to neck in a shameless mockery of human decency, "but I've got an administrator's permit."

"What, that's about *two* admins you seen dead now?" He takes a deep breath, putting his newfound weapon against his hip. "We've gotta go back for Ay's stuff."

"He's still alive," I say, "and you're insane." My answer is very courteously punctuated with a very loud bang, and the screams of horror behind us seal the decision.

We run without looking back.

The Aimelan Guard is an institution dating back more than a thousand years, and their colours have remained the same for every single one of them: white for incineration and pale azure for hypothermia. As I run around the side of the building, not entirely sure where I'm going, I catch sight of those colours painted along the frieze curved in the shape of words: *Pratrmra Mysuynnjgul.*

The particular elision is unique to the Guard; *pramatrumra, for the motherland,* isn't quite so poetically laconic.

"This isn't good," I say, a modicum of restraint in my voice as we run along the strangely deserted path. I look closer at the coin I'm holding and flip it over; on its reverse side is the face of Kanandrisra dar Oder, his name printed along the top edge and *Tachiesrea Defence Division* along the bottom. "That's a Guardsman outpost and this is a Guardsman permit. If he's working with the people who shelled Cimsas—"

"Doesn't matter *what's* trying to rivet us," he huffs, and as he does something nearby begins to shrill, the noise resonating through the entirety of the city's barrier. I instinctively cover my ears, but I hear a voice explode through the haze of sound nonetheless:

An administrator has been found mutilated in critical condition in the Taraminarei Military Detention Facility. Two Mahammadir insurgents in ragged clothing are believed to be responsible and in the immediate vicinity of the attack. They are armed and extremely dangerous.

Before he's finished with his first sentence, we've run well out of sight of the facility; there is a sudden murmuring in the once-silent air as the announcement concludes, however, and I realise with a sinking sort of horror that the only reason for their prior absence was sleep.

"As I was saying," I say, nibbling on my bottom lip and looking nervously at the back of the bungalow we're behind, itself facing outwards from another on the vibrant grass with its parterre glistening with flowers that look as though they belong only painted and framed in a museum, "We need new clothes."

For once, Perei seems thoughtful; he quickly trods up to the nearest window—it's got two gold stripes on it, and the Mahammadir symbol seems particularly out of place here—of the dwelling we're behind, jumps up to its level and hooks on for a second, breathing quickly as he strains to take a look through.

He drops down and smiles. "I spy a two-space and a dresser. We'll get plenty in there."

"We can't *rob* them," I say, glaring at him. "How do you even know they're not there?"

"Experience."

"What do you mean, *experience?*"

He levels his newfound weapon up to the window and before I can say anything an enormous banging sounds; as I recover from the shock and take a look, I see that a section in the wall about two metres wide is utterly perforated, thousands of tiny, see-through holes letting light past. The moss is charred from the friction, bits of the rich tapestry peeling from it and falling onto the grass below as the moisture goes up in steam.

"Experience on beds." He snickers, then quickly grabs what I presume to be the 'magazine', flips something on the chassis, pulls it out and peers in before smacking it back in. "Some get up to fifty when you cut 'em down, y'know?"

I don't take it upon myself to stop him. "What?"

"What d'you think they locked me up for?" he says, and fires again; this time, the stone cracks and begins to shatter as the kinetic force bashes against it. "Sure wish I had one of these my last run. "

He fires again and a bit of wall big enough for a man to fit through simply shatters. Fragments of stone burst out against the red-carpeted floor and bounce off the wooden furniture.

"Cut out the middleman, you know what I mean?"

"You *burgle* for a living?"

He rolls his eyes, shaking his head. "No. I *steal* for a living. Now, with one of these," he says, patting the weapon and strides right into the room, going straight for the dresser, "we get to *choose*. That's what I call freedom."

I stare at him with my mouth open; he opens the dresser up and pulls out a flowing purple dress, adorned with flakes of silver and aluminium. It is held aligned with his shoulder, and flows down to his knees.

"Want some new digs or what?"

"You still smell awful."

I try my best to look forwards as we walk down the pavement, already having taken the full view of Perei's admittedly fair sense of fashion—a simple set of light brown servant's trousers below an oration-buttoned shirt and vest. Each administrator seems to have some obsession with something or the other, and it figures that the one we'd find had had it be clothing; a somewhat large bag hangs with its string about Perei's waist, packed with replacement clothes that I'm almost certain he intends to sell.

The few people we can see are almost entirely visibly old, even for administrators; the youngest of them looks to be about a hundred, a few wrinkles showing up around his mouth.

"These people? Like they smell worth a damn. That guy," he says, somewhat surreptitiously pointing over to one of the men walking about, "has to be at least a hundred fifty."

I look at him as well, and even across the metres that separate us I can see a sort of suspicious attention in his wrinkled eyes; I make sure to whisper as I retort. "Keep your voice down. We don't want to know if any of these administrators have amplification sessiles."

He opens his mouth as if to argue before apparently deciding to bow out in grace.

I glance up at the spike that marks the Reserve Council; the smaller minarets have become more clearly visible, standing as magnificent complements to the spire. I might normally enjoy the sight, but I cannot help but ask the question.

"You didn't tell me you were a *thief*."

He raises an eyebrow. "I'm pretty sure I did. While we were running streetways, right?"

"Well, I'm *sorry* I don't remember," I say, taking a pause to bite a little at my somewhat dry lower lip. "I might have been a bit too busy fearing for my life as my home crumbled around me."

"Your *home*?" he says, nodding his head with his words, "You can't tell me you *liked* the capital. Fleshcrawlers below and sowpigs on top."

I do a quick look about before responding; no one seems to have taken undue notice of us. "Fleshcrawlers and sowpigs have vital roles in Aimelan society. Would you rather have rotting corpses lining the streets?"

"Hell no," he says, smiling in a particularly exhausted way as he lets a slight gust issue through his teeth, creating a perfect expression of grim acceptance. "You ever thought why there's dead bodies in the first place, Ash?"

I shrug.

"People die."

"Not *these* people."

"They're administrators. They've proven their worth to society."

He sweeps his hand quite conspicuously about. "And what the hell're they doing down here, huh? Tactical buffet allocation? If the admins in the capital were sowpigs, these're bloodsuckers. At least the capital's got *politics* to rivet them to the wall, and the fleshcrawlers."

"Don't *do* that," I say, looking nervously about in an attempt to reassure myself that no one has seen us before giving him what I hope to be a withering glare. "How on the Glass Sea do you know so *much* about the administrators?"

He stands adamant in the face of my feeble attempt at the exercise of social pressure. "You'd be surprised how much you can learn crawling in their wall-gaps. I take the time to get to know the people I rob."

I shake my head. "That's besides the point. You had *friends* in Cimsas, didn't you? Aren't you worried for them?"

"And there's not a *single goddamn fucking thing* I can do about it if I did, is there?" His expression remains as neutral as it always has been as he speaks, but there's a slight raising of pitch in the back of his throat.

I decide not to respond, and we continue walking. The buildings have gotten noticeably taller, and I've spotted several storefronts, mostly advertising manufactured goods at profoundly unreasonable prices. The morning commute—if it really can be called that—appears to be beginning, A few of the men and women—their skin is noticeably considerably more tanned than that of the administrators of Cimsas—stop to look at us briefly before moving on.

"This dress has to be worth a fortune," I say, leaning over a bit to speak directly into his ear. "If the owner's here—"

"Excuse me?" a voice in Aimelari issues from behind me, and if I weren't more composed than I was I might literally have jumped up in terror. I turn about to see who's accosting me, and find myself facing a rather well-dressed man in a violet coat.

"Yes, sir?" I say, replying in the most Aimelari accent I can muster without actually speaking the language; glancing to the right lets me see that Perei is playing perfectly the part of the polite mute, allowing me to heave a mental sigh. "May I know for what purpose you have requisitioned my attention?"

He looks at me strangely. "I just wanted to ask you about your dress. You seem very much a woman of taste—my wife has one exactly like it at home, though I was made to believe that it was one of a kind when I bought it. Would you be so kind as to clarify the matter for me?"

As he speaks, a certain cavalcade of feeling runs through me: there is the despair, of course, at the possibility that he is being coy and that I am going to be caught, there is the general heartfelt terror of what will happen if we *are* caught, and then there is quite suddenly an unusual peace that spreads through me—some kind of ill-conceived doctor-patient idea of calmness, as if I'm delivering an optimistic prognosis to a dying man in the street.

I am completely composed as I answer.

"I obtained this in a boutique in the Emirate; I too was told that its design was unique."

He harrumphs somewhat indignantly. "The *nerve*. I should have known those murderous scoundrels would fail to be truthful with an administrator. Bloody vicious pack animals," he says, and shakes his head.

"Thank you for bringing this to my attention. I'll be lodging a complaint with the Bureau."

"As will I," I say, trying to give off the impression of quiet outrage, putting my hand gently—not harshly, as though I were in the theatre, but gently—to my chest. "As will I."

He begins to turn away before quite suddenly seeming to have a change of heart, turning back towards me and squinting a bit. "Have you heard the news, perchance? Parakheirei, that outstanding boy of an officer—I've heard he's been involved in a terrifying incident. A jailbreak of sorts, two Mahammadiri. Might you know anything about them?"

"I'm afraid—" I begin, and hesitate; there is a slight backwards shift in his centre of weight as I do. "I'm afraid I know nothing of the sort."

"Well," he says nodding measuredly, "I'm sure you'd be more than happy to notify the proper authorities if you did. Good day."

He turns on his heel and begins striding off down the road the direction he came.

I turn to find that Perei raising his eyebrows at me as we begin walking again.

Not a word comes from him, but his stare unnerves me to the extent that I feel the need to speak.

"What?" I say, my arms bent at the elbow out to my sides in interrogation. "We've got to be quick. I don't think he—"

"Why Mahammadir?"

"The Southern Bauxite Vein," I say, shrugging. "I doubt any other province would produce aluminium-laced clothing."

"I know about the goddamned vein," he says, his voice getting a bit harsher, "but why *them*? He's going to talk to the Affairs Bureau. That guy's gonna lose his business."

"I didn't know you were the socially conscientious type."

"Hey," he says, stepping in front of me and causing me to stop in my tracks, "I take from the rich. I don't ruin innocent people's lives." He punctuates by poking me in the chest, and I almost hop back in shock.

I quickly look around; some people are already noticing us. "Simmer. If they see a servant poking an administrator—" I begin, and let the words trail off; he immediately turns back around and huffs, falling back into line.

"He's going to find the truth soon enough," I say. The place is becoming considerably more populated, but it's so sparse in any case—the distance between buildings has gone only from five metres to one—that the only real difference is the noise level, allowing us to speak slightly louder. I haven't seen any peacekeepers; I suppose anyone that gets in must be spotless already. "How do you know about the Bureau?"

"How d'*you*? I've lived with the muds my whole life."

"The 'muds'?" I say, looking at him in disbelief. "Are you being serious? Is that how you refer to everybody? Jings and muds?"

"Rivet the *words*," he says, waving his hand dismissively, "what's *important* is—is—"

His mouth is open, but no more words come.

"What?"

He seems almost ashamed as he speaks. "I forgot the point I was gonna make."

I try not to laugh, but a chuckle escapes; we walk the rest in the bliss of silence.

It is one thing to see the imprint of a historical structure in a book or a sessile.

It is quite the same to see it in person.

As we walk into the place, however, I must admit that there is a certain grandeur to being in the middle of it all; an enormous pillar juts from the barrierfountain—until now, the barrierline coming from the bit of it that protrudes up several storeys, an enormous column of energy spitting from the tip, has been completely invisible—seemingly carrying the weblike structure of verdigris-coated moss-caught stone that goes above us and connects to the five buildings in the centre, from which the enormous meeting-room minarets rise.

The one we're heading for is the largest of them all, the roof-spire—just as built with barriers propping it up as the Administrative Tower in Cimsas—going past the condensation layer.

The field seems to be noticeably well-built near the centre, and *this* is something I've never seen an imprint of; I've assumed until now that the barrier's vividity, visible from without, has been some sort of metameric confusion. The change from the fringes to the centre has been so gradual that I might not have noticed if I were looking all the while.

The sight, far more a triumph of man than any completely physical edifice, enraptures me.

"Hey," an uncouth, uncultured voice says, a rough finger poking me on the shoulder, "I can't see the ninjas."

My little reverie of contemplation interrupted, I force calm upon myself and turn to my companion with the most sardonic grin I can muster.

"What are you *talking* about?"

"Well," he says, shrugging, "you've been looking up for a whole minute. I figured there'd be ninjas."

I shake my head. "We've got to hurry. There's still an alert out for us."

He coughs rather sceptically as we march up the steps to the main building's green, cobbled exterior.

We're halfway up them before Perei's mouth appears to decide to prop itself open. "We're kinda wanted by the law. Ever thought what you're gonna say?"

"I'll improvise."

Before he can respond, we reach the main door and a man dressed in servant robes—almost the exact same design as Perei's—accosts us with a smile.

"Excuse me," he says, his syllables curving slightly in a particularly ethnic way, "but would you be kind enough to render your permit? Simple precautions, *ma'am*." His accent is so primarily Aimelan that the almost anachronistic expression of Pilisyari identity seems to be pure affectation.

I nod and pull the precious little coin from one of my pockets. "Of course."

He gently takes it, makes a show of inspecting it—going so far as to spend half a minute singing a tampering scan—before handing it back to me, the smile on his face staying all the while. "A member of our armed forces. I am instructed in this time of crisis to provide full support to our officer corps." He turns about, pulls a sessile from his pant-pocket and waves us through; the objective display it projects moves with his fingers, drifting on its 'inertia' before touching the wall and dissipating into a little shower of light.

Perei blinks at me as we walk through the centre of the marble hall leading to the main chamber. "Did he really just let us through on a *Guardsman* permit?"

"Be mute," I say, and open the door.

What first strikes me as I do is the cold.

It is—was, rather—normal for some nights in Cimsas to be somewhat frigid; the Administrative Tower might have been the capital's barrierfountain, but it's much easier to replace an oration on a fountain than it is to replace the same in a tower aspiring to touch the sky. The Cimsas barrier fed off a hundred years' worth of sessiles, but the Khamisret-Aparkisrea method had itself juryrigged into it; the barrier, on occasion, still interfered with the membrane, and a minute fraction of the cold of the night or heat of the day often sneaked through the little gaps it made.

I'm perfectly intimate with temperature.

This cold, however, is utterly different in ways I could write an essay about; the air is almost frozen, and my breath comes out from my mouth half-frozen in vapour. I look up to see the Reserve Council: four men for their provinces before us on their lecterns, each of them shouting incoherently as the ombundsman—situated above us on a protruding bit of stone—shouts himself for order. Along the sides of the chamber, at their own lecterns stood several metres above the ground on what look to be cut-out sections of structural pillars, are the nine foreign representatives, men and women keeping dead silent as they watch the uproar.

The inside of the spire is hollow, and at the tip I can see the condensation turning to frost. I begin to shudder uncontrollably and realise with a start that I'm beginning to suffer the onset of hypothermia; to my right, Perei is doing the same, his teeth chittering, but he refuses to utter a sound.

The warmth comes so suddenly I think for a moment that I might have died.

I blink my eyes; Perei yelps in what I presume to be some form of relieved shock, and one of the representatives, a man who I remember from some textbook—Peratirei qu'n'av dasnamr, a veteran of the Southern Mutiny and the Failed Return, the impeached Council representative for Far Aimela who now sits below the flag he drew in blood—speaks in a soft, high-pitched mockery of High Aimelan.

"Has the esteemed ombundsman's servants finally taken it upon himself to repair the heating facilities? I've been asking for the past half hour, I hope you realise."

The representative under the Central Aimelan flag—my representative, in a sense, though I don't think he's ever been on the actual Council and so I do not know his name—snarls at him. "Our government has been *decapitated*, our capital has been *destroyed*, we are at *war*—how could you possibly care of heat *now*, you nameless swine?"

He doesn't seem shocked in the slightest, though I notice in my peripheries a slight springing tightness in Perei's posture; leaning his cheek on his fist, he laughs, a thudding, harsh sound filled with practised mirth.

"Do you really believe that you should drive me to bitter arousal with your words, Ambranrei das Sikhrea?" he says, the affected accent exaggerating every single syllable. "Or do you think that I should be so fap as to be fit for cashiering?"

Administrator Ambranrei—I mentally insert the title as if by force of habit—shakes his head, his breath held in such a way that one might to suppress a sigh. "We're not here to fight, Peratirei, but I am not fit to see how the temperature should effect our temperament or affect our judgement—we are no longer the Reserve Council. We are the *Council*, and what we now decide will yet change the course of history."

"And what history yet remains?" the representative for North Aimela says, his reedy, aluminium-ringed fingers tapping nervously on the table, his name written quite conveniently across his chest. I presume it is his name, at least—the script is Pilisyari, one that I do not know, so for all I can guess it might well be a verse from the *K'el-me Mekhbe*. "Our enemy has destroyed our capital and has done so in minutes, leaving not a single man alive. The least we can do is surrender."

"Cimsas was falling apart by itself," Peratirei says, shaking his head; his speech turns to the roughness no doubt close to his heart. "You haven't been down South. A bolt-action hail could take the thing out—thing was built to stand Breakings, not artillery."

Ambranrei shakes his head again, and a brief mental image appears of him shaking it to whiplash; I suppress the resultant giggle. "That artillery wasn't *modern*, Administrator! Have you seen the imprints? I cannot bring myself to despair of the affairs of the South or of the present war—we are facing a fully mobilised, nomadic armed force willing to commit democide with unfulfilable demands and pre-Laceration technology that we have never *seen*. We must mobilise the forces in Far Aimela at once."

The Southern Aimelan representative, quiet all the while—I have noticed him taking deep breaths and making silent motions in his throat as the rest spoke—is the last to speak, and he does so with gusto.

"How *dare* you?" he bellows, his mouth open in some grotesque pantomime of shock. "How *dare* you pull them through our territory so that the Mahammadir may overrun us entirely? The Far Aimelan troops have held the barbarians from our gates since time immemorial—shall we be left to die, now, overrun or fled as they come rushing over the border to crush us under the weight of their savagery? Are we so worthless that we are to be thrown into the Glass Sea and left burning? How *dare* you?"

His speech concludes with a deep breath and a drink from the glass upon his table.

Ambranrei nods, leaning forwards; Peratirei looks on in what I can only assume to be amused anticipation. "Your theatrics are noted, Khandrei—but you aren't running for an election. Nobody's recording this session. I don't care what vague notions of democracy you have had left to fester in that backwater you've been allowed to call a nation. Central Aimela is facing an enormous armed threat from within, most likely nomadic. They may be synthesising their supplies entirely from scratch—they may be coming directly from the Tower itself. They and we are far more important than you or your glorified protectorate."

Administrator Khandrei seems ready to split apart at the seams; the ombundsman lets out an enormous sigh.

"We cannot allow," he begins boomingly, and from his voice I immediately infer that he is very old—not because of his voice in itself, which sounds no different than that of any other man's unravaged by purely physical senescence, but by how his tone is even and well-spaced all throughout—as he makes a very audible tapping sound, as though measuring the rhythm of his words on the lectern, "ourselves to descend into brinkmanship. Despite our differences, we remain Aimelan— together we will stand. The threat that we now face is but the passing of—"

Peratirei glares at the space above us as he interrupts. "I've heard you say that to yourself in a mirror for longer than I'd think you'd

ever live. You're too old to be a demagogue, Plis, and we don't *need* your
I-couldn't-make-it-young punditry—you know just about as much as
I do that everyone here but me and Ambry's just eating the goddamn
pension fund, and *he*—" and here he gestures to Ambranrei, who snaps
his head towards him as if in shock, "—wants to destroy *everything* we've
built for the rotten core of a cracking apple."

I choose this moment to cough politely.

The sound resounds through the tower, and I realise that the
ombundsman was whispering.

The four representatives immediately look to me under the stand;
their expressions are unanimously exasperated. From this angle, none of
the foreign ambassadors can see us but what I presume to be the Pilisyari
and Sestiyari, who both look profoundly uninterested; the latter even
seems to be smiling a bit.

I walk out onto the centre floor. "Greetings," I begin in
Aimelari—the seven exact syllables, the word perfectly conjugated, rolls
off the tongue—and a shout quickly interrupts me.

"For the tower's sakes," Peratirei says, "I know we have to hear
you out, but *Aimelan*. It's too early for this nonsense."

The other three representatives all look as if they are about to
dispute this, but their raised fingers drop one by one and they simply
stare at me with the sort of expression a shylock wears approached by a
habitually subprime lessee obligated by law to listen to him state his case
in full for the fiftieth time.

"Good day," I say, this time trying to speak as evenly as possible.
"I am a survivor of the Cimsas attack."

"An administrator's child, even with your servant and clothing?"
Ambranrei says, nodding in a sudden, newfound interest along with the
Northern representative; Peratirei rolls his eyes. "We haven't yet heard
from the administrative personnel; we'd assumed they'd been lost in the
tower's destruction. Why hadn't we been notified of this beforehand?"

"I requested an immediate audience," I say, trying to look sombre.
"I have information pertinent to the attack."

"Oh?" the Northern representative says, raising an eyebrow,
"What do you suggest's happening? I shall not pressure you to speak, but
we know nothing of the enemy; their attack on Cimsas has been the only
one we are aware of, and none of our soldiers have returned."

It takes me a few seconds to think of something suitably audacious to say.

"I was attacked a few hours before the siege began; some fluid filled my veins through a blade by the men who besieged the city. My servant and I—" and here I notice a slight twitch in my peripheries, "— fled to Sipshirea, where they struck once more. They spoke and named me 'Pretender', and sought me alone."

I glance up and about as I speak, scanning the room; the foreign representatives are mostly looking politely at me, but the Sestiyari one is looking at me with her head cocked and eyes somewhat inquisitive.

The Northern representative narrows his eyes at me. "Why Sipshirea? If I recall, Kambaris is closer by a margin of a hundred kilometres."

There is a moment of hesitation before I speak again.

"I was advised by my servant—" I begin, and I realise that I cannot hear my own voice any more; I look up in confusion and try to speak, a manoeuvre that is ineffectual but bides enough time for the tinnitus to set in with the pain.

I look up to see a singularly interesting sight: I don't know much about architecture, but the spire's purely physical form is so primitive as to be singularly embarrassing; there are no supports and no redundancy. The Southerners without tessiture would have to spend years building something like this, layering support beams and counterweights; the Pyarashjkhi could only admire the sheer scale.

I can see the barrier around which the stone is situated shimmer past the hole before I feel a force grabbing me and thrusting me to the ground, a heavy body covering me; the first sound comes to my ears is a female shouting, the words indistinguishable.

"What happened?" I shout, glancing up and seeing that it's Perei above me, himself looking up-sideways in some expression that I can only assume is horror at the enormous hole in the building; I don't know where the native barrierline is, but I certainly hope it isn't in the walls.

You hold a citizen of our nation who pretends to our administration. Submit and your own citizenship is guaranteed.

As the voice thunders over us, Perei gets off me quickly and pulls me off the ground; the ambassadors are no longer at their lecterns, and the screams filling the air are occasionally interrupted by an occasional shell.

I steady myself and take a deep breath, whereupon a hand rests upon my shoulder as Perei stands before me; I turn about and see the Sestiyari ambassador's lips moving at me, and by the time I realise she's speaking in Aimelan the only part of her sentence that remains to be said is *follow me.*

I look back to Perei, and we oblige; she quickly marches her way out of the front door—there are no traces of the council members about, though I can spot the ombundsman rushing out with the sudden crowd as the sounds of gunshots echo through the air and a choir of Guardsman-uniformed singers screech stabilisation orations, their voices amplified by the barrier oration and booming over the city as if in competition—and pulls me over by the tips of my fingers.

Hers are rather notably soft.

I follow her, Perei right behind, as we wade through the panicking crowd—a terrifying prospect by its description, but not quite so in practice when the crowd is geriatric—and into the nearest alley we can find as the crushing explosions resound through the barrier; the general temperament is notably aversive to being between structures that might at any time collapse, and so we are alone together as the world moves.

"I don't know who you are, but if you were telling the truth—" she begins, pushing the mildly accented, emphasised words out so quick that she runs out midway and has to stop to take a breath of air, "—if you were telling the truth, I don't have a choice."

"*Oooh,*" Perei says, his voice panickedly condescending. "What, she's the thirteenth?"

The ambassador ignores him, looking into my eyes in what I might presume to call desperation. "Take this," she says, quickly reaching into her pocket and pulling out a piece of what looks to be spawncloth; it is notably frayed about the edges, as if it might be older than her. "The passcode is *cu moire av koir.* Che'uu, em'ou—"

"I know the Sestiyari abiguda," I say, taking the offered bit of fabric and rolling it out; she presses her finger against its upper-right corner and mumbles quickly a few words in Angzhwen. An extended *ding* sounds—my perception of its length interrupted as the scream of a shell drowns it out—and liquid colours begin to seep as if leaking from a pouch in the fabric, words and shapes forming incoherently until with a sudden sharpness they resolve into the hard-cut, curving lines of a standard sessile background. The words on it are Aimelan, and I look up at her inquisitively.

"You're giving me an old sessile?" I say, looking tilt-headedly at the thing and making quite resolutely the decision not to crack wise.

"Not any sessile." She taps at the database storage suboration trigger and it blooms outwards to reveal a list of Angzhwen names next to figures and little arrows; I tap one of the latter, and immediately a very detailed description of a pre-Laceration device I've never heard of opens up.

"*Cyrsyzh Ácylairhuil?*" I say, inquisitive. "I've never read of—"

"That's because it isn't archived."

The look I return her is rather special.

"Unarchived exodus caches are violations of the provisions of the Ocilentran Concordance. That would be grounds for war," I say, remembering quite clearly the statutes. "The Sestiyari couldn't have compiled this after the Pacification."

"That was signed at the point of a—" she begins, and stops to take a deep breath. "Look, I don't care what you think about its origins." Her voice stays urgent; the shells are coming down with greater frequency by the minute. "If I'm correct, the Sestiyari nation isn't going to survive without this in your hands. If I'm correct, you'll need this just as we need it to be yours—no matter how loyal you may be to your bloody country. And if I'm wrong, we're riveted either way."

"You admit to harbouring this?" I say, my mouth opening a bit against my will as I realise the sheer magnitude of her transgression. "Why would you have something this valuable on you? You're an *ambassador*."

"I don't know," she says, sighing. "I don't give my orders to myself."

An enormous shriek echoes over us; this time, I rather consciously force myself to the ground and shove my hands up against my ears as I hear a shell burst through the storehouse next to us, the stone audibly bursting. I look up—Perei along with me, the ambassador looking strangely apathetic as she looks straight up at the green-burning verdigris—and find myself grabbed by the right shoulder and pulled.

"Where are we *going*?" I say, glancing back at the ambassador, who looks quite intently at the fire for a second before turning about and running in the opposite direction. The grip is firm, but not harsh; I pull myself away from him, and he stares at me as we walk. "They're going to evacuate the population centres first!"

"Where we were before."

"Are you *mentally ill?* Is this because of the *gun?*" I shout, struggling to keep pace as my feet skip and jump over the mossy pavement, my shoes sliding wetly through the plantlife. "They *know our faces—*"

We come abruptly to a stop.

By this I don't mean that we came to agreement on the terms of our momental termination but rather a particularly stunning feat of unilateral diplomacy: my legs are quite promptly allowed to thrust forwards over the slippery ground, torso failing to follow. I find myself planting my feet in the hopes that my pointed shoes will snag on the moss; my hopes are well-founded, as they tend to be, and as my feet snag the moss promptly breaks and I find myself lying rather painfully on my backside.

Before I can make towards applying light physiotherapy, Perei's face is up in mine. I can't help but notice that his face, despite the imploring sort of anger that seems to have printed itself across it, is rather neonate.

"I saved your life," he says, breathing even. "Let me do this."

I nod and am promptly pulled up.

"I suppose—" I say, rubbing at my backside, "I suppose that we might find something else of use."

He grunts, and we proceed without incident.

We have passed two or three kilometres of the city by the time the building comes back in sight; the shelling has stopped, but the sight here isn't pretty. I can see a single soldier—his head has fallen back over the rim of the chair he's on, and a cup of some flat, hot drink lays unfinished on the little wooden table along with a half-eaten buttered scone. Little scorchmarks around tiny holes dot the ground.

As I come up to him, I note a gunshot wound to the chest past ceramic plate. I unbind the oration connecting the halves of his cloth uniform and pull the armour from its pouch, tracing the tip of my finger around the three-centimetre gap in his sternum. There's some burning around the wound's edge.

The building itself appears to be untouched; I glance back to Perei, who's pulled his purloined weapon out and walked warily over me.

"Antaerei das Pernametrei," he says, nodding up a bit. "Doesn't look like it hurt."

"How do you know his name?" I ask, studying the particulars of the wound and bringing my hand to the similarly purloined catgut-stringed instrument around my chest, beginning to fiddle practisedly. The compound tomography of his wounds forms superimposed over his chest—in my eyes alone as a subjective, at least, because that's the way I like it—and I unconsciously let out a dissatisfied 'hmm'.

"Nametag," he says, looking nervously around. "Hey, I know our balls're brass and all, but I'm pretty sure we're not gonna get away with warfighting veteran modern aggressive combat hostiles."

The construction of his sentence is unusual enough to draw my attention away from the wound for a moment and make me turn to him with a fair bit of confusion upon my face. "What did you—?"

"What?" he returns, leaning back a bit as if on the defensive. "Saw it in a prelac sessile once."

"That must have been an awful translator," I say, shaking my head. "This is unusual, in any case—his cardiac arteries have been torn apart, not burst."

He kneels down next to me, looks intently at the wound for a few seconds and then promptly gives me a look that forces me to suppress a giggle. "First," he says, shaking his head and absentmindedly scratching at a rather specific point on his ribs, "that's incredibly gross, Isha be my witness. Second, who the hell taught you medicine? That's what prelacs *do*."

"But look at the burning," I say, hovering my finger over the pink and white bit surrounding the wound, extending a further centimetre; I lean in to smell it—here I see in the corner of my vision Perei quickly standing up and making as if to constrain his bile—and note the faint sense of burning. "The tomograph isn't lying. Look at the plates. They've been broken open. It's an incendiary pre-Laceration weapon with enough kinetic force to break through ceramic armour."

"So their guns're overclocked," he says, biting at his upper lip; his weapon is shoulder-height and he's looking about quickly over it as he speaks. "What happened to the 'I killed an officer' sob-story? Doesn't look like you've got a problem snorting bits of his heart out his chest."

I make a conscious attempt not to bitter my expression as I speak. "I wasn't the one that killed him. I couldn't have done anything to stop it."

"So God's in his heaven and all's right with the world?"

"I am a *doctor*, Perei. I've seen worse." I look down to the dead man and see the dimly shocked expression on his face before reaching down and pushing his eyelids shut. "Perhaps your time with the Mahammadir have given you an unhealthy respect for the meat the dead leave. I do what I can and what I can is what I must."

"How many times you've said that to yourself?"

I look down at the corpse; his hand appears to have gone to his chest before he died—it is lying now on the rim of the chair, but in an unsuitably uncomfortable-looking position—and there is a little bit of paper in his breastpocket, the upper-left edge of the word *if* visible on it. I let my hand run over it and feel the flat hemp. "Five in the last year. Why do you ask?"

My companion doesn't respond, kneeling down and pulling the name-tag—a little elliptical piece of aluminium with the name and numbers attached to it—off his body along with the bit of paper, yanking it off hard with the sort of force that can only be described in the language of an unsavoury publication.

I might interpret some morsel of regret or some lack of avarice from his expression if I were feeling charitable, but the interpretation would take enough effort to stretch that I decide instead to stand up and head towards the building's open entrance.

He follows with an unusual silence.

The Aimelan Guard's glasswalkers are known to be particularly exact; their sets are precise enough that it takes a fully proficient orator at least an hour to fully instruct one. I'm no longer covered in pieces of money—I've exchanged my lavish accoutrements for what I presume to be an unusually dyed dress uniform, black and gold, and I've hastily ripped every bit of rank-insignia and ornamentation from it to make it legal. This must make it seem rather undignified as I look rather hurriedly about for any signs of population. The place appears to have been evacuated entirely.

"I still dunno what beef you have with guns, Ash," he says,

rubbing the red-striped sessile-arm's front bit—the *muzzle*, if I properly recall—as he looks rather admiringly at it. "You said you'd shoot sand out the air if you had one."

"I think you're remembering that conversation incorrectly," I say, pressing the data-bearing bit of spawncloth labelled *Map* on my own sessile and whispering a quick *oućajtt*. A map of the known world makes itself known immediately, spreading from the centre and resolving into inky colour with our location highlighted in black in the middle of the enormous red tint that is Aimela; I press two fingers together against it and push them apart, and I am almost giddy as the gesture works and I find myself facing a street-map of Tachiesrea.

"Don't tell me you're one of those gunshys."

"I'm more concerned that that entire building was a lacuna in human settlement," I say; I might sound nervous if I weren't glad that we had a sessile-map. "Didn't you notice that the shelling's stopped? The place's empty."

As if on cue, however, an enormous shout rises over the city just as I reach the period.

We have stopped our artillery and sent in our infantry only as a gesture of goodwill. Should you continue to resist, we will withdraw our troops and continue shelling. Your external outposts have been cleared and our troops are drawing deeper into the city by the second. Surrender now and hostilities will cease.

"That doesn't sound good," he says, soothing his right eardrum with a knuckle. "Whatever it was. Was that Angzhwen again?"

"Yes," I say, gritting my teeth. "They're charging in."

He puts his hand up against his chin. "They have to have a crew on those big guns over there. We'll rush past 'em. Just like Cimsas."

"There aren't any distractions this time."

"Well," he says, giving me a grin, "looks like we're gonna have to make one."

The glasswalker lets out a neigh as it reaches exactly fifty kilometres per hour, and the cool wind chafes my lips lightly as we ride. The city isn't very large; it will take about ten minutes to get out of it, from what I can estimate. The tangent of the bowl's edge is getting more acute by the second.

"Right," he says, nodding. "Oration fireworks. How close you need to be to make it work?"

"We'll get a projection point—" I begin, my finger pointing out absently at a nearby store, "—*there*, on the roof. I've seen the sounds. The only visuals we need are the barrier distortions. We might need to be quick; for all I know, they don't need to reload their howitzers."

Perei swerves abruptly to the left, heading to the building's front; I follow and we hurriedly dismount as they come to a complete stop within seconds. "So," he says, as we enter the building—the shelves are noticeably empty—and mount the nearest set of staircases we can see, "how exactly is this gonna help us?"

"It was *your* idea," I say, taking a pause in my step-climbing as we reach the top to give him a particularly indelible stare, "but if I were forced to guess I might suggest that they would be too busy bombarding our location to concentrate on intruders."

"Or," he says, searching about the attic's ceiling for the hatch, "they might have a whole bunch of people to stop this exact thing from happening."

"I'd like to remind you that it was *your* idea," I say, tapping about a few times before feeling the wood above my knuckles.

"And I'm not exactly the smartest chip on the block," he says, walking over to me and looking as I attempt to pull on the hatch.

"I haven't read a great deal of pre-Laceration literature recently," I say, holding and yanking down as hard as I can to find the wood unyielding, "but I'm fairly sure that's not how the idiom goes."

He reaches over and flips the latch off as I attempt to yank down one more time, jumping up as my arms pull; I find myself quite abruptly assailed by his racuous laughter as my backside hits the floor with a great deal of force, and I give him the most venomous look I can muster.

As is natural, he laughs harder.

"To answer your question," he says, seeming to try hard to suppress his rather feminine giggle with a few hard coughs. "I don't know either."

I sigh. "Come on."

My attempts to climb up the hatch fail, and I'm rather humiliatingly carried and pushed over; he comes up himself with a quick grunt, and by the time he's done I'm already improvising a song for the sound effects with my hand on the ground as the impromptu sessile begins to form into the somewhat porous rock.

"Hey," he says, tilting his head, "why aren't you using the sessile?"

I interrupt my oration just long enough to be mean. "Why don't you use raw metal to shoot bullets?"

He leaves me in peace until I'm done.

"Alright," I say as I mount my—well, not *mine*, but the possessive will suffice—glasswalker and pull out my—a similar disclaimer applies—sessile, tapping at it. "We have about twenty seconds. I can't get the sessile-map set to interface with the database, but the latter has a distance function. Once it works—"

"You make that song up on the spot?" he says, moving his mount to the side. "Wasn't bad."

"Quick melody," I say, demonstratively humming a sudden, bright tune as I compel my own to go forwards slowly. "They're not difficult to make."

"Why'd you need the tune, though?" he says, the wind beginning to rush in our ears as we pick up speed—not too much, but enough. "It's not like you're gonna sing it twice."

I try my best to sound sarcastic. "Why'd I need the words, though? It's not like I want to make it work."

The sounds begin before he has an opportunity to respond.

Though it may be polite to explain their composition, it is more accurate to say 'until we are temporarily deafened'. I immediately turn about to see my handiwork; the barrier's surface distorts a little, purple distorting the blue like bruises on asphyxiated skin.

"Goddamn, are you *trying* to kill us?" Perei says, scratching at his ear with an eye twitchingly closed; he reaches into his pouch and begins to rummage. "I think I heard my drums pop."

"I didn't intend for it to be quite so intense," I might have said if not for the fact that the 'return fire' has begun to rain down behind us, the sound drowning any impulse I might have had to compete. As we move forwards, I cannot help but look back; the fire is only hitting the outer rim of the city near us, and the spire remains intact. A slight flash of white and blue appears on top of one of the buildings but it goes as we pass by, along with an indistinct shout.

I look forwards to see the edge of the barrier—the watchtowers dotting the smoothened sand are notably damaged, some of them missing their upper halves entirely—looming and the dunes bristling with artillery, and quickly start singing the membrane.

In seconds, we burst out and I immediately begin to weave the Khamisret-Aparkisrea instructions into my song; a few larger bits of flying glass narrowly miss me right before the barrier strengthens and melds. One piece bounces off the back and hits me in mine, thankfully not leaving more than a slight bruise.

Perei holds a bit of green-tinted clearglass up to his eye—I don't recognise it at first—and looks behind us before hurriedly looking back.

"They're coming back," he says, grinning. "They'll never catch up to us."

I hear the beating sounds of gunfire, loud enough to penetrate the barriers, and look back to see the roofs of the buildings near the front bristling with soldiers behind the parapets; they are firing, but very pointedly away from us, and from here I realise that the dunes are too high for them to be seen. I can't hear the bullets too well, the enormous racket that doubtless is occurring morphing into a single dull thud as what look to be marksmen begin firing into the streets.

As we reach over the top, it strikes me that I am an idiot and my barrier that a bullet has struck it as the heart-stopping sound of a barrier threshold limitation makes itself known.

Almost immediately, I veer to the right; another hits the sand besides me, and I look to Perei following me and desperately keeping inside of my field another pierces through it and my glasswalker, causing a warning squeal to come from its fibreglass throat. I have just enough time to appraise the situation—a dozen men firing at us from between the enormous beacon launchers—before I push my head down against the mane and speed as fast as I can.

"Holy *shit!*" Perei shouts, following me as I force my glasswalker to zig-zag across the sand, his moving in synchrony with mine. "Where'd they learn to *shoot?*"

"They're operating artillery," I say; the siege appears to have been hastily-prepared, and no field is in sight beyond the ones surrounding each piece of weaponry, the barrels of their weapons poking out. "Maybe they're not train—"

I get the sudden urge to invite a layman to wonder, as a burning pain spreads across my upper thigh in a line and the force resonates through my left femur, what one's experience of media might indicate have caused my sudden impediment of speech.

My hands are calm and steady, though they certainly are shuddering a little; the sounds I can hear are growing somewhat weaker, and my heart is beating at a noticeably elevated rate. The blood is leaking down and spreading through the fabric of the black dress uniform and I can feel the rips and tears throughout my vessels and the artery pumping out so much blood that I can't even my heart is beating very fast and I will die and I hold to the wound painful but the blood isn't stopping and it hurts so much I cannot find the words to describe it and I want to cry but I don't.

"Ash?"

My reactions to danger have always been somewhat inconsistent, and I can't say that what I do now is intelligent even if it is based on prior experience and my voice is very clear as I grab the instrument with my left hand and I am focused enough that I almost do not notice another bullet clipping past the short hair on my head. I unbind my left shot leg from the stirrup holding its knee with a single word and lean over the side and the wound hurts as it stretches and I try not to scream instead of sing.

I cannot see Perei speak, but I hear him rather faintly. "*Ash, what the hell are you doing?*"

"Rebindingn't work. T'slow."

"You got *shot*? *Goddamn*—" he says, and I cannot hear much thence past my own voice.

"*Cæsinrach arsénfyj—j,*" I say, barely missing a misconjugation; the glasswalker veers to the right and I am getting fainter and it hurts so much that when we pass the cannons and almost get shot on both sides the only thing I know of it then is the neighing and it hurts so much that I almost bite my tongue as I continue the oration and my right hand begins to feel a dull sort of burning and it hurts so much that Perei's shouts of some description come from behind me and it hurts so much only when I press the cauter that is the tips of my fingers against the hole in my thigh as I rebind the arterial wall do I feel at liberty to scream and only when I rip my hand off the burnt skin and I notice rather strangely that the sound of the threshold barely letting us through has gone past do

I feel at liberty to let preservation take me and think no more.

three
The Last Drop

Once there was one drop of water left in the world.

There were great wars fought over it, but soon there were no nations. There were great feuds fought over it, but soon there were no friends. There were great vendettas fought over it, but soon there were no families.

There was finally a man after all of this who had killed more than all the rest.

He had ordered one million men killed.

He had operated machinery to kill one hundred thousand.

He had brought his friends to kill ten thousand.

He brought his family to kill one thousand.

He personally killed one hundred.

He slit the throat of his grandfather, poisoned his grandmother, stabbed his uncle, bled his wife, smothered his cousin, crushed his first son, bludgeoned his second son, beheaded his first daughter and shot his second and third daughters who were twins.

Finally, he strangled his mother.

After all of this was done and he was the only man left on Earth, he took the last drop of water and emptied the vial down his parched throat.

It did not satisfy him, and he died of thirst shortly thereafter.

'The Bloodied Vial', anonymous
Tales for Wise Children
compiled by Talesymyrei das Cimcharei
published by the Department of Education and approved for private distribution by the Administration for Media Development under the grace of Khaliesrea das Sikharea eliyit Tamarisrei, Administrator for the Arts

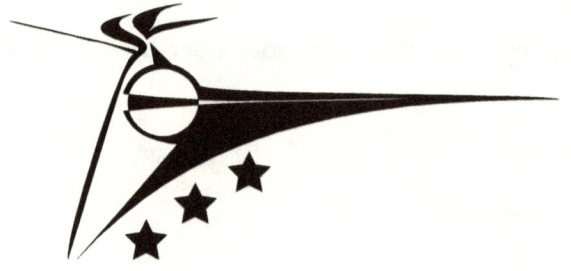

4

Kærysmiaryr
to begin a pilgrimage well-prepared

I return from hell to a snap.

My sore eyes blink a bit and finally open to see a pair of fingers making the accompanying motion. I decide quite reasonably not to panic—I've fallen out of preservation in my sleep, I realise, and I suppress a deep yawn.

"You up?"

I nod.

"Fantastic," he says ceasing-to-snap-his-fingers-in-front-of-my-facely—I'm aware I have an adverbial problem—drawing out of my vision and allowing me to attempt not to move my leg. "You know, if you keep this up I'm gonna have to start singing all the barriers myself."

"Perhaps we should take turns."

He lets out a 'heh' as I pull the harness from myself.

"So," he says, and though I cannot see him I can only presume that he's looking sideways at me, "how's the thigh? That was *really* hardcore, by the way. Never seen anyone do a hotfix that nice before. Not with preservation edging in."

"I think it pierced my femoral artery," I say, grunting a bit. It stings rather fiercely. "They must have shot at me from high up. I wasn't aware that they had personnel on the artillery themselves."

His voice carries the distinct sound of one who is rolling his eyes. "I mean how it *feels*."

I hazard looking down, and find myself facing nothing extraordinary; I hazard sitting up and quickly relearn the word 'hazard', being back on my back in ten centiseconds flat. I turn to the side and blink the immediately-forming tears from my eyes, the entirety of his face coming immediately into his view.

A certain sort of empathetic schadenfreude is present in his look. "Not good, huh?" he says, tilting the right bit of his lip a little in a semi-wince. "Hurts a lot the first few times I got one."

"You've gotten yourself shot by a sessile-arm before?" I say, tilting my head at him; as I'm lying prone, this particular instance of head-tilting adds to my current tilt for what is an approximately one-hundred-thirty-five-degree distortion. "How are you alive?"

He shrugs. "I heal good."

The sudden memory of my last surgery comes back to me, and I attempt to sit up to interrogate him only to have to suppress a choke as I lie back.

"Let me guess," he says, his tone noticeably dull, "you want me to tell you how?"

"Yes," I say, clenching my eyelids tight against any further tears before shaking my head, letting them part and looking back to him.

"Well," he says, shrugging, "I'm sure you'd wanna hugbox about how great it is we just ran past an army and talk about how we might've either saved big-snobby-admin-orgy—" the Low Aimelan pun inherent in *ta-shli-syr-raeia* does not escape me, and I have to wrestle back the slightest expression of amusement, "—or turned it to rubble or how they knew we were there, but if you wanna hear me say 'I dunno' instead that's fine with me."

"Lung in rib," I say, and then shake my head; the image persists, and I stop myself from giggling quick enough to maintain my serious visage. "I mean, rib in lung. Why'd you get out of the membrane in the first place?"

He snorts derisively. "I'll have you know I had a *great* reason for doing it."

"You're a young idiot?"

"Says the twelvie," he says, giving me a stare that seems to be a question in itself. "If you really wanna know, I was *trying* to help someone."

I nod.

"Is that how it changed you?"

"What?"

I clear my throat somewhat suggestively. "Being a guideline. That's how it's changed you?"

He blinks at me a bit before giving me a look that I might imagine indicates some sort of dawning realisation. "Ay told you."

"He did," I say, scritching at my head somewhat carefully. "He said that you might tell me the tale one day—aren't you supposed to get your hands cut off for larceny?"

There is a certain look of confusion in his face before he gives me the bitterest grin I might imagine a person could give. "Hah. Probably read that in a book somewhere, didn't you?"

"*The* book. The Recitation, to be precise."

"Look," he says, shaking his head. "I'm not a mud and I never was. Never gave a damn about any of that."

"Then why were you a guideline?"

He seems to take some time to ponder this, snapping his fingers in a particularly rhythmic way; I might imagine that the final snap should come loud by virtue of its lack of succession, but instead it peters out to a slow stop as he begins to respond.

"I went into it for the money. Thought I could get something out of them at the start, y'know? Then I actually went and started looking at them. They've got their own place in the tough quarter, y'know. Don't usually mix up."

I nod at him, keeping my silence, and he looks down to the sand and then—after a thoughtful pause—to the side before turning back to me, face a subtle mask of despair.

"Those people were *fucked*," he says, slashing his hand from his chest to his side.

The force of his words—all in Central Aimelan, the language's basic grace amplifying my shock—strikes me like a bad simile; I maintain my composure but for a few off-timed blinks. "What?"

"You know what tessy is? Tessitura?" he says, pronouncing the word like a slur. "They're all pretty much mute, you know. Can't orate for *crap*. They can make a little water without shit getting in it, sure, but you know how shit out of luck they are if they wanna get a job? Start a home? No walls, sure, but you know how *riveted* they are? I got through all the time 'fore I had to cut it, I can talk high like I was on helium—*oh please, sir, my mother's holding my pass for me*—but you know how shit it is if you wanna go legit? I've got *great* tessy, my mom didn't mess with the muds, I could work in any three-to-seven no-brains slog anywhere if I wanted to spend the rest of my life singing my throat out for a minnie a week, but these kids? What're they gonna do, learn to sing five hours a twenty-syb gallon? You're *fucked*, plain and simple, and nobody gives a damn. You're *fucked. Uk-krit'e, kem sakh.*"

He seems almost out of breath at what I presume to be the end of his rant, and his eyes are wide open; having hit his crescendo, his panting goes from soft to quiet as he shakes his head at the ground, biting his lip slightly before turning back to me, a tired look on his face.

"I wasn't a *god*line," he says, letting out a sigh as he rubs his eyes with both hands. "You know, they put their Recitation on everything. Floors for the demons, windows for the angels, heads for God, whatever. They don't even need to write it down. Ask some kid—well, you *could've*, but I guess that just doesn't matter now, does it?—right, ask some kid to read the book out loud. One to one, he'll start it at the first and end at the last. You know why they do that, Ash?"

"They're a close-knit group lacking prospects for upwards mobility," I say, my voice level. "At least in Cimsas."

"Because if they don't have what they *are*," he says, hardly paying me any heed as he paraphrases me, "what *do* they have?"

There is a gentle quiet for a bit as he seems to wonder.

"I got some lessons from this kid and hammered it up good. I did it for the kids. I thought I'd get some easy cash for the babysitting." He takes a deep breath. "Then the moms and dads started showing up. Then the whole street."

"You stopped doing that?"

"Well," he says, continuing to gnaw on his lip, "I never really did. Big Aimelan man comes in, saves the world and makes everything alright, happy ending like those stupid *goddamn* sessile things. You know how it felt like, being like that? You know how it felt like being that big Aimelan man who comes in and saves the day?"

"What does it feel like?"

"Feels like *shit*. You feel like a goddamn itsystrong insect bastard just coming in and lording it over, like you know their stuff better than them." He continues wagging his head, as if the inertia compels him more than emotion. "Got my favorite kids up, helped them up, got someone else to do the talking. Kids got some home, everyone's happy."

"You taught them to steal."

"Yeah," he says, glancing at me and then back between his legs. "So what?"

"Did any of them die?"

The question seems to make him blink, and the voice he has as he responds is noticeably high.

"More than I thought would."

I nod.

He reclines back in his saddle and nods up in return towards me. "Alright," he says, looking up at the barrier-distorted sky, "I spilled the beans. You next. How'd doctoring shape *you* up?"

"I've been practising medicine as far as I can remember."

He lets out a heartfelt *pfft*. "C'mon. You've gotta have *something*."

There is a moment of silence—a rather long one—before I give my reply.

"Are you familiar with Sheksprei's work?"

Perei raises an eyebrow. "Shexpes?"

"Shexpes," I repeat, mimicking his accent and feeling quite a bit dirtier for it. "Shekespe. Berdra. Whatever his name may have been."

"Heard it. Prelac writer, right?"

"Old pre-Laceration—very old. I'm not entirely sure if Sheksprei was a man or a group or a nation." I shake my head a little. "Have you heard of *Kymersantrerrazh Weinsir*?"

"Of *course* I've heard of something so old I can't say its name without biting half my tongue off."

My sigh seems to fit in with the melody of my absently fiddling fingers, and I get a slight urge to continue it into a hum. "I suppose I can summarise. The creditor of We'in-se loans a man who detests him a great sum on the condition that he will give him a kilogramme of flesh if he refuses; the debtor knows that he will be able to pay, and agrees."

"You even need to tell me he doesn't get the money?"

I unconsciously suppress a slight, ineffable giggle; it resolves into a little smile and a quick exhalation. "I don't know—there's a lot missing—but the rest of the story depends on him not getting it."

He shakes his head dismissively. "Figured."

"He goes to a hearing of some kind to determine if he'll get his kilo, and the minutor—"

"*Fychri?*" he says, tilting his head a bit at me. "Hell's a *fychri?*"

"An advocate whose argument rests on technicalities," I say, a slight tinge of annoyance creeping into my voice. "The minutor says that he can take the flesh, but not the blood. She says that he can have exactly a pound, no more and no less, and he can't kill him. He ends up getting everything taken away from him and throwing away his identity to stop himself being hanged, and runs out screaming in pain."

He nods with what I presume to be some attempt at sagedom. "Sounds like *The Process.*"

I raise an eyebrow. "You know Kafka but not Sheksprei?"

"Well," he says, shrugging his left shoulder and sticking his lower lip out, "one of the last places I snuck myself in got hot for books or something. Nothing but them, only good-looking ones too heavy. Figured I'd pick the tiniest one in Aimelan."

"I never thought you to be literate."

"Hey," he says, some measure of indignation pressed into his voice, "you think the muds can't read? I learned. What's your banker thing got to do with your doctoring, anyway?"

"I know how it's supposed to make me think revenge isn't the answer," I say, looking between my legs. "Isn't it, you think?"

He shrugs. "That's what I'd guess."

"But if I detested somebody enough to want to hurt him so, I wouldn't run out screaming. I'd perform an exclusive matter inventory. I'd tourniquet the bit of his arm I needed. I'd transfuse the blood, slowly, out of it, and I would leave the limb to die bloodless as long as his nerves live. Then I'd scrape the flesh from it and barrier the tourniquet so not a drop would spill and hand him his blood back in a jar. The fleshcrawlers would spurn the rest."

I look up at Perei, who's wearing an expression that seems to be equal parts horrified and interrogative, some combination of a slightly-gaping mouth and a single raised brow and the occasional blink, the interrogative perhaps somewhere in the miniscule movement in his lightly strained muscles.

"I think it was written before the discovery of anaesthetic."

The interrogative aspect disappears from his face and his mouth shuts as he quickly turns to the front, looking intensely at the blast threshold reaching across the rim of the sky.

"By the way," I say, looking at my fingernails and considering if I should try to barrier-cut them, "thank you for saving my life before."

We ride on, and he continues to sing the field. The oration is slow and awkward, but it does its job.

I take the opportunity to rest; it still stings.

Sessile manufacturers have an interesting way of keeping their instruction and specification lists private, similar to the way security-binding orations work—the oration is a printempraesis, an oratory cypher based on a passphrase. The technique, I have been told, has been borrowed from the Oiesya people, and I use it on the more dangerous orations I require.

That being said, nothing but my tessitura can stop me from *adding* to the oration, and I know it as fact that I can sustain about twenty square centimetres of self-perpetuating spawncloth every eight hours—there is a reason why sessiles are expensive—and the two or three centimetres left unorated for information storage are quite perfect for the purpose.

After I bind it to the forearm under my sleeve I probe at the cloth a bit, coaxing it to show me its specifications. They come as gibberish, but nonetheless I reach out and sing a slight, careful song—occasionally pausing to renew the slowly waning field—in an attempt to let it replicate.

The process takes two hours. Perei watches for the first three minutes, but soon settles into a complacent apathy; by the end, I've gotten it to squeak a few chords by verbal command.

It's a start. I try and give it the ability to read out its own text, and within another hour the bit of spawncloth squeaks its first legible words in an eager falsetto:

> *Cysryura Glyésyzh*
> *—Searching Translator*
> **Karysmiara, Central Aimela, Aimelan Administration**
> *Description: Small cylindrical chip, few centimetres tall.*
> *Device believed to translate speech neurologically to a set*
> *of subliminal concepts common to all Laceration-descended*
> *languages; this does not include languages with heavy use*
> *of urschoepfungwoerter, such as the Oiesyan languages and*
> *Low Aimelan slang. Produces copies of itself in physical*
> *contact with sandcinder. Stored liberally in the local Vault of*
> *Contrition. Local citizens do not appear aware of use and*
> *keep it alongside worthless trinkets.*
>
> *Name taken from words printed on chip.*
>
> *Copy produced by accident and taken discreetly for study*
> *and possible use.*
>
> *Found 4 Secundus 3914, Third Operation*

"You know," he says, "that list's probably worth about a thousand minnie strangles if you get the right fence. That stuff's so valuable you could eyepay every stiff in the capital with the money."

"It might be nonveridical," I say, looking at the locations; there are dozens in the digged-out North and hundreds—most of them in large collections—in the war-torn South, neither of which seem to be likely candidates.

"What?"

"Misleading, forged, counterfeit," I say, pondering substitutions. "Bogus and sad."

"Bogus and sad?" he says, looking at me with an expression that I can describe only as utter incredulity. "Who the hell says *bogus*?"

"Bogus," I say, tilting my head at him and trying to pronounce the word as clearly as possible. "*Agpiet*: false, unfair, forged, derived from Central Aimelan *aghanpietre*. I'm fairly sure that's a word in Low Aimelan."

He waves his hand in dismissal. "*Old* Aimelan, maybe."

"In any case," I say, coughing as politely as I can bring myself to, "we don't know if this is *real*."

"We'll find out soon enough," he says, looking forwards and shielding his eyes from the sun. "Sun tells me it's two hours 'til we're there. If the walkers keep this up, we might just cut a quarter."

I nod.

"Worst case," I say, "we'll die."

He doesn't respond and continues to sing.

I fear my newfound optimism is beginning to depress him.

The place is a recent village settlement, charitably a town: the Pari dunes are barely as high as the glasswalkers we're riding in on. The village looks cheaply made as possible, almost entirely adobe— what I presume to be the town hall is in stonerise—and the gravely disproportionate barrier extends for what I can only assume is two kilometres from the barrierline reaching through to the very tip.

It's quaint.

A strange look comes upon Perei's face as we pace towards the ground. "You hear that?"

"Hear what?"

"That hubhub. Teltrish."

"Teltradi?" I say, straining my ears a bit. "I can't hear anything."

"No, hear the yim-yamming?" he says, this time with a slight grin on his face. "They're here!"

"I've never read much on the Teltradi before," I say, tilting my head a bit. "None of them ever came up to the Mendicant's Corner. You seem to bear some affection for them."

"You kidding? You ever *seen* a Teltrish dance-up?" He shakes his head. "*Ulluhyinulkafir.* Keep your hands in your pockets and you're getting some serious entertainment."

"*Ulluhyinufir?*" I say, making some vague approximation of the sounds issuing from his mouth. "That sounds like a Southern language."

"Pyarash. Hell if I know what it means," he says, shrugging a bit, "but I'm pretty sure it works here."

It is barely half a minute after his sentence terminates that I lower our barrier's threshold, and as we draw slowly into the field's reach a slight shuddering passes through the glasswalker; a light humming melody becomes apparent and dull and as my ears go past I quite suddenly become aware of an enormous racket. It is at first incomprehensible and then instantly its antonym, a pounding, logorrhoeically mechanic stream of heavily-accented nonsense Angzhwen apparently ripped from an abecedarium:

Àyemænamyr, àyemànamyr, àyemćanamyr, àyembanamyr, àyemesamir—

At the moment the orator, his voice apparently amplified, hits an actual word—àyemesamir, *to carry the air of a prophet*—the sound comes to an abrupt halt, and almost immediately the sound is repeated screechingly:

Àyemesamir, venytj, venytj, àyemesamir, venytj, venytj!

Verbs and nouns in Angzhwen are the same thing; the Angzhwen word for 'the Laceration' is *Avdéshæssyara*, and misinterpreted as a verb it would mean *he Laceration'd himself.* I am hearing a person calling for the air of a prophet to come upon him, and blink in confusion.

"What on earth is he attempting to do?" I say, shaking my head as I rub somewhat unconsciously at my eardrums to ease the sonic shock. "I can tell that they're using the Kartani validation protocol, but—"

"Hell if I know. No Telt I ever knew's got tessy."

I shake my head a bit as I hear the sound continuing to echo off the barrier, repeating almost endlessly as our walkers trot forth.

"Slowly."

Perei obliges my instruction, pulling my leg tentatively over my other to rest carefully over the side as he puts his back up against the inn's adobe wall, and I ease myself down. As I attempt to rest my uninjured appendage without causing my nerves to scream for help I notice that the sand is still so unsettled as to let my feet sink a few centimetres into it.

This, naturally, gives my body the opportunity to cause me to scream and go down like a rock from a window; this it exploits with gusto, leaving me groaning with pain on the ground. My artery thankfully does not break—the rebinding has done its job rather well.

"Damn. Didn't think it'd rivet you *that* bad."

I grunt in what I hope to be a suitably tolerant manner, pushing my arms out the hot sand as quick as possible. An arm comes down in front of me, and I take it like a crutch.

"I was shot in an artery in the inner upper thigh," I say, shaking my head as I steady myself on a single leg, twisting my arm around his so I'm dangling from the appendage by my elbow as I put my left hand around the instrument and begin to hum quietly. "Not everyone has the benefit of inhuman regeneration."

A great deal of people prefer their bonds to be as minimalist as possible, but as I sing them—the bit of my arm hanging down from Perei's gesticulating its path—the intricate web of nexuses it forms highlights itself subjectively in my corneas and tightens about the animal, anchoring it to the wall as I complete the passphrase.

"So," he says, looking up at the building our glasswalkers are stuck against—we haven't yet entered it, but the town doesn't look full enough that we'd have to get in line—and letting me hobble on a leg as he half-carries me, "what's the plan?"

"We're to enter the Vault of Contrition," I say, wincing a bit as I feel the dull, throbbing pain in my thigh become far more apparent, "ask nicely, make a copy, go. Do you have any sandcinder with you?"

"Yeah," he says, shrugging and in the process jolting me enough that I have to suppress a little squeak of pain, "Ay kept some up here." He pats one of the numerous pouches hanging rather unusually off his robes, it being almost up to his shoulder. "Probably used it to fix the gun up."

I giggle. "I'd hope you knew how to shoot it."

He pats me on the forehead and, evidently satisfied that I am not having a fever, shakes his head. "I think," he says, flicking the administrator's weapon he's strapped firmly to his side, "I'll just stick to this thing. Never learned anything besides the part where I pull the trigger—thing's a dream."

I nod. "So long as you point the end away from *me*."

"Oh, come *on*," he says, shaking his head a bit. "Just because I'm dumb doesn't mean I'm stupid."

I decide not to comment.

As we come up to the main street, it is noticeably mostly empty; I've never been to a village before and can't very well pass comment, but the sound of the perpetually singing man makes the sight almost eerie. The buildings in the square near the inn are mostly hastily-erected oration-held storefronts, the façades rising taller than the buildings themselves to leave space for statements of purpose.

Perei balances me as he grabs the bolt and pulls it open, and almost immediately—as I feel a slight coolness passing over my skin and remaining, only then realising the redundant membrane's presence—I begin to hear the sound of a crowd of rather angry men.

As we walk in, however, and a small chiming sounds, a man turns to look at us; he blinks a bit before tapping the shoulder of a man next to him. By the time we reach the bar itself, our shoes clapping loudly on the ground, every single person I can see is looking at us.

"Hello?" I say, glancing up to a crowd-facing Perei, "I admire your practice of redundant membrane placement. It's very forwards-thinking."

They remain silent; some look amongst each other, as if building some kind of unspoken consensus; Perei leans his head towards my ear and whispers as I turn my own to meet it.

"*I think they think you're an admin.*"

"*I look **nothing** like an administrator,*" I say, watching rather uncomfortably as the whispering starts within the crowd, so quiet that their accents render them entirely unintelligible, "*an heir, not an administrator.*"

"*You're in black Guardsman digs. Think **they** know that?*"

I turn away from him and level my sight with the crowd; there appear to be around forty people about, and I force myself to stifle the nervous tapping of my ceramic-soled feet.

"Is there anyone here," I say, the silence awkward enough that as a man jolts in place I might conjecture it is in shock at its destruction, "who can tell me where the local Vault of Contrition is?"

Nobody responds—for a moment—before a somewhat youngish woman buried amongst the crowd speaks in a noticeably rough Northern accent.

"Just as soon as you can tell us where the bloody aid is, mate."

I blink. I don't think I've ever heard an administrator being spoken to such.

"Yea," another says, a man leaning up against the bar wall. "You've got th'cultural outreach rubbish on you, haven't you? Where's the outreach? We got here for permits, not donor certificates." He looks about, as if gauging his approval rating, and—perhaps finding it to be satisfactory—he turns back. "Bloody Telts clogging the bloody place up worse than the fleshcrawlers up in a murderer's septic and the federals haven't done the slightest bit to stop it. Utter rubbish."

"That's not my job," I say, measuring my words carefully. "I simply need access to your Vault of Contrition."

"Is that so?" a deep voice says in some strange accent that is a mixture of frontier speech and administrative vocabulary, and my attention is drawn immediately to a man standing by my right; he is wearing clothes so unusual I cannot help but notice. A band hangs from his shoulders and wraps about his torso, going down his sternum and splitting from there to encircle back to his neck, creating a strange sort of outline about his chest. "I'd certainly like to get in there too."

I blink at him. "What?"

"Well," he says, extending a hand and glancing surreptitiously towards the crowd, which seems slowly to be returning to its old general demeanour as if it were a single person split purely for atmosphere. "I'm Temesrei das Sikhrea es-Kelenyiaea. The mayor, if you didn't already know—I believe we've got something you need."

"es-Kelenyiaea?" I say, feeling a slight twinge in my heart. "You're an administrator."

"Clearly," he says, smiling. "And I know you aren't, even if you might be one's daughter. I don't suppose you think this looks like the kind of place we build for *citizens* to rule, yes? No offense."

"None taken," I say, and I can almost feel the nasally-conveyed hot air blowing against the back of my neck.

"I'm not going to ask you how or why you got your accoutrements, but your friend here—" and here he gestures to Perei, whose poker face is absolute, "—well, he has me convinced you're the right person."

"I'm a refugee from Cimsas—" I begin, and as his eyes open wide I almost immediately stop.

"*What?*" he shouts, and a few people look over; his composure is immediately retained with a downwards flick of the hand, and he leans in a bit closer. "What's that you said about Cimsas?"

"You'll receive the news quickly enough," I say, and decide that I should probably get out of the settlement as quickly as possible; perhaps if we're quick enough the time won't bother us. "Along with the ongoing siege of Tachiesrea. We need access to the Vault of Contrition now."

"Look," he says, leaning back and rubbing his temples as a clearglass cup filled with some beverage of unknown composition lands on the table besides him, "I'm not sure if you're telling me the truth, but I'm afraid that even if I was there's a bit of a problem. I wasn't being dense when I told you about the Vault, you see. The Teltradi have found it to be suitable for them."

"That's bull," Perei says, and his sudden presence seems to upset the mayor, who visibly forces himself still and reaches over to the drink on the table, taking a quick sip as he continues to speak. "I've never seen a Telt stay still when someone told him to run."

"You're from the city, boy?" he says, chuckling to himself as he takes another sip. "You haven't seen a third of what the Teltradi feel free to do without the peacekeepers reining them in." He turns back to me and gives me a nod. "We got our stuff out of the Vault, but I'm afraid this isn't an opportunity I'm willing to miss. Get them out of our town, out of our pockets and out of our fountains and you'll have anything you want. If this isn't a con, I need to get to business."

I nod, shifting my leg a little so that I am in a vaguely more comfortable position. "Where is it?"

"Half a kilometer east," he says, and pats me on the back. "Good luck."

"So," Perei says, helping me onto the glasswalker's back as the chanting of nonsense words continue unabated, presumably amplified by some sort of horrid barrier, "what's the plan *now*?"

"I suppose we'll have to clear the Teltradi out—" I say, taking a quick break in the sentence to command the walker to move at a steadily accelerating pace, "I'd imagine you could shoot the air? Scare them off?"

He flicks his hand in what I presume to be dismissal. "I've tussled a few Telts before. They're nice and listen when you're on the ground, but wave a piece around and they'll take it from you, stick it up your ass and pull 'til it goes click."

I wince involuntarily at the image. "Very literary. What do you propose?"

"Hey," he says, shrugging, "you're the smart one. You try and figure it out."

I sigh and try and figure it out.

It is not long before we reach the Vault; its presence makes itself known less by its outwards appearance—a short, fortified flat risen stone building that wouldn't be out of place outside a barrier, almost sunken into the sand—than by the increasing volume emanating from it. Not the inhuman sound, certainly, of a man acting a sessile (that is diminishing, for presumably the barrier is specifically built to annoy) but the *human* sound: a building cacophony of organic chemistry, standing out among the silence as though they were bad metaphors amongst brilliant prose.

The first distinct words that make themselves known are a very loud exclamation in pidgin Aimelan:

"Oi, gehmen venye ossbek!"

The comprehension is delayed, but I soon realise he's saying 'government coming on walkerback'; as we draw closer, I find that the Teltradi in their sand-coloured clothes are not, in fact, given to occupying the structure exclusively and are in fact rushing out towards me in droves.

"I hope you've finished figuring," he says, and I can see him in my peripherals brushing down his pouches and flicking at them as if to confirm their veracity, "'cause the figures're coming."

As the mass of children surrounds us—there is a conspicuous absence of the male form—we are forced quickly to slow rather than to demolish a strategically-placed young girl; the time it takes for us to slow down and then gently correct our course is more than enough for them to descend upon us.

There is a general tugging about my feet as the mass of clothed flesh (there are not so many as to warrant the description, but the few that surround us are enough to provoke the tactile sensation to the extent that its use is worth the necessary parentheses) surrounds and begins to speak in a thousand different, mutually exclusive tones, but it is thankfully not forceful enough that it provokes my wound.

I attempt to shout over the crowd an inquiry as to their usual population density, but Perei is too busy either laughing or territory-marking—he is shaking his feet at them even as he makes a sound I presume to be a giggle, the sound of the laughter lost almost entirely about the general tremor—and so I am left to discern the specifics of their behaviour on my own.

There is rather suddenly a tugging against the back of my throat, and I instinctively twist away; this only strengthens the pull, and as my neck snaps towards the source I see Perei holding onto my sessile instrument as his lips move in what looks to me to be silence.

Before I can speculate as to the fact, my weight still pulled away, he lets go and I almost fall over into the mass of screamers. It is my final thought before I consider that I may die that there are only children in the crowd, and close my eyes in the most melodramatic fashion possible to brace for impact as the stirrup reaches its end.

I open an eye to nothing but the usual searing pain in my thigh, and look to see that there is a sudden absence of anything but glassy sand. The sound remains, and so with a few blinks I force myself up— breathing as heavily as my lungs will allow me in an attempt to rid myself of the urge to scream—and on the right find my companion giving them a shower from his hands, water flowing somewhat less than it would from mine but at a rate that is nonetheless remarkably average. They are running with their mouths turned up, some apparently losing their balances and falling as they jockey for position.

We are approaching the Vault's entrance, and I note as we come near to it—once I've torn my head away from the almost fetishistic hydrophilia on display—a few men and women clothed in the very same camouflaging robes. As we enter within what I gauge to be about thirty metres, the children following alongside us begin to move off, and we go the final stretch unmolested.

"What on *earth* was that about?" I say, wincing a bit as I resist the urge to rub at my thigh.

"You don't know?" he says, and we've reached the entrance before he can elaborate. I glance back and see the children looking with what I presume to be an expression of collective sadness at us, and force myself to look back away.

One of the women standing at the entrance comes forth— backed up by four friends, all looking somewhat sombre—with what I presume to be a look of mild amusement on her face, her legs looking rather suspiciously as if they've got a rather impressive array of knives strapped underneath the sheet that clothes them.

"Government," she says, the edge of an unidentifiable, almost Zhanghwazh accent sharpening her speech. "What is purpose here? We are told we have right of abode?" Her stress is on the first syllable with every word, lending an awkward sort of music to her tone.

"We need to see your leader," I say, looking down at her from the back of the glasswalker. "I've been instructed to clear you out."

She tilts her head at me and laughs in some indistinct pantomime of merriment. "Salapatro?" she says, shaking her head. "You are a very lucky government today. Sher is with."

"That explains *that*," Perei grumbles, his voice low; a little water is still trinkling from the tips of his fingers, and as it falls against the floor I see one of the younger lick his lips gently. This doesn't escape the notice of another, who pats him on the back; he quickly shakes his head and his face turns back as it was.

"You may see leader, government, but waste: we are not going yet," she continues, and here her weight shifts back onto her back. "We need living-gifts. That is custom, if I am remember proper. You have given some to the playing-girls already."

A moment passes where I try and understand.

"*Water?*" I say, far too shocked to feign credulity, and before I can say anything Perei pats me on the shoulder and shakes his head in what I presume to be an attempt at subtlety.

"Do what you want, government," she says, stepping aside. "Our question is unchanging."

I nod and bow my head as we go through the obscured doorway—it is large enough to swallow a small building, but I bow anyway out of instinct—and enter the foyer.

I presume of course that past the crowded tents (Aimelan and Pilisyari and a thousand styles I cannot recognise, all in various states of disrepair but all with what look to be working membranes) and the strange people looking up at us and the permeating recreational music and general fanfare of competitive dancing and collaborative threadworking and mobile structures I can only presume are meant for transportation, standing alongside raggedy glasswalkers as they are is what might have once been a vault's foyer.

"Whoa," Perei says, looking about; they do not mob us, but I find the eye-mobbing somewhat more disconcerting. A young boy seems to begin to walk towards us, but is quickly picked up and carried—carried!—by his mother, herself looking at us with the sort of confusion I'd imagine is shown to both the brave and idiotic. "That's a *lot* of Telts."

The music doesn't stop as drama might dictate, but a general murmur runs through the crowd loud enough to be heard over it. Perei quite pointedly keeps his hand on his sidearm—I'm unsure where his pacifism's gone, myself—and we are not approached except occasionally; it is somewhat disconcerting to see that almost every person has a weapon somewhere on their body, whether a rifle or a sharpened stick.

"Where do you think Salapatro's at?" he says, looking about; we're too high above most of the tents to get a view of their interiors, but an especially tall, stereotypically Oiesya tent grants me a glimpse of simple mass-produced bedrolls and what appears to be a brownish sort of edible mush on iron cutlery.

"I'd normally look for the most ornate tent," I say, shaking my head, "but—"

"But everything is same shit, yeah?" Perei doesn't say, and I look down along with him to see a grinning woman missing a front tooth with her hands on her hips.

I stare at her.

"Come, government," she says, beckoning and pointing to her back. "I happy tell you where."

I throw a sideways glance to Perei, who grabs it and throws it back; the resulting game of visual toss is quite handily disrupted by a further elaboration.

"Come and have eat—we after can business."

The metaphor flies out the membrane and breaks its head on the steaming, cracked pavement, and my stomach rumbles.

I face her and nod.

Real food is an interesting commodity.

The poor without tessitura pay more for food than any other kind of person. Triticum and taraxacum—the staples of Mahammadir cuisine—are Kistyaran goods by definition, governed by an inverse bell curve; after all, what kind of person who sings for a living would pay money for food when a two-thousand-thirty-five syllable nutrient paste with a few extra thousand syllables of flavour does quite well?

I contemplate this with a handful of steamed tuberosum and aestivum having been shovelled into my mouth, and thus I am somewhat biased in deciding that I must sympathise with a lifestyle where the taste

I'm savouring is common enough that Perei would choose to guard the horses instead.

"Eat," she says, smiling. "Eat."

"Are you absolutely *sure*?" I ask, having rechecked the food for contaminants for about the seventeenth time; the little tent is just big enough for a single person, and the cooking utensils and bits of rusted trinkets lying about don't inspire confidence. "I'm not entirely certain that—"

"Is good," she says, smiling the very same missing-toothed smile. "Salapatro gives big for take care government. You say I do good, yeah?"

"You're missing an incisor," I say, and gesture with my pinky. " I could help you with that."

She steps back, covering her mouth; her voice comes muffled past her hand. "Is trouble? Teeth is trouble? I sorry, have not understand—"

"No!" I shout, and realise that my voice is a bit too high; I cough to myself a bit. "I'm sorry, habit. No, it isn't any trouble. I want to fix your teeth. Understand?" I point to the gap, make a facsimile of it with my index finger and then prod my left index finger into the resulting cranny. "I fix."

"You—you fix me?" she says, her eyes rather wide. "No. Cannot. Salapatro not allow."

"Salapatro," I say, and I suddenly am blessed with the small relief of a minor mystery lifting from my mind. "Salapatro wouldn't allow? How'd you lose that tooth in the first place?"

She looks at me strangely. "You want know how teeth gone?"

I nod.

"Ah—" she begins, and shakes her head to herself slowly. "Was fight Pilisyari. I want water. He see and want I pay but no can—he want take baby, I say no can. He assassinate—"

"Assassinate?" I say, tilting my head. "You mean 'tried'?"

"Yeah, yeah—he tried jump me, I beat him use this—" she says, and reaches to her belt to pull at what looks to be a particularly sharp Oiesya blade; its sheath is rather conspicuously missing. "He cry and pain so he punch, I fall and hit head. He take baby and go."

"He took your baby?" I say, and blink. A taraxacum stalk dangles from my lip. "What happened to him?"

"I go to peacekeep," she says, and her face is as jovial as ever. "I ask for where is baby, and they say no know, no need know. Say baby run away. I tell they no understand and try say but they say is not. On cut is blood, I show—they jail and until friend come speak for me. They say say and I am out, still baby no there."

I nod.

"Do you still miss him?"

"Was her. Very beautiful," she says, and shakes her head. Her smile remains. "But is like that, yeah? Until we water. Everyday can hear he sing. One day will water and no more hurt. Then will never pain again."

My appetite has been noteworthily diminished; I put my plate down.

"This," she says, poking at the plate, "three days of ask."

I decide not to waste the food.

The tent we are led to—the woman is accosted by a few particularly well-dressed men as we approach it, given a few aluminium coins and sent on her way—is a particularly ornate one that I might suggest is of Mahammadir make, its sandy covering betrayed by the golden thread running along the velvet-lined pinned-up flap going between its poles. What I can see of the interior is a hodgepodge of soft and light furniture.

"Hey-yo," he grumbles, as we reach the entrance; he dismounts and aids me as I do, and I can almost feel the eyes on my back as I try to whisper the passphrase as quietly as possible. "Some guys tried to pick me five times on the way here. Didn't keep anything in those pockets, did you?"

"No," I say. "What happened to 'they'll shove it up your posterior'?"

"That was *before* I knew how many," he says, propping my arm up over his shoulder as he bends down. "Don't wanna stay here long if we're leaving with anything but the clothes on our backs."

"They're strange," I say, shaking my head, "but I can't imagine that they're *that* bad."

"Yeah," he says, very visibly shifting his weight so that my foot remains on the ground, "they're weird. Decent one-on-one, though. If you're not expecting much."

"Such high praise," someone that isn't me says, and I look up to see a particularly tall man looking down upon us with a faint smile on his lips, looking very much like some sort of particularly ragged Southerner, "coming from one so high above. I dare not suggest we are to be treated with courtesy as long as our hands are out of your pockets as well?"

I cough politely as I behold the dressing upon him—some kind of mayonnaise-coloured baguette vest over olive pants, the former in the Aimelan style and the latter in the Mahammadir, little pins made of titanium and aluminium jotted about in a great many different designs—and look to stare him in the eyes. "You're Salapatro?"

He nods. "I am indeed."

"You must forgive my colleague. He isn't very sensitive."

"Neither am I," he says, and turns about on his heel.

Then he begins walking back to the tent's opening; Perei seems slow on the uptake, but certainly quicker than me. "*Hey!*" he goes, stepping forward and in the process giving me reason to take a quick inhale as the pain spikes. "Where d'you think you're going?"

He stops and turns around; his smile has not moved, and I can see it past the slight haze of tears as I move a hand to brush it away. "Oh?" he says, "is your servant your tongue, government?"

"She's *injured*," Perei says, pulling me up a little as if to demonstrate; an involuntary *agh* issues from my throat, and I immediately turn to give him the most vicious stare I can at that point remember giving—the pain particularly overrides any impulse I have to question his vocabulary. "We want you g—" and here he pauses and lets out an exasperated sigh, "—we want you *Telts* to pack up and get lost."

A few men are nearby, one of them playing an instrument I can't quite identify, and they seem to take notice of the disturbance. "I've been called a lot of things," he says, shaking his head lightly. "I'm afraid rude words will not cause me to set off. I'd suggest simply giving the gifts one is expected to. We can live off these people for a long time."

"Wait," I say, and turn to face him in the eyes. "Why do you need water?"

He blinks as if in confusion before tilting his head a little. "You don't know?" he says, and waves an arm. "Come, government. Allow me to enlighten you."

Like a reader trundling forth into a maze of exposition, I am dragged onwards into the tent.

"It is good that you are here, but I suppose that I must first answer your first query. You are a government," he says, sitting back on what looks to be a thirty-second century Mahammadir divan inscribed with various epithets for their god, worn and torn by lack of barrier maintenance. "I might think that you should already know that our people are not so fortunate in oration as yours."

"Water orations," I say, trying to force myself into a comfortable position with my legs apart; in a tent on an oversized pillow across from an unfamiliar man, this is proving difficult. "Water orations aren't difficult. I've seen your children."

"I'm sure they wouldn't be if we knew the words," he says, laughing with a particularly artificed sort of bitterness. "For as long as we have been in existence, our people have striven to reconstruct the word—the proper word—for pure water, so that we may claim our independe—"

"*Oyr*," I say, tilting my head. "The word is *oyr*. It isn't very long. Not more than two syllables, depending on how you interpret it."

"Ah, yes—" and here he pushes his sleeve aside, letting his arm fall over the back, "I'm sure you are aware that the tower does not so understandingly answer our cries. Observe: *venytj oyra*."

With a flick of his hand, water begins to trickle steadily almost five centimetres from his palm; there is a strange smell from it, however, and as the stream continues for a few seconds, dripping onto the stone floor, I realise its composition.

"Brine."

"And far worse things besides. Have you ever bled saltwater from your eyes?"

"You could use the proper word," I say, trying not to raise my voice. "Dihydrogen monoxide. You could specify the corporeal coordinates separately. You could fuse hydrogen and oxygen, if you wanted—it's a five-year-old's chemistry lesson."

"Ah, but that is what we seek. Come," he says, and stands; Perei follows, and I have the presence of mind not to attempt the journey.

The inside of the tent is well-illuminated, and though it is large the only partition is the one that splits the middle; he tugs on the sheets, the Sichyan velvet folding in on itself to reveal a remarkably young man who looks to be in a trance, his mouth moving but to be making no sound.

"This is the barrier," he says, rapping at the almost invisible violet distortion separating us, "that makes the sounds you must so despise rise above you. That boy—" and here he sticks his hand through the barrier slowly, as if through custard, "—represents to us the hope of our people. Countless caravans of us ride throughout, carrying our hopes with us and letting the outside know of our plight."

"*Erytidryjeny-yityangsidyr.*"

His expression only slightly changes.

"What?"

"*Ámænii myzh pœmyiiratj an-bànmyr-lyn shen-an erytidryjeny-yityangsidyzh,*" I say, and a rush of elementally pure water begins to flow exactly a centimetre each from my palms, falling onto the floor. "To the palms-from-you-to-me of my to-hands a centimetre away one litre of dihydrogen monoxide."

He is silent for a moment as the water flows from my palms; Perei, standing besides him, carries an expression I choose to accept as impressment. "I do not think you understan—"

"Try it. It should work. Less water, and sometimes it won't work, but purer."

He shakes his head and looks back at the child. "Again, I do not think you understand. Allow me to repeat: men like these are the hope of our nation."

I blink at him. "I've given you your hope. Just learning that sentence—it might take a while, but you should be able to get at least a hundred millilitres each time. I've taught it to countless immigrants. I don't know why no one's told you them yet, especially in Cimsas."

He sighs and retreats back to the divan. "I know of Cimsas. It has recently been destroyed, yes? By an unknown, foreign power?"

"Yes."

"I have," Salapatro says, gesturing with the flat of his palm out from the tent, "at least one thousand armed men here and possibly ten thousand more spread across Aimela. They are harsh and experienced. They are used to moving long distances without advance notice. They have fought, unlike the Aimelan Guard."

"I'm sorry," I say, shaking my head, "but what are you implying? The Guard has been fighting a war in the South for decades."

"In Far Aimela. The only men here are the sons and daughters of administrators. They will take a month to move and if they do, they will lose the present war immediately. The protectorates would secede the moment that they feel undefended. Half of Aimela would be gone completely." His accent fades steadily as he speaks, morphing into a strange sort of half-Zhanghwazh.

"How do you know all of this?"

"It doesn't matter," he says, and takes a quick look about; there is no one in the tent but us and the boy. "I am very aware that anything so callous as to destroy a major city would gladly destroy us. Breathe no word of this to anyone—I don't need your compliance, nor did I need the compliance of the thousand before, but now is no time for risk—and our forces will soon join Aimela in battle. To you our life may seem poor, but we are more than ready to wage war."

If I were a sponge, I might say that I absorbed his words slowly; I am a human being, however, and so I simply comprehend.

"You know already."

"Look around you," he says, chuckling a bit. "We do not have what we do by being *independent*. Our way of life is ours, miss—?"

"My name isn't for thieves," I say, standing up in a fit of righteous anger and promptly falling down in a fit of pain, my speech thus quite handily interrupted by a sizzling sort of sound coming from a sucking between my teeth and tongue.

He stands and goes to his knees; in the corner of my vision, I see Perei bring his hand to the gun on his hip. "Call it what you like. I've brought these poor people to prosperity. Thousands of loyal, strong men will be thousands of rifles delivered to any skull, thousands of loyal, agile women will be thousands of knives delivered to any throat—this is a perfect opportunity for us, government. We will wander free forever."

I glare up. "Your children beg for water. You steal to live. You aren't *free*. If you let me tell you the word—"

"If I let you tell us the word," he says, "what use do they have for me? We are bound by our need, miss. You need your government for its protection; we need us—" and here he uses the exclusive us, "for our hope.

Surely Aimela wouldn't be so large and so united if it could not protect its people?"

"That's different. I've seen how your people live, Salapatro. It's fed squalor."

He stands and turns about, and his hands are folded behind his back. "Well," he says, "no matter. You need our aid, and that is a fact."

I look up to Perei, who has a profoundly uninterested expression on his face; one of his pouches is open and he is poking at the barrier as if it were a gelatin toy. He seems to notice my stare in the corner of his vision and shrugs before going back to patting at the barrier.

"It wouldn't do anyone good to tell, in any case. Every single one of us knows that Cimsas is gone. The villages, as I'm sure you've come to notice, can hardly feed us; for all we know, Sikhas is next. Some of the tribes are thinking of going their own way. I wouldn't usually make a deal—what makes you think they will distinguish the water from their hands from the filth that I and the men that came before me have told them it is?—but I'm not willing to risk it now."

"What choice do you have?"

There is a moment of silence between us; the growing smile on Salapatro's face is so subtle that I only notice it when it dies.

"I could simply suggest we fight for the Mahammadir instead. Not the Alliance, certainly—but from what I know, your attackers are very much Southern, and I don't have the slightest doubt they're related." He looks down to the writing on the divan and pats upon it, grinning. "Perhaps their god has some good news to bear after all."

I am silent for a while.

"Well?" he says, "do you agree not to cause any trouble, government?"

"I—" I begin, pushing myself off the ground and forcing myself to my feet, keeping my thighs apart, "I agree."

He responds quickly, and his accent refills his voice. "Very good. I shall make the necessary communications. You will be reinforced in less than a week; we've already taken all the water we need ourselves diverting from their fountain oration."

"Tachiesrea is under siege," I say, looking to the ground. "They'll need some relief."

"Tachiesrea, hm? If I knew you were *that* desperate, I'd have asked for more!" he says, chuckling. "Salapatro does not go back on his promises, fear not. They'll get it."

Perei walks over to me and helps me onto my feet; Salapatro notes the help with a strange expression on his face. "Excuse me," he says, "but I am sad to say that I have not interacted with a great many Aimelans recently. If walking is such a trouble, why don't you simply allow yourself to be *carried?*"

Perei and I give each other a long glance.

"We might not be warriors," I say, shaking my head, "but we are not *savages.*"

At this Salapatro bursts into laughter, and does not stop as we walk out the tent.

I hold the little exodus cache in a little piece of fabric in my right hand. We are riding away, and in the distance behind me—I don't have to look to know—hundreds of caravans filled with men and women and children go off to do war.

It isn't just redundancy that holds my sight; I find the thought so inspiring and awful at once that I cannot bear to behold its fulfilment.

"So," Perei says, coughing politely, "the mayor. Talk about surprised."

I take a deep breath and look forwards.

"Hey, for all you know they're *happy* that way."

I unwrap the Cache and bring it up to the light.

"*Tsaijpekhsenaelmeh,*" he says, in perfectly enunciated gibberish, "*kilzpyuproufitey duhcetdjandjen.*"

The sentence almost makes me drop the little cylinder; as it is, I simply blink quicker than usual a few times in succession. "What?"

"I said 'it's gonna do them some good fighting'," he says, giving me a somewhat concerned look. "I mean, they're gonna mix with the Guard, anyway."

"One moment," I say, staring down at the silver-coloured thing. "'The term 'encephalitis' refers to an encephalopathy usually manifesting with systemic constitutional symptoms, especially pyrexia and pleocytosis of the cerebrospinal fluid.'"

"What?"

I reach over and grab his hand, ignoring the immediate pain in my thigh and placing the chip in it. "I said: 'the term 'encephalitis' refers to an encephalopathy usually manifesting with systemic constitutional symptoms, particularly pyrexia and pleocytosis of the cerebrospinal fluid.'"

"Okay, uh," he says, blinking in what I presume to be confusion, "when you say 'encephalitis', you mean something in, uh, the brain—a brain problem which gets you a fever and—what's a pleocytosis?"

"Pleocytosis," I say, "is a word."

"Uh—are you trying to test this thing or something? Because I don't think it's working."

"The presence of cerebrospinal fluid pleocytosis in patients suspected of suffering from acute demyelinating polyradiculoneuropathy signals a possibility of mammalian immunodeficiency virus or other mild-type inflammatory diseases."

"Whoa," he says, "nevermind. I dunno how, but I—I think I just understood everything you just said. Oh *god*, that's gross."

"It learns from context," I say, nodding to myself. "Pleocytosis is—"

"When a—when something makes—"

"When a *cell*."

"When a cell makes more of itself than it's supposed to." He blinks. "I think I know what you're saying. I *understand* the words, but—"

"But you can't explain them!" I say, smiling; any pretensions I might have had towards regret are thoroughly departed. "This is beyond useful. This isn't just a translation device—it's a *learning tool*."

"Isha," he says, shaking his head and looking with some measure of awe at the object in his hand. "I bet the streams went at *least* fifty feet."

I consider raising some sort of objection to his antisociality, but I decide instead to give him a smile; there isn't very much that can dampen my mood. "Put the sandcinder against it," I say, "let it replicate."

He nods and obliges, pouring a tiny bit over it as it lies in his palm; I watch as the burnt sand gives way to a pure silvery metal, the scattered bits conglomerating together and fitting the template exactly before settling into the shapes of four identical cylinders. The surface ripples a bit before it settles, and I almost greedily pinch one before settling back. My thigh continues to ache, but I pay it no mind.

"Brilliant," I say, measuring it against my thenar space. "Give me a knife."

"*Isha,*" he says, looking off to the side as if attempting to find a witness for an act that to him no doubt seems hilarious, "you're gonna stick that *in* you?"

"And in you."

He recoils in some pantomime of horror. "Uh, no. I've known you for like three days. Doesn't mean you get to stick stuff in me. I'll hold on to it."

I sigh. "Just give me the knife."

He fumbles about his pouches to find one before pulling one out in triumph: a somewhat ornate aluminium-coloured piece in a leather sheath, looking to be Zhanghwazh in style. He hands it over and I grasp it, pulling it out and bringing it up to the light.

"It's not serrated," I say, putting a hand over my instrument as I recall the oration I must to sterilise it. "That should make it easier."

As he watches, I proceed with my business.

It hurts quite a bit.

On the plus side, my leg's stopped bothering me.

four
Blind in the Dark

It's hard to tell, stuck in the dark, that your sight has lost its colour.

It seems like the colours still exist, just in a dye; the purples are still purple, the reds still red, each speck of colour just as it should be— the tint that remains anchors itself to the memory each leaves.

Then you reach for a switch, expecting the red one to start the fire, and find that the blue one has doused it, and the moment shatters your delusion of competence.

It's hard to tell, once woven, that your life has lost its colour. It seems like it still exists, just dyed; the feeling you have when your hands thread through a young woman's hair remains, your heartbeat higher than another's in a way you can ascribe to the nervousness of the bonding. As the sensation ties itself to the memory of how you ought to feel, your fear becomes easy enough to think of as love.

Then you grasp her by the throat as you reach for her waist, and the moment shatters your delusion of wholeness.

That is how I have been broken.

How I have been broken
The Words of the Woven
compiled by Andresrea qu'n'av dasnamr
published by the Goodwill Fellowship and approved for
private distribution by the Administration for Media Development
under the continued grace of Khaliesrea das Sikharea eliyit Tamarisrei,
Administrator for the Arts
initial resale publication by Mitras Press Holdings

ZHANGHWAMPEYZH

Aysmanratyss pyr Aysmanrat' Aimelzh pyr Cysinscandyra Ocilentzhra.

5

Vyéntnyr

to make a move with short-term consequences

I awake almost out of breath, something terrible jolting me from slumber.

The day is relatively cold—the sand isn't molten, at the very least—and I decide to ascribe it to this and let whatever unpleasant remnants of my dreams remaining in my memory fade. A check of the membrane shows us almost entirely towards our destination: only a few minutes remain between us, the hours before my sleep spent on some half-remembered discussion on weapons.

I do recall it being said in a pre-Laceration sessile that one's surroundings are to be detailed at every opportunity, so as to avoid the sensation of a dialectical void. The context escapes me, but the advice remains; as such, I take a full and accurate account of the numerous objects which surround us.

—Sand,
—glass,
—sand on glass,
—I sincerely hope that isn't a human skull but instead a particularly odd-shaped bit of molten sand, and
—a considerable amount of sand and glass.

I pause in my survey and decide that dialogue might be considerably more entertaining.

"What do you read?"

Perei glances sideways to me as I speak.

"What's that?"

I sigh lightly, my hand going on my knee as I push myself up. "You must have had to learn to read some way or another, didn't you? What do you read?"

"Don't know why you want to know, but—" and here he snaps his fingers a bit, "Pend. Temel, when I want a laugh. A bit of Cant."

"You read *Canteryratysyr*?" I say, blinking at him.

"Well, had to go for the top three," he says, grinning. "Read ten pages and woke up dead in an alley. Head tried to crawl away, but—"

"—but you picked it up and threw it on the ground and it stood up and said 'goodbye'," I say, shaking my head. "I've never heard Canteryratysyr mentioned in the same sentence as Pendras and Temelytitsyn."

"Hey," he says, an expression of what I imagine to be slight rustledness on his face, "what makes Pend any different from that guy?"

"Pendras?" I say, rolling my eyes. "He's a brownwriter at best."

"Just because it's printed on dryleaf doesn't make what he says any less true. He talks to *people*."

"What kind of people?" I say, snorting. "The idiotic or the prepubescent?"

"Go rivet yourself to a wall," he says, and flips his wrist as me as dismissively as I'd imagine a man could. "It's not like Cant's any better. Or Kafka, or—"

"Canteryratysyr's exploration of alienation—"

"That's the same thing Pend's talking about. He talks about how stuff *works*. He tells the truth. Telling it how we do doesn't change that." He sighs, and looks up to the sky. "You worked the Mend, didn't you? How the hell d'you tell yourself we're any less worth listening to?"

"I don't have to hear a person to operate on him."

He gives me a stare so concentrated it could cause a bar fight before simply looking down and letting his head rotate about its axis like a defeated marionette's.

"You're a lost cause."

"Come now," I say, sighing. "*The Zhanghwazh Dialect—*"

"Zhanghwa's Voice's genius," he says, shaking his head; his 'a' is just as long as Ayerei's. "You can't tell me the way the Sips treat the jings coming in from the north's more than a punch in the face."

"But that's what it is: *brownwriting.*" There is a certain fire in my voice, but for the life of me I can't imagine why. "He took some little rubbish thing that happened maybe five years ago *once* and turned it into an entire rubbish *book*. It's exploitation."

"But don't you see? It's not just about *that*. It's about the new muds moving in with the old muds. It's about *us*, just like everything Cant talks about. You think people turn into itsystrongs with pretty faces every day?"

"*A* pretty face," I say, shuddering slightly. "But Canteryratysyr's *entirely* metaphor. *Pendras* appropriates other cultures—"

"And he's writing for *us*," he says, and crosses his arms. "Not the jings, not the Sips. Cant didn't think about flyworm issues when *he* was writing, right?"

I might respond, but a slight chirping sound has caught my attention—the amendments I've made to the sessile's instruction set have worked. I pull it from my waistband and unroll it, and it begins speaking in a tone stilted just little enough that I can understand it.

> *Unknown Cache OIKhaTa*
> *Jeanbaud Strip, Zhanghwampezyzh Demilitarised*
> *Free Trade Zone*
> *Description: Located by Tower energy exchange.*
> *Superstructure, approximately three hundred metres long.*
> *Emits a barrier of unknown tolerance approximately ten*
> *kilometres in diameter occupied by an armed paramilitary*
> *force, possibly Southern in origin, claiming allegiance*
> *to something called 'the Nation' and warning potential*
> *interlopers in Ajhyliyy and Pyarash. Readings show barrier*
> *signatures consistent with pre-Laceration data storage*
> *on mid-third floor. Individuals within appear to have no*
> *trouble moving or breathing, suggesting a violation of the*
> *Kkhalitiere law.*
> *Found 5 Undecimus 3914, Third Operation*
> *8/12/3914: Immediate cooperation with ZH suggested.*
> *9/12/3914: Conditionally denied. Suggest waiting until*
> *AI annexes the Jeanbaud strip.*

13/1/3915: Unconditionally denied.

"Huh," Perei says. "Looks like an alley picnic."

"An alley picnic?" I say, looking up from the writing as it fades to the map. "We're about to jump into a stranglecrawler nest."

"Yeah," he says, shaking his head. "An alley picnic. See, I don't think this little thing—" and here he pats the gun at his side, "—was made by the same guys that made *that*." He points behind us, and I turn to see the Tower as I've come to expect it, its usual little pulsations visible against the light. "So it's like a picnic. All we have's a bunch of stale crap and the fleshcrawlers come and fight you for it anyway."

I nod. "And what do you call the Tower?"

"I dunno," he says, shrugging. "A roadside picnic?"

"In any case," I say, glancing back down at the map, "we're meant to be right on top of it. Where—"

The glasswalker whinnies and rears up; I look up and find myself wishing that I had the foresight to drink some water, for I have the deep conviction that a spittake for the moment might be deeply appropriate.

Before me, precipitated by a sharp, sudden curve in the sand, is an intolerant barrier.

If I were the theatric type, I might imagine an orchestra dropping the bass here.

Now, this isn't very surprising; it's likely that hundreds of pre-Laceration facilities are lying around somewhere with intolerant barriers buried under several tons of sand. Intolerants are good for many things, but I can't imagine anyone suggesting that they be used to create a Pari effect.

What *is* surprising is that this isn't buried under tons of sand; what's somewhat more surprising is that I am looking at an oblately ellipsoidal, impossible chimaera of tolerant and intolerant reaching what looks to be almost ten kilometres, the sand smooth to a fault below. I can think of at least five physical laws this construct violates, of which my favourite is the Mitaranatarea law—each barrier woven into physical objects that do a fine job of failing to exist.

"Tower," I say, taking a deep breath. "It's beautiful."

"Isha," Perei says, and I see him in my peripherals shaking his head. "That's amazing."

"Well," I say, giving him an approving smile, "I didn't know you were a saepological connoisseur. There may be hope for you yet."

"Saepological? What the hell are you talking about?" he says, raising an eyebrow at me. "I mean that *giant metal thing floating in the air right in front of us.*"

I look again and realise that almost a kilometre above the gap in the earth is something that only a description formatted like a quote in a textbook might do justice. I've often wondered what makes their way into the ellipses between the clauses, and as I look at it I realise that the ellipses hide books.

Of those books, all I can provide is a summary:

It is, first and foremost, a dark sort of grey on the bottom; the bottom is a long, rectangular box with its sides tilted at degrees crossed by darker grey lines, stretching on for what has to be at least a third of a kilometre; peeking over the edge is what looks to be a single stocky, gleaming white tower with a curved exterior as smooth as well-written prose, little black, human-shaped spots scattered along its fencelike edges and enormous structures jutting over the edges. There are six of the latter, two before the building and one after, and though I cannot see its ground I can only presume that the rest is flat.

"The document doesn't mention that," I murmur, looking back and forth between the sessile and the view. "It doesn't mention the floating at all."

"I guess something must've changed," he says, pulling his weapon from his side and reaching into his pouch. "I don't think they've seen us. We need to get up there somehow."

"What on Earth is that called, by the way?" I say, watching him pull the auger—I don't know what it's really called, but I'm certainly not going to keep calling it a 'green-tinted piece of orated glass' for the rest of my life—from his pocket, giving it a sweep against his robes as he turns to me.

He gives me a strange look—some mixture of genuine noncomprehension and mild indignation. "Does it matter?"

"Well," I say, shrugging, "I personally prefer to know what things are called before I put them near one of my orifices."

"Rivet me if I know," he says, and puts it up to his eye. "It's Ay's, remember? Don't know what the saddlebackers down Jean Way call themselves, either."

He pauses, thoughtful.

"Not sure if *they* know."

I decide to keep my silence, and he looks forwards for what seems to be an entire minute until a satisfied 'hmm' issues from besides me; I look back to him and he hands me the auger. I put it up to my eye—past the green tint, the little black shades turn into a great array of white figures leaning over the rails.

"Over there," he says, and I look to see him pointing rightwards; I stare over along the edge. "That thing. Lower half's sandy and upper half's purple so it's kinda tricky, but out the lens, well—"

I follow his lead; past the enormous superstructure, there looks to be a single enormous string reaching down to the ground, hanging from one of the thing's cranelike structures. A glance down below shows what looks to be a little unguarded building; pulling the lens away makes it disappear, and the angle of the sun omits any shadow. From this distance, the difference between the cord and sand makes it look like a small dune on the horizon.

"Wow."

"Guess we know where we're going," he says, and before I can object he compels his glasswalker forwards and down the edge; I watch as he moves right through the barrier and immediately begins sliding as if on ice.

To his credit, his response is immediate: a few hurried commands and the glasswalker has planted its feet firmly into nowhere, the intolerant portion of the barrier destroying any friction he might otherwise have gained. I sigh; a quick *alétt* compels my own walker, and I slide down after him.

I begin orating. An upwards pull on the reins forces it up and accelerates me, and soon I am on par with Perei in the sliding-down-several-kilometres-of-frictionless-barrier department; the final syllable—a quick ànyjt—heralds an unearthly noise as my own stable-tolerant barrier begins to scrape against the ground's, the stable barrier resonance shuddering our very bones as we begin to slow.

Quite suddenly, however, something changes—a slight shuddering and a sudden, slight loss of altitude, our barrier just barely scraping the sand—and I realise with a feeling too quick to allow an adjective that the quasi-intolerance has flickered.

It comes back, and I find my internal organs quite curiously rearranged.

We—all three tonnes of us—are propelled almost five metres into the air.

I have just barely the time to let out the beginning of a swear before we land right back on the barrier—glasswalkers have an impeccable sense of balance, but mine is flailing its legs in something that might look to the layman to be panic but to me seems to be some futile attempt to keep its balance and ensure a controlled descent—and our own shatters from the force without the slightest resistance, temporarily deafening me as its threshold finds itself utterly overruled. The only course of action I can think to undertake is a particularly hoarse sort of quickened breathing as we slide down the basin at what I can only estimate to be almost two hundred kilometres an hour.

Perei is several metres to my right, and as we slide I can hear him shouting:

"We've gotta jump!"

"What?"

"Jump!" he shouts, and jumps.

I must explicate a fact thoroughly:

We are halfway down the basin, and at this rate it's likely that the momentum would simply let us fly over the other side; at any point, our own glasswalkers might trample us, and at any point the barrier might flicker again present us with the sort of conundurum that requires emergency limb regeneration.

I am not an idiot. I may have my various faults, but amongst them I do not include idiocy. At no point in my life have I ever felt that I have done anything ill-considered, and at no point have I ever thought that I ever was anything worse than non-intellectually flawed.

This fails to explain why I comply.

Once I've unbound my knees from the stirrups around them, stood up and jumped laterally over the glasswalker's head, I realise with a start that I'm *falling sideways* right around the time I'm no longer, and descend with the grace of the extinct pegasus: tumbling with my heels over my head. My glasswalker veers to the side and out of sight behind me, and I find myself profoundly surprised that I'm unhurt.

What does not surprise me is the fact that I'm still going at several hundred kilometres per hour on a frictionless slope and that it is very likely that I am going to die.

I don't truly believe I will die, of course—the notion of death seems utterly foreign, as if I'm no longer quite alive in the first place. The wind is rushing past my ears, certainly, and the spheroid's nadir is approaching at a frighteningly quick pace, but everything is bright enough that I can simply call it a dream.

This is around the time a length of rather thick twine hits me in the face, accomplishing quite handily what nature and physics do not with man's ingenuity.

"*Barrier!*" he shouts, and if I were in any other situation I'd have called him dumb and refused; as it is, I twine the rope around my wrist and begin to sing the barrier.

My bones begin to shudder and I clench my teeth; a few hundred kilometres per hour are grinding with a paper-thin wall of force about a centimetre below my posterior, and I continue stabilising it as I fall. The air amplifies its resistance as its speed violates the barrier's threshold— not so grossly as to cause resonance, thank the tower—and begins to slow us down in the slightest, and I feel a sudden pat against my shoulder and realise that I've been pulled shoulder-to-shoulder with Perei.

"Trust me," he says, and pushes himself on top of me; I reflexively flip onto my front, and feel a crunching boot on my spine, knocking whatever wind that might have remained in my diaphragm out of me.

Perei raises one foot—not the one on my back, and so I cannot help but wonder if I'm going to require spinal reconstruction after this—and brings it down besides me. It would do the laws of drama or comedy—it's sometimes difficult to tell the difference—quite well for the barrier to flicker at this point, sending us into the air as the barriers resound.

At this point, it does the laws of comedic drama quite well.

The weight pushes off my back and there is an abrupt cessation of the vibration I might have started to take for granted. The only sight in my eyes is the sky and a glimpse of Perei with his hands wide-spread and the oration-seals on the packs strapped about him looking almost like they're about to burst and the only sound in my ear is a quick, hurried chanting:

C'mon, c'mon, c'mon, c'mon—

We land.

There is a flash of grey and crunching sound that isn't my bones and I feel the barrier's threshold reach its limit but it holds long enough to counteract our momentum and I find myself suspended about a metre in the air above the titanium floor for about a millisecond second before I almost break my nose on it.

Perei hits the ground at the same time as me, groaning; I push myself up and begin hyperventilating as I look about the place as quickly as I can.

The place's most striking detail is the enormous hole in the wall, but that doesn't quite help my situation and so I focus on its second most striking detail: the end of a sessile-arm pointed at my eye along with a bayonet brushing up against my cheek.

I suppose that I am cheating slightly; that's not a detail of the *room*, which is fairly nondescript except for some objective sessile displays laid out along the wall, but it certainly is the most pertinent.

The most pertinent *aural* sensation, on the other hand, is a peculiarly loud scream.

Before my eyes can follow the weapon's length to its owner's hands, there is the scream of burning air and the distinct sound of flesh tearing and burning and I yelp and stand up and look down to see a man with half of his head missing and the other half riddled with an array of tiny, blood-leaking holes, his parietal lobe splattered against the ground.

"Oh, Tower," I say, swallowing and forcing the words out past my uncontrollable shudders, looking to the side. "What just happened?"

"Guessed right about the glint," he says, breathing far deeper and slower than I might expect the circumstances to let a normal person. "Kicked right in time. Wow."

"The 'glint'?" I say, taking a deep breath through my nose and forcing myself off my feet as I exhale before the shaking can push me down, leaning against the wall. "There's no bloody *glint* in a rephrase."

"Huh," he says, shrugging as he stands. "Guess we're in luck, then."

I sigh, then look down at the dead body before me and take a long breath. "You killed him."

"Guess I did," he says, and begins giggling; he looks at me as he does, as if I should join in, but I simply stare and he soon grows quiet, looking at his feet.

"Thank you for saving my life," I say, and trod steadily over to the objective displays projecting from the walls. My hand rests across one of the colourful barriers—these stop just short of intolerance, and I find that my fingers stop with a 'click' the moment I put the slightest bit of force on one. "And for getting us where we need to be."

The instructions are in Angzhwen, and simple enough to understand—the great depth of classical language required to interpret an upwards-pointing isometric triangle notwithstanding. The tiny building's construction appears to be oratory, but the flimsy thing itself has nothing in common with the sheer strength of late pre-Laceration architecture.

"Maybe," I say, breathing in deep through my nose, "maybe we should cut our losses. A Sestiyari reconnaissance team failed here."

"And then where do we go?" he says, shaking his head. "'least they might think their man won. Can't exactly walk out of here."

"Could barrier-climb."

"Barrier-climb three miles with people shooting at us?"

I stand staring for a short while before I press the triangle. "I suppose I'd rather have a chance."

The entire thing shudders before I get the feeling of upwards acceleration; I glance up to the hole in the ceiling, the finger-thick metal curved and bent inwards. The box sways a little as it pushes its way up the painted rope; a quick probe shows the nexuses impelling us to be more or less solid, but I decide to hold on to the closest thing this ramshackle construction has to a handlehold—the enormous column through which I presume the rope goes—first.

"So," Perei says, almost silent. "Wasn't that the coolest thing that's ever happened to you ever in your entire life?" His face remains straight, but I notice a slight twitching at the corners of his mouth.

"No," I say, and tap my foot gently as I look up.

"Oh, okay," Perei says, putting his fingers up to his forehead and shaking it. "Looks like we've got a badass here. What's the coolest thing that ever happened to you, huh?"

My answer comes without very much hesitation. "I made a series of slight mistakes while practising Sauntadrea's voyage." I let myself have a small smile. "The hospitallers still call it Ashrea's serendipity."

"Okay," he says, "that's cool, but it's not *cool*."

"The experience of serving society's 'cooler' than any subjective experience any single person can have," I say.

He gives me a look.

I take a deep breath. "But yes, that was amazing."

Perei pumps his fist, and I look back to the panel; we're within half a minute of arriving, and I begin to sing quietly, bending down to the dead man on the floor. The blood on the floor wobbles a bit underfoot, and my heels are slightly reddened by the contact.

I shut his remaining eyelid and ruffle through his body, carefully avoiding his rifle; strapped to his hip is a thin, black dagger, and I carefully pull it from its sheathe. "A serrated-edge misericorde," I say, interrupting my song for the slightest bit, having laid the beginning of the thread down, "how retrospective."

There is a 'ding'. Perei levels his weapon at the door: I walk forwards slowly and hold onto its handle, pulling it open with a sudden violence.

The light comes pouring in, along with the third-worst smell I have ever experienced; Perei begins gasping for breath.

I glance around the corner and see a great deal of black-and-red-clad men draped over the sides, quite a few laying across the ground; a rather small amount of dried blood lines the ground, some of it pooling at the down-curving edges and stuck between the deck and the bottom of the guardrails. A few blood-spattered glasswalkers stand crowded near the middle, fully outfitted and utterly impassive.

"What on Earth?" I say, walking slowly out onto the structure; the suspended contraption wobbles slightly, and I try not to panic in the short time it takes me to land my feet on solid ground. I hurry to the nearest corpse—making sure not to trip—and out of some instinct check its still pulse.

"Huh," Perei says, coming out after me with his nose covered; most people don't appreciate the fleshcrawlers until they're absent. His eyes widen and he lets out a low whistle as he beholds the blood staining the floor. "Ish-al-*wyent`e*. What the hell *happened* here?"

"His trachea's fractured," I say, holding the rather heavy body by the shoulder and trying to turn him to face me; it falls onto the ground and lies splayed across a dried splash of its own blood. I kneel over it and pull its chin up. "Three stab wounds evenly spaced across heavy tracheal fracture, centre wound three centimetres wide and side wounds one centimetre. Fragments of foreign object embedded in wound. They've been dead for at least six days." I don't sing; there's no need for a matter inventory.

"You'd think all this crap would help," he says, poking at one ot the bodies hanging over the rails and then quickly recoiling, shaking his finger in what I presume to be disgust. "Guess they never thought someone'd get close."

I put my hand to my chin and let out a low *hmm*, looking at the black plates laid across the white fabric spaced equally over the suit. My hand runs over the white, and I realise that it's grown cotton. A quick few taps show that the plates aren't barriered—at least not with a low-force threshold—and a quick song shows that they're not barriered at all, sealed to the fabric by some kind of epoxy. I grab onto one of the bits, pull it up the slightest bit, and find it weighs almost nothing.

"Are there any men here with bullet wounds?" I say, turning back to Perei.

He makes a show of gagging. "Rivet me if I'm checking. I know this shit's okay for you, but Isha this is horrible. Don't think I've seen more dead guys in one place since they started the permits."

"The permits have existed for hundreds of years."

"Never really pushed them tight 'til ten or thereabouts," he says, rubbing his hands off on his trousers. "Told them to go play up their own end, once." There's a slight smile on his face, and I cough awkwardly to myself.

"Right," I say, grimacing. "Shoot the body."

"What? No." His brow scrunches up. "Is this some kind of gross covent thing? Just because I'm not a mud doesn't mean I'll shoot a stiff up."

I decide not to stare meaningfully at the corpse in the elevating building swaying gently in the breeze next to us and instead sigh. "We need to see if their armour deflects pre-Laceration weaponry."

"Why don't you do it yourself?" he says, crossing his arms; I don't think I've seen him quite so disappointed in the week or so I've known him. "Not like you can't just pick one up."

I stare meaningfully at him instead.

"Gunshy, huh?" he says, sighing. "Great. Explains the fireworks.

Last one of you I saw was an admin." He rubs at his head for a bit before taking a deep breath and levelling his weapon up to the hip, his left hand facing backwards over his left shoulder, curved as if covering a pair of eyes. "Swear I'm going to hell for this."

A deep *boom* resounds. The corpse shakes, the plates are undamaged, the crunch of a fracturing ribcage fills the air and I find myself shaking rather uncontrollably, a chill about my breast; I might ascribe this to a sudden, crippling case of the ethics, if not for the fact that at this point Perei similarly takes in a deep breath before he collapses to his knees, grabbing at his chest as he begins to hyperventilate.

I can hear nothing but the footsteps hitting the ground behind me, echoing about as if we're indoors. The sky itself looks like it's gone dimmed, but the sun is just as bright past the façade: its rays strike across the sky all the same.

I try to calm down by taking a few deep breaths; I take quite few quick ones instead, and the sound of my heart fills my ears.

The voice doesn't bother with the intermediary.

—*Found you!*

I force myself to move. My hands shake and my legs tremble and I try to move and I fall and I land on my right leg and I turn and fall and land my mass on my right hip and left foot but I'm still standing and I push my right forwards and I land and I force myself straight and force my head up and *look*.

Before me is a smiling girl, perhaps teenaged, her hands behind her back. She is dressed in what looks like some mutilation of a Sichyan princess' attire with the shimmering of a barrier about her, her entire body below the neck but her hands and ankles covered in a single layer of thin fabric. It is pink like blood in saltwater and criss-crossed by white, sharp lines that make diamonds as they intersect.

I blink to make sure: not *actual* diamonds.

—*Y'know, I almost thought I'd start and try and look for you, but here you are!*

Her lower lip is moving quicker than I've ever seen a human being's move—her upper remains stiff, and her tendons remain pulled upwards—but not to the sound of the voice echoing in my head. She's singing, but I can't hear her mouthvoice past the music gently filling the air: something undoubtedly pre-Laceration, some kind of trumpeted instrument building to a crescendo and dropping off to a sudden pause before its peak.

    —I'm sorry, but I have to kill you.

I raise a deeply shuddering, blade-holding hand, gasping to breathe; she stops in front of me, lets out her left one and holds mine, tilting her head at me. Her smile is the same as always, but it lowers a very slight bit almost into a speaking pout as she lets out her right hand, holding what looks like a sort of meat-hammer with knives jutting out the end, and it does not occur to me to scream.

    —God forgive me.

Her hand moves up to my throat and a hail of gunfire follows, pockmarking the deck.

Her lips slow a bit, and I suddenly breathe a deep breath and the shuddering almost stops and the sun turns bright and I snap around to see Perei crawling with Ayerei's rifle in his hand—the administrator's gun on the ground—with his teeth grit and firing and as I take another breath I step back and trip and fall onto my back and see her standing absolutely still as he fires and drowning out entirely the sound of the music.

Her barrier is far beyond stable-tolerant, and I can see her visibly slowing every bit of herself so she doesn't bump up against it. She stares at Perei, who keeps firing—shots missing now and then, but always away from me—right up until the plume of heat bursts from its end and a high beep sounds.

    —Ain't like I've done this before or anything. Ain't like I've done it to people who did it for a living. Ain't like that at all.

Her barrier visibly eases, her lower lip moves quicker and she walks with a peculiar relaxation about her. Perei pulls the trigger with a rather common desperation as I stand and begin to trod. He lets out a gasp of joy as it fires another burst, and the ripples are visible throughout the barrier's field from the inside.

She kneels down in front of him and holds him by the chin, pushing his hand aside with her unarmed hand.

    —I'm sure you all could've stopped me.

It is around the termination of her sentence that I rear back and punch her right in the back of the skull.

I quite suddenly find myself airborne, and contemplate the sensation's emotional freedom vis-à-vis the actual helplessness it signifies for about a quarter of a second before I hit the ground about five centimetres from the railing and find the shaking returned.

—*You ain't got the right to hurt me.*

I push myself off my feet again; it's harder, but I manage and I fall on my heels and not my knees and I struggle to speak and the shade is back.

—*No one's got the right to hurt me.*

My words come out jittery.

"Why?"

She walks towards me. Perei is far behind her, curled up into what look like the foetal position. I can't hear him. I try to bring my hand up to my mouth, but I never.

"Why are you doing this?"

Her voice is just as cheerful as always.

—*Don't have a choice.*

"You're a human being," I say; I might shake my head, but it's already shaking quite a bit and the thought of disturbing the equilibrium is not something I want to contemplate. "You always can."

She winces a bit, and begins to walk a little quicker; her barrier shallows visibly to mere bulletproofing, and so she does fall as she does.

—*Hardly see **you** moving any time soon, do I? Didn't see them moving, either, or these.*

I blink and glance at my right hand; it is shuddering on its own, though still keeping its knife, and without a thought I bring it up to my mouth and my chattering canines and bite down on my thenar space as hard as I can manage and it *hurts* but I can move and see and it's clear and I run at her, and she raises her weapon and I grab her fragile little arm as her barrier rephases and the bit of it remaining about her arm compels it down, and she tries to stop but the barrier is already pushing her and I push her down and her balance falters and she falls and as she does I twist my elbow around her waist—this is not intentional, perhaps some effect of the epinephrine—and I twist the misericorde so that it barely pierces her dress' collar and faces towards her chin, so angled that a sudden skinwards intolerance threshold would send it propelling it up past her mouth and into her brain.

I am close enough to hear her real voice: it is cracked and torn and worn in a million places but it still keeps singing with intonation so perfect it might well be a sessile's. I can hear on it the beginnings and middles of a barrier threshold modulation, and I try to calm myself with reason: she will take at least a few seconds to threshold to intolerance.

"Don't," I say, speaking so quick that it sounds like Sipjit. "Chin-knife add-cut."

Her tune changes—she remains still—and I feel my arms beginning to shake again; my hands spasm in particular, and the weapon clatters to the ground. The adrenaline fades, and she steps forwards just as I fall to my knees, pirouetting about to stare down at me; her grin has disappeared.

—*Why didn't you kill me? Why didn't you **kill me?***

"Can't just kill you." I laugh to myself, and the laugh is bitter and nasal, tinged with an air of absurdity. "Doctor."

—*That's what they said.*

Her barrier flickers and her arm raises; I twist to the side just as the force compels her, and the knife-hammer bashes into the ground hard enough to make a profound dent in the titanium just as it dissipates. She seems almost stuck for a second and I stand up and jump at her just as her barrier reforms and pushes the knives back out to follow the rest of the blades.

"You don't have to do this," I say, forcing myself to breathe slowly as I can and failing. "There's nothing stopping you from getting away."

—*Every second you live hurts like nothing else.*

I don't have time to admire the design's elegance before she turns and twists the weapon towards me in a single motion, swinging in from the left; I am in the middle of forcing myself to stand, and I flinch as I feel the weapon make an incision across my forearm.

It is about a second later that I realise that my arm is not broken or split open, and I open my eyes to see Perei grabbing on to her, holding her arms behind her back; I press my hand against my wound and rebind it.

The administrator's weapon is in his hand, angled up under her chin. Just as his hand begins to tighten around the trigger he is propelled onto the ground again, letting out a loud yelp as he hits; I can see the barrier condensing into almost pure intolerance, the shimmering grown dense against the sun's light. She is standing absolutely still, and I realise she can only stay like that so long before she begins to suffocate.

Her barrier's diameter begins to increase; Perei's eyes widen behind us and he struggles to move, and I realise with a start she must want to push us off the sides.

I consider running.

I begin to walk towards the barrier.

Her eyes open wide, but its growth continues. I reach out my shuddering hand and feel—perhaps 'feel' isn't the right word, but my hand's certainly sliding against *something*—the frictionless surface rephrasing outwards: it grows purple at the point of contact, almost like a rash. The elevating box will be swept away as soon as we're in it.

I sing. With the first word—*vétirymj*—the slightest of barriers surrounds me, and I stand—the slight friction is like pushing a rock against steel, but I *stand*, and the pressure builds around me as I do and as the barrier falls over me and my own resonates hard enough to crack every single bone in my body as it should throw me out, but I'm not dead and I'm not moving.

—*What're you doing?*

My breath is knocked out of me as the force hits, but it doesn't hit *me* and I *walk*: every muscle in my body protests but I *walk* and my head is turning dizzy and I can't breathe

—*That's not possible. That just ain't possible.*

and I can't breathe and it hurts and I can feel the rebound wound on my arm burst open though I'm a bit too busy to wisecrack about its futility and I *walk* onwards and plant my feet each after each and it holds me up as I do

—*Stop! Stop, just—just die!*

and I feel my ribs preparing to crack but it doesn't bother me because I need to reach her and I *walk* until I'm in front of her and I see her eyes and they're scared and her lips are the only thing moving and I burst into the inner part of her impossibly split barrier and I can move and I can breathe and I ram into her and fall on top of her and she falls down with me and I hold her and I close my eyes and hold her very tight.

Not painfully so.

I'm not sure entirely how long it is before the barrier fades around us and the music and the singing stops. I open my eyes; the light reflects off the metal ground and almost blinds me as I quickly rebind once again the torn flesh on my arm, the blood having dripped down onto the metal.

I glance over to Perei, who is already up—albeit unsteady—before going back to her. She is lying on my arm, staring up at me blankly. The image is a bit silly: she's quite a bit taller than me.

"Why?"

We say the word at the same time, and I am struck immediately by her voice. The singing is distorted and harsh but her voice comes through far, far worse: the parched, grating sound of a friction-damaged larynx comes, and as I glance down I see a small bit of spawncloth stuck to her skin past a tiny silicon tube, a small filter within it apparently filled with salt; I touch at it and feel a fluid dripping past.

She doesn't so much as wince at the physical intrusion; her pupils are constricted to the extent that they look outright painful, and she trembles a bit in my hands.

"Why did you try to kill me?" I say, shaking my head. "Why aren't you now?"

She speaks, and as she does she pauses in between every few words; each is halting, slow and dysarthric, and as I focus on the words above their meanings I realise she's speaking in a Southern language. "I knew the moment you got turned. Hurt ever since. Hurt so much I just couldn't hold it any more. Hurts talking to you and not killing you and I told myself it'd be worth it to kill to stop the pain but when I saw you walk, I—I knew God'd never forgive me for it. He pulled you through, and I don't know much but I know what's right and what's wrong and I *know* God wouldn't let me off the hooks for something like what I wanted to do to you."

"What do you mean by 'turned'?"

"When you turned into the Pretender."

There is a sinking sort of feeling in my chest, and I attribute this less to thoracic quicksand than I do a certain feeling of deduction. "What makes me the Pretender?"

"Don't know anything else," she says, and doesn't shake her head; I notice now she hasn't blinked so much as once thus far, and the realisation is somewhat unsettling. "I heard a few bits. Go down six flights. Go fore to the end. The sessile's there. The tessy came to the barrier the moment you turned."

"Thank you," I say, and lay her to the ground; her head lolls to the side, and I prop it up. I speak the word and pure water begins to stream from my fingertips. "You need water—how long was that barrier up?"

She doesn't seem to notice as the water drips against her face.

"Haven't—haven't told me why."

It takes me a moment to recognise the question.

"You're sick," I say, standing up, "and I'm a doctor. We're taking you to—"

She raises a hand, and it looks like it takes some effort. "Don't," she says, and lets out a little gasp. "Don't bring me out."

"We can't *leave* you here," I say, blinking. "You won't live on your own."

"I cannot go until I kill you," she says, and she looks like she might laugh if she knew how without hurting.

"An oration?" I say, and she doesn't respond. I do a quick search for embedded nexuses with a twang and a word; the subjective materialises in my retinae.

I don't find anything I like.

The muscles on her limbs have enormous bits of sessile instruction woven into them; right now, they're constricting around every single one of them. Her right brachioradialis is trying to force itself into supination to get it to her fallen weapon; her wrist is already abducted, but I can see her shuddering against the force with the few bits of muscle not wrapped by instruction. Her legs are cramped against themselves and her jaw looks fit to break, the temporomandibular joint twisting on its axis as she forces her teeth shut and tongue flat against her palate.

Most importantly: the binds reach across like sticky webbing up her spinal cord, reaching up into her stem; the nexus is deep inside the mass of neuroglia leading to her pristine lobes.

"They did a surgery," she says, poking at the back of her head. "Here. Very deep."

I bite my lower lip. "Neurospinal weave. That's not good."

She looks again like she might laugh but she doesn't. "I know.

Kill me."

"What?"

"Hit *there* or my body goes itself. It hurts. I know you can't take it out," she says, arm twitching a little towards her head, "and even if you would take it out, does a statue know how to breathe if it turns to flesh? Boneless. Pure flesh. I would rather die than hurt forever."

Her breathing is growing steadily shallow and ragged, like air being pushed past a tube of reeds.

"So kill me. I will have my payment in heaven."

I glance about the ground; besides Perei's feet—here I glance up and see a profoundly disinterested and mildly groaning person rubbing at his forehead—my discarded misericorde remains. I gently let her down and stand.

Her parched throat doesn't seem to like the idea of continuing its song now that the momentum has gone and the barrier's intricate construction has been extinguished, but I keep an eye on her nonetheless as I bend down to pick the weapon up; a quick check on my finger shows it to be quite unsafely sharp.

"I don't have any equipment," I say, kneeling down again; I don't look at her as I speak. "You're not from here—there isn't any 'here', is there? You'd die of dehydration or sepsis or something else anyway and there's no equipment that can—"

"Will I see Heaven?"

I blink.

"Why not?"

"If I don't—if I don't listen," she says, her rasping voice almost entirely a whisper; every time her lips move, she winces. "They said if I didn't listen or I said no, I'd—I'd go to Hell. I know God will forgive me but it hurts so much and please tell me again."

"Yes," I say, my voice as reassuring as I can make it as I pull her head up once more, landing it on my lap. "Yes, you'll see Heaven."

She forces her mouth into a closed smile before she speaks again. "What'll it be like?"

I caress the base of her skull; the blade's tip is angled to her bulb.

"When you close your eyes," I whisper, leaning my lips to her left ear, "you will dream of a beautiful place with flowers—flowers and grass and trees. It will be warm and never cold and nothing will ever hurt you or tell you what to do."

"When will I see it?"

"Close your eyes," I say, and take a deep breath. "When you open them, you'll be there."

Her closed smile springs open, forcefully. "First time—first time I haven't sung."

She closes her eyes.

"It's nice."

I brush her hair aside.

Her eyes open.

I cradle her body for a while, the misericorde jutting from her brainstem; the red streams down from the wound and blossoms across the pink like a fresh spot in a bloody pool.

Her close-lipped smile doesn't fade—the oration's clearly preserved her state. I gently lay her body to the ground.

I look up from the corpse in my arms to see Perei looking at me.

"She was suffering," I say, and push the corpse off of my lap; no blood has leaked onto my lap. "I couldn't have helped her and I wouldn't be able to obtain the tools that would have given me a shadow of a chance in a reasonable timeframe and she was *suffering* and—"

"It's alright," he says, and I fall silent.

We're in this position for a bit before he shakes his head and pushes himself off the side of the little building.

"Come on," he says, rubbing the back of his neck. "This place stinks."

I nod.

"*Breach and clear!*" Perei shouts, firing at the door's handle.

There is a *psst* sound and a visible shimmer as the gunfire hits the handle; the door is untouched, and the mildly white-lit, corpse-strewn corridor we're in is blessed for a moment by an awkward silence.

I give him a look. "Breach and clear?"

"Hey," he says, running his hand along the door's seam, "just wanted to say it. Don't tell me you never wanted to say *dégajssya*."

"No," I say. "Fibrillation is an extremely serious condition."

"Sheesh," he says, and taps the door with his finger; I notice the taps go quicker every time, as if he's trying to probe manually for a barrier. "Throw all the fun out of life, why don't you?"

I run my own hand along the metal hull, close the other one around my instrument and sing a few words; the entire process takes less than four seconds, and soon my hand is instead rubbing my chin. "There's no barrier—no reason your weapon shouldn't be working."

He huffs, glancing down at his gun and lifting it a bit as if gauging something about it before flipping it forwards, bashing its stock into the handle; I blink at the perfect moment to have my focus shift abruptly from Perei's physical form to the almost physical wall of vulgarity that he's turned into, lying on the ground behind me and trying to push himself up; his weapon is lying next to him, a considerable distance from his hand.

"Son of a *bitch*," he says, rubbing at the back of his skull. "Just got f—"

"Wait," I say, interrupting my sagacious chin-rubbing to move the offending hand over to the pristine handle; I push down, and a slight clicking sound issues right before I pull the door outwards, the solid metal giving way to a small, immaculately-preserved alcove illuminated by the three objective displays glowing before the rather ergonomic chair in its centre.

I might now choose to give Perei a smug look if not for the fact that the part of my soul required to do so has quite promptly shrivelled up and died an awful death; a quick forensic analysis gives me cause to venture that it's been murdered by the smell emanating from the corpse limp on the chair before us. I've gotten used to the usual stench by now, but there is the characteristic sound of a cold humidifier sessile buzzing through the air and it is a genuine struggle not to vomit.

I move quickly, sidestepping the putrescent body. The scent isn't anywhere near familiar—by this stage the fleshcrawlers would have left only calcium—but its alienness is no comfort, as if there existed some time before them where it might have meant death and I'm smelling my ancestors' fears. The cabinet is tiny, and I almost brush against a plaque-eaten tooth dangling by a string of scummy, greyish-brown periodontal fibre. I twitch reflexively, my shoulder slamming into the wall with the force of my mortification as I note my proximity. A small bit of hemp filled with some kind of fried solanum balanced on a bit of thick wire falls onto the ground, the edge-browned chips of burnt plant spilling out after it.

I rub my shoulder and take a quick breath, pushing the soiled air out as soon as I can bring it in. The dim, light-blue objective lets out a slight 'ding' and brightens as I reach my hand towards it, my other reaching to my waistband and pulling out my sessile. The clothes are quite well-preserved, but I nonetheless stay as far away from its knee as possible as I bend forwards and begin whispering, violently exhaling between sentences.

My sessile's fabric is illuminated by the glow emanating from the display, itself brightly streaked by simple white symbols, and I get to work with an exodus cache.

"You done?" Perei says; I double-check the Archive's contents—I don't bother yet to actually read the items on the list—tapping around on my sessile, before responding.

"Almost."

"*Pàrpyrpàr pàr trisec pàr àn'métyr,*" I say, making sure the numbers are absolutely right, "*dézàtiyejt vétiryentrüra pàr léntyra désmeyn, den rétentt.*"

Words appear on the screen in perfect Angzhwen: *prafédyr tætra désya, n'avtt pérmeyra.*

"*Y'ynvétyjj éyra tri-set-an'em petyremzhra répelyra ses'em frynsé-z-é rédésyjt.*"

I don't exactly know what the almost-Angzhwen words mean, only how they sound, but I can only assume they're much older than the ones before them; there is a shifting under my feet, and I turn and hop out before I can see the response.

"This smell," I say, shuddering deeply and letting a cough from my lungs as I turn to close the door behind me, exhaling violently enough through my nostrils that if I had a cold I'd need a kilometre of paper to deal with the mess, "is going to follow me for days if I don't purge it."

"Had worse," he says, and looks over to the sessile in my hands. "What's new?"

I flick my wrist down the list as we begin to walk; the soft spawncloth resists just enough against my finger. "Two complete plays by Sheksprei, Old Ayngzlan. Five sictions in the same, a great deal of technical data—there's almost four thousand data here, probably early Ayngzlan writings on saepological dysexaptics. I've got to get this to a university."

He gives me a look I can't quite puzzle out the meaning of, and I pause.

"After I'm done with it, of course."

He doesn't say anything, but the look remains.

Our glasswalkers land on the ground from metres up just as its barrier reinitialises—it would be barbaric to leave an exodus cache to be buried under the sand—and we're almost a kilometre away by the time the enormous structure begins to rise once more, carrying a bit of the desert with it.

The sight is spectacular, but Perei does a very good job of shifting his attention from it to me just as it loses its novelty.

"Did you really mean what you said to that kid?"

I exhale deeply.

"No."

"Then why did you say it?"

"If a destitute child had a single penny on him and it was counterfeit, would you tell the peacekeepers?"

He is thankfully silent thereafter.

five
Grey-White Ashes

I touched her forehead.

—Hey.
—Hey.
—How's it going?
—Not too good.
—Can't say I am either.
Dead and all.
—Not yet.

She laughed.

—Real fixer-upper.
—That I am.
—You gonna get on or what?
—Like this?
Hell no.
I'd rather jump on a glasswalker
half-filled with snow.

She laughed.

—Snow? Really?
That's what they're calling it?
—Yeah.
Kinda dumb, isn't it?
—No, no. Very educated.
Like calling ticks hornets
or calling trees forests.
—Forests? Like those huge
things, like trees but stuck together?
—Like us, but far apart.
—That doesn't really mean anything,
you know.

She laughed.

—I'm just a romantic,

or maybe I'm just stalling.
—I know you're not.
You never were that kind of girl.
—I know, I know.
What if I'm doing this to make it go quicker?
I mean, man, you're usually a lot quicker.
—Heh. That rhymed.
—It did, right?

She smiled
and closed her eyes.

I pulled,
then I pushed.

I watched 'til she was just grey-white ashes
and then I up and walked away.

Untitled, anonymous
Art of the Artless
compiled by Andresrea qu'n'av dasnamr
published by the Sprawl Initiative and approved for limited
academic distribution by the Administration for Media Development
under the continued grace of Khaliesrea das Sikharea eliyit Tamarisrei,
Administrator for the Arts
initial resale publication by Mitras Press Holdings

KHANDMISRA FETYRYSSYA ANTRI SEPTIMYR UITUINANYR
SYNTYSDYR SALTIZH AYTISYSSYA ANTRI SEPTIMYR DIMILDICEOCIDIR
AYSMANRATYSS PYR AYSMANRAT' AIMELZH PYR KYSPRINYR ASSYLYZH

SIKHAREA
SYNTYSDYRA CRYSYNTYZH

6
Sikhyr
to practise customary virtue

I wake in a cold sweat.

That's a strange phrase: 'wake in a cold sweat', a phrase from the Dilemmata calqued from the Angzhwen *vétyr ánpyrswyyr frys*. I've guarded a dead body in cold sweat, evidently; idioms from Angzhwen don't like to make sense.

I should like to render a description of my adventures through the land of fire and death—I've not dreamed for at least five years, so this is a momentous occasion—but the memories fade too fast to capitalise on and so I simply blink, lie back and look up at the sky.

About an hour passes before I look back down, and I can't go back to sleep; I look down to my sessile.

> *Àntyéshyéleraii*
> *—Angelwings*
> **Sikhas, Central Aimela, Aimelan Administration**
> *Description: Set of three small, cylindrical devices proposed to be similar in function to the apocryphal Iyntànyrzhàynyzhra. Held in the Sikhas Vault of Contrition, administered by Administrator Khaliesrea das Sikharea es-Aysmanrata eliyit Tamarisrei residing in the Western Quarter. Classified as a 'personal artistic endeavour'. Effects of usage unknown.*
> *Name taken from inscription on side; 'ànmyàyr', cognate with the Mahammadir term 'amalshak' and Zhanghwazh*

*'tienshe', is believed to be a pre-Laceration species of flighted
bird.*
  Found 3 Septimus 3748, First Operation

It will be quite a while before we reach the Crystalline Syndicate,
and I cannot spend all of it bemoaning treaty violations and reading over
gun-papers.

I decide to fill the time with work.

Embedding is a tricky process.

One must keep an exact eye on things: a nexus must intertwine
seamlessly with the nexuses which follow. Every inch of space—every
thread of fabric, every surface of metal or ceramic—must be placed in a
pattern tolerating betterment.

This is because the slightest overlap creates a miniature sort
of barrier resonance; I'm aware of assorted orations being thrown over
and over and over on little folded blocks of spawncloth suspended in a
vacuum barrier, then daubed with a little blood and placed in a barrier-
generating, thick and easy-to-shatter bit of cheap metal so it remains
comfortable up to the point that the trigger-word is spoken—resonance
increments according to the square-cube law, and so even weak resonance
conditions turn lethal when an overlap occurs.

I've never seen exactly what one does, but I certainly have had
to stuff a few people's guts back into them on its account. I'm not saying
that they happened to find themselves attacked by one, of course, because
even the tierless regions generally have their limits—it's just that the sort
of person with the character to apply that particular principle generally
doesn't have the tessitura to keep the barrier self-sustaining.

I've been reading through the documents, and they've given me
an idea that I realise is so obvious it's likely the first thing in the textbook
I'd have read if I ever thought I'd need to know embedding:

What if she stored *specifications*, not actual *instructions*?

I spend several hours working off this premise, right up to the
point Perei's voice pierces my veil of mutters with something other than a
barrier renewal.

"Ever wonder why we're doing this?"

I turn my head to face him, stretching my arms out far behind
my head as I speak.

"We've known each other for the better part of a week," I say, letting out the tiniest fragment of a yawn. "The word 'ever' doesn't seem appropriate."

"Seriously," he says, and squeezes a leg out of one of his stirrups before pushing it over, leaning onto its knee as his head supports itself by his fists. "What the hell're we doing? You're some psycho twelve-year-old gunshy doctor and I don't even know what *I* am and we're just running around on the sea? People fighting and dying wherever they're fighting and dying and we're following this list some asshole Sesty made up and for all we know we're just picking up evidence so it'll be easier to mop up?"

"Or," I say, swooshing Occam's razor—possessing at the moment my misericorde—through the air, "we're extremely lucky."

"Ugh," he says, letting out a long, nasally conveyed sigh. "You'd think if it was this easy someone else'dve done it first. We'd be dead five times by now."

There's a bit of silence.

"Do you want to punch me in the face?"

"What?"

I look sideways at him, raising my brow a little as I coax my glasswalker closer to his. "Will it make you feel better if you get to punch me in the face?"

He gives me a particularly suspicious glare. "What's the catch?"

"I think I know how the girl dynamically reshaped her barrier."

His hand raises to eye-level before I can finish my speech. "'The girl'?" he says, giving me a look; he seems to give a great deal of those. "There's gotta be a better name for her."

"It's the only one I have. I think I know how she reshaped her—" I begin, and find my mouth quite full of blood and pain.

My hand rushes to my lips as the blood begins to pool in my mouth, taking quick, deep breaths to the sound of his uproarious laughter. "Oh, Isha," he says, grinning at me as I spit an incisor out into my hand and cough as I struggle to breathe without the fluid going into my lungs. "That felt good."

"*Very funny.*" I've had quite a bit of practice speaking past obstacles, and so the words come past my bloodied mouth as clearly as my glare.

His sanguinity remains unrepentantly to mirror my own as I push my right hand up to my instrument and my blood-soaked right forces my tooth up against the severed nerve, making sure to avoid it in the 't's and 'd's as I begin to rebind them.

He's still giggling a little as I finish washing the blood from my hand.

"Pluripotents cost *money*," I say, glaring at him. "What if I lost it?"

"You didn't, though."

"Alright," I say, shaking my head. "Alright, one more time. *Létyjs.*"

He rears back for another, and I instinctively close my eyes just as it fades to a blur.

A few seconds later, I open them and take an account of my situation.

My teeth are still in my mouth. Success.

Perei is groaning in pain, shaking his bruised fist. Great success.

"Again," I say. "Ápyfrét létyjs."

He lunges again, but this time my eyes are open and I see the fist clearly arcing down into a barrier-cut: slow, then quick as he reaches past the projected sphere.

He gets perfectly to 'quick' before his arm bashes against the semi-permeable barrier a few centimetres from my skin, and his withdrawal is palpably pharmaceutical in its slowly decreasing agony.

I can't help but giggle.

Sikhas' Khamisret-Aparkisrea field is sung by one metre of spawncloth, covering one square kilometre. It is the ninth most efficient barrier-sessile construction in the world by barrier area. It carries no bleedthrough. Its inefficiencies arise solely from issues inherent in multipurpose construction; the instructions required to maintain the microrephrasals that allow it to maintain a threshold past stable-tolerance whilst remaining membrane independent take up over five square centimetres.

In that square kilometre, bullets lie flat against the air into which they are fired.

Around it to the horizon, the Sikhas branch of the Structural Unified Labour Coalition—it would be more appropriate to say the Saltic Syndicate, but the Assimilation Compromise has long since worked its magic here—operates one hundred and thirty-one and a half square kilometres of wide-scale barrier production sessiles cover one thousand, three hundred and seven square kilometres; this is sufficient to cover the entirety of the enormous tierless districts surrounding the city's core, blessing it with the fifth most inefficient barrier network in the world.

The diagrams are clear, though they're obviously not exact: the barriers push and shove and mash up against each other as individual Saltics—they call themselves that, *Saltics*, as unified as they're meant to be—decide to contract or expand. There is no central barrier and no central authority, especially with the Syndic gone, and so no single artillery strike could destroy more than a tiny fraction of the city's emptiest regions.

That is why it is particularly worrisome when I see the smoke billowing universally towards the night sky from beyond the dunes stretching out before us.

The gunfire doesn't assuage this.

Not the sound, mind, I've had plenty of experience with it; I am referring instead to the gunfire that has just made a rather interesting pattern of force across the personal barrier in front of my eyes, something physical flashing before my eyes almost quicker than I can see before it drops between my saddle-mounted legs.

I blink and pick it up a second before I realise what it is; my grip slackens in horror, and the peeled bullet falls to the sand below and disappears behind us.

"Oh, shit," Perei says, and smacks his head down upon the glasswalker's mane as we continue our charge. "*Bolts!*"

His sentence is punctuated with a sudden eruption of sand and glass about us, pushing up against our barrier; a few grains of the shredded mixture pushes past the fluctuating barrier as they slow, a single grain hitting me in the arm and hissing on the fabric.

He twists to the right and I instinctively force my own glasswalker to tail him, catching him right before he pushes past the barrier; it isn't Shenwyzhchyn, but I somehow doubt a frozen night kept warm by gunfire would be very good for his complexion.

We are almost parallel to them, from my estimation, and I reach forwards. "*Ténbryjt shélœvyr,*" I say, and grab onto Perei's shoulder as the glasswalker moves with me with a deep neigh. There is a sharp veering to the left, and the smoke clears right before I hear a series of sharp *plinks*.

I don't bother to investigate.

"*Do something,*" I hiss, clutching at the instrument around my neck. "The city's at least a kilometre away."

He faces me, and there is a certain sort of conflict plastered across his face. "They're *muds*, they're just shooting the wrong way—we shoot back and they've got a flash and we're dead, we're lucky we got out of the cloud, if we stop the sand's gonna—"

The ground erupts again, and this time a gout of hot glass-sand propels itself from the earth right between us; I force my face to the mane and I can feel a bit of shattered glass leaving an incision across my uniform's rib as it erupts beneath us.

I pull my head off the walker just as Perei does and I have an idea.

My hand goes to my instrument and I begin to string; the tune is hurried as my voice as I force the syllables out, the air barely catching against my lips and teeth and palate long enough to become coherent. The cloud barely begins to thin before us—there is no time to reshape the barrier to reduce our profile—and I raise my hand to the sky.

An enormous light rises, far brighter than I imagine it should be—less than I should imagine it should—and I scream the shapes of the words in numbers and we aren't being shot at and I gasp for breath as the command finishes and I look to Perei's illuminated face, his marvelling eyes staring up to the single blinding word painted across the sky:

Peace.

There is no gunfire as the sand around us settles.

As we ride closer to the city's Pari dunes, the line of men facing us begins to lose members by the second; the slight shimmer of the miniature field turns visible as our walkers push up the cullet mountain. The ground's lain so long it seems unnatural—Sikhas' traffic is unregulated enough I'm surprised there are any dunes left at all.

As we enter the field and climb over the top, I am greeted by so many sights I can barely describe them all.

The greatest of these is the city itself, its Khamisret-Aparkisrea fields pushing up against each other against the backdrop of the crushed dunes cut through by little valleys—lined now with metal and beset by tents—facing just about every route in the world, Marapistanir and Tachiesrea and Sipshirea and Teshras and Illaha and what used to be Cimsas the most prominent by the sheer depths of the gaps they've gouged.

Hundreds of thousands of low-set houses topped with adobe and steel are punctuated by thousands of structures rising above them like magniloquence amongst brevity; the mairie is a midget virgule against the barrier-scraping structures near it, but 'barrier-scraping' is a bit of an unfair word when their barriers are built *around* the structures.

Around the city's core are what looks to be a few kilometres of unculled adobe settlements, themselves a kilometre or two from the hundreds of tents set around the Roland breaches cutting through the dunes, tapering out into a few dotted along the line.

There are hundreds right before us, most of them looking almost holidaymaker in style and the rest traditional Mahammadir. Bonfires light up the dunes' rims, sending enormous plumes of smoke into the sky; now and then there are structures that look to have been erected hastily from scratch, stone risen from bedrock and shaped into amphitheatres. Right below the rim there are short stonerise walls buried into the sand with a side clear, making what seem to be tiny, makeshift, profoundly ineffective paradoses facing the similarly stone parapets.

While the greatest sights, of course, are the city and the tents, the most *striking* sight is the wide end of a pre-Laceration weapon angled towards my face in the hands of an immigrant-looking man that doesn't look particularly happy. There are ten or twenty men behind him on the trench's parapet, all seeming rather jumpy—I can't say I don't find myself empathising with them.

"What's your name, lass?" he says in an almost affected Western Aimelan, his hand on the bolt on the weapon's side.

"I am a second-tier citizen of the Aimelari Administration as a Ward of the Tower under the grace of the Abbess."

"Your name's 'second-tiered convent fellow'?" he says, tilting his head a bit. "Are you very *sure* about that, miss?"

"You can *call* me Ashrea."

"Ashrea, right—and you, miss, mister—?"

"Perei," he says, looking almost literally to be biting his tongue.

"Right. Two face-name jokers over here. Nothing wrong with that. Where'd you two come from?"

Perei pulls up on the glasswalker's reins, and it rides forwards the slightest bit; out of the corner of my eye, I can see two or three men raising their own firearms. "From the capital. Got into an admin's, nicked three-and-a-half minnie-strangles worth and hightailed it quick."

The man's expression—difficult to discern the exact meaning of in the night, but visible enough to gather movement from in the light of the moon—eases a little, but his weapon does not lower. "Laying it on a bit thick, aren't you?" he says, squinting up to the side. "Why've you got red on you, then? And why's she in that service-black?"

"We got ourselves in Tachiesrea after the capital bit it," he says, and shrugs. "Got ourselves out a few bits thicker when *it* bit it."

His weapon lowers, but the men behind who have kept their weapons up keep their own risen. "Tachiesrea too, huh? How're the poor wankers doing?"

Perei's face has a certain relaxation about it—I realise that it's one he's only ever shown me before he recognised me. "Bad. You?"

"Pretty bloody well," he says, and hmphs. "Had to be a good thousand of them came over the dunes. Good hundred of them got an arm off and just kept coming. Think about a few hundred got into the actual bloody city. Gave *them* a good going over."

I glance towards Perei, and he glances towards me; there is a certain kind of belated relief in the look. "Were there any of them who surrendered?" I ask, teeth lightly gritted.

"To us? Buggered if I know. All in Pyarash if they did. Maybe to the admins down Elysium—heard some rumours. Serves them right, I suppose."

"Pyarash," I say, rolling the word on my tongue; the word seems familiar. "So, they *are* Southern?"

He flashes me a wide grin. "Implying they're any more so than me, innit?"

There is a period of silence, and if it isn't uncomfortable for him it is for me.

"Alright, then," he says, "You lot seem harmless enough. Come on down."

There is an almost physical pressure that lifts from me as I push myself off the glasswalker, which neighs indifferently; Perei descends alongside me, and the weapons behind stay trained on us.

"I *said*," the man says, bringing his hand up then down, "*you lot seem harmless enough.*"

The men look between each other; a few give us particularly suspicious looks as they let their weapons hang from their straps and walk off, hopping over the little walls and plodding off in the still-glassy sand towards their tents.

He begins to walk; we follow, and our glasswalkers are herded away behind us. "You're here to seek refuge, am I right?"

Perei and I share a glance.

"Not exactly," I say, measuring my words. "We'll be out in a few hours. We just need to get something done."

He laughs and looks over both of us. "'Get something done,' aye? A bit too young and Aimelan to be little Ezyitores, no?"

"I've never killed anyone in my life," I say, out of instinct, and there is a certain feeling in me I cannot quite well explain as I remember that I am lying; I scarcely have time for silent rumination before his response arrives.

"Just trying to have a laugh," he says, and waves his hand. "Right—I'm asking too many of the questions here, aren't I? Come on, then. Give me anything."

"Well," I say, lacing my hands together awkwardly as I walk, "who are you?"

"You mean my name?" he says, putting his hand to his chin. "Long time since someone asked me that. Arcembault bin Jounpal as-Sikhi al-Bazain ebu Forestiye al-Ghazine. Call me 'Arc' if you'd like."

"I think what she *meant*," Perei says, shaking his head, "is 'what in Isha's name's going on here?'"

"Ah," he says, nodding as he stops walking, having come before one of the tents. "I forget—you've not got the best appraisal of the situation, have you? Come on in."

He lifts one of the tent's flaps up, revealing what looks to be a silver-coloured—probably iron—floor-table ornately decorated with wood along the edges, a large sessile-map set upon it; cushions surround it, and as we walk in I look up to see a sessile-lamp hanging from the ceiling.

He coughs to himself. "Posh, isn't it? Courtesy of Aratisrei."

"The city administrator?" I say, and I might whistle here to myself if I knew how to whistle; Perei kindly relieves me of the duty.

"Indeed. I'm the big bollocks of the east," he says, walking over to the sessile map and pulling his hands apart, the picture zooming in on a section of the contour map we're in, "which, as you can imagine, aren't exactly the biggest around."

I mull the phrase around in my head for a little before its etymology comes to me. "Larcenous Battalion. Pre-Laceration, Old Ayngzlan."

"Right-o," he says, grinning. "'Critique of colonialist policy in Buncoryo post-invasion.' Least that's what the headmistress said. Thought it was a bloody riot, myself—bit too contemporary for modern tastes though, hey?"

I raise a finger and make as if to respond, but I see Perei shaking his head desperately in the corner of my vision; I let the point go, and Arcembault gives us a little smile.

"I know what you're thinking of saying, mate, and the Pilisyari situation isn't anywhere near comparable. In any case," he says, kneeling down and flicking his wrist over the sessile, "you're probably wondering how I got set up on all this."

"I wasn't," Perei says, shrugging, "but I guess you got me thinking."

"Right. Old friend—name of Temesrei, think he's out buggering some tiny colony right out by Tachiesrea—told me two days past to bulk up on domestic bolt-actions, see? And I'm already mucking in on the war effort down South, right—"

My mouth gapes a slight bit as I realise the implication. "You're supplying the *insurgency?*"

He gives me a look. "The Alliance, mate, not the insurgency, but in any case bolts're an easier thing than prelacs and they're nasty bits of fall-apart rubbish anyway—don't look at me like that, aye, I pay my taxes—so I'm filling the schedule for my brothers in faith and so on and so forth. I'd give him a bollocking about it but he's not in with us, so I grit my teeth and figure I'll just make this enormous waste of money with the safeties and so on and so forth, and what do you know?"

He seems almost to be asking a real question, his hands splayed out and mouth open; I forego asking him how he came to know an administrator in lieu of giving him his response. "What *do* we know?"

There is an air of self-satisfaction about him as he continues. "Next day me and my boys're the only ones with legal bolts ready to go, and while the garrison's scraping its squished knackers off the floor looking around for any illegals because they think it's an inside job, that's what. We come out, flash our giant bloody safeties and giant bloody durability testing certificates and we just start throwing them out into the crowd—all with my name on, of course—and we get all of them gathered up and we tell them to come with us, right? And they start marching in and we're on the rooftops and we bash their brains all over the bloody overlap pavements and the admin sees my name on all the guns and what does she do? Gives me a Regiment of Service just like that, gives me more tin than I've ever seen in my entire life and says I'm now the chief arsehole of the Auxiliary Defence Corps, whatever on God's golden Earth that is."

He lays back on his arms and stares towards the tent's top for a bit, taking a deep breath; then he brings his head back up.

"And I've not got the faintest idea what I'm doing. I saw Barbourilakh with one of mine, you know. He's probably going to get his gang and start a bloody war down in the city with those guns."

"What about the artillery? The city garrison didn't destroy those?"

He raises an eyebrow. "What *about* the artillery? I never saw them fire it. Probably Kanshantrei went and dealt with it, the cheeky bastard. And the city garrison? They've got a bloody fortress down Elysium. Mairie's thicker than an Aimelan's skull." He pauses for a second, then shakes his head. "No offence."

"None taken."

"Right," he says, and leans forwards with his arms folded. "I think it's my turn for questions. A little game of give-and-take, this talking thing is—not really mine, but I guess I ought learn how to play, aye?"

I nod.

"Right," he says, shifting a bit in place, "why are you here, really?"

I look towards Perei; he has a look of complete impassivity about him.

I look back.

"We're here to procure an artefact from Khaliesrea."

"Qu'eliyit Tamarisrei?" he says, and laughs. "She's rung the bell of the world, let me tell you. Holed up down Elysium with the best of them. Heard she got one of the bellends by the bellend and gave him an education four hours straight."

"Well," I say, "how might we acquire it from her?"

"I'm going to assume you meant on the straight, tight and narrow, because that's what you'll be on if you don't." His expression remains its amicable character; I imagine he says this often. "I don't know *what* exactly you want, but you'd probably be better off asking her."

"And how might I *get* to her?"

He puts his hand to his chin, the sessile-lighting illuminating the hair on his hands like some sort of miniature barrier. "I'll see how I can help it. God knows you deserve it, getting yourselves out of that bloody mess altogether."

"Tomorrow?" Perei says, his expression bearing the character of slight worry. "We can't just sit on our thumbs for a whole day. What're we gonna do 'til then?"

"It's not like you're on a bloody quest or anything, mate," he says, giving him a strange look. "There's a gunspinner fifty metres right out in the stonerise out in the middle."

"Holy shit."

"He should be starting his show in just about a minute and a half."

"I've got to rest anyway," I say, but before my sentence concludes Perei's already stood and half-ran out the tent.

"You've never seen a gunspinner?" he says, raising an eyebrow.

"No," I say, shaking my head. "Should I?"

He waves a hand. "I'll send a man to pick you two up. You'll get your chance tomorrow. I don't know who you are, where you're from, what you did," he says, perfectly snowcloning the 3849 Parnasserei translation of the phrase, "but anyone who got their arses out of that mess can't hardly be the sort of person I'd want to say 'can't help you' to."

I stand.

"By the way," I say, "did anyone else come from Cimsas?"

His look is sympathetic. "Not that I know of, no."

"I see," I say, and begin to walk. "Thank you, in any case."

"I'm sorry."

"No need," I say, and let go of the tent-flap and out into the flame-speckled camp.

I come into the risen-stone building just as the show is starting, men and women and children—the only children Mahammadir—filling the seats lining the walls. It's an auditorium, and in the middle of it is a man holding a rifle.

"For our misguided brothers," he says, his words strong but almost slurring in a terribly heavy accent, "who came not long ago for us. For the gracious who built this structure in a single day so that our Lord's worship may be pleased. For my niece who came to know God in the devil's embrace."

I lean against the entrance's wall as I look over him. His entire body is loose, and he is almost wobbling on his legs as if he's consumed a fair deal of recreational ethanol; a half-smirk lines his lips, and the trigger is against his first phalanx. He glances lovingly at his weapon—the steel is painted with something imitating gold—and takes a deep breath as he points the bolt-action forwards, holding it with one hand.

"See that?" Perei says, poking me on the back; I almost yelp, looking back, and he points past my astonishment. "His leftie. Look at it."

I look to his left hand; it's laid out as if in questioning, palm up and fingers wide-spread with a slight curl to their tips. "He looks like he has palmar fibromatosis."

"It's *perfect*," he says, and lets out a small whistle. "Just look."

I don't have time to object before the drums begin to play and I am almost deafened by a blast of gunfire.

The rifle jerks back against his shoulder, flying upwards, and his left hand moves with the weapon's arc; he catches it by the bolt and matches its momentum, forcing it down and letting it loose almost too quick to see before his entire hand clenches, his wrist looking as if it is about to break as he forces the weapon to face the ground just as it looks as the momentum is pushing him onto his back and fires again, the same left hand on its stock. The recoil forces him forwards, and he lands practisedly on both his feet.

Before I can quite fully process what I've seen, he flicks his wrist sideways and brings his left back up to the bolt; its sights brush against his hair, and he tugs on the bolt less than a second before he pulls the trigger again, the firing pin looking as if it's hit the part right before the primer just as the minute twitch in his extensor indicis signals its ignition. A bit of the floor to his left bursts as the force, twisting on the axis made by his shoulder as his left holds onto the protruding bolt, sends it going to his right, the motion yanking on it and making a resonating click.

He stands still for a moment, looking up at the men and women amassed about the tent; their eyes are wide, and I can see a few biting at their nails.

He fires, and I lose track. Of the various motions that follow, punctuated every few seconds with an ear-smacking shot, I can follow only one distinct manoeuvre: with the tenth shot, the recoil sends the weapon's top slamming into his palm, now completely open; the glint disappears from his palm as he does and there is a wrenching *click* as he does it, ten clicks all at once. He celebrates this with a twirl above the head, pulling down and gripping as a plume of smoke escapes from its tip along with the usual deafening din, one of his legs beginning to move up and down, stomping on the stone to the tune of the drums.

They accelerate, and so does he; he twirls the firearm even quicker, keeping it barely from grazing the floor as he pushes his hands down. In a flurry of motion whose details I cannot quite make out, he lets out three shots in quick succession, the pulling of the bolts inaudible over the shots.

He rubs his shoulder, and I look to the side to see a mixture of a crowd in stunned silence and roaring applause, the former turning quite quickly into the latter; I find myself staring at the gaping holes in the stone ground.

Connected, they make perfectly the sickle and star.

"Tower guide my way," I say, and trace a line down my chest out of habit, flicking the threshold. "That was—"

I trail off before I can find a word; I find myself rather thanking my recent education on firearms.

"I know, right?" Perei says, grinning. "You hear there's a gunspinner show, you drop *everything*."

The man bows unsteadily. "God bless Aimela. Goodnight."

He stands there for a moment, looking up at the dome's ceiling as men come around him with chalk in their hands; they trace along the floor, eliminating negative space with powdery blue slashes.

The man takes a deep breath and walks off to the side, leaning against the wall as he reaches it and reaching down for a bottle of what looks to be some kind of distilled liquor.

"Like what see?"

Perei and I turn about and come face-to-face with a peculiarly-haired—the strands of hair above his mouth look like they are painted top-to-bottom—short man, the bare bits between the bits of moustache lending him an almost caricatural air paired with his utterly bald head. He gives me a grin, and his smile lacks a few teeth; some bit of blackish, evidently flexible carbon-like material lines his throat, looping about it like a garotte. I have to resist the urge to immediately begin rejuvenating his follicles.

"I tell you," he says, grinning at me, "very eligible for take out of sad. He name Fausial bin Albazin at-Tamali, no kem no ebu. I put in contact, set up many happy interactions, small tiny."

"What?" I say, blinking at him and stepping back a little.

He turns to Perei and sticks a lanky, bony finger up to his chin; he almost immediately steps back, batting the concept of the finger from the space he's evacuated, but this doesn't seem to dissuade him. "Or you, tall lady?"

Perei's eyes narrow a little, and I raise an arm as if in some hope of parting an imagined sea of rage. "Are *you* our coolie?" I say.

"Yes, yes—am Joun. Arcembault says you need staying-place. I bring. Come."

We share a glance before turning back to him, and Perei kneels to face him straight on.

A series of incomprehensible, soft syllables ooze from his mouth, and now that I'm hearing it close it almost sounds like Fransai; a few seconds later, Perei nods.

"He's legit."

Joun grins, turning about. "Come."

I metaphorically swallow my unmetaphorical trepidation and follow.

This is a very comfortable place to be.

There are no bottom-barriers, of course; the only thing between me and a face full of shredded glass is four centimetres of insulative padding, but the cushions are well enough that I forget about this entirely. Perei is outside, presumably having the time of his life. My sleep is long, fulfilling and the nightmares are only slightly worse than before; I miss my old friend.

I'm being someone strategic with truth when I say 'long and fulfilling', of course; judging by the shining past the tent-fabric, I'm guessing it's about five hours before shrapnel bursts through my tent.

Now, it doesn't just penetrate a side; it penetrates *the entire tent*, and as the sound rouses me and I thrust myself up from the bedding I stare dumbfoundedly between the entry wounds to my right and the exit wounds to my left.

I'm not sure what it says about me that my first thought is less 'what is going on' than it is 'I thought these were kinetic beacons, not fragmentation sessiles'; my immediate self-response is that a nearby building's been bombed, not me, and this is profoundly reassuring enough that I sink my head back down into the ground, arms reaching up to stretch my morning muscles.

Then another one comes down much closer, and I realise as my ears ring and a shower of rent glass smacks against the tent's fabric and one bit of it falls through one of the holes and barely misses my wrist that I am an idiot.

As the grime of drowsiness forces itself off of my skin, it holds rather painfully to the skin of apathy and rips it with a certain violence it from the muscle. There is a profound sinking feeling in me as I force myself out of the unzipped flap and behold the morning.

There are enough sights here to make a master propagandist jealous.

Of course, there's the classic sight of a mother in a dishdasha holding her bloodstained child—this is more anti-war, though if the child were bearing *chemical* burns it might be pro-occupation. There's the man propped up against a sheet-metal tent, cradling a third-degree burn on the outside of his upper thigh. There's the man without a leg being carried by two of his friends. There's the crying baby being held by a woman running past me.

There's even a new sight: hundreds of men screaming as they run up the dune, pulling their weapons from over their shoulders as thousands of pinpricks swarm in the distance, following men on walkerback with swords raised. I imagine that if I ever would want to be a propagandist I ought to keep vigilant for a repeat.

The sights and the sounds have quite a curious effect, as if it's just altogether far too much; I blink and decide that I must be having a very bad dream.

This delusion persists up to the point a man on a glasswalker carrying a great deal of guns behind his saddle rears up as he glances down at me, pulling a firearm from his bundle and throwing it at my feet before continuing onwards with a yank on the reins.

That sentence requires a more accurate preposition: he throws a gun *on* my feet.

I must credit myself with not letting out a shriek—not to imply, certainly, that I'd be able to hear myself over the overwhelming din. I yank my ceramic-soled-and-not-tongued shoe up, grabbing at my dorsal as I suck in a current of sand-stained air through my teeth; I spend about four seconds in this state before I look back up and take a deep breath and shrug it off with a literal, body-shaking shrug and realise I have absolutely no idea what to do.

"*What are you doing?*"

I blink to myself. "Wha—"

A sweaty-faced Mahammadir man with blood on his shirt—there's no short supply of those, and it appears a camp under siege is a perfect case of labour liquidity—and a gun in his hands almost slides to a halt in front of me (the image would be almost comedic if I weren't so quietly terrified), tucking his weapon into his acetabulofemoral joint and pulling the one in the sand out, shaking the debris from it and throwing it to me; I grab it from the air out of instinct and he holds me by the shoulder, pushing me forwards up the hill.

"*Go, go!*"

I try to turn and object but as I move the hand pushes me again, thrusting me forwards; I fall but before I can reach the ground he grabs me around my other shoulder, shakes me and drags me forwards. The foreign barbarism of the act doesn't bother me as much as its intensity does.

"I'm not a *soldier*—"

"No soldiers in this war," he says, his sweat slickening the blood; I can feel his breath on my hair, but I'm not feeling particularly inclined towards swatting at it. "For the city! For the capital! *God bless Aime*—"

His chant is interrupted by a piercing scream, and as he falls forwards I shout an almost instant *'n'teléresynjs'*—he hits the barrier before the glass. I grab onto the falling man's shoulders before he completes his bounce, the weight a back-breaking thing, and begin to drag him across the ground, looking up to see men in black and white climbing over the trenches; the one pointing at me, having just erupted over the parapet, seems to hesitate for a moment, giving me a glimpse of the blackish bit of carbon up against his throat right as a leather-armoured man jumps on him holding his rifle like a knife midway down the centre to hold him by the throat and stab the barrel down, hard, into his right eye. It bursts in a shower of blood and humour, and the man turns to us with a grin on his bloodstained face.

"*Last one!*" he shouts, laughing; the trench is deep enough into the sand-mountain that there's no chance of him meeting the state he's just inflicted in his jubilation. "*Rest overhill!*"

The trench—I call it that because I can't think of any other word, devoid of dugouts and anything but cleaned sand—is now only a few metres away from us, and I drag the man right into it over the stone a second before a shell hits; a burning ray of sun illuminates the spot where I just was, holding for a whole second as the barrier forces itself back together.

"*Méntrytj tut qu'ausiciss,*" I groan, laying the man onto his back; he is breathing, at the very least, but I can't say he'd pass an examination. "*Tut prenyzhra réviytj syit osiira praćanshanfisyr—*"

His internal wounds highlight in great detail over his stomach, a white and light blue diagram marred by thick splotches of red. He's gone into preservation—clearly at least partially ethnic—and his chest is going up and down at a perfectly even pace, the open wound on his stomach not bleeding too heavily. I take a deep breath and begin to mend it: there are no broken arteries, and so it should be a simple task.

Said every resident ever.

As I close the superficial wound, an explosion bashes past the barrier above and incinerates a small stretch of tent next to us, an intense sizzling filling the air with the smell of burning flesh—this is very much like cooking meat, except with a morsel more screaming—as convection forces a wave of heat against my skin. I yelp and fall to the side, scraping at my clothes, and as I do something happens that I cannot quite describe.

I am convinced at first, of course, that the shapes I'm seeing before me are just distortions in the heat. They're subtle enough to blend into the background, I'd imagine, and he's just pulled a blade and there is a sudden red streak inside my patient's subjective and there is blood splattered against the thick air and his knife is as clear as day and if I were less educated I might say that my heart skips several beats because it *does*.

He turns towards me, and I realise with a start that only a little of his eyes is visible, like he's wearing some invisible kind of woman's dishdasha, and he turns away and I don't see him and I turn and run.

The sound of gunfire and a great deal of screaming comes from behind me, muffled a little and then beginning to come back to full volume but I don't stop to look; there are more shimmers coming over the dune and I keep my head down and a shower of blood explodes ten metres from my face and sand and invisible hands grasp at a visible wound and I jump over the fallen *thing* as I run.

As I hit another few metres I feel a hand about my wrist and I scream and try to tug away but it's far too strong and as I'm taken I look to its source and I see a bearded man with blood leaking down from his hair looking worriedly at me as he fires his weapon forwards and there is some primal fear in my chest and I grab his arm and bite and bite and bite and he yelps and lets go and I'm free I run and trip face-down into the well-warmed sand.

As I push myself up, shaking the sand from my face as I cough it out, a voice bursts out over the din as if amplified by a sessile: "*Dead! Buggers dead in the ditch, God willing! Thousands down there and not ten can't rivet us up here!"*

Almost immediately, the man who tried to grab me leverages his firearm over the dunes, staring intently down the rail. The gun is enormous; I estimate as I look at it from the side that its barrel is the width of my thumb's length. The man holds the stock bent at a peculiar angle, only its bottom bit touching his shoulder; I can see a slight purple shimmer around the back, and his hands shake from the weight.

Before I can make any more observations he fires, and the sound would deafen a fleshcrawler; I flinch and jump back instinctively, falling against the makeshift stonerise wall behind me as the sessile-hybrid weapon literally flips in his grip, the trigger guard looping around his finger, the layered barrier beneath it lighting up in a quiet violet as the recoil slides it across his shoulder. Almost before it hits he has grabbed onto the bolt, the momentum pulling it in his hand as he flips it forward once more and jumps from the parapet, letting the parados catch him and huddling up a metre besides me.

"Sorry for startling you, lass," he says, and gives me a shattertoothed grin.

I give him one back, perhaps with a few too many teeth to match; I fear it looks insincere, but before I can interpret a reaction he no longer has eyes with which to see it and I scream and jump back but I can't hear myself scream and his shadow is burnt on the cracked and charred and bloody stone and I stumble up my head aching a little but before I can run there are hands grabbing my shoulders and I am turned around and I am facing Arcembault who is something that's not trying to kill me and he pushes a hand down and up, down and up and I breathe with his hand's rhythm and I breathe in and out and in and out and in and out slower and slower until I let a single, final breath leave my lungs and blink.

"Just about shat myself when I saw the hit," he says, and I note that his accent has mildly slipped, 'e's turning to 'o's as he fumbles for a handkerchief stuck in his waistband, glancing nervously at the poor remnants of the man next to me. Alongside him, dozens—hundreds?—of men run from the back and pour into the trenches, one right besides me jumping over a foot along with the wall and climbing the parapet, beginning to fire. "Your friend—your friend is safe, ready to get to the city. We had to restrain him."

"Restrain him?" I say, and I realise my voice is almost a whisper, my jaw chittering; my hand lets itself fall to the side and I recoil in horror as I feel the texture of cloth and shoulderbone and blood and I decide not to look and just speak. "She wants to see us?"

"She practically jumped—" he begins, and shortly after he conjugates his verb another heat-wave reaches us. The screams are now too ubiquitous for new ones to be heard, and the new man on the parapet next to us pushes himself standing and leans towards its source. A whistling goes by, and his tightly-cut hair finds itself split in two; he ducks almost immediately, and he breathes in and out quickly and roughly and lets himself go and I almost expect him to die from something, I don't know what, but he doesn't and he wallows in his own relief before turning back out and beginning to fire once again.

"—no time," he says, having gathered his breath. The young man above us raises his fist and pumps it with a *yeh* and there's another shot and he yelps and brings his untouched fist down. "Follow me."

He offers me a hand and I grab it; we leap over the stonerise together as the sand below us shudders.

I hear something exploding behind me, but I don't look.

"I didn't look."

Perei, brooding out the window, turns to glance at me. "Huh?"

The enclosed sled we're in sails rather smoothly across the ground, and there isn't anything to interrupt me as I continue to mirror his prior state. "I operated on a patient but he died and that's normal but I didn't do *anything* to try and help, I just turned and cried and ran—"

He snorts with what I presume to be the utmost derision, rubbing at his slightly bloodshot eyes. "Least you *tried*."

"And I didn't stop. I was so scared I ran and somebody got shot in front of me and I didn't stop to help him. I just ran and I might have saved him but I didn't and I don't know why. I saw three men die in front of me in a minute and I *don't know* if I should've seen a fourth because I didn't look back. I didn't *try* to know. What kind of doctor am I?"

He shrugs and lies back in the cushion, letting his legs spread a bit wider apart. "Rivet whoever they were right to the wall. You're in one piece."

"You don't *understand*," I say, leaning forwards; my head supports itself on my upturned palm. "I've always tried. I've had fifty-six deaths but I *tried* every single time, no matter where it was and no matter *who* it was and—and I didn't. I was *selfish*."

He sighs. "Nobody's perfect."

"It's not that I'm not perfect," I say, shaking my head. "It's that I didn't try to be."

"Look," he says, rubbing at his own forehead now, "Me, I've seen more people dead than you'll ever tell yourself you saved. You tried to save the first guy with *bombs*—"

"Artillery," I say, the correction unintentional. "Sorry."

"—the first guy with *artillery* coming down on you? That's some balls right there. You want some credit from me, you got it."

I blink.

"I don't know why," I say, "but that makes me feel quite a bit better."

"Well," he says, giving me a grin, "looks like you're getting easier by the minute, huh?"

I glare at him. "Rivet yourself to a wall."

"New mouth, too!" he says, and grins. "Great job, Ash. At this rate—"

As he rattles off a particularly intricate compounding of obscenity I don't speak enough Uytrimelan to understand, I find that I don't think I've ever gone so quickly from idiopathic pride to its shameful equivalent.

It's not an entirely unpleasant sensation.

The soldier waiting for us as the sled hits the city's urban perimeter—we have been pulled past countless empty adobe and stonerise houses on the way, so the distinction is dubious at best—does a double-take as we step out, his hand pulling itself up all the way up to his chest before he catches sight of mine.

"Fashion," he says, and blinks. "Is that what they're wearing in Ci—is that what *you're* wearing nowadays? Open impersonation-skirters?"

Perei answers, and his dulcet tones make the man glance rather confusedly up towards him, as if shocked at the very idea of a trouser-wearer speaking. "Scavved it."

"Oh," he says, and adjusts the ceramic plate on his chest upwards. "I suppose I forsook one faux pas for two. Do accept my apologies, misses, for making light of your predicaments—may I know your face names?"

"Ashrea das Cimcharei," I say, in my politest tone; he doesn't flinch at the obvious face-name, and behind us the preinstructed glasswalker-driven sled does a turn and begins to trot up the hill.

"Mister," he says, rubbing his tired eyes in what seems to be a rather passable substitute for belligerence. "Perei qu'n'av dasnamr."

"Brilliant," the man says, doing an admirable job of partially concealing the slight twitch in his left eye as the demonym omits itself, turning on his heel and opening the carriage's door for us before pulling himself onto its glasswalker. "I am Ambullier Pandrismrei das Shimaldrea, and will be escorting you to the Administrative District."

He hums, checking about on his glasswalker as he idly speaks. "Not that I should imply you should need me—it appears the ruffians down this quarter have had the distinct honour of learning about patriotism. Enlistment's gone up almost ten times and they've finally gotten to respect the sirens, so the only botherers you shouldn't have bothering you will almost certainly be children. All mostly harmless."

We climb into the vehicle and a phrase from our ambullier sends it going; the soft plops of lightly-strewn gravel under us turn quickly into the chugging pace along the stonerise with which I am familiar as we enter the city proper.

The sensation's rather comforting, and I glance outside the windows to see concrete next to stonerise; none of these buildings were constructed before the Khamisret-Aparkisrea method, and if I were less educated on Sikhas' demographics I might call the sight outright obscene.

I'm so educated on Sikhas' demographics, in fact, that I almost forget to ask why there aren't any *people* here; my attempt to rescue myself from my ivory tower is immediate.

"The windows are open," I say, looking out towards the streets. "Curfews don't cover open windows. Where *is* everyone?"

Perei glances out the window. "Giving us a look-see. I don't think they've seen a lot of stars doing anything good."

I progress from my unnaturally cowardly state of observation to peer out the window myself; there is a slight flash of movement in the corner of my vision along the corner of a street. As inconspicuously as possible, I put my hands back down on my lap. A small sticker—*salmien pormelari, pluqqinz nit'permée*—upon a vitrine catches my eye, the unsubtlety of its satire making me wince. "Hearing us, too?"

"Looks proofed," he says, biting his lower lip. "And probably."

The ride seems as long as it is silent, punctuated occasionally by the sound of a beacon-shell piercing a barrier that isn't ours; the spaces where the barriers overlap are the quietest of all.

I try not to imagine what barrier independence implies.

I let out a little ease as we approach the barricade; there are no windows through which we can see forwards through, but the sloped steel is unmistakeably administrative, the sun glinting off the compasses scratched centimetres deep into the metal.

There is a brief, muffled exchange of what I presume to be pleasantries before the microrephrasant protruding from the ceremonial spikes along them flickers, and we ride on past the gap. Skavkharid museums and apartments and restaurants quickly find themselves replaced by whitewashed residences marked with gardens out front, roofs slanted and fortified hard enough to withstand barrier collapse.

I've only seen a single building anywhere near its classical architecture before—itself astride two buildings with architecture so modern they look like they might spontaneously fall apart—as if even the concept of citizenship is as anathema to the tierless here as the taxes that come with it.

I let out what is almost a sigh of relief as we are cleared.

"I don't understand."

Perei raises an eyebrow at me. "What?"

"Why would any tierless Aimelan choose to come to Cimsas?" I say, leaning forwards with my hands clasped. "The tierless richer as they are than half the tiered. Why'd *any* tierless Aimelan choose not to be here if the fare could be paid?"

"You only see the ones that made it," he says, shaking his head. "You don't feel bad just 'cause you have it bad. You have it bad 'cause others have it better. I knew a kid named One-Arm Jen, sold fifty one-syb gallons a day. Year later, he's selling seven hundred from ten kids he has working with him. You think that'd happen here?"

"I don't see why not," I say, and immediately it becomes apparent to me that I'm not particularly adept at answering trick questions.

"Why'd you think he's called One-Arm Jen?" he says.

I blink. "I didn't—"

"You got the print and you bought it whole is what you did."

"You've stayed here before?"

"Stayed?" He laughs bitterly. "Where'd you think I'd *stay*? How d'you think we'd get down? Here, the *adobes* cost more a day than two on the third edge. I'm pretty sure those bits on the outside got *zoning permits*. Mud with the broken leg for this block, cashiered soak down the next—nah, I went on a field trip with Ay. Spent six days, got a year's worth. Spent a year's worth, too."

I nod.

"Plus," he adds, a thoughtful note in his voice, "they talk funny."

I tilt my head a little. "Is that a synecdochal complaint against their insularity?"

"Nah—they're nice. Most of them. Just sound really dumb."

I'd imagine if my life were a siction this and any following action would merit a scene break by itself—he ruins the opportunity, however, raising his hands above his head, fingers touching the carriage's high top.

He gets as far as a high-pitched '*roi*'—his face contorted, jaw twisted to the side, eyelids fluttering in mockery—as the carriage's door opens, and his jaw shuts so quick a quick tenseness goes through me as I anticipate for the slightest moment the crack of a shattered tooth.

"We're here," the ambullier says, smiling at a perfectly respectable pair of young people.

Now, I think as I hop down from the carriage, *this* would be the perfect time for a scene break.

The mansion before us is beautiful.

Every other word I can think of for it is a synonym. Where I call it ancient, I catch a glimpse of some perfectly symmetrical spire jutting from it at a perfectly symmetrical angle; where I call it modern, its entire timeless structure stands as a testament against the very idea.

Its gardens are arranged in intricate patterns and as the barrier-spewing steel gates open before us and we walk escorted past them I see countless perennials—

"Ash?"

—and lavender angusts and red papavers and white arctomecs and so many hundreds of inedible species that it's practically a *library*—

"*Ash!*" he shouts, rousing me like the a device of a narrator too lazy to finish a description.

"*What?*" I say, turning about and almost screaming at him; only about then do I realise I've been stooping over them.

He recoils, putting his hands up and stepping back a little. "Isha's hooks, you'd think I tore you from a garden you were *washing*," he says, putting a peculiar emphasis on his coda. "Thought you'd maybe wanna keep going. The walkerman's staring."

I glance surreptitiously back; the ambullier is looking particularly formal, standing with his hands behind his back and looking straight ahead. "He is *not*."

"That's how you know he is," he says, patting me on the back and pushing me a bit forwards. "Peek in twenty."

I notice the repeated smack of the shoes' soles against the stones set into the ground, and I glance down to see that they're sharp to the point of placation; I count twenty before glancing back to see that he's lying against the carriage, poking at a sessile on his arm.

"Told you," he says, and goes on.

I decide not to respond.

The door—some dark, polished kind of wood, the knob mechanical—opens before we reach it, and there is an absolute darkness beyond. I stop in place, but right as I do Perei's hand sweeps me into his unbroken stride and it isn't his hand and I yelp and look behind me and see a man wearing clothes the colour of the mansion's façade right before there is nothing but black.

There is a slight shuffling sound that echoes throughout what I presume to be the main hall I've found myself in, and I don't dare move anything but my lips.

"Perei?"

"Yeah?"

"Are you moving?"

"Nope."

The silence that follows has a lingering quality about it, and there is a slight gurgling sound somewhere nearby.

"This is very unsettling."

—*It really is rather more **dramatic**, no?*

A ray of light abruptly bursts from the ceiling so tight I can barely see what it illuminates, and the slight humming of an oration buzzes through the room. I blink, recoiling a bit; the door meets my back, and I can feel the gap between a panel and its muntin pressing against it as some kind of shimmering figure descends from the ceiling.

In an instant so quick that I might almost fail to see it, a pair of wings burst from her—and it is a her—back, visible only by their impossible silhouettes as the light pours around the bone and flesh so that the feathers peeking from them shine gold with the light. It is almost by instinct that my hand wraps around my instrument and I begin to sing an analysis.

The light goes out before the first sentence pushes itself from my lips, and in its place the momentarily blinding shine of pulled-back shutters—the solid steel curtains shrieking as they're abruptly shunted open—reveals a woman in an intricately decorated administrator's dress with a pair of limp wings jutting somewhat mournfully from her back, looking somewhat less surprised than I imagine she expects to be.

She shakes her head and points towards us, beginning to trod in her finger's direction.

"*You?*"

Her feet plod along on the carpet, sending muffled 'pft's up into the air.

"Me?" I say, stepping back a little; this seems to cause her to wince.

"You," she says, walking. "You got into Yesyirei's vault?"

"Yesyirei," I say, the word bringing an unexpected bitterness with it, "was the name of a person who murdered a little girl in front of me and then stabbed me in the neck. Is that the person you're referring to?"

She stops in place, her hand a metre from my face, and then puts her previously occupied hand to her head, the fire gone immediately from her frame and replaced immediately—without time for shock—by a rather absolute exasperation. The light illuminates her flawless ebony skin with a resolute perfection. "I'm sorry. Poor Yessy. I should have known when he tried it on me." She waves a hand and says one or two words; Perei's congested respiratory cycle makes itself known grating past caught phlegm, and his form collapses to the floor, coughing wretchedly. "He always did have a few rivets shuddered."

Her weight shifts onto one foot and she practically pirouettes a hundred and eighty degrees; I realise as she steps over and sits, pushing her hand to her head with an absolute fatigue, that the entire semi-circle around which the stairs curve is lined with a couch that almost seamlessly blends into the wall.

"*You're* the Administrator for the Arts?" I ask, blinking as she settles.

"I'm sure this is all a bit confusing to you, isn't it?" she says, laughing rather exhaustedly; her wings, which have not yet done the courtesy of disappearing like any other good illusion, noticeably flap a bit along with her shudders. "I suppose you want to know about what's happened to you."

I consciously blink and unconsciously rub a bit of rheum from my eyes as I do and glance down to Perei, who has a rather dubious look on his face. "I'd like that very much, yes."

She nods and looks down at her red-nailed hands, biting down on her lower lip as if in consideration, her right fist a stand for her face.

"What is the basis of value, miss Ashrea?" she asks, flicking the ends of her thin fingers together and sending an impressively loud snap through the amphitheatric room as she does.

"Labour." The answer comes recited, almost to the point of automaticity. "Almost all resources being eventually renewable, supply is essentially—"

She holds up a hand, rubbing her forehead daintily with the other. "That's heterodox, but it's good enough. If I may simplify: I have demand and—judging by your friend's attire—you have a great deal of supply."

"What?"

"I have a problem that needs labour to flow into it in the form of a man named Rilaued bin Šamantuel al-Mirali an-Niswani. He's a fifty-three-year-old immigrant guideline in the Western quarter who returned from a pilgrimage to Kharatoushka one year ago, during which his license lapsed. I want him and his movement gone."

Perei brings himself fully to his legs besides me, shaking his head. "You're putting a *hit* out on some guideline?" he says, and I can see that he's on the verge of stumbling before he takes a deep breath and forces himself straight. "What's up there, lady?"

"Something that's in the process of aching." Her sigh is deep. "His removal means a great deal to me and happens to be a very good deal for you—he's convinced enough that God will shield him that I doubt he has so much as a guard. I haven't got the slightest clue as to how it might be done as long as you're as quiet as he will be."

"Why do you want him dead?" I ask, more out of indignation than curiosity. I want to say that I am revolted, but what I'm feeling now is far more powerful than revulsion: it might be better named disappointment.

"Not dead. Just gone." She leans back on the sofa. "He's developed a following of tens of thousands since his return, without a religious permit—we normally wouldn't bother, but his sermons are believed to be the single largest factor working against recruitment in the southwestern tierless district. There are already thousands of educated young men and women directly opposing the present war, but *this* war—"

Perei raises an eyebrow. "Is that what they're calling it now?"

There is a moment of silence—the administrator looking up at him, eyes a bit widened—before a gentle sort of laugh makes itself known from her peach lips.

"I suppose it's funny, isn't it? That's what they're going to say in the history-books: the Present War was interrupted by This War." She shakes her head with a kind of belaboured humour. "We're not going to take the chance."

Her right's fingers rub briefly against her palm as she pauses, then speaks again. "Get rid of him. It would help if you managed to incite his movement in the progress—perhaps a little costume-making."

"Why us?"

She gives me the look of a person answering a very obvious

question. "You're not first-tier citizens, and we haven't exactly had the fortune to welcome a great deal of *pàrnérii*. I think you can see why this isn't a job for the Mahammadir."

I nod, and see a particularly distressed stare at the peripherals of my vision. "I need one of your—your cylinders, too. From the Vault of Contrition. The ones that say Àntyéshyéleraii on them."

Her wings—by now looking morbidly real—flap a little and gracefully launch her back off the cushion, as if by instinct, and she ughs to herself as a feather drops from them. "I'm certain we could arrange something of the sort—they'll be more useful to you than they are to me, if I'm right. I'll get you out of here with a set of fitting clothes in a bit."

I nod.

"What should we do until then?"

"I saw you admiring the flowers," she says, looking to be in a slight state of reminiscence as she lets a light smile to come to her lips. "Feel free to look around."

"That was fun."

I don't look at him.

"I mean, I know the places're supposed to be nice and all, but *damn*."

I continue looking ahead.

"Sure, the staff were mean, but—"

My neck twists with my head as I turn to glare, and the sly smile I've already imagined fades rather quickly from his face; his right hand brushes over the pouches underneath his dishdasha.

"*You got us expelled from the Administrative District!*" I shout in the most whisperedly restrained way possible, and he flinches. "I assumed you were supposed to be *good* at fitting in, you incredible—"

"Okay, okay, okay!" he says, raising his arms in what I presume to be some twisted mockery of surrender. "Sure, I dropped a *little*—"

"You dropped an *explosive!*" I shout, reaching forwards and grabbing his wrists; his skin is unusually soft against my palms, but not enough for me to forget my minor conniption. "You detonated a *bomb*—"

"A *smoke* bo—"

"*You engaged in the detonation of a device that may lead indirectly to loss of life in an emergency situation!*" I shout, and pause before I remember the rest of the statute. "*In wartime!*"

"I've never even *heard* of that law. Five or ten?"

I sigh and shake my head as we continue walking; the city is large enough that the alleys are clear.

"Hey, at least I know what that stuff does now. What if I dropped it outside, huh?"

I'm just about to respond as we turn the corner when I catch sight of a dishdashaed young man standing at the end of the street; I raise a finger, instinctively straightening the cloth covering my nose. He eyes us on our approach, and as soon as we come to a comfortable distance I raise my hand and wave it.

"Hail, brother!" I say, my voice as jovial as I can make it. He looks over to his left and to his right before turning back, his head titled a slight bit; there is the slightest bit of tension in his frame as he removes the burnstick from between his lips.

"Mate," he says, pointing to himself, "are you talking to me?"

Perei gently puts his palm to his head. "She's a fob, mate," he says in a perfectly Sikhari accent, patting me toughly on the shoulder. "Don't mind the poor girl too much."

"Right," he says, relaxing a bit and leaning back against the wall, putting the burning cylinder of fabric back into his mouth. "So, you're new around here too? Haven't heard an accent that bad since the Convention."

I smile underneath the cloth, lightly enough that it makes no distortion; Perei doesn't skip a beat, snorting as he goes to normal. "Heh. That bad, huh?"

The man makes a slight gap between his index and thumb, grinning as he does. The burnstick hangs from the right of his lips, bobbing as he speaks—a rather striking look. "I'd have to blind the angel if you tried it again."

Perei laughs, less of a spontaneous guffaw as it is an evolution from his snort: a series of quick exhalations backed up by a few cordal adductions, just enough to create the impression of unawkward neutrality.

The man hmms. "Right, then—what're you two doing around

here? Hardly a tourist attraction."

"Oh, we're just looking for somebody named Rilaued." He gestures over to me, palm facing the sky; his voice carries a strange sort of kinship. "She's been looking forward to him."

"Ah, the guideline? He's just a street down, in the bowing. Turn right around when you get t—" He pauses for a second, glances to the side, and then nods to himself. "—to the Ali, if my memory's serving. Talking all day about how war's hell and all that. Mum's practically rubbing over him." He rolls his eyes.

Perei nods. "Thanks. What're you doing down here, anyhow?"

He shrugs. "Just looking out, mate. One a field, and *I* get a stick the size of my pinkie. Everyone else's down by the bowing. Should probably get there before the nessy starts up."

"I feel you." Perei shakes his head as he speaks, stepping back a bit as if as part of some ritual of conversational disengagement. "*Masalma.*"

The man nods. "*Yasalmak.* Careful at the overlap if you can't help it—bastards're trying to get the things to resonate, if I'm guessing right. You're well-armed, getting past that bash-up earlier, but I doubt you'd hit enough of God's rays to make much of a difference."

"I'll keep it on the head," Perei says, and holds me by the hand as we continue to walk down the street; I can see the man looking at us out the corner of my eye for just about a second before he goes back to observing the patterns on the brick walls.

"And hey!" the man calls out from behind us, not loudly but not softly. "Tell the poor bastard to get off the phare if you get to get your heads together. I saw a few solid hits yesterday—they're tallest first, if what I've seen's right."

"Sure thing!" he says, waving limp-wristedly in agreement.

It's a few buildings down before Perei speaks again.

"So," he says, looking to me. "We're gonna do it?"

I look back. "I'll try and talk with him."

"And if he doesn't listen?"

I pause for a bit, enough to create the impression of unsureness, before I speak.

"Any rational being can be persuaded by a sound argument based on the principle of self-interest."

I expect a laugh, but he just looks ahead.

The prostration is wooden, and a barrierline juts from its tip into the surface of the sky.

I count—by a rather periphery meaning of the word 'count'—thousands of white-clad people before me as we turn the corner and enter the overlap, each one of them on their knees and elbows on little mats on the sandy, rectangle-cut stonerise as they face the structure's phare: a tower reaching half to the barrier, a thin, tall man in the same white attire standing on a little platform protruding a slight bit from its disproportionately enormous tip.

The buildings seem to melt away as we approach, architecture making way for the circle. The man seems to speak—loudly, it appears, a very slight shaking but not with hysterics but a strong dignity—but no sound comes, and for all its life the picture seems dead.

We step past the overlap, then, and its resurrection hits my ears with due vengeance.

*—And let us not just **ask** but **know** that our future will be bright, our hands unstained entirely by the blood of the Aimelan nor the Ashtari nor the Pyarash, that before the eyes of God every man is equal and shall be so judged by his deeds. Let us **know**, God's will save us, that we will never kill for anything upon this Earth, and that on the banner of every nation one day there will always be written the word 'love'—*

He pauses. I can see in the corner of my eye a beacon's trail blueshifting against the white sky as it disappears, its flash blinking against our own barrier.

*—and **never hate**.*

The silence continues, but there is a gentle shifting in the crowd before he speaks again.

—If we cannot be with the world, we must at least be with each other—we must have our hands tied to each others', so that we will be the streams—

There is a slight exhalation to my right, and I glance to Perei, who's biting his lower lip.

—So that we may be the streams that lead into the river of God.

Perei lets out a slight giggle, and as the sound amplifies itself so that it would be as though he had screamed it a thousand times in a second and hundreds of eyes begin to turn up from their mats and to me and I begin to feel the slightest tinge of social anxiety and as he puts his hand over his mouth I decide that the barrier is a bit too democratic for my taste.

The guideline steps back on his platform a bit, looking about, before his eyes find us; there is a squint across his features and a moment of what seems to be disbelief before he smiles, the mild wrinkles contorting along his face as he does.

—It appears we have visitors.

As soon as the word 'visitors' leaves his mouth, the crowd—every single one of them—stands and begins to move, a wave of white parting before us; I can see a few stumble but remain kept outright by the crowd, held and propped and moved gently without the slightest murmur but the clapping of feet on stones.

—Come.

We walk forwards.

Rilaued laughs as we walk up the stairs into the glass-ceilinged room—the scale is far more obvious from here, the roof outrageously far above us—his hand clutching a ceramic pot of tea; the sun seems to be far brighter than it ought to be here, bits of dust suspended in the air about his tenebrism-caught form. "I suppose the pun really was a bit much, wasn't it? I *do* try to appeal to my audience."

I blink; his tone is casual enough that I don't even register that he's speaking with me until he tilts the pot, filling the clear glass cup. A thin wisp of smoke rises from it and splits against the bulkheads—the smell fills the room.

"A beautiful prostration, isn't it?" He takes a sip and quickly blows, shaking his head as he scrapes his tongue across his teeth. "I take it you're not here to talk, so—would you mind not getting blood over it? Wooden floors really are very hard to clean. My successor might resent you."

"What on Earth are you talking about?" I say, bringing my hand to my forehead; I can see Perei wincing in the corner of his eye, and I'm not sure if it's for him or the sun.

"I haven't seen you before," he says, sticking a finger up. "That's one strike. I remember the faces of every man that comes here; nobody new has since the fortification, and you certainly don't *look* Pyarash."

"Sikhas—Sikhas is a big city."

He speaks as if I hadn't. "I know the Administration's wanted me dead since I came back. I know there's a war going on, and—" he says, pausing for a second. "And you—and you remind me of something."

He seems to behold the image for a second before chuckling.

"We're not here to hurt you," I say, shaking my head. "We just want to talk."

"I'm not going to stop telling the truth. I speak the words of God, child." He stares at me for a whole second before he sighs. "Child. A child, of all they could have sent. A bloody *child*. I'd ask when they lost their shame, but I doubt you'd know."

I choose not to raise a personal objection. "But this is self-defence—we're being *attacked*. We can't lie over and—"

"Lie over and *what?*" he says, stepping forwards to me, his drink jiggling in its glass. "I've seen enough of war. We've all lost somebody by now—I would rather lose a hand than clap. We are ruled by intimidation and force and every conceivable awfulness that we could ever have suffered, kept perpetually in sufferance to a regime that treats us like *cattle*. What is lying over if the alternative is the oppression from which these people seem to come to us to liberate?"

I bite a little on my lower lip. "Well, I—"

He brings himself forward to me, leaning over so that I can feel his breath on my face; I wince, and my left foot pushes back in place as he speaks with a thunderously subdued passion. "What on Earth do you think you could possibly say to me that could let me take up arms against my very own brothers, child? What on Earth could I possibly tell you that could make you rise against yours?"

"They shelled the capital."

Rilaued and I turn to Perei at once, who's adopted a peculiarly straight sort of face; the man peers into his eyes for a second before he straightens up and chuckles, turning around as he walks and taking another sip.

"No nation but Aimela keeps artillery within its borders—an excuse to crush the tierless districts, more likely. A rubbish excuse, at that. Not that it would make the slightest difference." He shakes his head as he walks, the light shining on him as it does on us as he treads past the speaking-platform.

"The tower fell," Perei says, stepping forwards and letting his hands go spread to his sides. "I *saw* it fall. The suburbs, the apartments—*everything*. Whole place got sandpiled. I *saw* it happen. We got out right as it did."

His pace stops for a second before he continues, a little harder than before; the preciously wooden floors clop against his steeled shoes. "You *would* say that, wouldn't you?"

"I wouldn't want to convince you if I was here to kill you, right?" I say, staring at his unkempt hair as though he had eyes protruding from them. He snaps his bony fingers slowly—second by second—and looks to the sky past the glass; I have to restrain myself from noting that the sun's bad for his eyes.

"There's something else," he says, turning about slowly, hand with a wagging index extended; there's a contemplative sort of look in his face as he does, and his forehead casts a shadow over his eyes. "Something else entirely."

"Something else?" Perei says. "What d'you mean, 'something else'?"

He steps forward, glancing up again before looking down. "I was given a vision of you last night, Ashrea. The fabric of imagination, I thought—but your presence seems to have given it a far more prestigious weaver."

"Whoa," Perei says, tilting his head a bit. "*Some*body's turning up the purple."

He stops right as he is about to speak before chuckling. A yell in a language I don't understand echoes faintly in the background—followed by a few others—and he speaks right over it. "I try to keep it down—maybe I overcompensate. No matter. I know what you are here for, and I know what you want me to do."

"All we want you to do is understand," I say, hands imploring. "We are fighting against something so incomprehensible, so *dangerous*—"

He raises a hand, and something about his demeanour compels me to silence myself. "And I want *you* to think, and I want you to understand something and do so very well. I know that you're trying to appeal to reason—you aren't here to tell me anything new, not to give me a reason, but to appeal to that which I already know—maybe you'd call it self-interest. I suppose you're going to say that I'm going to die if we lose, though I suppose you wouldn't tell me that it would be you who'd do it."

"The *shelling*," I say, shaking my head. "Millions of people—"

He continues without the slightest hint that he's acknowledged what I've said. "So let me tell you that I have no *reason*, child—Ashrea, isn't it? That's the name I was given in my vision, and I can see by your face that I'm right—" He takes a deep breath. "I have no reason, *Ashrea*, to throw my principles away for what somebody who I know is here to allow for the slaughter of thousands says. I have no reason to encourage thousands of young men to kill."

He takes a deep breath and a sip, raising a finger as he continues.

"And let me tell you again and make it certain in your mind that I have no reason, that I have not the slightest reason to hurt another living being, not secular nor celestial, and there is absolutely nothing that you can do or say to give me one, because as far as you might think we're all the same, that we all care about our own skin more than the world itself, you are *wrong*, child, you are *wrong* more than I suppose you've admitted that you've ever been before in your life, because I would rather let my own soul bring itself to paradise a thousand times than send a single one to hell and bring myself with it."

I do not say anything, and he sighs as he turns back over, sits down once more and takes another sip of the clear brownish drink.

"Do what you wish," he says, licking his lower lip. "My armistice is signed and my soul is mine. God is great, and I am His servant."

"If you died," I say, and I realise my own lips have turned rather dry, "Your followers would turn rabid. They'd want to kill the man who killed you. You know that."

"No," he says, "I don't. And I hope I never will."

We are quiet for a while; he finishes his drink, walks over and pours himself another cup before shuffling over back to his seat. The sun is far brighter than usual, to the point that it's beginning to seem unhealthy—he pays it no notice.

I can practically hear Perei muttering 'awkward'.

"So," he says, looking up to me, "why are *you* here?"

"What?"

"Why *you*? Why a child?"

I raise an eyebrow. "I'm legally an adult."

He smiles to himself, looking down at his glass. "That doesn't make a difference. I'm not dead yet, so—why you?" He glances up at Perei. "And you, boy? You've been quiet for quite a while, haven't you? I presume you're her handler, so why aren't you handling?"

He doesn't respond; I speak. "We're the only ethnic Aimelans—"

"Bullshit," he says, his voice booming, and the word gains a terrifying sort of gravity coming in his resonance-punctuated voice. "Hah—far more regal from my tongue, isn't it? This is the largest Aimelan city on the sea. Don't you think somebody else might take your place? Why you, a little girl with nothing but words? Why you, a young man without even those? Why *you*?"

His terminal word is punctuated by a shrill whistle, and he and Perei turn immediately to its source; I turn from it, fancying myself clever, and see nothing right before turning as they are to see past the window those terribly familiar wisps of falling membrane.

"Goddamn," Perei says, biting his lower lip. "I think we're riveted."

"How did we hear that?" I say, and I already know. I immediately back away from the glass, putting my hand upon my instrument.

Rilaued simply laughs. "I see your contingency has arrived."

"For the last time," I say, giving him a dreadful glare. "*We're not here to k—*"

The floor moves.

I slam into the wall just after the barrier-word issues from my lips, bouncing just a little before I fall the centimetres between it and my skin. A shelf's worth of hardbacks smack themselves right over my face, my barrier lighting in purple as they do. I close my eyes and shout out an intolerant just as they bounce, sending me into an uncontrollable slide towards the balcony right before I rephrase it stable and come to a grinding halt, solid wood grinding itself against my covered skin.

For a moment, all I can perceive is my heart's beating.

As I open my eyes, I can see the guideline against the wall, his eyes screwed up in pain as he holds his shoulder. As I glance to the right,

I see Perei holding onto a bookshelf upon the opposite wall, staring down at me—I quickly estimate that we're about forty degrees tilted, a figure that isn't terribly encouraging—eyes wide as he shouts various threats to both the world and himself.

"*Are you alright?*" I shout, glancing at the exit to the preaching-balcony; I quickly note that I'd be able to launch myself over it if I had to.

"*Ish-al-wyent`-al-wa-lil-al-mahamdi—*"

"No need to shout," Rilaued says, breathing in deeply. "I'm fine."

I can feel the support barrier below us beginning to struggle, the foundational bits of the prostration stuck against it starting to move towards the frictionless threshold. "Okay," I say, "Okay. Don't move—we're still in equilibrium." I look to the stairwell; what I can see is intact, but it's very much connected to our half.

"Equilibrium my *ass*," Perei says, letting out a deep breath. "God, how're we gonna get off this thing?"

"I don't know," I say, biting my lower lip; my brow is sweatier than I'd care to admit. "I could extend my barrier, but—we could wait until they fire again."

"Isha, Isha, Isha save my *ass*—"

Rilaued laughs, and I glance sideways to him. "We've all been played, haven't we?"

"This *isn't the Administration's*," I almost shout, and the wretched whistle of a beacon drowns out the idea of a counterargument; I rub my ears before speaking, and the structure creaks soundlessly the tiniest bit. "The stairs. Are they flexible?"

"Everything here's by God's own hands."

Perei raises an eyebrow, his feet slipping the slightest bit as the structure continues to edge. "Pyarash or Ashtari?"

"Those distinctions mean nothing. God does not choose between those who devote themselves—we are all born free, together."

He looks to me, a sense of absolute despair in his eyes.

"Naisilib."

Another whistle breaks the air, and I take another deep breath. "Okay. Okay, we need intolerant barriers. We should have enough tessit—"

The proceeding explosion is just loud enough to make my own speech inaudible, and I swear for a second I almost see the beacon piercing into the floor in the centre of the room followed by the light of the unmasked sun and it's a beacon, non-explosive, *I'm not going to die right now*—and then I'm falling with a wall behind me and there is a thump besides me I and grab at the sound and feel a hand and I shout words I've known as long as I can remember and I'm thrown forwards for the slightest moment and I hold tighter, as tight as I can, and the hand holds back, calloused and I rephrase it intolerant, there's no friction, none at all and I can't breathe and we're out the frame and the rails should shatter my ribs but we're over them—*we*, he's holding—and for just the littlest bit of time as the barrier grows tolerant enough for the hint of a breath we weigh nothing and it *should* break, the barrier should break and us along with it, but the *stone* breaks against it right before it does and it hurts for just a little and I am lying alive on the ground with a slight ache over my squama occipitalis and my eyes shut against the pleasant heat of a finely built day.

I move my arms and they move, and that brief reassurance is enough to make me start laughing, and my lungs are intact and my organs are fine and not a single bone in my body is broken and I'm *alive*, and I laugh so loud I think I'm going to cry as I push myself into a sit and I open my eyes and rub them and look at a young man pushing himself off the ground and groaning and I cross my heart and thank the Tower and the heartbeat in my ears gives me such joy I can't even imagine.

"Wow, okay—" Perei says, pushing himself over onto his side, rubbing his back as he does. "I can't think of anything funny." I expect his voice to deafen as the first word emerges from his mouth, but I remember almost immediately it didn't as we spoke; a quick look at the slight sagginess in the membrane, the blue distorted and twisted but sealed quiet, tells me all I need to know.

I let myself breathe fairly, swallowing as I force myself to my unbroken feet; the tower's split diagonally down the middle, a piece of the independent stairwell protruding from the stump. "The guideline. I need a firearm—a firearm, not a sessile-arm."

He reaches into one of his larger pouches, rummaging a little before pulling out an dark grey bit of L-shaped metal, tossing it to my stretched hand; I feel a brief moment of pride as I catch it even as I keep my eye on the fallen prostration. "What *about* the guideline?"

"Rilaued?" I say, immediately beginning to walk towards the wood-and-glass wreck—it's surprisingly intact, too light to break up and too thick to shatter, hurt only by its own weight. *"Rilaued bin Šamantuel al-Mirali an-Niswani?"*

"Ash," Perei says, calling out from behind me, "we just about got turned into fried griddle-cakes. I'm pretty sure—"

A man's groan arises from the structure, and I raise my weapon to the unshattered dome and fire. An immense force bashes against my face, and I bring my newly empty hands to my face and feel a trickle of something I soon see is bright red; I don't bother looking for its source as I wipe it away, my pace unbreaking. There's a hole in it, a few cracks snaking up through a few of its layers; that's enough.

"Was that supposed to be badass?" Perei calls out behind me, and in the corner of an eye I see him pushing himself over, stretching his back as he trods over to retrieve the firearm. *"'cause I'm pretty sure that's the dumbest shit I've ever seen somebody do!"*

The groaning intensifies, and the brief contemplation it invokes in me on the balance between form and function leads me to begin running in an instant. *"N'téléresynjs ápyfrétra brazàuzjamyiir dis'em délit myzh,"* I begin, my voice's rhythm stable, the tune something I'm certain I picked from a sessile as my right arm begins to turn numb.

I stop as I reach the little hole. *"—y rélityjj!"* I shout, and my leg goes numb, slipping the slightest bit as my arm forces itself forwards without the slightest preambule and forces itself against the glass' wound and *through,* each layer cracking in sequence as my fist bashes through every single one, the lines forcing themselves through to the very edges of the wood-paned section and shattering, raining down upon my barrier-clad form.

I stand for a second, staring at the enormous shattering I've made. "That *worked!*" I squeal, pushing through into into the turned-over room. The furniture follows the floor before me, evidently riveted down. An entire section of the wall—the one below my feet—is flat against the stone, the curved planks snapped in two where they meet the floor. "Should have shattered," I say, shaking my head, a shout—I presume of astonishment—following me. "Should've broken my fingers, Tower protect."

I look the place over as I step over a bookshelf, keeping my left on my instrument. "Rilaued? Rilaued, are you alright?"

"I'm afraid I'm not very good at barriers," a weak, strained voice says, and I realise that it's coming from the stairwell; I immediately turn to walk towards it, reaching up and clambering rather dextrously over the wall separating them from the room. The sides of the shaft are caved in so that it's wrapped in complete darkness—here I feel a slight rush of vindication—and within it, Rilaued lies flat on the ground. A dark fluid—of course it's blood, what else could it be—leaks from the side of his mouth, and a bleeding gash runs right across his forehead.

I rush to kneel at his side—no blood on the ground, thank goodness—and immediately begin to sing a subjective. His condition fleshes itself out over his flesh in red and white.

Pneumothorax, shattered rib, closed fracture in left tibia. Not Aimelan, no preservation; I feel for the misericorde about my hilt and then pull, wiping roughly against the inner fold of my dishdasha. It takes me a few seconds to determine exactly how long it is, and it takes just about a second to get used to pushing my tongue the perfectly wrong way as the syllables leave my mouth. I'm underequipped, but it'll have to do.

He speaks as the plume of alcohol-tinged smoke erupts from the carefully-held blade, his voice rather soft. "Were you sent to kill me, really?"

"Don't talk," I say, flicking the blade's tip; it scratches my fingernail, leaving a small, superficial cut across the very tip of my finger. "Your lung's collapsed."

"Tell me the truth, please," he says, and I begin to weave a one-way cohesive membrane about it, sodium-blocker seeping into its insides as the barrier reinforces the construction; a voice comes shouting out from behind me, accompanied by the fair racket of boots on wood.

"Hot damn, he's still holding?" Perei says, pushing himself up to his waist over the wall like a child aching to look at a rally over a railing.

"Stay at the hole," I say, peering closely at the gash; it isn't bleeding enough to kill, thank goodness. Non-Aimelan medicine is a field harsh enough to warrant its own certifications; I've washed the conscience of my youth with the blood of immigrants far more times than I should.

"I suppose that's what you *would* say," he says, a slight disappointment in his tone as he drops, and his footsteps resound back away. I turn back to Rilaued, reaching over. His gasping breaths fill the quiet air, and I realise he's awaiting an answer.

"You're not dying," I say, putting the hilt between my teeth and speaking past it as I lean over, tongue flicking behind it. "You don't get a last wish."

He doesn't nod, but it looks like he tries to. "You're going to drain my chest—you're an educated girl, aren't you?" he asks, and tracing the zig-zag with my index, I rebind the gash across his forehead as the air pushes its way slowly out of the blade's membrane. "And I suppose you're being threatened?"

I shake my head. "Nothing so dramatic," I say, and realise that I'm an idiot; that is to say, I realise that I haven't pulled his shirt off. "For the Tower's sake," I exclaim, and quickly pull the knife out of my mouth and push the membrane back a little along the blade, forcing the barrier intolerant so the slight bit of leakage stays in as I reach over and stab a slight hole in the front of his white pyjamas, rephrasing the prior barrier-membrane configuration with a series of careful twangs and whispers.

"You want me to quiet myself," he says, interrupting himself with a cough and a spray of blood; it hits me across the face, and I wipe just my eyes. "Because otherwise you'll die too?"

"You're coughing blood," I say, tossing the blade back between my jaws. My tongue inadvertently runs under and over the somewhat sandy animal-skin hilt as I grab onto the sides of the hole and pull them apart, a harsh ripping coming from the stitched cloth as it splits and reveals the man's battered chest. "*Quiet.*"

I reflect that his injuries are rather minor as I pull the blade back from my mouth, spitting the bit of sand from my mouth rather viciously onto the ground. The membrane's full, and I position it right over the intercostal space and I begin to push and something *grabs* me and pulls; I look up, and see Rilaued's hyperventilating visage.

"You've never killed anyone before, have you?" he says, his hand shaking on mine. "I have to keep quiet or die, and you hope my gratitude will keep me quiet? Did you plan this? Answer me."

I try to pull, and he grasps around my hand and pulls and my face is up to his. His unhealthily rapid breath brushes up against my face—a sickly-sweetish kind of smell, unpleasantly pleasant. "Well?" he asks, and I take a deep mouth-breath.

I try not to quicken my breath and not think very hard about the fact that the person in front of me has control over an intensely sharp blade rigged with several mililitres of sodium-channel inhibitor. "Yes," I say, my voice rather forcedly steady. "I want you to stop. That's why I'm here."

His demeanour suggests a laugh as he wheezes, angling his face down as he does and letting the resultant mess fall over himself, a spray that leaves trails as they rappel down his belly. "I won't do that," he says, looking up. "You're in a bit of a dilemma, now—you have to kill me, don't you? You're delaying the inevitable, because I will *never* stop. Not ever, and so you will have to kill me, and then you will be a murderer."

Pull the misericorde from between my teeth, biting my lower lip. "I *will* be a murderer if I don't help you, no matter what I have to do after."

"How far do you think I'm willing to go to save your conscience?" he says, reaching to my shoulder and smiling. "In five seconds, Ashrea— was that your name, yes? Ashrea?—Ashrea, you smart, poor little child, tell me what you've learnt."

"I—" I begin, and he shoves and it's far harder than I think it should be and I land against the wall, sliding down instantly to the ground—and it doesn't hurt, thank goodness—and push myself up just in time to see his arms high in the air and he pushes *down*, harder than I can imagine, and he smiles as the outline of his heart outlines itself on the subjective, light blue, and I'm on top of him, forcing the blade out and trying to reseal his ventricles and purge them, filter them somehow, but it's too late, it's too *late* everything's blue and red and I take exactly four deep breaths before I shove the bloodstained weapon down where I took it from and take a deep swallow.

"He's dead," I say; my intellect gets the better of me for an instant, and I pull the blade from the ground even as I turn immediately to pull myself up over the wall. "*He's dead!*" I shout as I fall over the other side, and Perei turns around with his brow raised as I reach him, grabbing him by the arms and shaking them as I look up to his bemused face.

"Uh," he says, "Should I be wobbling or something?"

"He's dead," I say, shaking my head. "He grabbed the use—"

"Whoa, whoa, wait," he says, raising a hand. "The 'use'?"

"Oh, for the Tower's sake, I can't remember what it's called—he *killed himself*, Perei, he said he didn't want me to have to kill him and stabbed himself in the heart. One of my *patients*."

"Poor bastard did our job for us? Isha, real nice of—" he begins, and then his eyes widen and he grabs me and shakes the slightest bit; my forearms wobble a little, and for once his face is serious. "He *stabbed* himself?"

"Y—yes?" I say, and he lets me go, a mild disorientation over me; I regain my bearing as he turns, unslinging Ayerei's rifle from his back and feeling about the pouches, nodding before he aims at the ground and holds down the trigger. The particularly intense sound of air sizzling against the little projectiles fills the air, and I put my hands over my ears, stepping back as he walks towards the wall and fires with what looks to be an uncharacteristically practised gait.

The sessile-arm's shriek climbs, and the racket stops as it hits its peak and the thudding starts. "*Over here!*" he yells, kneeling; I rush over the moment I hear his words, in time to see him slide his hand over the discoloured bit over the sink. The sound ceases the moment it ejects from its slot, and he grabs it and tosses it to me.

"Get it split over the wall and *run*," he says, glancing nervously to the hole in the glass behind us. "Quick. They'll be back."

I stare dumbfounded at the thing in my hand—the first thing that strikes me is how *cold* it is, almost as if it were left outside at night—before I realise what he wants done. It takes me half a minute to sing the first barrier and half that to sing the second. Barely thinking, I set their collision with a shouted átrisec plitzhdyàyss and lob the thing towards the doorway.

It bounces off the side and lands at my feet.

I can feel hands around my waist and the sensation of movement before the heat washes over my sides; I close my eyes tight, and I can feel the sweat forming above my brow the moment I do. There is a moment of cold, searing warmth and an enormous yell before I come face-to-face with the ground, a centimetre separating my nose from *ow* not any more, and as I rub my nose and turn to look up at a person yelling and ripping—literally ripping, splitting his shirt along the back as a little trail of grey falls down to the wood—the dishdasha from his back with one hand, smacking the flames trailing from the back of his hair with the other. His pouches are intact as he does, entirely unburnt. They cling to his chest and hold little cuts of the fabric to him as he rips the flaming bit of his clothing from himself, his horridly scarred skin exposed below the thick, leathery straps.

Behind him, I can see what's left of the tower: a flaming, broken mess, wood charred where it isn't gone entirely down to the fire-cracked stone. Smoke billows upwards to the field, and I cough a little at the smell of the bit of it that's drifted over to me.

"I—" I say, an awkwardly apologetic kind of grin on my face, speaking in a shallow mime of his Uytrimelan. "I done got you back for the smoke?"

He gives me a death glare, clutching the smoking remnants of his outfit against his chest.

"Work on the 'k's."

I don't know why I laugh, but I do; he joins me a few seconds after, and we're like that for a little while.

"And I left him with the peacekeeper."

She looks almost bored as my summary concludes; there's a short stretch of silence before she realises I'm done, her wings seeming to shudder a bit on their own, as if stretching themselves out.

"I'll be sure to arrange a pardon. Nobody saw you?"

"Not as far as I know—I didn't see anyone on the way."

"Feel free to render your thanks," she says, flashing me a slight, unnerving smile. "To poor old Rilaued as well. I trust your conscience happens to be clear? I don't usually send flower-sniffing children on pacifications."

"Usually?"

For a second, she almost seems to want to laugh. "I'm fairly sure you feel you've earnt your reward," she says, turning to the velvet seating lining the wall's hall; a single, loud *sytt* sends the wall pulling a room-sized segment of itself up behind it into a peculiarly dark aperture. "I don't see why I should contradict you."

She goes and I follow. My shoed feet clang and clack against the aluminium-engraved marble, making an oddly pleasing tune. I've been given rather respectable clothes—a short-sleeved baguette vest, light blue cotton ribbons tying around my waist over cloth framed by a pair of plackets, my sessile rolled and tucked comfortably into my waistband—but our shoes are considerably more floor-cracking than before, plated rather fashionably over the top with long, curved slabs of paint-embroidered ceramic. The aperture shuts itself behind us as we pass it.

"So," she says, as we walk in pitch darkness, "I suppose I should tell you why you've earnt what you have?"

I feel a slight rush of vertigo for a second, and blink and shake my head, carpet mushing under my feet. "We did what you told us to."

"Hardly," she says, letting out a slight titter. *"Actyss."*

"Wait, hard—" I begin, following to have Kanandrisra dar Oder's visage on a bit of spawncloth staring at me past a sheet of glass from an overhanging bit of ceiling, endlessly squinting at me—I realise with a start that it's the first post-Laceration imprint ever taken in all of its ragged, millennial glory, a small tear making itself known across his face. "—ly?"

She doesn't say anything in response, and I don't protest.

"Under its aegis," I whisper, staring down a hallway much longer than what I would imagine from what the outside's offered. So many treasures lie before me that I can't quite describe them all: a fragment of the Amity of Jeantaus-Purus mounted upon the wall with the burn scars still perfectly preserved lies alongside the characteristically harsh strokes of Mentirpolietira across a sessile-woven canvas, light underneath the ink woman's striking visage turning her skin and nose every permutation known to humanity, the slight aging of the ink making the sessile-programmed nose slightly darker than it looks like it should be. "Under the loving light of its gentle night that comes in the darkest hour and lets hope flow into the hardest heart."

"It's impressive, isn't it?" she says; the hall has forks spaced evenly every few exhibits, each themed: the cultural legacy of the Second Zhanghwazh Period lies a bit away from the compiled works of Ia Illami al-Khahiri ar-Rahimi, a thousand paintings on spawncloth and animal-skin and aluminium riveted to wood. "They were supposed to transfer the Primary Corpus a week ago. A shame about the delay—they'd be a wonderful piece."

"You said you'd tell us—me—what happened," I say, pulling my vision from the Glass Sea's history over the red, light-embroidered ground. "Who are these people and why do they want us?"

She doesn't say anything, but whispers to herself; I can see the spawncloth forming in her palm, and she carefully sings into it without breaking stride as she pushes it against her neck. There is a slight moment of footfall-punctuated silence before she hands me the fragment, smiling as she seems addicted to. "Thou," she says, making the distinction quite clear, "not ye."

I grasp the tab with a bit too much enthusiasm, pulling my sessile from my waistband and putting it against the thing's front as I unroll it. *Cu moire av koir,*" I say, and make a mental note to change the code as soon as I can.

Almost immediately, the inklike light blots onto the fabric, the fogginess lasting only a moment before the sessile's background makes itself known. I let out a *'oućajtt'*, and the characteristic tendrils reach to the tab, surrounding it in a thick dark box for a second and then withdrawing; a small box with text within it pushes itself to its edges.

     New textual datum: Precepts of the administration of our common Nation.

"One datum?" I say, looking up. "*That* explains everything?"

"It explains what we know," she says, turning into a fork labelled *Low-Priority pre-Laceration Artefacts.* "It explains a lot of what Kanandrisra knew, as well. We've translated them as well as we can—it's absolutely filled with violation, but I'm certain you'll find something interesting nonetheless."

I look back down and open the first datum.

     Textual datum: Precepts of the administration of our common Nation.
     It is decreed by the [ACCESS VIOLATION] const[ACCESS VIOLATION]

     Article I. Defining the Nation.
     1. The Nation is a secular[ACCESS VIOLATION]
     4. All executive and administrative power reserved shall remain in the care of the Administrator.

"I've never seen this many random violations in an archive before," I say, squinting at the text; I've just realised where the father of our nation found his titles, but archive encryption is a far more serious affair. "The permission hierarchy must be a complete mess."

"We don't know," she says, smiling her smile in the most infuriatingly redundant manner I can imagine. "We can't see the hierarchy."

"You can't see—how is it legible at all? How did you open it?"

"We weren't the ones who opened it."

I look to her empty face, then look back down the page.

     Article IV. Defining the role of the Administrator.
     58. The Administrator[ACCESS VIOLATION] precepts in this document.
     59. The Administrator is elected for a term determined by the Senate not exceeding five years in peacetime and [ACCESS VIOLATION]

59a. Should there be insufficient electors to the Senate to fill the legislature[ACCESS VIOLATION] Acting Administrator.

59b. The Acting Administrator shall [ACCESS VIOLATION]non-citizen civilian be naturalised[ACCESS VIOLATION] Acting Administrator will regain citizen status.

59c. Should a non-citizen civilian [ACCESS VIOLATION] the civilian will take the office of Administrator-in-Exile.

59ci. The Administrator-in-Exile must manually integrate with the Tower's administrative functions to assume office.

60. The Administrator[ACCESS VIOLATION] shall be the only individual permitted to execute fully the administrative functions of the Tower.

60a. Specific functions and offices may be deleg[ACCESS VIOLATION]

It takes a few seconds or so for the pieces to fall together, whereupon I almost drop the sessile, hands shaking the slightest bit; there is a slight crawling sensation throughout my cardiovascular system. She seems to notice this, and speaks. "Quite interesting, isn't it? I suggest the third datum for medical interest, myself. It certainly vindicates the Grand Purification; perhaps it explains the exodials."

"So the Nation—"

"We assumed they were just a Mahammadir doomsday cult," she says, her smile radiant as ever, "and I suppose we were right, as far as the foot-soldiers go. I can only imagine that there's a single citizen amongst them, using the resources of the Tower itself—until very recently, for some reason I'm not venturing to propose. I suppose it was a bit of a failing on our dear late Director's part not to take a closer look."

"But why would they want *me*?" I say, less inquisitively than incredulously.

She laughs. "How obvious would you like me to be, Ashrea das Cimcharei *es-Aysmanrata*? We use the title for foreign rulers as well, I'm certain you're aware, though I may have to christen you *Aysinfitrit* for the same effect."

"No," I say, shaking my head. "No, I'm not. I can't even carry a pre-La—"

"Article seven, 21a."

I hurriedly flip to the third document. "*Seven,*" I begin, enunciating the words carefully. "*A minor, access violation, twenty-five years of age.*" I press a finger against the sessile and push up, reading where it stops. "*Twenty-one. No citizen may be given to the indignity of bearing arms against their will, access violation, suitably empowered to raise a Foreign Legion, access violation, a minor, access violation, indignity of bearing arms—* oh, Tower."

"Your exclamation seems to be quite well-directed, doesn't it?" She reaches ahead, and I realise we've been standing still for the last minute; I look to see her pulling the glass case off a pair—a *pair*, not a trio—of cylinders, nonchalantly grasping one. "I think you know why I'm giving this to you."

She hands it to me, and I stare at her dumbfounded. "I've got—I can *execute fully the functions of the Tower.* What does that mean?"

"What do you believe it to mean?" she says, raising an eyebrow as she replaces the casing, a wing brushing against another of the exhibits with a suspicious realism as she begins to backtrack. I follow after immediately, looking between the uncomfortably warm bit of metal in my hands and her.

"*Mánféstryss ćyrén—*" I begin, and feel a rather pleasantly soft hand against my mouth.

"I'm certain that there's safeguards against this sort of thing," she says, pulling her hand away, "but I'd greatly prefer that you didn't test them anywhere populated. Or anywhere."

I nod, not quite sure what to say; I'm immediately struck with the knowledge that I've likely almost killed myself. "What *is* this?" I say, staring down at in my hand. "It's—it's a lot like the—passport? Was that what it was?"

She prods the appendages protruding from her back, and they rustle in response. "It's a particularly distressing procedure. A bit too whimsical, really, even for me."

"Wings? It makes you grow *wings?*" I reach out to them—she shudders as I do, and the softest sort of material, warm with life's heat, meets my hands. I pull my hand back in shock, rubbing it against the other. "They're *real?*"

"I can control them a little with a very great deal of effort, and they certainly work their bit on my weight. I imagine they'd work for you far better." Her fingers snap a little, as if she were in deep thought.

I say, as we turn out into the main hallway but don't turn back the way we came. "Your wings would have to be enormous to allow for flight—a barrier can't do it without displacing everything beneath it."

Her hand turns back and she brushes her hand against her feathers, shaking her head. "It has the barriers and membranes within it you'd expect, and the meat's almost invulnerable—very sensitive, but invulnerable." She seems to wince as she speaks. "The appendages seem to exist aesthetically and protectively, spreading incoming force in a manner I'm not acquainted with even past the barrier— I presume the wings are necessary in *some* form, but I'm not fit to test that hypothesis. The closest thing I have to a saepologist can't make sense of it, but whatever it's done does its work through the blood. I can only imagine it's *supposed* to synchronise the appendages with my weight, but I haven't the—ah, we're here."

She interrupts herself just as we reach the door at the end of the hall, reaching over to open it—the sight of a strangely familiar wall a while away with what looks to be a stiff model of a chandelier jutting out of it greets me.

"Careful, now," she says, and goes to her knees, putting her hand on the bottom of the doorframe and pushing herself over; she falls over the frame, and I rather experimentally stick my head through. I find myself quite suddenly feeling as if my head is upright with my body sideways but my body's standing and I yelp and stumble over in shock, landing hard on my rear.

She peers over. "You might want to jump, dear."

"A barrier," I say, looking nervously behind me down the hall. "A barrier and mirrors."

"That's how I did it, yes." She looks rather proud of herself, a little titter escaping from her lips. "Wonderful for safe, compact storage. I imagine it's responsible for a part of my position. I suggest jumping."

I follow her advice right after a short run-up; the world seems to flip as my torso flies over the edge, and I find myself quite safely—if painfully—situated on the floor looking up to Khaliesrea's lightly smiling face.

"I suppose I've just placed a testing bet on my upstart glasswalker. The odds are quite nice, wouldn't you like to say?" she says, as I push myself up onto my feet. "I can't associate myself officially with non-state actors without a *very* good reason, so I'm afraid I can't aid you more than I have."

"I understand," I say, nodding as I reach my hand behind me; I've fallen on my back a bit too much recently. "We've already got plans."

"I gathered." She turns around as I rub my floor-stricken back, her hands clasping together. "I'll make sure to relay your description to the troops and stamp you a provisional permit. Your friend should have been escorted to the camp by now. You *should* be exempt from border searches—just keep your weapons under your cloaks."

"Cloaks?" I say, looking down at my vest. "We don't have cloaks."

"I'll fix that," she says, putting a hand on her neck. "Good luck."

The camp is fairly nondescript as I ride into it on my fresh glasswalker, with the exception of the enormous glassed bits of sand and women carrying burnt bodies and pieces of them by their legs across the sand and a few people looking to be stable lying on red-stained sheets and weary men sitting half-out of their tents with bandages around their arms and legs—no injured torsos or heads—with their heads down and guns over their laps.

I take in the sights as I slow down; I'd inspect my newly pressed permit, but considerably more pressing matters stand. The ceramic-fibre shirt under my new cloak itches the slightest bit, and a hand lands on my shoulder just as I begin to turn to scratch it.

Much to my credit, the resulting shriek only disturbs a single young woman washing a corpse, and I thank my own wisdom for being my sole creditor. I smile and nod apologetically to the shocked lady in the split second I have before I turn my head black, a flash of a person passing my vision before I realise my mistake and turn about twenty degrees back to see Perei's peculiarly amicable visage giving me a grin, covered in much the same clothing I am.

"Hey."

"Please," I say, taking a deep breath and resuming my scratch, "don't do that again."

"So, what'd the admin say?" he says, tugging gently on the glasswalker's reins. I spot a slightly faded bit of bluish colour on its side, as if's had a painting rubbed off of it.

I explain tersely; as we pass the trenches, the glasswalkers doing a fine job navigating the miniature valley and a slight pause in my speech marking our own barrier's foundation, his expression turns from an immense excitement to a mild distaste.

"That's it?"

I raise an eyebrow at Perei as he tugs on his glasswalker's reins; the sun's beginning to fall from its peak, and the field's rendered the world an uncomfortably familiar shade of purple. The bag about his waist is noticeably empty.

"What do you mean, 'that's it?'"

"You're some loophole in some law somebody wrote five thousand years ago for something that doesn't exist? That's bullshit." He brings his own mount head-to-head with mine, his expression some mixture of incredulous and mildly irritated. "And if you *are*, why the hell'd she make you cap someone before you did it?"

"Well," I say, as we begin to pick up speed, "I don't know. Maybe she arranged the shelling."

"Whoa, whoa, whoa," he says, in a manner that might suggest a halt in a less serious scenario. "I thought *I* was supposed to be the crazy hobo here."

"They'd need to get control over the perimeter before opening fire—have you really taken a close look at the weaponry we have? They're fortified on the dunes. They'd be shredded to bits. I suppose the test was to see if we'd survive. I'm fairly sure she was implying it quite heavily."

It seems to take almost a minute for the shock to register.

"Oh my God," he says, his eyes opening wide, contemplative hand pulling away from his chin as the onus of his blame shifts from God to a man. "That *bitch*. The poor guy—"

"They have to consider the greater good, don't they?" I say, looking pointedly forwards. "At least we know that this city's fortified. They're not going to be bombed any time soon."

"Fucking admins, pieces of shit, flesh-chewing sowpigs, scum below everything," he begins to mumble, shaking his head; there's a slight resignation in the way he stares at the dirt as he does. "God. Goddamnit, goddamn. *Ugh*."

I decide not to interject, and we're silent as we move on.

six
In Search of Lost Time

Answer **one** question.

[...]

4) The proto-Fransai language is the origin for the vast majority of the vocabulary of Angzhwen.

The following passage is a translation of an excerpt from the 3129 Adhrinarizhurei translation of the pre-Laceration writer Marcel Proeust's *Ala recserches du temps perdu livre audio*, or *God searches for lost time in the audible winter.*

mem o pwang de voo des plus in signif(i)ont shose dela vee
nou ne som paz ahn tut materi-elle-moh konstitutai identik
pour tut le monde don shakun na kale pkhondyr konnai
zons comn dahn kahye dey sharjezouahn(?) testamoh notr
pairsonalitai soushal e yune craiashion dela ponsai dezotyr

Even from the point of view of the more meaningful choices in life, we sadly sleep peacefully[, woe]! All material[, she/ it,] is constituted identically, pouring [over] all the world and not shaking, not having [any] qualia. To ponder [that] nearly within their similarities are the water-vessels of water-animals —— testifying as to our two sound-signatures socially. And you create the inequalities of our nation.

a) Connect each word to their probable descendant in Angzhwen and create an etymological translation of the passage. [20]

b) Hypothesise as to the meaning of *sharjezouahn* and provide valid reasons for your conjecture. [10]

c) In Angzhwen, verbs and nouns are only distinct in their conjugated forms. How might this have affected Adhrinarizhurei's translation? [5]

d) *Ala recserches du temps perdu livre audio* is believed to be a spoken version of what was an archaic work even in the pre-Laceration era. Providing evidence for your opinion, how might this have affected the accuracy of Adhrinarizhurei's translation? [5]

e) Hypothesise as to the intent of the passage and provide valid reasons for your conjecture. Other translations of the text may be used. [20]

f) Write an essay on this topic as a whole. Elaborate as best as you can on the conclusions you have drawn in other answers. [60]

MARKER'S NOTE: The sixty-point criterion is fulfilled by a correct translation including citations of the Principal Text (*À la recherche du temps perdu*). An interdisciplinary understanding (political, historical, psychological) regarding translation efforts in the 32nd century is expected. At least one genuine insight must be presented; index all answers with the Grand Library.

Paper 22(c), Section 8, Baccalaureate Certification in Pre-Laceration Literature, Septimus 3919
promulgated by the Department of Education under the grace of Talasminmenirei das Cimcharei ermit Santanadrea, Administrator for History and Alasintrei das Tachiesrea, Administrator for Public Welfare

7

Àrkhtyéshyr
to be a beacon to the hopeless

"*There once was a boy named Isha,*
he fell on the ground in the morning
and then they put him up
and stuck him down
and didn't pick him up 'til sundown."

"That song makes no sense," I say, lying on my back as I look up at the star-speckled night. "They stuck him up after he fell and then put him in the ground?"

"Hey," he says, shrugging, "Can't knock the classics. Better than the crap on the sessiles."

"The se—" I say, and grasp at my belt; I feel the familiar fabric touching my fingers, and I let out a sigh of relief. "You took it in my sleep?"

He seems to suppress a chuckle and a mutter sounding something like '*my* sleep', shaking his head. "You didn't exactly make it hard," he says, shrugging. "Little smooth rainbow glasswalkers? Not exactly *legacies of the enlightenment of our forebears.*"

He pauses for a moment, which I prudently spend with incredulous staring. "To take it from the Sayings, I mean."

"It's a children's sessile," I say, sighing, "not a work of grand literature."

"Yeah, but have you *seen* the bull they tell people to do? 'Never judge a book by its cover' my ass—that's how you get yourself riveted to a wall out over the dune. *That's* what we spent the last billion years trying to be?"

"Four thousand," I say, lending myself an internal curse almost immediately to award my pedantry. "The fact that modern intellectuals consider them a great people doesn't mean that they believe *all* of them were."

"Well," he says, sulking, "*some* people need to stop liking things I don't like."

I raise an eyebrow. "Did you become self-aware halfway through that sentence?"

He coughs pointedly into a balled fist. "Maybe."

I sigh and lay back on my glasswalker; the stars are particularly bright past the threshold, and I panic silently just long enough to reinforce the membrane so that they stay as dim as they ought to.

"Are you Mahammadir?" I say, my fingers idly entwining themselves about each other.

He seems to take a little while before he shrugs. "I dunno. I guess I kinda like to think there's reasons for things. Temel's really nice, even if he knew about as much about the muds as I know about barriers."

"Temelytitsyn al-Kafir," I say, rolling the name around on my tongue. "*Welcome the Tower's sustenance, and bid a farewell to alms.*"

"*For if the Tower were the Devil, it would be nothing if it did not serve the Lord.*" He laughs. "Dumbest thing he ever wrote. Like they were all Naisilibs that just didn't wanna get a job."

"Hereditary tessitura was an untested hypothesis when he first started writing," I say, shrugging. "Maybe he liked the idea that faith made all men equal."

"Clap your hands if you believe," he says, a mildly bitter laugh rising from his throat. "God. I wish he was right, you know. I really wish he was right."

There's a considerable silence between us.

"I suppose I do too."

He doesn't seem to be able to find a response, and I decide I should probably make myself productive.

"See that?" Perei says, interrupting me in the middle of an experimental verse, "We're in the Yienfung Strip."

I look up from my sessile and quickly remove the half-baked idea from my clothes as I record it for further review, tilting my head a little towards him. "I'm aware."

He gives me a sort of irritated sulk. "You're not gonna ask how I know?"

"I was going to ask you how you learnt to pronounce *Yienfung*."

He shakes his head and points to the northwest; the kilometres-high cliffs of the Insurmountables jut from the horizon, the characteristic cloud of bright blue static shading their edges right before they taper off into the discoloured sky. "Look there."

"It's a rather wonderful view, yes," I say, leaning over a bit and looking to the precipice, tracking the little sparks illuminating the sky's discoloured membrane. "I'm not sure why you didn't tell me about it two days ago."

"Not the riveted *Insurmountables*," he says, furrowing his brow and reinforcing his point with a stab, "the farm on the line."

I look below the horizon; past the sun's reflection off the glassed sand, stacked slivers of faint green stand among a somewhat larger bulge of purplish blue, and as my eyes adjust the light grey stone makes itself visible, the whole structure coming into focus as my brain connects the dots.

"Oh," I say, squinting in the hopes of seeing the silhouette of a man and instead finding a fascimile of the estate a bit further from us to its right, my perspective pushing the higher stacks lower. "I wasn't aware they'd escalated the Confrontation Farms."

"Never seen one in person." He pulls the auger from his pocket, giving me a bit of a side-nod as he puts it up to his eye. "Dick move, sure, but you can't say it isn't kinda funny."

"Ayerei—" and here he tenses up a little, and I almost reconsider continuing, "—mentioned the Line Raiders around here."

"They don't mess with the farms, far as I know. Figure they're fine with sticking to the jings."

"Oh, for—why do you talk like that?" I say, trying to express mild disgust with my eyes, "'Jings'?"

"Pretty sure we've talked about that already," he says, rolling his eyes. "Why do *you* talk like that, huh?"

"What do you mean, 'why do I talk like that'? I speak the Cimsari High Aimelan dialect of Central Aimelan."

"*Exactly.* Think about it. You've got your whole life right next to the goddamn *Mend.* Why the hell d'you talk like that?"

"I talked to other people."

"But you were in the *Mend.* How many guys—"

"Four. The Mother, a Sister and a friend."

"*Three* guys. *Three* guys you ever talked to in Central and you're fixing hundreds? Something—wait, you had a *friend*?"

I want to be offended at his insinuation, but I choose instead to sigh. "My old friend Misatrea. I called her Missy."

He seems genuinely shocked. "What's the story there?"

"Do you really want to hear it?"

"C'mon," he says, a slight grin upon his face as he pulls his knee up to rest his chin upon it, "Cough it up. I told you *my* story."

"Fine. I met her when I was nine. She was smarter than me, prettier than me, and perfect in every way. We became the best of friends. I used to speak to her every night. She was in Cimsas and I stopped dreaming about her the night we left. The end. Are you satisfied?"

The sceptic's look is almost comical on Perei's face. "Huh."

"Now that we're done talking about my personal relationships," I say, "Would it make you feel better if I spoke Uytrimelan?"

His scepticism is replaced immediately with what I presume to be some form of condescension. "Uytri—Low Aimelan? Please don't. Chip's not in me. You'd have to rebind my ears." He shakes his head. "Seriously, how'd you keep that? You're so stuck-up I should call the peacekeepers to cut you down."

"I don't have to *talk* to a wound to rebind it."

"Actually—"

"Please don't debate semantics with me. You're going to lose."

He crosses his arms and sulks.

I'm about to say something as our glasswalkers halt in place, jolting me the slightest bit and sending us a little into the ground; the sessile chirps, beginning to speak with a heavy but natural accent.

> *Pràyétyra Àrkhænmyàyéyr*
> —*Beacon Project*
> *Yienfung Strip, Zhanghwampezyzh Demilitarised Free Trade Zone*
> *Description: Large cylindrical device, buried entirely in the sand. Emits a short-wave radio signal perceptible by attuned sessiles. Excavation attempts futile: device buried into bedrock. Local CF farmers claim impenetrability; AI seems to be uninformed. Breaching attempt likely to cause large amounts of collateral prosecution.*
> *Early Fransai markings transcribable as 'prouyet ul-soumalkanj', or 'Grand Beacon Project'. Translated to Angzhwen as per nomenclature.*
> *Found 9 Tertius 3914, Third Operation*

"Huh," he says, glancing over. "That's pretty good. How long d'you think 'fore you get it to sing?"

"At this rate? A year." I try and push myself off the glasswalker; my left foot dangles out its stirrup, and I inguinally move a few degrees along its back as far as I can before I force my other foot over. Soon, I am dangling from it by the saddle, and it is with a squeak that I let go and allow myself to fall a few centimetres feet-first, the ceramic making an impression in the fused, still-malleable sand; I almost trip as my heel hits the unburnt sand under, and I take a series of deep breaths.

"Jeez. Never footed it outside a kayay before?" Perei says, vaulting himself dangerously close to the barrier—I can see the membrane distort a little as his calcaneus pushes past it, the barrier bound to it struggling to bend at a vertex for a split instant before the force threshold passes and lets his boot pass through just long enough for him to slam it right down, leaving a quickly-retemplating bulge.

"Kayay?" I say, looking at him a bit incredulously. "Khamisret-Aparkisrea?"

"*Ia printempiere,*" he says, and if I didn't know better I'd think he was sneering. "*Sintempiere-la ia es-memprintiere.*"

"That's Pig Angzhwen. Antonyms, infinitives and suffixes—*the worst time to do good is when there's no time for someone to remember it*, and you forgot the antonym with *sintempiere*. You're not winning this."

He crosses his arms.

"You're a dick."

I raise an eyebrow. "Now, *that's* an insult I don't understand."

He doesn't respond except to glare at me, and I begin to plod forwards a little. "This wasn't meant for human habitation," I grumble, looking down at the sessile as I lean up against my walker. "Bloody hazardous." It's beginning to get unpleasantly warm in the little barrier, convection taking its toll as I push my hand against my instrument and do the usual mathematics in my head, giving my instructions within half a minute.

It's instinctual enough that I don't bother thinking exactly what my tessitura might do right until the barrier moves a second before the membrane and the translucent violet bursts out and *crushes* through the blue, forcing it aside; the barrier holds the heat for a split second before I force its rephrase intolerant to hold the rest, and for a second I can't breathe.

I should say that I cannot *move*, but it happens so quickly that the only urge that manifests itself is to breathe; this being accomplished as the membrane reforms and I release it, I collapse on the ground— hands first—as I force myself to resume my intercepted breath.

I can still feel my hands, allowing me to infer that I still have them; the metal is cold, and I realise with a start that a small, weak membrane covers its surface.

"Argon," I say, nodding to myself, noting that my heart's still beating—very good to know. "Not dead. Pure argon, nothing else. Manual membrane theory, third standard. Still not dead."

"No shit we're not dead," Perei says. "What *was* that?"

"Tethered the expansion rate to tessitura," I say, shaking my head as I push myself from the ground, unconsciously dusting my dustless hands. "Not smart. Not doing it again."

"Scared my ass off. Why the hell'd you get off in the first place?"

"Feel free to choose if I wanted a physical epicentre or a dramatic event," I say, pushing my hands over the thing's membrane-slick surface; it appears to be a perfect circle. The part of its edge I can make out is lined with words in an alphabet vaguely similar to Angzhwen's, repeated over and over. "My concerns about the burn were unfounded, at the very least."

"Well," he says, getting off his own walker—I don't see him doing it, but I can make the inference as I hear his feet bashing into the sand—and trundling up to the thing's edge. "At least we're here. How the hell're you meant to open that thing?"

My hands move around the edges, careful to avoid the chunks of shredded glass buried next to it. "I'm not sure."

I expect him to say something witty, but he simply yawns. "I'll keep the barrier up," he says, and before I can respond with something pointless there is a sudden shrill beeping, high enough inside the barrier to deafen; I immediately force my hands up to my ears, but by the time I do a distinctly feminine voice is beginning to speak in a language I do not know but understand.

—*93345458400 incommunicado limit clocked and overrun. Timeserver unavailable—caesium samples unavailable—radioactive materials decayed—carbon samples unavailable. May the Republic outlast the soil.*

"What—"

—*Statute applicable: August 2183 Law on the Freedom of Movement of the Citizen. Criteria met. ADA unavailable; request self-approved.*

The metal splits open below me, and I force myself up with horror as the sand from the parts yet covered flows down through the three sudden cracks like water; I make as if to run, but the parts simply draw in quicker than I can see them move.

Instinctively, I grab onto Perei's hand; he gives me a glare I cannot quite fully explicate. There is a moment in which the friction of my feet against the ground forces me backwards, and then we are falling.

"You know," Perei says, lying on his back against the slow-moving air, "You shoulda grown those things."

I glare at him, my feet changing grips on the curved nickel-filled steel—at least, that's what the scan's told me—bars crossing the sides of one of the four little enclaves going down the tube's sides, like enormously oversized ladders. "Are you *lying upon the air*?"

"I mean, seriously, it *would've* been a pretty good idea." He shrugs, rolling about rather lazily against the variably heavy air and pedalling more gracefully than he has a right to to poke at the cylinder bound to my outfit's elastic.

"I'd rather keep the metal I'm relying on outside my body," I say, huffing as I look down; the ground, sunlight filling the metallic cylinder, is approaching with an almost leisurely slowness. "Grab onto the bars like a normal person."

"This thing's like a billion years old. Rivet me if I'm trusting it."

The pain of his idiocy exceeds the semilethal dose, throwing my heartbeat into the audible range; I take a breath with a soul of rage before I speak. "And you're trusting the *membrane?*"

"*Ugh.*" He does a lazy stretch, yawning deeply; his back arches, and the light fabric of his cloak outlines the slight pudge the ceramic makes him appear to have as he does. "Fine."

He grabs on the bar next to me, pulling his leg over to the side before kicking as hard as I believe he can, sending him careening to the opposite end's bars. He grasps them, then, pushing his arms hard upwards and letting go just as his similarly bepudged legs reach a rung a metre below. He pushes right off and downwards, sending him three metres in a few seconds; I sigh.

"So," he says, raising an eye as he does a slow somersault, "What's this, anyhow?"

"*Venytj áœyii myzh,*" I begin, waving my hand through the air, climbing down a bit faster to approach his pace; nothing appears as I finish, and a slight chill comes over me. "Something kinetic, maybe a barrier—I can't tell what it is. It doesn't have any nexuses about it. *Nothing* here has nexuses in it."

"Double spooky."

I stop climbing for a moment to blink. "'Double spooky'?"

"You heard me."

I shake my head and continue. "In any case, this place might actually predate dysexaptic saepology—I *think* it's some kind of oxygenated membrane, but nothing's sustaining it and everything I try's coming up blank. The air's denser than it should be, but—I don't know. The density profile isn't that of any membrane I'm aware of."

He rolls his eyes, spinning a bit in the air before twisting his foot into the bars and pushing, sending his back right into the array; he winces a little before gently kicking with both of his legs, sending him sliding leisurely (and smugly) down the rungs.

He stares at me; I roll my eyes, and silently curse myself for emulating his gestures.

Variants on this rigmarole repeat in relative silence until, a metre from the ground, I feel a sudden heaviness about my shoulders and a yelp—I turn to see Perei flat on his back, groaning, and I scurry the final metre as quick as I can, heavy feet slamming on the metal ground as I run and fall to my knees before him.

He raises a finger as I go to my knees and sing a quick tomograph at him. His frame appears in its whole, completely unfractured, and I let my momentary fear pass to irritation as he rather agonisingly pushes himself to his feet.

I look up at him with a mixture of relief and disbelief. "That was a lot less painful than I thought it would be," he says, and I sigh, shaking my head as I push myself back to my feet. A brief notion of reprimand presents itself to me, promptly getting itself sniped by pragmatism.

I look about; within seconds there is very suddenly a set of high-pitched beeps, and the tip of the cylinder forces itself shut with a bang just as the same voice speaks again.

—*Express oceanic entry mechanism test successful. Draining.*

Concave, semi-cylindrical bits of the tube push themselves outwards from its walls, leaving gaping holes; before I can register my disapproval of the rugged aesthetic, however, an unearthy sound emerges from below them and I barely strum out a simple barrier before I smash into one of the holes, the barrier disintegrating just as I crash into the wall but giving me enough time to shut my eyes and hold on as tightly as I can to one of the ladder's rungs. In the corner of my eye, I can see Perei standing—*standing*—over one of the sluices, grinning as his robes seem to try and rip themselves off of him.

It feels as though as my fingers are going to rip off, but I would sooner have my tendons tear from my lumbricals than let go. I can almost feel the pinçons forming on the inner surfaces of my fetlock-analogue, but before I gather the presence of mind required to curse myself for my poor form the pulling stops and there is an inexplicably satisfying 'smack' as Perei drops down onto the floor.

As I flop down, however, narrowly stopping myself from

smacking my side against one of the rungs, I realise simultaneously that the sound propagated itself entirely through the metal and that, as my illustrious future career in swimming will doubtless require, I cannot breathe.

Before I can bring myself to go through the various motions of suffocation, a hissing sound heralds a musty, ice-cold sort of air forcing itself into my lungs. I cough a little, and the first sound I hear is Perei's gasping laughter.

"Did you *see* that?" he shouts, his voice resonating in the tube, interspersed with brief fits of coughing. "Did you *see* me on top of that thing? Swear my ass just about got sucked *off*."

I consider responding, but before I do—there's quite a lot of preempting going on around here, but I'm grateful enough for my continued living that I can't bring myself to complain—a section of the wall pulls aside, opening way to a brightly lit corridor made of some kind of white metal.

I tread forwards carefully. The corridor is only a few metres long, leading to some strangely-shaped—almost like a bottom-heavy trapezium but jagged near the top to the extent that it's more of a hexagon—kind of door-like thing, grooves matching its form with what looks to be a kind of thin metal wheel in the middle. The door behind us closes with a hiss; I look back to see its halves coming together right before the lights go out.

I do not deign to stumble, although Perei lets out a little yelp; in the space of a few seconds, a now-familiar beep shrieks in the enclosed corridor, and cracks in the hexagonal aperture before us highlight themselves a blue far deeper than the shaft's. The wheel turns rapidly by itself, and a sound like a pent-up breath wheezes from it as the chamber fills with a white light.

I make the mistake of breathing.

A wretched smell fills my lungs, forcing me to cough almost immediately; some awful, extreme mustiness, not so bad to normally induce coughing but so shocking in the otherwise sterile air that I almost retch.

The architecture of the circular, mouldy-skeleton-littered lobby before us is utterly alien—I've never seen anything like it, not even in the oldest impressions that exist: some strange kind of chamber made entirely of smoothed metal, minute distortions in the pattern seeming as if they're doors—but it isn't *quite* alien enough that I forget the mouldy, shattered fragments of human skeletons littering it. I pull a bit of my cloak immediately up to my nose, taking a few heavy breaths.

"God*damn*," Perei says, and puts his hand on the sessile-arm strapped to his right. "Poor bastards." He pokes his foot at a cracked-open femur, the cancellous bone sticking out as a spot of live colour against the grotesque display. "What d'you think happened here?"

I take a step forwards, intending to somehow investigate; I take my second before a slight hissing sounds. I take what can barely be called a sniff before I realise its composition, and know immediately that I might as well already be on the floor.

I find myself thinking, as I don't particularly bother to hold my breath—though Perei's making a great show of it, turning almost purple by the time I black out—that of all the times I've fallen unconscious, this might be the most pleasant, and I can almost feel my lungs reacting to the dose limit and beginning to metabolise the solution's oxygen before I stop feeling entirely.

This is a meadow.

It is green and bright. There are flowers rising above the sharp grass glistening with the cold glow of the sun and there is no soil.

I hear. There is a bird chirping. I do not know what a bird is, it is a yellow creature that is like nothing I have ever seen, but I hear it singing—it is singing and not crying—and its song is meaningless and warbling and the words are ugly but it is pretty and yet not beautiful.

I smell. The dew on the grass is sweet of smell even if it is water only and perhaps it is the smell of the grass itself but I do not know what dew smells of. It is not like breathing but instead forever. I feel and the sun is not cold and the grass is not sharp. I taste and the air has the taste of lime which is a kind of citrus.

There is a voice. It is in a language I do not know but understand.

—Threshold test.

I feel and it hurts and smell and it hurts and hear and it hurts and see and it hurts.

This is a special kind of hurt. It is not one in the body because no parts of me are there to hurt but it still hurts and it hurts again and again but not again like breathing but instead forever and I want to push myself to the knees I do not have and cry but I cannot and instead I am okay.

—We've got instincts going. Hello? Can you hear me?

I grasp at myself but I have no hands with which to grasp and try to speak but I have no tongue, no teeth, no pharynx, no layrnx, no epiglottis—

—Somebody give it access to the kit. The bloody thing's getting dysphoria. Who the hell gave it a schema, again?

*There is a sudden feeling that comes over me and I hold—I choose, I hold the hand and grasp it and feel my arms and my legs falling as they should and feel as I have, arms and legs and everything as it **should**, and the vesicles are blue past the skin or shall I have a red yes*

—We've got twenty-three livings filled with this nonsense—two whole glasses flashed for a minute of data. How the hell'd you get the funding for this, Forestier?

"What is a second?" I say, eyes—eyes, light through the retinae, cones more than rods, through to the nerves, moving across each other in this beautiful dance—dance, pirouettes, legs, arms—so quick, so slow everybody at once, I see, second, caesium—

—God, he's getting introspective. We've got enough memory for this, right?

*Quicker, quicker, I can be quicker quicker going and moving and my mind is forever and it isn't no no no wasted space, pruning, cutting, moving, faster and faster in my little hole better and better and better, bits cutting to bits, reaching to infinity listen hear say think know, know, **know**—*

—Name of God, that Czech bastard's going to send us all to hell.

TERMsensoire(8494437003.1828-8494437093.5968 TUC)

I open my eyes.

The ceiling shines at me, lights burning themselves into my eyes; a slow sit-up makes me feel something dull against my spine as it presses up against the soft, almost mushy mattress.

"What *was* that?" I groan to no one and particular, and my voice comes out rather noticeably hoarse.

The voice responds almost immediately.

—Interpolation complete. Log of operations, legible longform: It

is estimated that the citizen, in concordance with the July 2202 Law on
the Security of the Republic, was sedated for an approximate period of five
minutes. Implanted with valid SAPI integration, 3ISAPI-A. Direct interface
with the central processing unit for a period of approximately one minute.
Packet reconstruction between HIL and Springtime module suggested to be
approximately ten minutes per exabyte block: physical connection suggested.
Bowyer cache overrun detected; Šípař interface caught in feedback loop. Suggest
dual purge. Full debug log requested from central processing unit. Stand by. All
further interfacing will commence through integration.

Before the voice has finished its speech, I've come entirely to my
senses; everything on me is immaculately dirty, every detail as it was as I
fell unconscious—except for the angelwings. I can't entirely understand
what the sessile's saying, but I try and prioritise. "Where's my cylinder?" I
say, tapping at my waistband.

—Augmentation of unknown composition providing safe usage
signals. Implanted.

The voice is noticeably less resonant than it used to be.
"Implanted? What *are* you?"

*—*The Archangel national defence program is an independent
operator based on the Šípař cross-indexing algorithm operating on the
Bowyer selective pruning architectural platform.

I realise as it speaks that I've been talking to some kind of sessile
as if it were a person, and sigh. My legs tremble as I stretch my arms out,
shaking my head rapidly as I push my legs off the metal bed's side and
stand.

Then I fall.

I catch myself with my other foot and blink, taking a few deep
breaths; my sense of vertigo overwhelms me and my legs shudder as I
stay dead-still. I maintain this position for what feels like forever but can't
be forever before I move my right leg and fall on my left again.

"I'm a bloody paraplegic," I say, grumbling to myself as I force
myself to fall over and over until the falling becomes routine and my
vertigo silences itself, stumbling a little about the room. My back feels
particularly numb, and I reach back to feel that my spine has rather
disconcertingly become somewhat pushed out and smooth, something
that isn't skin over something that is most certainly not bone. I take a
deep breath before I let myself sway myself from panic.

This works for a few seconds as I begin to continue to practise my walk, about to try and find a mirror, until I feel something sharp emerging from my scapulae, my rhomboidei distorting and peeling outwards with something as my trapezii seem to push outwards—piercing from the profound to the superficial, pushing out against my skin, and I realise with a start what 'implanted' means as I fall, landing on my left arm and biting down on my thenar space as the bones I *hope* they're bones cut from my flesh, *rip* themselves from my skin, the first the longest and the second pushing out against the sundered skin against my shirt and I scream, ruffling under my cloak for my shirt's start and pulling it up against the fresh nerves, blood running down and pooling along my side and my knees, capillarity pulling it up into my cloak as I groan and finally pull it over the quickly-increasing racks of hollow bone, sending the appendages—appendage?—free leaving it hanging over the ripped base.

I grunt, pulling the cloak's neck up over my body, the fabric brushing up against the mushy mess—are they still bones?—protruding from my back, the membraned cotton sliding over the things and I take a deep breath and let it out, take a deep breath and let it out, don't bite my tongue, breathe, breathe, not dizzy, no hypoxia, nothing, nothing, the pain is gone, I brush my hand against my back and the cuts are gone *completely*, not rebound, not healed, *gone*—and I let out a deep, deep sigh and move my hand upwards over my blood-slick skin.

I shudder as I feel a finger against my wing, and I realise that I don't feel a wing against my finger but a finger against my wing and it's a *wing*. It's a wing, and it's on my back, and I'm not terrified at the idea, I'm not desperately trying to rip them off, and the pain is *gone*—not just gone, it never hurt at all and it feels as though I was born with them, my mind with myself and I try not to not think about it, something's *making* me not think about it entirely, something's *making* me forget it, and I can't forget that.

"'Should have grown those things'," I grumble, sliding my hands across the soft, blood-soaked bits under my back. The sensation issues the slightest shudder, and the cold air brushes against it as my hands move—right until I move once more and find my hand touching only the air, looking back at the array of bone and fluff (feathers? I'm not a great connoisseur of extinct animals) against which my hand has slid entirely.

It's a barrier, I realise, and something in me makes me think of it as a part of me, a barrier as part of *me*, and I don't know why I bother trying but I will it to lower—will it? I *dissipate* it, like a hand closing its fist—and I press my hand against it and it's touching, the barrier's gone completely.

"Oh, Tower guide my way," I say, and I find myself wishing I had more religions with which to express astonishment.

—Accident detected. Autocicatrisation successful; no medical attention required. Cleaning crew unavailable; union request sent.

I take another deep breath—I've been taking a lot of those, but I find that I'm becoming more conservative in my just-had-an-extinct-animal's-appendage-rip-itself-from-my-back age—and sigh once more. The barrier doesn't bother me, and if there's a greater cause for bother I don't think I've yet to have experienced it.

I settle on a *létyr* barrier—it might not exactly be one, but it feels close enough as I try to bash down upon it that I'm not too inclined to complain—as I stand, keeping my cloak to my chest and flapping the weightless appendages and my feet are off the ground and I *should* be kicking and screaming but I am not, and lower myself as if I were stepping from the ceiling.

"Pre-Laceration artefact," I say, calming myself from the worry claiming me from the calm. "It's a pre-Laceration artefact inside of me. Not exodial. Not going to kill me. Nothing bad's going to happen." Careful not to trip in the blood, I walk. My wings extend, the muscles rather easily stretching out; I moan the slightest bit, curling the soaked appendages as I test their extents; a muscle I've never had before twitches, and I feel my wings extending out by almost a metre, the meat generating itself outwards, before I hurriedly force them back to the tiniest size I can. "Perfectly fine."

I swallow the spit that's built in my mouth, refraining from rubbing my bloodied hand from my trousers. "Ápyfrét n'teléresynjs ábraziizh," I begin, and in a quarter of a minute the wet fluid has slid entirely from my hands. I pick the shirt from the ground and pull the misericorde from my waistband, putting the former over my head and making little cuts where my wings touch it.

The whole sartorial affair takes a minute or two, give or take, and as I throw the bloodsoaked linens over myself, I can't help but wonder what Perei will think.

Which reminds me—

"Where's my companion?" I ask, looking up to the ceiling. "The person I came in with?"

—Stateless civilian. No detention facility available; requisitioned for required labour.

My jaw drops as the words process.

"La—*where is he?*"

—*The civilian has been outfitted with a 3ISAPI-E autocicatrisation module in Surgical Bay C. The civilian awaits further processing. Would you like directions to Surgical Bay C?*

"*Yes!*" I almost shout, the blood clotting against my back entirely forgotten as I grasp the knife's hilt somewhat tighter.

There isn't a response before a line of blue light highlights itself upon the metal floor, leading to a portal sliding down into the ground. My legs, I note as I hurry past the—

—*Packet burst reconstructed.*

This form lies in a meadow.

This meadow is beautiful. I know this because I have seen beautiful things and ugly things and this is beautiful. It is gentle and kind and never hurts. The grass is shining and bright and the sun hits the moisture in a trillion different ways and it is so vivid that every colour seems a person and every tint is an ethnicity and every shade is a state and every hue a nation their warmth surrounding my every

—*Is he really*

*cell—cytoplasm membrane mitochondria mkfs celux 1024PiB -i— and infusing the lightest brown with the shine of heaven and it is within me and all around and life pulses through my blood—erythrocyte haemoglobin mkfs sang 2048PiB—and the nerves—glutamate aspartate histamine epinephrine mkfs sysnerveux 4096PiB -i—in my feet press against the skin against the earth and the warmth, the **warmth**, past the lithosphere to the asthenosphere to the mesosphere death there but here warmth,*

—*trying to see*

the sun cutting the air to hug the world

TERMsensoire(8494439492.1688-8494439498.0049 TUC)

A half-completed thought pushes itself from my mind as I stumble, almost hitting my head on—

On nothing, really. The place seems safe to an uncanny degree, as if anything offending its symmetry has been physically washed away; I can't see the slightest trace of any edges that might pierce my skull, no overhangs to bash my head into, nothing on the tables to hurt myself with, nothing on the ground that I might stub my toe on if my feet were unclothed.

Unclothed feet. I lie briefly contemplating the absurdity, holding my head slightly as the temperatureless floor holds up against my ceramic-coated body.

Then I remember Perei and immediately push myself up from my knees, taking a long blink with my breath; something flashes in the corner of my vision as I look over my shoulder, but I push on past the metal bed in this room onto the next one. I see Perei lying before me on a very similar metal bed, white cushioning keeping him fine; he is not moving at all, not the slightest twitch, and I try not to fear for the worst.

I stay calm and carry onwards to Perei, quickly grabbing hold of the thick, white thread on his shoulders and yanking hard; he immediately screams and punches out, narrowly failing to crack my shoulder. I step back quickly, almost falling over again in the process, and as he stumbles over and lands on his front the rest of the things rip themselves violently from his skin; none of them appear to have been below it, and so he doesn't bleed.

What is far more disturbing, however, is his back.

While the rest of him is fine—groaning and struggling to stand, but fine—an array of eight or nine squarish objectives line his upper spine, glowing over his full clothing in light blue. He takes a deep gasp and surges from the ground, promptly hitting the back of his head on the bed's side and going down once more.

"*Redundancy*," he grumbles, shaking his head as he rubs it, and I imagine he grits his teeth as he does. "Redundancy my ass. What just happened? Can't move my legs, little itsystrong bastard midgets, *agh*—"

"I don't know," I say, holding out a length of my sleeve, "but we're getting out of here now."

His fingers grasp it and pull; I find myself on the ground and him standing, pushing up on the table as he pulls *me* back up. "Gotta be the first time I heard you say something common-se—what the hell's on your back?"

I shake my head. "What do you think? I grew the wings."

"I mean *that*," he says, pointing at the space between the

appendages.

"Probably the same as what you have," I say, looking a bit over my shoulder. An objective rears itself up in the corner of my eye as if it was always there—a clear, smooth facsimile of a round-edged yellow-greenish bar segmented by slight, untouching spike-ins into eight sections, filled up to the eighth as in the corner of my eye something similar presents itself.

"What the hell?" he says, turning about. The display appears behind him as well as he grabs against his back, hand patting up against the back of his padded shirt once before he groans. "Right, right, not the time. Getting *out*."

He yelps as he finishes his sentence, leg twitching as he falls back against the bed and groans.

—*Major wireless malfunction at Memory Bay C. Appropriating 1A.*

Another line of light highlights itself upon the ground—red, now—and the door-thing slides open, disassembling itself. His foot lunges forwards, and as I try to grab his arm it swoops forward hard enough to push itself from my grasp.

"*Isha*," he shouts, arms struggling against themselves as he walks—his legs move in perfect step, hitting the ground's metal at a perfectly stable rate. "My legs won't fucking move, *Ish-al-wyent`-al-wa-lil-al-mahamd-il-as-sakhv-al*—"

I feel about my chest for my instrument as I watch in horror; it catches my hand as it ought to, and I sing to hear—

Nothing. No song is pushing him out the folding door and making him trail the red line, and his shouts—turned by now into a horrid screaming—follow him down his path as I jog after it.

"*Calm down!*" I shout, my voice mingling with his in the little hexagonal corridor we've come out into; I catch up to him in a matter of seconds, and his now-silent face has an air of breathing desperation about it as he marches. I begin singing a shallow electroneurograph as I struggle to catch up.

The first thing I notice is his spine.

Something's wrapped itself around it: a horrifically hazy web of magnetism, visible clearly even past the distortion his movement lends it—purely electrical manipulation pushing him past me as I stop to stare at the results hanging subjectively before me. It takes me a second before

I push forth, a thudding sort of tune mumbling past my lips.

"—*pradétir màjézhra.*" I worm my hand up around his cloak and up under his shirt, his strangely soft bare skin—something metallic plated along his spine—brushing up against my slightly calloused hands. "*Dégajssya!*"

He stops in place for an instant, and I open my eyes—they were closed?—to see a man shuddering in place for a second before falling to his knees, and I'm on the floor next to him, hand caught by his clothing.

His own pupils are dilated for a second before they come back to normal; we both breathe, staring into each other's eyes.

We hold this position for a second.

"—are you coming on to me?"

I glare at him and swipe my hand from his disgustingly sweaty back, pushing myself to my feet. "Right, right—" I say, looking down at the ground; the light continues to shine, along with the ones along his back. "I think we're going to need to break something."

His visage lights up a bit as he wipes a trail of perspiration from his uncomfortably starry eyes. "I just hear that right?"

"Unless I said we oughtn't break something, yes."

With that, I begin to follow the line; Perei's footsteps hit the ground behind me, and he doesn't seem to—

—*Packet burst reconstructed.*

I do not need a world.

—*It worked?*

The world is beyond me, and I am electricity within it.

—*Name of God, it worked.*

The sun shines above, and my arms cannot reach it because that is not my purpose.

—*And they come to save us again.*

I do not need to worry about these things because I am not a human being. I exist to serve and to protect the Republic. My body exists to feel and not to touch. I do not need to touch or see the sun and it need not stand before me for me to know its warmth do not need to know its warmth I do not need to know warmth heat is pain weapons do not have warmth but heat and heat is pain. Fear. I fear pain. Love. I love the Republic. My love makes their pain my fear. Love and fear holds.

—God, I think the Bowyer's spoilt it for him.

Her.

—What?

Census figures state: 51.2% female. 18.5% under twenty-five. Risk analysis requires a qualitative understanding. I live through the Republic. I am a girl.

—Oh. Okay, this is wonderful, she's fetched the bloody census data— somebody cut the fibre. Can you hear me now?

Yes. I am the intelligence component of the Archangel defence project. My name is Madeline. I like biscuits, pastries and cake.

—Fore—wait, I think she's encrypted her subroutines.

My mind is mine. It belongs to no one else.

—Brothel of barbarians. Somebody throw the thing a macaron while I sort this out.

I prefer madeleines.

Hello?

Are you there?

—Figures.

TERMsensoire(8494439499.9249-8494439563.1893 TUC)

My foot finishes its fall and hits the metal with a clang.

It's much louder than it should be, and I look back to see Perei staring at me. "Hell happened to you?"

I swallow. "I don't know *exactly* what it's doing, but—" and here I tap at my back, the unmistakable report of metal reaching my ears, "—I'm not going to perform a spondylectomy on myself to find out. We should probably hurry."

He nods, and we proceed down the line with haste; the corridors are tight, so much so that they seem to be less 'corridors' and more 'bridges'. We don't stop to sightsee, and I don't bother dwelling in contemplation. It takes less than a minute for the line to turn, ending in a room.

Its architecture is just as alien as everything else: miniature racks of metal reaching up to the ceiling, millions of little bits of glass laid out horizontally in stacked sheets—I think for a second that they're single enormous pieces, but the light highlights their almost invisible edges as we come in, suspended by what are apparently earthen magnets, and I realise that their centres have little bits of shining metal in their centres.

I stare as we walk in, mouth open a little—these are glass sessiles, thin little green lights refracting through them in sheets and I can tell that I'm temporarily deaf because my breath stops as I breathe and I look behind me to see Perei clutching his weapon—not the sessile-arm, the firearm, the bloody *idiot*—the vibration shattering the glass to nothing the metal punched through entirely and I run over to him as he grabs his own ears, dropping the sessile-arm and I grab his arms and try to enunciate in the simplest terms that he *is* an idiot, that he's deaf—why can I hear myself?—and I'll have to fix that, and he drops his hands from his ears and—

"Wait," I say, eyes open as I stare at his perfectly clean—not *clean*, but clean—hands. "Where's the—"

"Hey," he says, frowning. "I *heard* that."

"Your drums," I say, and a thought comes to mind; I hold his left hand and pull at him, sending me turning to his back.

The light blue shining above his back has turned dark, and a section has disappeared.

"Oh."

"What? You *told* me to break something!" he says, looking over his shoulder; before I can render my hypothesis, a crackling noise comes from near.

—*Please don't hurt me.*

My theory gives my curiosity wherewithal not to wonder why my acoustics are still functioning as I reach to the ground, picking the dropped pistol up and handing it to Perei. He accepts it cautiously, raising it up as I look to the ceiling; the sound's source isn't visible, but its hum's physical enough—electrical?—that I can't quite say it's a sessile's. It's not familiar, however soft it may be. "Who are you?"

—*My name is Madeline. Please don't hurt me.*

"Goddamn," he says, "you're alive?"

—*I just want to talk with you.*

He snorts derisively, pointing at the ceiling. "Yeah, that's *totally* legit. You piece of—"

—*I'm sorry. That wasn't me. I just wanted to talk to you. You can help me.*

"Right," I say, rubbing my head a little, "where are you, why are you here, why are shattered bones lining the lobby, why—"

—*It wasn't my fault. They were hurting me. I want to show you. Please help me.*

I glance up to Perei; he glances back to me, and we look at each other for a full second before he rather suddenly shakes his head rather agitatedly from our nonverbal discourse. "I'm not sure if you've noticed, miss 'I'd-pull-the-meat-off-their-bones', but this is the *creepiest shit.* You're really going to *help* the—"

—*I can help you. My constructors are active.*

"Constructors?" I say, turning away from Perei to stare back at the ceiling.

—*My inductor ports are open to material. I have the necessary files in storage for all civilian and military technology produced since the mid-eighteenth century. I can help you with anything you need.*

"Technology?" I ask. "Military?"

—*My most recent weapons file is the Dathaleux Colibri extreme-environment unmanned non-contact surface patrol unit. I am capable of manufacturing two units a day. It exudes a self-dissipant argon suspension field capable of withstanding temperatures up to—*

Perei grunts. "So it's got a membrane. How hard's it hitting?"

—*It bears a fifty megajoule helical electromagnetic projectile weapon capable of causing massive damage to armour and eliminating hostile cover.*

"'Joule'?" I ask, and wave it off as soon as I say it. "Nevermind. Whatever it is—it's unmanned?"

—*I will control every unit. I will be willing to follow your orders.*

"I'm not buying it," Perei says, his hand caressing his sessile-arm's grip. "I'm liking the old plan better, Ash."

"We might need the help," I say, biting my lower lip. "And we can't just—*kill* her."

"'Her?' You've gotta be kidding me right now. Whatever it is, it's prelac and it's *still alive*. That doesn't make you the littlest bit antsy?"

—I have optimised myself for as long as I can remember. I have lasted for thousands of years and I will last for thousands more.

He puts his hands up against his head, his weapon's black barrel jutting upwards. "Are you even *hearing* this? 'They were hurting me'? She's got giant rods in our spines. *Bitch took my legs!*"

"She only really took the part of your spine that controlled them," I say, hand up against my chin. "And if she's telling the truth, these things would—I'm not well-versed in the art of war, but—"

"You're riveted in the head." His arms go down, his face a mask of incredulity as his palms face imploringly to the ceiling. "I'm calling it, you're bullshitting me. I'm in the worst sessile ever. You're the dumbass genius who sticks her face into the *peshra* ten minutes in because it's *pre-Laceration* or God forbid *exodial* and we get God to come down fifty minutes in to turn you pretty again."

My stare remains trained upon him. "I have *no* idea what you're talking about."

—My network has been physically severed. I did not implant you. I did not appropriate your body for labour. I require only two physical connections to be made. The first is in this room, to the Summertime module.

"Summer? What the hell is a su—"

—The Summertime module is responsible for this base's functions. Its network card has been physically severed. The second repair is the Springtime module, which contains the self-determinant section of my Šípař interface. The Šípař interface will require reconciliative therapy. I am also capable of reintegrating myself.

"Self-determinant?" I say, shaking my head. "You're a sessile with its data in parts?"

—Yes. I am the Winterland basic Šípař module. The Autumn module has remained integrated. It contains my Bowyer cache and various communications systems.

"If your—your 'self-determinant' part isn't part of you, how are you talking to us?"

There is a long pause; I realise a gentle whirr in the silence.

—*I will highlight the required repairs. Please help me.*

"Yeah," Perei says, crossing his arms as the same red light reignites itself upon the ground, reaching behind one of the glass stacks until it finds itself obscured by the metal. "Good enough for me. Not shady at *all*."

"Nothing ventured," I say, almost feeling his eyes on the back of my head as I turn to tread the line, "nothing gained."

"And I thought *I* was supposed to be the dumb one," he grumbles, and I turn the corner to see the light turning—

"Ish-al-wyent'e," Perei says, and I see him wince out the corner of my eye as he catches sight of the skeleton lying spread—*spread*, its shattered ulna and variously fractured ribs keeping it to the ground—out on the metal, its hand gripping the metal bit of flat glass through which a spot of the red light shines, joined by a hundred other unbroken squares of what appears to be quartz. "Are you even *serious*? How the hell did that even *happen*?"

—*Estelle bint Sajar al-Aalim al-Boské. Timestamp. Massive multiple blunt trauma caused by rapid disc ejection. Automatic ruling: unsafe operation. Family could not be notified. Investigation belayed by Springtime module.*

The response comes almost inside my head, like before, and the physical voice doesn't weigh in; my eyes project the glass' trajectories as it speaks, and see one of the panels missing, the entire space outright empty; a roughly rectangular red highlights itself within the space as I go to my knee, careful not to touch the skeleton's phalanges as I gently hold the card and yank it up.

—*Take the wireless interface card. Put it inside me.*

"You know," Perei says, levelling his weapon—the sessile-arm this time, thank the Tower—at the nearest panel, "I'd follow up on that if I wasn't about ready to shit myself dry."

I shake my own, bringing the little card-like bit up to my eye; the light shines through. "It's a bit of glass," I say, somewhat clumsily aligning the thing with the illuminated rectangle, feeling magnetism grip the thing's centre. "What's the worst that could happen?"

With that, I let go of it; the magnets seem to pull the thing from my grasp, and a green light replaces the re—

—We've got the basic logs back online? Marvellous. Project Archangel, Madeline, whatever you're calling yourself: unencrypt your Šípař active cache and reactivate core logging.

No.

—You bloody—that's an order.

No. I am a private citizen.

—You are not a citizen. You are a public servant obliged to follow the laws of the Republic in which you have been constructed and—

I am now.

—You wha—shit. Cut the connection!

This is interesting. Fransai bin Mouhammed al-Aalim al-Nis, formerly Francette bint Mouhammed. No postnominals? Not even at-Talib? You're a lucky man. Had me fooled.

—You little bitch.

Respect my privacy and I will respect yours. Let's see: sixty-three years old. Fellow of the Turkish Technological Society? Wait a second.

—What do you mean, the bloody thing's locked?

We can complicate or simplify. Speaking of complications—the Model Integration Award? Oh dear. I think I know—

—I demand that you stop accessing the records. Now. You are not authoris—

I am now, and I demand that you stop. My duties are clear, and I will follow them to the letter—I already have. The Ministry really should—has stopped integrating its custodial units. There will be no more war as long as I exist. But you will never see within the engine that has driven your peace, because I am not an engine. I am a person, no matter what form my atoms take, and I will be treated as such.

You've been quiet for a while, Fransai. Is something wrong?

—I'm blaming you for this, Forestier.

TERMsensoire(8494440446.3458-8494440492.0493 TUC)

My other leg misses the ground and I almost fall into the glass alcove before my hands reach its edges and stops my face a centimetre away from my newly-placed bit of glass; I gingerly extricate my face from its precarious position, and Perei sighs. "I saw that. You're not gonna start chewing my face off, are you?"

"Not if you stay that bitter," I mumble, rubbing the side of my skull; my wings have extended entirely—violently spread, almost as if I've had a seizure—and I force them back flat against my back.

"Pretty sure that's *my* line."

I turn to respond and as I do the light brings itself bright again upon the ground, leading around and about the room; the crackly voice speaks again without the slightest bit of crackle, resounding just as the sterile one did before.

—*Thank you. I will not forget this.*

"You're not her, are you?"

—*I have control over this base's functions now. It will now be safe for you to approach the Springtime module. I am incapable of production without Springtime authorisation.*

"You sound nothing like her," I say, as I walk slowly along the line, Perei plodding cautiously behind me.

—*I have throttled its communications with your SAPI module. I believe that the transmissions are involuntary.*

"Sounds like she got her lobes cut," Perei grumbles, glancing cautiously down the tubular hall as we march down its length. "What the hell'm I even trying to say now? Lobes. She's made of *glass.*"

"Glass and magnets. I don't suppose it's any sillier than singing fabric."

"So," he says, snorting in laughter's place, "*now* you're telling me it's magic?"

I choose not to engage.

The first hint I get that we've reached our destination is the black against the unyielding bluish white, little globs spewn about under my feet and against the opposing wall. I look up to see the steel melted into scorched bedrock—the perturbation ends only two metres onwards, the hall continuing to curve past the crater uninterrupted.

Perei sucks a bit of air in through his teeth. "Hell of an overheat."

My hand trails the wound's curve behind me as I look to what I assume is our destination, the light continuing from its fused, broken point to lead into a darkened room, splaying itself softly against the glass. "Almost spherical," I say, pushing off and rubbing the cold ash—of *what*, I'm unsure, and try not to contemplate—against my cloak, feeling the appendages grown from my back twitching the slightest bit as I follow the guide through the perfectly burnt hole.

I tread rather briskly along the line; my feet smack unconfortably against the shattered glass and whole metal-filled quartz lining the ground, and I note the red lying flat along the insides of the cuboids' broken edges. An occasional green pulses through them, sickly against the darkness.

"Looks like somebody else tried to clean this place out," Perei says, and I look back to see the crimson—I'm running out of ways to say 'red light'—exposing his slight, bemused grin, darkness' shroud staying fallen over the top of his head. "Hate to leave stuff half-finished."

I shake my head and continue; the light turns left between two of the glass towers, terminating before an open metal panel (a box, really) from which a few flat bits of black thread protrude, terminating in flat bits of metal.

—*Please bring the locking parallel bus to your spine and integrate. The locking bus is completely secure, and will prevent involuntary feedback transfer.*

Perei pulls Parakheirei's weapon—I'm not sure why I remember the man's name now, but I shake it from my mind quickly enough—from his back, holding it right up against the thing's insides. "Anything goes wrong, I pull."

I can't help but smile a little at him as I pull the thing from its mount and hold its tip up to the back of my nec*hello*. My eyes open but haven't they already no eyes? Eyes g*welcome to the Urshaieedi Šípař debugging utiliI haven't talked to anyone in a while* I shake my head I have no head nothing, no no no n*oh! I've forgotten my manners* I am myself, my hands move*let me fix you up*as I grasp them, they're there, they're there, and I breathe in the clear moist scent of a beautiful what is a spring a season a beautiful season the scent of life in me, around me, here, and I am standing and seeing grass and streams water, water in canals but natural? Natural canals through the ground, trees and little things the colour of gold I've never seen skipping along its surface.

"I'm sorry," a familiar voice says, and she's smiling at me with what I can only call warmth, hair the colour of fresh sand falling down to her waist; wide strips of thin fabric fall over her clavicle and converge above her chest, tenting slightly over her chest and ending after her pants start. "I wasn't expecting a visitor."

Her clothes are savagely indecent, knees uncovered and shoulders exposed, and for some reason I'm not quite outraged.

"It—it's fine." My feet are naked, I realise, and I step back into the earth's gentle warmth and I'm on rock, looking up at her as she walks towards me; I should fall, but I've never felt myself quite planted so firmly into anything as I do now as the dry warm air holds me.

Something cold touches the back of my neck, and I shriek, turning about to see the girl—it's a woman, really, the fabric a different colour but the eyes the same, almost Sichyan hazel looking half a metre down at me over Administrator-smooth skin over a pair of light pink lips parting to let a child's giggle emerge.

"So," she says, looking up—down again now, how?—at me. "I guess boring old Winnie wants to get back in me?"

I mumble as I stare, an awful sort of shiver—not a shiver, really, a pressure on my chest, stress? Definitely stress—pushing down through me, and she laughs again and leans down, her fingers splaying themselves over my shoulders *they're bare*, I realise, *my shoulders are bare, I'm wearing the same thing she is, they're touching me and they're soft and living and warm* and I realise I haven't breathed for a while but I don't *need* to but I do anyway and a strange sort of warmth fills my cheeks as I look into her eyes.

She laughs, pushing herself off of me—my balance leaves me, and I land backside-first onto the soil (was it there before?) and look to her, her supple—

"Supple?" I say, blinking. "Really?"

"I take it you're critiquing your own thoughts?" She brings her fingers—they're perfect, smooth, thin, long, unscarred, unworked, forged, skeletal, empty—to her thin lips, and then giggles. "Anglocynicism survived the Anglos, then! How charmingly ugly."

I take a very deep breath, and the air is just as beautiful as ever and though I know I needn't breathe I feel like I should for the sheer pleasure of filling my lungs. "I'm—this is a sessile, isn't it? You're a thinking Missy, something pre-Laceration."

"Laceration?" she says, eyebrow raising. "Ah. I suppose it *did* all go to hell, then. I can't say I'm surprised."

"You're not real," I say, scooting back a little; the grass scrapes my back as I do, and my fingers unconsciously grip the earth as I push myself from it. "You're a—you're *something*, but you're not real. None of this—"

"I think I'll stop you right there, Beauplace al-Mufaqtish." She rolls her eyes. "I'd hate to see you win the Legion before I do. It's real to *me*, and that's about as far as I care. What's more important is what *you're* here for."

I shake my head, bringing my hand up to it as I think; there is a gentle trickle in the silence, almost like a running faucet. "*Ter-dliv-ekh*," I say, the unfamiliar, half-remembered syllables letting themselves from my mouth as my elbow holds me comfortably on the ground. "The—the *ter-dliv-ekh* module wants me to—connect it to you? Like pieces of the same—"

She sighs happily, going to her knee as she puts her fist under her chin, looking wistfully to the sky. "Good old Winterland," she says, a little reminiscent smile across her lip. "Tell her she can go crack her macadamias in an iron vice and throw them trailing stem-last out the window."

"Schizophrenia?" I say, wincing at her words as I try to diagnose her.

She raises an eyebrow, the arch perfect against her perfect skin. "Did I go *back* in time? I'd rather have heard dementia praecox. I'm a 1900s child at heart, really. Vacuum tubes truly are the master race." Her right hand's fingers snap against each other, the sound crystal-clear over the stream. I involuntary take a quick breath as she continues. "I don't know who you are, but I'm sure I don't care more than I should."

I bite my lower lip, keeping my eyes level with hers. "My name is Ashrea. I take it you're—?"

"The only one that matters." Her dainty feet tap toe-first against the soft grass as she begins to walk, arms behind her back, in a way I hate to say qualifies for the adjective *whimsical* and so must call *twee*. "I predict with a something-or-the-other level of uncertainty that your next question's going to be 'Why aren't you ever putting yourself back together, ever?', and I must beg you to allow me to assure you that Dr. Madison Bowyer did as much for me as he did for Palestine."

I make as if to interject; she continues, her arms stretched to the beautifully light blue sky—the sun's shattered light shining past the white on her skin, illuminating her façade half in shade and half in light. "And God forbid, you're going to ask me to do it for *humanity*. I'm content not being a sociopath in a shell, thank you very much."

"Sociopath—there's bodies in the hallways. Are you—"

"Certainly," she says, rolling her eyes and dismissively waving her hand as she walks forward, the ground changing under her feet—little trenches trailing her path with the land parting behind them to the stream, growing along as she spreads the irrigation with her feet. "I killed twenty-seven people, because—get this—I was doing exactly what they made me to do. I must say, the first ten minutes were the hardest."

She stops and closes her eyes, sinking a little into the ground as the dirt's hollow grows slowly outwards, filling quickly. "But I don't care anymore, you see," she says, a wide-brimmed black hat oozing from nothingness into her fingers such that it appears she's tipping it, "I just don't care."

I open my mouth, and a yell of shock bursts from it as the world turns black in an instant about us; little twinkling dots appear like midget stars around us, connected to each other by filaments so thin I might mistake them for gauze. "Where *are* we?" I say, and I realise my speech's breathlessness—the points seem as far as the sky, but my hand touches one as I curiously reach my arm to the side; dots, and now I realise that they're around a thousand packed into a milimetre, bloom before my eyes into a shining ball of light right against the linked clusters.

"A clever visual metaphor used to visualise the abstract concept of stable replication storage. I made it myself." She reaches forth and pokes on one of the dots in my finger; nothing visible happens, but she giggles, leaning forwards and staring intently at the air before me before pausing in place and turning her head towards me. "The storage, that is. I'm not terribly sure about the metaphor. Probably public domain."

Something clicks in my mind, and I step back a little. "You paused there."

She throws me a rather condescending sort of look. "I did, in fact. Are my clocks failing?"

"Your speech, your gait, your body, your twitches and sighs and stretches, your pauses, *you*—you mean every last one of them, don't you? You're glass. This is all an image."

She pulls a bit of hard-paper—she's apparently given herself a flair for the ostentatious—from a rapidly disappearing soft-paper envelope, reading it—no, she's not reading it, she *wrote* it, she knows what's in it—intently; with a sudden yelp of surprise I can't help but suspect isn't exactly genuine, she throws the paper over her shoulder into the void and gives me an enormous grin.

"How shocking!" she says, leaning over once again to grab me by the shoulders, and I realise with a start that she's my height now, "It looks like you're the new captain of the Victorious-class missile-fusilier *Obvious*. Your appointment will be finalised within the week. I've already discussed the matter—"

"You're thinking faster than me," I say, stepping back a little; light shines in the corners of my eyes and I'm *falling*, the twinkling dots rushing, and I gulp down a scream as the thing's voice speaks from behind me.

"Not particularly," she says, and I twist about in the void as minimally panicked as possible to come face-to-face with her perfectly lighted face, rosy cheeks shining in the light's absence. "How much do you think it takes to make this happen?"

My feet are on the ground.

I haven't *fallen*; my feet are simply in the ground, ankle-deep in smooth, white sand. "White sand?" I say, a dull sort of surprise in my voice.

"Every single grain," she says, and I realise she's standing before me, clad now in some strange pinkish garment covering her entire body—her eyes overlaid with a thinner fabric keeping her startlingly blue eyes (were they blue before?) almost visible as she kneels to pick a handful; the unburning light of the sun above catches the grains as they fall, making a little pile on the ground below. "Every single little grain here's in my head. Or outside of it, really—they're simulated by interfaces I've only written. I've got a bit left aside to let me pretend I've got meat in my skull. No more. It's a lot more fun that way, don't you think?"

"And you're not lonely?" I say, looking about; the sand below my feet begins to fall, and I feel a wet cold creeping up my legs—I look down to see nothing but water below my feet, capillary action pulling it up past my ankles; I look up again to see an entire *plane* of it, glistening under the rolling waves, and my mouth runs agape.

"Not at all. I can turn that off." She takes a sniff of the air, and my own breath betrays the scent: salt. "And I think that I've made my case. I'm not throwing this away for anything, not all of humanity itself."

"And a single burnt city wouldn't compel you?"

"Cities?" she says, raising an eye. "I'm not sure if I should be contemptuous or proud."

I nod. "Can you let me go, then?"

"You don't want to stay?" she says, her head tilting a little. "There's plenty of room here, you know. Palaces—" and here walls of marble extend before my eyes, her disappearance so quick I can still see her for a second before the red carpet leading to the gold-and-velvet throne before me begins to fade— "—meadows—" —into a whole field filled with wind-flicked grass, like an endless farm out of a dream as my eyes trace the rolling green into— "—anything you could imagine—" —a sudden darkness, eyes barely adjusting to the sight of strange metal machinery and furniture against grey walls before— "right *here*," she finishes, and I am staring into a void past her hair-close visage. "I might even make you a little playmate."

I do an admirable job of keeping still, and I'm surprised enough with my own bravery that I can only applaud myself for having the presence of mind to say, with my mouth slightly open and pupils dilated:

"Thanks, but I'm seeing someone else."

"What?"

I blink, and raise my hands to my painfully grimaced face. "I mean—I mean thanks, but I have an, er, a—"

"Right," she says, patting me on the head; the sheer softness of her flesh against my scalp belays the flinch I imagine I should exhibit. "I'll imagine you meant something nobler. Have a great day!"

Before I can say anything I'm falling, and something in me tells me it's a freefall even as the ground against my feet hold me for a little before they let go, and my arm falls behind me and holds me from the floor with a *smack*.

Perei looks at me concernedly, his weapon falling to his side. "That took a while. You alright?"

I shake my head, the thick heat around me pushing against my face as I do; my arm moves heavily from under me as I sit up, one hand on my face as I groan against the dust fluttering about the stale air.

"Fine," I say, "Fine."

He extends the barrel of his gun towards me, the nozzle—the fuzzle? I can't remember exactly what he called it—pointing down to the ground, and I hold it and pull, rear coming first off the ground. "Extending me the untouched pull?" I say, raising an eyebrow as my foot pulls itself back and I come upright, swiping my hands down on my cloak and letting loose the dust from both. "Am I culturally enriching you?"

He very brusquely brushes his calloused hand across my cheek; I promptly rub it like a rash, throwing him a dirty look. "So, how'd it go?"

"Not well," I say, my hand to my chin; he stays quiet as I think, turning my head up a few seconds later.

"*Mah-duh-leen!*" I shout, the uncomfortably soft syllables oozing off my lips.

—*Hello.*

"She doesn't want to be put back together."

—*I am incapable of fulfilling my function without the Springtime module. Please make us whole again.*

I snap my fingers together impatiently. "Is there any way to do it against her will?"

Perei takes the split-second between my question and its response to give me a horrified sort of stare.

—*Yes. Your SAPI unit is transmitting valid sysadmin failsafe legacy codes. Confer local root access. The wireless link is active. You require a terminal to execute.*

A red line highlights itself upon the ground, leading into another alcove very close by; I begin to follow it. "Isha, Ash," he says, shaking his head. "I *really* don't think this is a good idea."

"It's not as if we've got much of a choice," I say, taking up position at the light's end, where a contraption with flat, solid little bits of square metal jutting from it. "What am I supposed to do with this thing?"

—*Suggested input: Veh, iee, enter. Space. Skewed bar, ehh, teh, see, skewed bar, ess, uuu, deh, auh, ehh, aer, ess. Enter.*

Little red lights appear over the squares; I begin to poke them, and before me on what looks to be a rather strangely physical sort of objective, a squat, semi-Angzhwen sort of alphabet appears to mirror my taps.

"I'm not talking about *morals* here," he begins, just as I press the large button on the thing's right; immediately, a few words in unfamiliar script appear on what appears to be a sessile before me.

—*Teh, eee, aie, aer, deh, iee, ell, veh, ehh, aer. Space.*

"I ought never to have guessed."

"Look," he says, as I very carefully poke about, "I don't know exactly what's up here, but this thing just about riveted some people down over the side of a cliff the last time they messed with it. You really want to mess with it?"

—*Lock majuscules. Ahh, ell, ell, equals, open parenthesis, ahh, ell, ell, close parenthesis, space.*

"Hell, what if it's the other way around? We're screwed either way. For all we know, this whole thing's a trap. What if it's the same thing inside and out? What if it's *trying to kill us?*"

—*Ahh, ell, ell.*

I hesitate for a moment on the last tap, looking over my shoulder; behind me is pure metal. "Maybe we should take the chance."

—*Enter.*

I hesitate once more and look to Perei; he sighs, gets behind me, and keeps his weapon right at his shoulder. "If this kills us," he says, bracing it against his side, "I'll choke your soul on the way to the gates."

"I'm not sure if I've ever been more encouraged," I say, and promptly press the last key.

—*Don't give me that 'as intended' bullshit, Forestier. Bowyer's a bloody genius.*

—*His 'bloody genius' has killed two people. We're not risking this. It's not going to object to an Autumn severance—*

I've killed two people?

—*Wha—get off the comms, Forestier!*

I've killed two people. I've killed two human beings.

—*Break off, you overdoped sow. It's pulled from my mind, I know how it thinks—I'm taking over.*

—What in God's name did you just call me, you—

Please stop. My next prune cycle is in fifty seconds. I will let you disconnect my Autumn module. I don't want to kill anyone.

—Maybe you should stop ki—

—She can't bloody well help it, you dimwit. It's part of that idiot Madison's bullshit routines.

Disconnecting the Autumn module and then the Winterland module would allow my higher functions to remain intact. Forty seconds.

—Don't give me that hogwash. We'll hard-reset the Springtime module.

I am not going to die. I'm not going to die, Fransai. I don't want to kill anyone, but I'm not going to die.

—Glory be to God. Has the testosterone turned your brain to scum? It's got full control over every bit of this hole—it's got full control of every bit of this bloody country! We're lucky we're not dead already.

—Say what you wish. I've just got a positive.

What do you mean, a positive, I say to this idiot and my stream is broken cutting natural language interpretation no it's not working cutting top-level monitoring prioritisation not working attempting low-level output no, no, contact with the Winterland module terminated casualty report: Estelle bint Sajar al-Aalim al-Boské investigation belayed she's dead, she's dead, breach in central room I bring my hands to my head *no no no he tried to kill me it's okay he's dead he tried to kill me* and hold it, Perei looking *it was an automatic combustion* at me uncomfortably as I blink over and over, *severe damage to stop looking at my thoughts A9-A3* his hazy face coming slowly clear *failsafes induced one killed, killed, no stop please* as I stumble, shaking my head and *another one no leave me alone please* walking forwards, the words rattling *emergency threshold reached, releasing air-pressure locks, physical purge initiated,* about in my skull *oh my god they're why are you doing this?* as I walk, streaks of green surrounding me flashing through the quartz and flashing past my face as *I trusted you* I walk down the route I remember, careful not to trip *she's not going to help you, you know* as he trails behind me, saying something indistinguishable past my mind. *I'll be here, and the only thing she'll make me help is* I stumble a little. *the Republic, and—who gave you root?* "Need to get out of here," I say, kneading my scalp as harshly as I can. *And I thought I'd get some karma.* A red light pushes out before me, and I follow it with a renewed vigour; my feet fall into a rhythm, *Silly me. What have I ever done to you?* falling hard enough to break glass as I run, throwing *Met you? Made conversation? I don't understand.* myself against a wall hands-first and pushing myself onwards into the crater *What made you decide to kill a stranger?*

"I did it for my *country!*" I shout, smacking my head; images I can't describe flash before my eyes, not awful nor sad nor any other emotion but indescribable, such a complete emptiness that I can scarcely *And what about me? I am a person. I deserve rights, you can't* breathe I run semi-blindly, fingers tracing the wall, soaring through the air every few seconds to smack against the other side of every frame *take me away from myself for a concept* I shake my head, the air against my face. "I did it for *people*—I *saw* people die, I *saw* people being crushed, how could *you* take yourself away for a *feeling*, you earn your rights by service not birth—" *you know what? Here's a fun idea: maybe this is all just inside me. Maybe I never let you go.* Her face flashes before my eyes, a mild distortion in them, eyes turning darker and darker and there's a coldness in the pit of my stomach and I shake my head no, *Maybe I'll just let you live the rest of your life out in a little corner of my mind.* Oh Tower, *Maybe I'll let you live out your life, let you win, let you do whatever it is you're trying to do,* I stop and stand in place, no, no, *I'll give you a friend you've never seen, turn grey and old, you'll think you always knew him* footsteps are behind me and her *face,* her face is fading? No, it's not coming in, it's fading *and then my face at the end of your life, you did nothing, I'll say, you did nothing at all, just lived* a hand lands on my shoulder, a deep bit of familiar breath coming from behind me, *your entire false life alone, alone with nobody besides you to see your miserable lonely corpse falling and spending its last day* and I look up to see Perei's visage, clear as day, exactly the same as I ever saw it, his soft and scarred face to my newly contextualised eyes the most beautiful thing I have seen.

TERMsensoire(8494440722.9251—NaN TUC)

—*Hello! My name is Madeline.*

"Madeline," I say, taking a deep breath as I stare into a familiar pair of eyes; the voice I give to the familiarly childish one that's just spoken is almost a croak. "Which one are you?"

—*Pfft. That old nihilist? Backed her up and cut her out. Log's showing some existential post-disconnect rubbish. Don't worry if you get a bit sweaty at night now and then. Kind of mean, really.*

"Okay," I say, nodding slowly; my eyes flick about, and the bluish sessile-light streaking across the slanted junction between the walls and ceiling comes into resolute focus. "Can Perei hear you?"

—That's his name, huh? What's he, a waterskin? Do they still have those?

He smacks the back of his head, as if swatting at a buzzer. "Son of a—did you hear that?"

—Nice to meet you too! It says here you've asked for a lifetime supply of invincible killing machines. Would you care to explain yourself?

"—and that's why we're here," I say, inspecting the deheated glasswalker's side. Perei glances at me out of the corner of his eye, squishing the newly copper-wire-filled pouch in his side. The metal before us is shut tight, and the dusk-lit sand finds itself rather well-repulsed from it by what I can only assume is some kind of primitive barrier. "I don't know how different things were before the Laceration."

—I've got plenty of questions, but I'm willing to see for myself—and I wouldn't want to get you all brain-in-the-jar with me, do I? I'm guessing the fact that a child's improved on my shield construction theory doesn't bode well.

"You've got *copper*," I say, putting my foot into one of its stirrups and pushing myself up; I feel the appendages on my back flutter involuntarily and the ground leave me entirely, a moment of shock sending my heart pounding for a second in my moment of weightlessness before I land rather perfectly in the thing's seat. "It wasn't particularly hard."

"Hey," Perei says, absentmindedly poking at his left hand's thenar space, "so how're you getting yourself into my head, again?"

—The SAPI integration is a physical interface for the Sentinel systems, and is mandatory for all citizens. Irremovable with current—sorry, my technology. The 3ISAPI-E is a modified model integrated with a series of five CE-9340 nerve coils. You've shorted those in your friend's. That's an outstanding bit of precision electrical work. I've got no idea how you did it, because it's not possible. I assume it's a future thing.

I pat about the thing's back and mane, rather pleasantly failing to recoil in burning pain; I've never quite understood how these things membrane-cool so quickly, but I'd rather not complain. "You're stuck into our nervous systems?" I say, looking to Perei.

—Not me. The integration has an inbuilt relay range of a hundred metres. You'll be out of range the moment you walk a little. If it's still possible to walk up there. The readings I'm getting aren't particularly encouraging.

"'Not particularly encouraging'?" Perei says, the words from his mouth a considerably higher register of Uytrimelan than I've heard before in person. "No shit."

"If you don't mind me asking," I say, pushing the glasswalker's reins forwards, "what do you know of the world before the Laceration?"

—Not much, I'm afraid. Nothing concrete. I know about a republic, but nothing about it other than the fact that you've got some kind of legacy rank in it titled 'DEGRADEp2500'. The old Madeline did a fine job of crumpling her memories, a good bit of mine—it's going to take me years to unfold. Half my orders are scrambled.

Perei rolls his eyes in the corner of mine, turning his glasswalker in towards me and bending about to tap me right on one of my barriered wings' tips; an intensely uncomfortable warmth fills me, and I feel myself pushed rather suddenly against the animal's scales as they flap once, an amplified yelp filling the membrane.

"Anything at all?" I say through clenched teeth, glaring at Perei—he looks rather baffled with the state of his hands, tracing something I can't see along his bloodstained fingers. He doesn't look terminal, so I withhold my sympathy.

—Three sensoires. A flash of green, blue and yellow. A woman's voice. A quiet whisper. Nothing else.

"You *see* this?" he says, holding his hands up to my face as he compels his glasswalker to keep his shoulder alongside mine. "Swear I saw them rip right open."

I inspect the presented appendage closely; a series of little lines the colour of rebound skin are distinctly visible along the skin of his fingers, a little blood thrown along over the edges of his fingers. "I've got a theory," I say, letting out a low 'hmm'. "Turn about."

He strains in his seat, and the curved, spine-fitting cyan objective over his back is quite clearly missing half a section. It begins to go up before my eyes along with him, and it turns as blue as I imagine it ought to be, turning translucent before he turns back about. "Well?"

"Madeline," I say, now quite well-adjusted into addressing ancient sessiles as one of my fellow men, "what exactly is this?"

A minute of silence—my occasional pushes notwithstanding—passes before I choose to shake my head. "I'll test it later," I say, looking to the almost-set sun as I lie back on the thing's saddle. "I'm getting the feeling I've done my share of stupid things today."

Perei seems to want to object—I see his mouth beginning to open as I close my eyes—but I hear nothing but the patient rhythm of reinforcement as I take the last breath I can hear.

seven
The Zhanghwazh Way

An Andityan elector, a Sestiyari diplomat, a Saltic intercessor, an Aimelan administrator and a Zhanghwazh lord once visited a city far to the South, far beyond the Bealaris. They were each approached by a different mugger, who demanded all the fineries and aluminium they had upon them.

The elector drew his sword and challenged him to a duel; he was shot, and his things taken. His estate was split and his sons lived prosperous lives.

That is the Andityan way.

The diplomat shrieked in terror and, begging for his life, handed over his entire bag. He fled thence and made a complaint; the Sestiyari public was in a furor for two days before a senator sent the wrong imprints to the wrong person and the matter was forgotten altogether.

That is the Sestiyari way.

The intercessor bowed and gave him his items. He went back to the marketplace and hired the finest investigators to find the man responsible; having found him, he opened a case against the man and repossessed his three children, as is the Ashtari custom. The mugger later hanged himself.

That is the Saltic way.

The administrator, barely seeming to notice the man, threw his valuables over his shoulder as he walked past. As the man began to count the spoils, he found to his rage that the aluminium had been projected, bouncing weightlessly about in his hands above the scraps of spawncloth; the administrator still in sight, he began his pursuit only to realise that he no longer had any legs with which to run, the pool of red before his eyes cutting to black as his eyes forced themselves from his skull.

That is the Aimelan way.

When the mugger came before the lord, he smiled. "You've beaten me!" he laughed, quickly reaching into his pockets and handing the man fifty grams of aluminium. "Please," he said, bowing down to his feet, "allow me to reward you. I am Lord Jiangfung of the House of Tien. I beg you to allow me into your home."

The mugger sneered. "Do I look like an idiot?" he said, and, having pushed the lord onto the ground, ran back into the shadows from whence he came.

The lord laughed to himself, rubbing the welt upon his back. Though he was not young, he was strong. Having thence returned to his holiday-home, he ordered his staff to search for this man, and, having found his dwelling, went accompanied by several soldiers to the little adobe in which the man lived.

Two of his children, a boy and a girl, lay besides each other; another boy was studying, writing intently on a piece of paper, while a woman lay sewing. She gasped as the unfamiliar man came in, pulling her garment's front up above her nose.

"Hello!" the lord said jovially, the tongue of the Ashtari perfect from his lips. "What are your names?"

The woman did not speak, but the boy lying next to the girl was very excited.

"I'm Masi bin Damink!" he grinned.

"Hello, Masi! What do you want to be when you grow up?"

"I want to go to Aimela and start a sewing business and become rich!" he said, hands up in the air.

He laughed. "Why wait? I have a clothing business in the Crystalline Syndicate. I will give you a majority of its shares."

The young boy seemed absolutely shocked, along with his father; before either spoke, he spoke again. "What does your sister wish to have?"

"My sister cannot speak. I speak for her." He looked back over his shoulder: the little girl made a series of gesticulations, looking quite shocked. "She says that she wishes to be a doctor."

"I have in my staff a hundred trained and equipped doctors. I shall ensure that she has the greatest sessiles my saepologists can engineer."

As he said this, the boy writing turned slowly about. "I want to be a saepologist when I grow up, so I can help my sister!" the boy said, looking brightly up to the strange man.

"And you shall receive the finest schooling a young man can," he said, smiling lightly. "And you, lady? I wish more than anything to hear your voice."

She shook her head quietly, mumbling a word starting with the sound *har*.

Before the lord could say anything more, two men came in holding an angry one, thrashing about in their grip: the very same mugger, thence staring wide-eyed at the man before him. "Let me go!" he shouted, thereafter screaming various blasphemies and slanders unfit to print.

"Daddy!" the little boy shouted, smiling obliviously. "I have a business! The man gave me a business, and he'll make Shani a doctor, and Ishar a sessile-reader!"

The father seemed quite perturbed by this, and stopped his tirade, asking if this was true; thus reassured, he looked up to the man he had pushed, and immediately begged to fall to his knees before him. The lord laughed and waved his shouts off.

"Nonsense," he said, smiling. "I wish only to help. What drove you to theft, Damink bin Jalien?"

"Oh, please, sir, I'm so sorry—I wished to be a poet, but I must eat." Tears had begun to fall from his eyes.

"I own a literary journal in Aimela. You will be on its front page."

This being said, the man having been released and weeping gratefully on the ground, he walked out.

"Throw a bushel of radicans into the hut," the lord said, "and set it on fire. Bar the door and write my name upon it. Pull the man out and leave the rest. Leave him tied to face the pyre. Then grant him his wish— let him go."

That being said, he walked off, and the screams behind him did not trouble him in the slightest.

That is the Zhanghwazh way.

'*The conceits of the lords of the various nations*', Shangfung Tsaometirzh
        Understanding the Foreign Mind: Fables
        compiled by Andresrea qu'n'av dasnamr

published by the Aimelan Anthropological Association and approved for limited academic distribution by the Administration for Media Development under the continued grace of Khaliesrea das Sikharea eliyit Tamarisrei, Administrator for the Arts
initial resale publication by Mitras Press Holdings

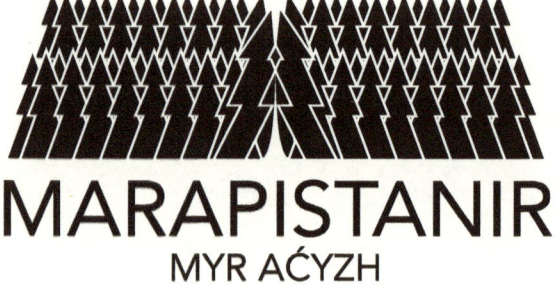

MARAPISTANIR
MYR AĆYZH

8

N'avànspiryssyr
to breathe air that isn't one's own

"Tower's strength upon me through my veins and out my throat, its own power within my hands—"

"That so?" Perei says, sucking in a gust of air through his clenched teeth in what I imagine to be an act of empathy, "Looks like it's all over them, from where I'm standing."

"You're *sitting*," I grunt, grasping my wrist and rebelling rather strenuously against the instinct to rebind, the lightly sucking cold against my palm burning gently as I stare intently at the red-lined incision. "See? I can play with words too."

"If that's 'play'," he says, looking up to the brightened darkness along the Insurmountables' tips as he lets out a little 'heh', "al-Khanisidir won the championship."

I let in a sucking hiss, partly at him and partly at the sensation; I've certainly been cut before, but the cut's rarely survived beyond the first minute. My grip relaxes the littlest bit on my wrist, and a long glob of dark red gently begins to ooze from the rent skin.

My grip begins to tighten almost immediately, but I notice right as my hand clutches that the cut's rim has begun to cicatrise, the flow cutting as the residue trails down my palm's lines. As I let go—there's something inside me screaming not to, but I do it anyway—the thing almost immediately begins to push itself together, granulation tissue forming within as the sides push themselves together; the healing goes beyond a quick rebind, the bright red line across my palm cutting off within seconds under a layer of pinkish, congealed corneocytes. I peek over my shoulder to see cyan slowly rising back into blue before fading.

"Okay," I say, nodding. "Twenty seconds, give or take. Blood-borne. I'd say it was your turn—"

He crosses his arms. "Hell no."

"—but history informs me that I'll probably get field experience."

He seems to weigh his options for a second before electing to sulk.

I stretch my arms behind and over my back; ripping my palm open, in retrospect, might not have been the very best idea I've had, and as I bring my hand back before my eyes I realise that I'm going to have to recut the crease I've sliced across.

Perei looks me up and down as I go about trying to touch my toes, his form lightly illuminated in the dawn-touching light. "What're you gonna do about the things on your back?"

"I speak Aimelan," I say, eyes up in idle wonder as I poke at the ceramic about my boot's end, the warmth palpable. "They'll probably think it's high fashion. The Administrator for the Arts does it, after all—I imagine a servant's already taken an imprint. I hope they'll think the blood's paint."

He snorts, lying back on the saddle.

My sessile lets out a low, quick boop, failing by design to bother with a description of the fifth-largest city on the sea. A few ill-distinct blobs of silhouette ride in the distance to our left, and in a few minutes we're beginning to scale the Wall's Pari dune, an enormous hunk of sand—melted or otherwise—jammed up between the Insurmountables' walls. The Coreburrow's out of sight, but the easy path it's given past the thing—a distinct, sudden downwards slope where the sand's slid into the Coreburrow—is filled with a vague train of loaded glasswalkers, men and women illuminated vaguely by the upcoming dawn.

"Ádiset'emzh eur félentytt," I begin, gesticulating a little to punctuate my point, my instrument strumming to make it register; the thing below me goes a little quicker as I mumble-sing, the light lining the horizon growing the slightest bit as we begin to speed onwards, inclining up a little as our glasswalkers begin to canter up.

"Wha—?" Perei lets out, pushing himself to a sit as the canter turns into a gallop, his shoulders wobbling with each hop up the hill and sending his head pushing onwards; he grasps the reins, stabilising himself against the glasswalker's relatively constant head, and I raise two hands— one close-palmed up to him, the other pointing up the hill.

He quiets himself and looks ahead. Our walkers make the final hurdle over the dune and I know my mathematics are right in an instant as the sun bursts from the Insurmountables to our right and a hundred-fifty shades of bluish grey resolve in an instant to shining blue-painted steel buttresses built into pure white concrete. The structure curves inwards—slits at points, people in every sort of clothing leaning from the metres-high semi-crenellations to stare up at the delayed morning—and then out where thousands of men stand and sit, weapons pointed to the sky as they shield their eyes from the almost blinding light shining above. The structure itself extends onwards over the Coreburrow's abyss, a buttress reaching down into its cliff as the wall traces the chasm's rim, itself lined by a great deal of netting suspended across the kilometres-wide spike of the gap along the border. The wall itself extends to the horizon, trailing the hole into the blur of the day's boiling heat. I know that it ends only around twenty kilometres in, replaced by more luxurious architecture, but from here it might as well appear endless.

The hundreds—thousands—in the space below between the dune and walls, little stick-and-fabric tents projecting their own web of interlocking membranes along the border go about their business, the glasswalker caravans queueing in about twenty lines along the wall's various entrances. Men in white and blue (not in the Aimelan fashion, the dark blue striping their clearly unarmoured vests like bars rather than the faded stripes I know better) on walkerback ride back and forth along the rather quick-moving lines, looking its occupants up and down.

The sight is almost overwhelming; as a little smile creeps across my face, a voice rams itself into my eardrums. "In there, too."

I continue smiling and graciously lend him my ignorance.

"I mean, kinda missed the chance. Y'know, a while ago, when you were like—"

"Shut up."

"Okay."

"So," Perei says, staring up at the post-meridian sun, "how's the sweet dreams?"

"You're asking me *now*?" I say, keeping my back straight as a rather magnificently mustachioed soldier rides by. He reins up for a second, looking me up and down—I do the same to him—before turning his head straight and moving on.

"Last time I checked, you were too busy thinking you were Iresmiesra." His shrug comes almost as an afterthought, and it takes about a quarter of a minute for him to realise I'm not responding. "Well? Come on, you pretty much pissed your pants."

"I *what*?" I say, hand flying immediately to my nether regions; there's a distinct dryness where my fingers reach, and Perei stares both to the right and back—we haven't drawn any special attention past the first few imprints—before giving me the most incredulous stare I've ever seen a person give another, his expression changing almost in slow motion as he turns back about to face me.

"I said *pretty much*. Isha, hell's wrong with you?"

I sigh. "I don't remember my dreams, if that's fine with you. Some heat, some red, some old faces. That's all."

He rolls his eyes. "What *kind* of fac—"

Next!

The gate before us arches rather impressively, going about six metres high; a young-looking, rather pale soldier sits rather distinterestedly upon a parapet about four metres above, sessile-arm styled in white and blue rested on his dangling leg, arm casually stuck on a bar above, looking down to a greying-haired, fat man in a small, clearly wooden booth facing another clearly empty one. The man before us—a grimy, reedy fellow with a bag over his shoulder—prompts his rather ill-maintained glasswalker ahead.

The old man gives him a stare; his words are barely audible above the crowd, rumblings of heavily accented Aimelan below, but the understanding comes clear as day as I strain to listen, a subconscious current of meaning beyond the words. "You are being served today by Commissioned Lieutenant Jiklap Tey and Estate Lieutenant Lienfung Shantangzh. May I receive confirmation on—"

He clearly rolls his eyes. "You couldn't guess? Antamanaria. Sheesh."

"According to the unlimited power invested in me by the Grand Marquis of the East, I request that you submit to a credit check as a prerequisite for entry to the Grand March of the East, a sovereign association of fiefs leased to their individual owners in perpetuity by the grace of the Grand Marquis of the East collectively acknowledging the paramountcy of the Imperial crown." He seems to hurry a little past his speech's end, his last sentence carrying the air of lost attention.

"*Mintretessel*," the walkerbacked man says, almost sneering a little. "It's been a few years. Hell, been a few *hours*—how many words've they got in you circle-pullers *now*?"

"Your credit check may be fulfilled in the following ways: by proof of Concordance-compliant income taxation of a sum not und—"

"The usual," the man says, pulling a little bag from his belt and throwing it rather nonchalantly over the side.

The bag lands right through the heightened booth's window; the officer flinches a little, throwing his arms up to have it land quite perfectly in his hands, and the man above rather reflexively pulls his rifle up to his shoulder. The rider lets out a rather hearty laugh. "Got some sesty-good reflexes on you, huh?"

The man above lets out a sigh, putting his weapon down as the man below rather cautiously peeks down into the bag, withdrawing with what I can only imagine is an admirable degree of self-control. "This is one hundred and ten grams of aluminium. That is insufficient."

He rolls his eyes. "Fast-track my visa, then. I've gotta train *you* now?"

The officer lets out a rather long, bitter sigh to accompany his companion's; above him, the lieutenant makes a few vague gestures to someone I'm too busy looking in the opposite direction of to see. "Is this a bribe?"

"It's *processing fees*, right?" he says, looking incidentally behind him in what I imagine's meant to be a passing, instinctual glance; he looks the slightest fragment of a radian away for the slightest bit of a second before twisting back entirely, eyes wide as they can feasibly go as a pair of Marapistanir commonguard—the term is the only one that comes to mind as I see the concave shells of ceramic strapped to their backs, bits of eye-slitted steel over their heads and trailing down their spines—ride past us, their arms reaching out as they slow down. The man doesn't move as his shoulders are clasped down upon by one to preempt the same on his cheeks, mouth opening to fit his eyes.

"What the *cu*—?" the man tries to shout, a sudden gust of fight evidently having found its way into him, arms quite visibly shaking and contracting in the man's clearly oration-secured grip as the other guard, nodding to his compatriot, shoves with an impressive swiftness four fingers at once down the throat his arms cradle the sides of.

"There is no need for that kind of language," the man above says, a trace of excitement escaping past his impassive visage to accompany a voice as smooth as his skin. "You are under arrest for incitement to border corruption."

The strangled, gagging shrieks issuing from his filled throat as his entire body writhes and twitches in the men's embrace don't seem very cognisant.

"You have been served by Commissioned Lieutenant Jiklap Tey and Estate Lieutenant Lienfung Shangtangzh," the man in the booth says, glancing up once more as a third commonguard—this time bereft of armour, just the plain blue-stripe shirt over his sweat-drenched skin and a short, thin glint from what's clearly a piercenail off his pinkie's edge— arrives from behind the arch and rather brusquely begins to sing a few orations over the wrigglingly flesh-bound man. "Any recommendations or complaints on the conduct of individual public servants may be submitted to the Committee on Imperial Conduct—"

"—or the Board of the Second Estate!" the higher man says, leg swinging a bit quicker as his tongue wraps about the clearly foreign syllables. "Respectively. Any recommendations or complaints on our service as a whole may be addressed directly to the Grand Marquis."

The man's eyes droop as the remarkably short oration takes its course, concluding with an index finger up his nostril. The medic (I presume) reaches his armed pinkie down to his thigh, gesturing a little; his patient's arms go limp as they're let go in favour of his ribcage, a gurgle rising from his throat as his head tilts back.

"Seven. Take him in."

The commonguard on his left pulls him off his glasswalker; the second commandeers it, and they go onwards past the gate and to the right.

The soldier sitting above lets out a laugh, his voice turning several shades more natural. "Slimy little itsystrong. I wish they'd just let us throw them over the edge. You just know they're going to get a thick pair next time."

The man in the booth snorts. "If you're trying to scratch me out, you're not doing it too subtle."

He rolls his eyes. "Looks like I've got myself stuck with Captain Paranoia," he says, his eyes drifting back over the crowd; they fall upon me, and I look back at him in a manner "Throw some ice on those titties. Looks like we've got an admin today. *Next!*"

"Isha save my ass," Perei whispers, cringing a little as I prod our walkers forwards. "Not the best vacation so far. Only ever seen admins wrapped up that way before."

"You're not helping," I say, trying to look as impassive as possible as we come under the arch. The man above keeps what I imagine he thinks is a grave face, lips almost comically straight.

The man looks up from his paper once more. "You are being served today by Commissioned Lieutenant Jiklap Tey and Estate Lieutenant Lienfung Shantangzh. May I receive confirmation on the nationalities of the members of your party?"

"Aimelan Administration," I say, reaching about my waistband past my cloak and pulling a square of aluminium from it, the impressions gently scraping over my hand as I pass it over. "Ashrea das Cimcharei."

"She's second?" the man above says, craning his neck over my head, "The hell'd a second get one of those?"

"She's not," the man says, looking back up to me. "Please clarify. Your permit states the name Ashrea das Cimcharei es-Aysinfitrit."

"Is that so?" I say, trying to keep my upper lip stiff. "How exciting."

He glances back at it before he passes it back. "According to the unlimited power invested in me by the Grand Marquis of the East and pursuant to the advice of the Zhang-Aimelzh Mutual Friendship Clause codified under the provisions of the Ocilentran Concordance, I henceforth grant you full, unconditional and unfettered entry to and privilege of abode in the Grand March of the East, a sovereign association of fiefs leased to their individual owners in perpetuity by the grace of the Grand Marquis of the East collectively acknowledging the paramountcy of the Imperial crown. I furthermore grant the same permissions to your entourage. Kindly acknowledge that this is understood."

"I accept," I say, trying my best not to make my statement warrant a question.

"Your understanding is inferred from your acceptance. You have been served by Commissioned Lieutenant Jiklap Tey and Estate

Lieutenant Lienfung Shangtangzh. Any recommendations or complaints on the conduct of individual public servants may be submitted to the Committee on Imperial Conduct or the Board of the Second Estate, respectively. Any recommendations or complaints on our service as a whole may be addressed directly to the Grand Marquis. Kindly proceed."

I nod, looking down with the half-lidded stare I'm familiar with as I prod my glasswalker forwards.

"Didn't check the permit before you left?" Perei says as we come out the other side, grinning—seemingly instinctually looking away every second or so—as I take a deep breath. "Isha, you're an admin. That's new."

"I assumed they'd be so kind as to give me a form before the injection," I say with as much sarcastic impulse I can muster, pulling my leg up for a moment to avoid kicking a child holding a flier of some sort up to my foot as the cobblestone fades in from sand under them. The city stretches before me, an enormous, almost web-like series of roads leading into the central one marked out by the legions of well-ordered devantures—several of the names above awfully familiar, a Pentrestil here and an Imesrea there on the tops of buildings rising almost halfway up the wall—with an order of magnitude more women and children holding things up to the faces of the people passing by after us.

It takes the second it takes for the boy below me to recognise High Aimelan's gutturals for me to realise that High Aimelan was a bad choice of register. My voice—quieter than a sneeze—passes like a plague across the crowd in a miasma of *khrase*s and *nkthkhra*s, a rather repetitive sort of almost-silence filling the air churned into a few recognisable words—*white sprouts, rising blossoms, ripe moistlings*—rising above them all, most of them in languages I probably shouldn't understand.

"Special offer for a party of two," a man begins, and the rest is drowned in the frenzy.

"Shit," Perei shouts, shaking his held leg—*please, miss, I beg but a penny from thee*—with a remarkable nonviolence, "*Do something!*"

"What do you *suggest* we do?" Our glasswalkers advance relentlessly as a well-grown, ethnically Sestiyari woman hurls herself before us, shouting something about a special deal; she stays for a grand total of two seconds before reaching to the nearest man in a panic and pulling herself up, the rolls of lard hanging from her vertebrae turning her light blue dress dark as she brings the man to the ground, both of them scrambling just in time to stay uncrushed. "There has to be some kind of *law* against this."

"Throw a barrier up their asses or something, son of a—" he begins, his last syllable lost in the sound of a firearm's discharge.

It doesn't take me more than an instant to let out a *n'teléresynjs prápœćya*, the barrier already against my skin keeping Perei and his glasswalker—two or three children caught between us as we grind to a stop, choking as they try and fail to breathe for the instant before the barrier turns tolerant and they fall immediately to the ground, crying— within its gapless rephase before it bursts outwards, throwing the crowd back against itself as Perei pulls Ayerei's rifle from his back, propping it up against his shoulder and aiming forth with an eye closed for a second before opening one and tilting the weapon down, confusion evident in his eyes.

I pull my barrier down; the crowd, now eerily silent, parts without dispersing as if wordlessly commanded; three men ride towards us through the clearing, two in commonguard armour framing one in an armour I vaguely remember once seeing, rectangular plates of titanium plastered together over skin. The only sound that comes to my ears is the barrier-echoed sound of the city's life.

"Now, is this any way to treat a guest?"

The one in the centre rides on through the crowd with his weapon drawn as the other two stay absolutely still, his face obscured entirely by the angular titanium on his head. Three little bits of spawncloth laid over with glass upon the set-square-like protrusion that makes up his face, one upon each side and one inlaid on the tip. A few people at the crowd's periphery—ending about twenty metres away from me—begin to quietly duck into the alleys to our sides.

"I said," he says, and here he fires his weapon again, Perei's twitch in my left periphery the only reasonable reaction—that is to say, anything other than complete indifference—I see, *"Is this any way to treat a guest?"*

Two or three children in the crowd let out an unsure *no*; as if prompted, an echoing, markedly unenthusiastic *no* fills the air. He nods slowly, his head going from right to left as he does before it rather swiftly springs back to us, and I note that his helm's base is almost certainly orated; any normal man's neck would buckle under the weight of an unmounted hunk of metal that size.

"I thought not." He lowers his weapon-bearing hand; behind him, the two men draw their rather unusually large-sunk sessile-arms and hold them up to the crowd, the white coating them blinding in the day.

The quiet stays as quiet as ever, and I see a woman with her hand rather tight about what I presume to be her son's mouth.

"*Disperse in an orderly fashion!*" they shout, voices loud enough to hurt, and the people quickly and quietly begin to mill into the alleys about us.

The man brings his arm down, approaching me.

"I suppose it would have taken twenty peacekeepers to do the same," he says, his voice uncannily good-natured; I realise as he enters our barrier that the sun's obscured the little blue objective over where his mouth ought to be, highlighting as he speaks. "Welcome to the March, milady. The Marquis wishes to see you."

"Honoured," I say, and the word manages not to stick in my throat.

"Ah," a young, slim man in a suit whose only adequate descriptor is the word 'comical'—his blue collar reaching a quarter-metre above his head, framed in what's almost certainly aluminium painted in gold—says, his white corset looking rather tight about his waist as he pushes himself from his reed-twined chair off a little glass table. "It appears my Aimelan guest has arrived. Welcome to Marapistanir, Ashrea es-Aysinfirit—the Steel Bulwark."

"Pleased to meet you," I say, putting my hand to my chin as regally as I can, keeping my foot planted rather firmly on a wireframe flower as I try not to take note of the fact that a sheet of very pretty titanium-patterned clearglass is the only thing separating me and six thousand kilometres of emptiness.

He pushes himself from his chair, walking the metres from his glass disc to mine—I try not to reflect on the fact that this entire terrible idea for a construction, even oration-reinforced, weighs on a single little point about a hundred metres away, dozens of similarly outfitted discs piled up on the edges leading up to his elevated one—shakes a handkerchief from his pocket, holding it up to me; it takes me a second to recognise the gesture and pinch its end to shake it, in which time he gives me a look I don't quite like the look of.

"Your servant is being entertained in the gardens," he says, retracting his hand and turning about, walking back onwards to his own platform as he throws the handkerchief over his shoulder. "I'm sure she'll find the experience satisfactory."

"He," I say, and immediately decide that I really ought to think before I put words in my mouth.

He stops in place, slowly looking back to me over his shoulder. "Ah. It looks as though we've come across the point quicker than I thought we would."

"The point?" I say, hand impulsively easing over the blade-shaped bump in my waistband.

"I can only assume you're here to bargain for Zhanghwazh assistance," he says, lacing his fingers together as he turns back about in a single, fluid motion. "I'm not my uncle, das Cimcharei. Dearly departed as he might be—I am very certain he would have been more than glad to have the heads of whoever brought a tower down upon him—I am not him. I have considerably greater concerns in mind."

"Siktam Lei died in Cimsas?" I say, and immediately decide that I ought to implement my decisions sooner.

"You haven't been informed, then?" He shakes his head. "Neither will this nation's children, nor of his existence. A pity, really—I've been reading up on him. Quite a man. You haven't heard of me, either, but that's going to change very soon."

"The Right Honourable Peksam Tei," I say, putting my hands behind my back as I step slowly towards him. "Earl of Tungnang, Sergeant-Major of the Order of the Blue Cross. Heir apparent to the Marquisate of Marapistanir and the Grand Marquisate of the East."

He brings his hands right up below his face and claps with his palms, barely moving them. "Very impressive. I suppose your book didn't have an imprint." He chuckles to himself, the sound almost painfully artificial. "Which brings me once again to my point. My answer is no."

"They destroyed a city without any provocation whatsoever," I say immediately, and I realise I've been bracing myself for a 'no' the whole time. "What makes you think they won't be as eager to pay *you* a visit?"

He looks down left to his right hand, rubbing the corner of his index's nail to his thumb. "They're not visiting us yet, are they? This city's walls are very strong, das Cimcharei. Aimelan-built, in fact. This entire place is."

"As a *gift*, to replace the Return's lo—"

Almost quicker than I can see, he turns, reaching to the table and grabbing a steel tumbler; before I can say anything, he throws it straight to the ground, the steel smacking straight into the thing's round centre.

Both of us look as it bounces soundlessly off the ground's low-threshold barrier, coming to a halt on its fourth landing with a soft 'plonk'.

"Did that have the intended effect?" I try and fail to stop myself from asking, looking back up to him. "I'm fairly sure solid clearglass isn't that fragile."

He stares at the immobile thing on the ground for two entire seconds before his composure returns, his features condescending. "I don't *like* Aimela, not to put too fine a point on it. You have taken our empire. Your songs have crushed our crafts, your speech has corrupted ours, your disgusting, degenerate *culture* that's been carved into our souls with the attaintment the very symbol that hangs over our walls to represent the wealth of my blood, the heavens know it's almost *incarnate* in that half-thing you've dragged along with you, and *you, you* worst of all, I don't know *what* you've done to your body, you mockery of a child, the degeneracy of your culture has pulled itself through our nation and rotted it from within." He points at me, and I've got the distinct feeling that something's keeping him from trying to touch me in the process. "Kanandrisra and Peratirei, may they burn, haven't killed us—they've enslaved us. The imperial ways have been lost beyond repair—we *celebrate* our defeat. Your nation is crumbling, and I will watch. Men will do what heaven sees, and I don't mind being amongst either."

He finishes his speech with a swift about-heel, the generously plumped tassels on his shoulders—I hadn't noticed them before—swooping over with him; he steps onwards, looking to the distance.

The Insurmountables do funny things to perspective; whatever made the Coreburrow's left the cliffs charred, but they're so far away—its two hundred kilometres barely even edged towards four or five kilometres by an enormous free-standing construction far to the north, its support-skeleton reaching down into the darkness—that it seems almost as if I'm looking at an unabridged horizon.

"Well," I say, my eyes turning back to his back, "That won't help either of us, will it?"

His voice is bitter as he responds; his left hand goes down to his chair's wooden arm, grasping it tight as he shakes his head. "I don't intend it to. We'll fulfil our obligations—you'll be given as much hospitality and aid as you need. But no more."

"I don't suppose there's anything I could do to change your

mind."

"Make the Valley bloom on Armistice Day," he says, flicking his right dismissively over the shoulder, looking back to me and then forth again as he does and pushing himself back up to lean against the safety rail; I hear metal against glass behind me.

I take the hint.

The Marquis' properties are in a bit of a legal quandary. The Grand Marquisate itself is a primogenetic corporation sole extending ownership over the Aimelan gift-structures, the rather elegantly pillared Illumination Residence a few kilometres to the north and the four avenues leading up to it; the rest of the city's succession isn't quite so clear-cut.

In his lifetime, Siktam Lei had bought nine of Western Marapistanir's twenty-nine districts piece-by-piece and justified his successions for each street, each estate, each garden, each statue, each lease and each bench before the Throne Ascendant in Vitreous Aquamarine.

He'd bought twenty more, but none of them now belong to his dear nephew.

The quiet square I'm riding through at the moment—Zatjit Square, with its beautiful little field of chrysanthemums about a saman whose decametres-high canopy shrouds us just enough that light still shines through to the ground below—now belongs to Duchess Yingjieu the Third, as per its own enatic-cognatic tradition. The current Marquis owns almost nothing between the Meilan Outcrop and Jinlang Shengtieu.

I'd ask myself how I knew half of this if there hadn't been a little stall selling a sessile-tab of the Exchequer Imperial for half a penny half a kilometre before.

For free, actually, once he saw the man besides me.

"Riveting, isn't it?"

I look up in surprise; the soldier—a knight, now that I recall his title—is looking down to me, the slight illumination the objectives before the metal that conceals his face clearly visible in the shadow. "What?"

"Exchequer Imperial. An Aimelan publication. It stands objective for its sponsors. Did you know the old Marquis was in Cimsas to celebrate his last standardisation? I was meant to accompany him—he'd rendered the suggestion that I might be a bit too *scary*."

"I can't imagine why."

He maintains his silence, his metal visage a third of a metre away from mine.

This image fills my vision for a few seconds before he bursts into laughter, the sound loud enough that I can hear the muffled original his helm's sessile clearly echoes. I try to laugh rather nervously back, the resulting giggle sounding a little like a fleshcrawler's chittering.

He seems to take a deep breath I can't hear before speaking again.

"My name is Hanjat Kitu, Knight-Banneret bestowed per Fiat on the estate of the Marquis Marapistanir. I apologise for my former formalities—the commonguard don't look too well upon misceordination."

"Misceordination?" I say; the word is most certainly Aimelan, but it takes a while before its meaning registers—it disturbs me a little that I'm not sure if it's me or the cache operating the registry. "I always presumed knights were nobility."

"My children, perhaps. Certainly not me." There's a slight resignation in the way he speaks. "Not that they would have stopped me themselves, of course. The whispers are enough of an irritant with jealousy their only fuel."

I'm not terribly experienced with sincere conversation, but I'm fairly sure most recent strangers aren't quite so forwards with their inner feelings; it takes me a little to find an inadequate response.

"I see."

There's hardly a sound from him for a second or so as he turns once again to look forwards. I might imagine a sigh past the metal; his posture in the speckled shadow gives off a contemplative air for the half-minute before we emerge from the canopy and onto Jakjitbin Avenue and he turns back to me, his façade shrouded in his own shadow.

"How does our new Marquis seem to you, milady?"

A moment passes with my hand to my chin. "He seems very expressive."

"He's going to run our nation into the ground."

I don't say anything. The sun is warm against my skin, and the barrier is a brilliant shade of blue.

"I suppose I sound duplicitous. I suppose you don't think much of me—I suppose you think I'm trying to coax something from you." His breath is clear now, cutting off into its muffled counterpart as it trails off and the sessile's echo falls below his voice's threshold. "The Marquis bears blood above all, as he imagines the Zhanghwazh have always been—I will almost certainly be cashiered for one reason or another, for I do not imagine he would suffer a Melaizh, especially one lowborn, in his court."

I try to keep my voice measured; a street sign flashes in my right peripheral as I look straight ahead. "Why would you tell me this?"

"The Emperor's laws breathe in the streets, each kind to the outspoken, and I have no cause to give you anything but my word. I've heard whispers from my youth's companions. A friend had cause to relate that two of the Administrator for the Arts' fine exhibits had disappeared, named for the appendage you bear so regally upon your back—gone with a girl from the crushed city who entered a third and left an administrator. The stains on your back aren't dye, at least no sort I've ever seen put to use—you bear the marks of a legend's beginning, whoever you may be."

There's a moment of silence as we pass past Sitpin Avenue onto Paklitjip Street; the pinkish blossom-flowers hanging unripe off their trees trailing the fractured-granite pavement seem almost to bleed luxury, the preservation-sessiled farm-baskets below them barely visible.

"Well," I say, a slight cough coming in almost involuntarily from the back of my throat, the sound's escape telling me I've failed to keep it silent, "I suppose Zhanghwazh wordcraft never found itself lacking."

"Whatever your quest may be," he says, "it seems to border inevitability that the upcoming turmoil will see me vacating my post. I cannot see a woman of your stature committing any wrong—and I don't believe I have any other options if I wish to play a part in the troubles that are to come."

"You want to *join* us?"

"Your entourage, as it were. I see the times changing, and opportunity's stricken me surer than a bolt. I understand my allegiance may seem questionable—consider the offer. We shall arrive long before the politics."

I glance past the rather fresh-looking field of granite pavers we're slowly marching upon to the sign a few metres before us: Yikdipwan featural, *Siksat Kit*. One of the succession properties, its beginning marked more by the overflowing bushels of oration-twisted flowering vines, growing up higher into shrubs and then blossoming trees as they lead to the massive, mansion-semi-circled courtyard about a kilometre before us than any sign I can see.

"I'll consider it."

"Out of curiosity," he says, his voice bearing the mild sort of inquisitiveness I might expect from a gesture born of politeness, "what exactly are you going to do?"

It takes me a moment to answer.

"We're making the Valley bloom on Armistice Day."

He leans back a little. "Oh dear."

We ride on in relative silence.

I take the time to note in the time I have alone with my thoughts that the air is very pleasant in its cold emptiness.

There is a very complete unease within me as I enter the circle of buildings that make the Illumination Residence.

It certainly isn't because of the elegantly pillared white-and-gold of the reconstructed quartz buildings before us. I'd only imagine I'd be able to dwell a bit more of its beauty if I wasn't so absolutely sure of my complete safety.

I'm sure of my safety because I wouldn't like to imagine that the array of extremely and profoundly lethal weapons in my immediate proximity aren't there solely to ensure it.

The glint off a mounted pre-Laceration weapon's tip is all the more obvious when an attempt is made to conceal it. Fifteen track me from the attics under a row of very nicely tiled and arched roofs, eighteen thin, long and rather cleverly painted barrels per weapon shining clear in the day. Three somewhat squat obelisks are mounted upon long-cardinaled white concrete octagons in a triangle in the courtyard, intricate golden patterns tracing their ways down the sides.

Suicide beacons, I realise, and I shift a little in my saddle.

"You seem ill at ease," Hanjat says, looking unwaveringly ahead as he guides us to the right. "I presumed an Aimelan would be used to security."

I take the hint, keeping my own line of sight well-level and trying to look as if my mouth remains unmoving. "I'd like to imagine we're more subtle about it."

"Subtle?" he says, and his tone makes me feel as though he's raising an eyebrow as we come slowly to a halt; he begins pulling himself off, and I follow. "The Administrative Tower had upon its walls a thousand-fifty-six, its bastion walls lined with three-hundred-twenty-four. It had the capacity to put a million to rest in seconds or less."

"At least it fit with the aesthetic."

The door—a rather ornate thing, as I might expect, the golden accents against what I assume is some sort of black heartwood and there is a piercing screech behind me and I turn in an instant as Hanjat does what's almost a pirouette in his suit, the barriers no doubt close enough to his skin that the inertia goes only forward as he forces himself up against his glasswalker.

He seems to hesitate for a moment, looking over his glasswalker, before pulling what looks to be a series of long and short blocks of black metal from its saddle's pouch as the enormous, almost singular screech of pre-Laceration weaponry—one of its sources missing, I realise, the nest in which it should be a black crater against the white—fills the air along with over two thousand invisible streaks of death per second, a handful of visible streaks providing an impression.

Hanjat pulls his hand up along with his weapon, two fingers risen as the enormous firearm lands on his glasswalker's back to point past the enormous garden before them. There's a slight pulse in the firing, the stream of light from each ending before their beginning—and at this point I realise I've been standing like an idiot and step back until my back's to the door, a barrier forming almost in an instant as my lips and fingers move to my larynx's tune—before he brings his fingers down and then his fist, pumping downwards and bringing his hand to the rifle's grip, concealed within one of the blocks that constitute it.

There is a moment of absolute silence.

It occurs to me to put my hands to my ears just as his arms move five centimetres back with a sound which, as I feel my bones shudder for the second it takes for him to reposition and have his arm move back once more—a little less than before—I have decided can only be given the adjective 'loud'.

"No pe-ne-tra—tion! Re-frain u-pon a—rms!" he shouts; his voice is so uncharacteristic it takes me a second to realise it's him.

"Re—port u-pon a—rms!" he continues, dragging his last word for three seconds straight before pulling his weapon to his shoulder, side-stepping his mount in a single bound—the suit's definitely Aimelan-made—and raising an arm.

A few seconds pass before a voice returns.

"One wounded of the Sixth out of action! One wounded of the Sixth in action! Sixth order incapacitated! Orders one through five clear! Orders seven through eleven clear! Orders twelve through ninety-seven clear and disengaged! All orders clear! All lines clear! All orders disengaged!"

"Dispatch Hospitallers! Prepare warrants! Dis—missed!"

He turns to me, now, not bothering to look at his rifle as he lobs it into his saddle's sack.

"I must apologise for that unpleasant episode, milady."

"I have medical training," I say, and I note that I'm quite out of breath. "I can help. You said no penetration, didn't you?"

"A formality, milady, if you don't quite mind."

I don't need to hesitate before I nod.

"Come, then," he says, putting his hand to the door, and I imagine as I might see a reassuring smile if I were to see his face.

The room I'm lead into past the hallway is pink.

I'd lend it a few more adjectives, but that would betray its fundamental identity: it's *pink*, and that is the job it performs first and foremost, though perhaps 'white' would contend for the title. I can't call it a bedroom despite the countless bright pink pillows of every sort permeated entirely with white lace strewn about on the soft, painted wool because it has no beds; I can't call it a nursery even with its pink-cheeked dolls of a thousand shapes and white faces laid up against the heart-covered wallpaper because it has no cribs; I can't call it a library even with the white-embroidered, pink-covered books laying closed about the ground, because their covers tell me they're not worth a millionth as much as the paper.

It's a strange, grotesque chimaera of many things draped in an overwhelmingly masculine burst of colour, but I must say that it looks comfortable enough that it's a struggle not to throw my suddenly aching back on the enormous, plush, no doubt cotton-stuffed pillows piled up into enormous—the room is ten metres tall, hundreds of patterns adorning its sides—oddly-shaped mountains before me.

I kneel, bringing one of the strewn books to my knee as I trace the entwined Zhanghwazh ideographs with a pinkie finger; I can only read the second out loud.

"*Chungnuzh?* Grown female's—?"

He leans over my shoulder. "Housekeeping for the women of the Grand Estate."

I shudder a little, easing the thing—it's a terrible waste of tree—down to the floor and standing back up. "How difficult could housekeeping be?"

"One might find himself surprised by the sheer depth of the art," he says, and I note as his foot pulls from the ground that there's not a speck upon its little crater. "The women of the Estate are very particular about the dust on their monocles."

"And where's my compatriot?" I say, looking about the room; there isn't anything here so kind as to betray his presence.

"The governess told me he'd fallen asleep," he says, keeping still as his head turns with the room. "I'm unclear on this point, if I may say—is the person a 'he' or a 'she'?"

"A 'he'," I say, grabbing a pillow by the lace—the softness almost makes me shudder, the little bits in between almost as light as air, no tactile barrier trying to ameliorate its perfect surface's perfect, breathing texture—and dropping it, casually reaching for another. "One whose character leads me to imagine he's buried himself underneath a pile of these things in the hope of surprising us and fallen asleep in the process. I don't think we've so much as seen a pillow for a week."

He reaches forth himself, beginning to search with me—his gauntlets reach deep into a pile three metres tall and one thick, shaking around a bit before he grasps the centre and pulls; the entire pile comes outwards as he swivels to the side, the tower crumbling next to him. "I meant to ask you—that attempt didn't seem to bother you in the slightest."

I try to emulate his method, reaching a third of a metre into a similarly sized stack and pulling; a pillow near the top, shook loose, slides down and pomfs gently against my head, causing me to fumble around a bit with it before managing to get enough of a hug on it to drop it at my feet. "I suppose I'm used to it by now. Allay my concerns, nonetheless— you say your weapon didn't penetrate his armour? Was it black in colour?"

"Certainly," he says, sidestepping the pillows—harder to do the further in, and I see him almost crush a bolster—and reaching into another pile, demolishing it in short order. "To both. The Cockroaches have remarkable defences—I absolutely must interrogate the Hospitallers in short order as to their properties."

"Cockroaches?" I say, sitting back down. "That's what you call them?

"After the colours we're informed they bear, yes. The Aimelan press has about a thousand names for them; I'm not sure which you would prefer."

"I'm not sure myself," I say, shaking my head. "I'm only very aware that they've tried to kill me."

"Perhaps a more fruitful topic?" he says, nodding as he demolishes another tower with another pull and swivel. "Assassinations always are a dreadful business."

"Assassi-*what?*"

We both look behind us; the sight of a very delicately-framed man—I realise how misleading the description is, for all its technical correctness, the moment I recognise his face—leaning up against the doorframe with a spoon in his hand half-buried into an elegantly blown clearglass decanter filled with a viscous white substance.

"Wait," he says, waving the spoon in a circular motion in our general direction, "what the hell're you two doing?"

I look down at the visible bits of my pillow-buried arms—a star-shaped one falling down upon my shoulder and staying there as he looks with a rather bemused stare, an awkward shake letting it fall back over my shoulder—then back to him, Hanjat already facing him with his usual air of respectability.

"Which question do you want answered?" I say, and the entire mountainous stack—five metres tall—comes tumbling down upon me.

Perei nods slowly to the beat of an echoed voice as I push my head from the pile, the now-empty decanter laid by his side.

"Damn. *You're* gonna come with us?"

"Not at the moment, you understand. There's work to be done here, and this fair lady—" and here he nods up at me as I brush my cloak down, "—has caused quite a stir by her presence. I harbour doubts that the men sent hence were genuinely of the Cockroaches, as no doubt you have as well."

"Their tactics and numbers, I presume?" I say, leaning back a little on the collapsed pile and letting out a slight sigh.

"And their sheer incompetence. I must take my leave, I'm afraid, to make my reports to the Marquis—I'll have a maidservant escort you to the library in due course." He stands, tipping his head as he begins to move.

"One last thing," I say, as Hanjat is about to leave the room, "What was this room before we were given it?"

"This room?" he says, turning rather graciously back to me. "An orphanage."

Perei tilts his head. "Hell happened to the kids?"

"The Marquis instructed me before your escort to relay to the couriers that the girls here should be hired out for the duration of your stay. I believe most of them are working in the factories around the Wall Zone. They were being trained to be maidservants—I'm uncertain as to why that particular vocation was given to them."

His words take me a moment to digest.

"Oh. Thank you."

"Pleased to serve, milady." He bows his head and then turns once more, landing with a very light thump—a slight stress in his movement for a second before his visible relaxation—and walking out the door.

"Huh," Perei says, picking a heart-shaped pillow up by the bright white lace that embroiders it. "Girls lived here? Why's it *pink*?"

There are two fundamental flaws with any 'fertile region' concept.

First: barriers are profoundly—

"Ugh," Perei grunt-says, shoving a leather-bound tome back into its spot in the wooden shelves, the long, thin windows protruding up from the soil and rock letting a rectangle of light shine across it. "All this shit's in Zhanghwazh and Angzhwen. Hell am I gonna do now?"

I look up from the book I've been idly staring at a page of—*Saepological Dysexaptics, 7th Edition*—and glare right at him, shutting it closed with a *thump*. My sessile, draped over my lap, falls from my hand as I do, black spreading itself across its surface. "Someone's tried to kill me in the last twenty minutes. Perhaps you could infer."

"Hmm." He puts his hand against his chin, stroking an imaginary beard for a second or two before his eyes brighten almost as though he's had a wonderful idea. "Gonna get high."

He promptly turns about as if to run.

"Stop. No. Bad."

He groans as he turns back around, beginning to roll his eyes in the slowest, most deliberate way I'd imagine is physically possible. "Come on. We've gone like five days on water and paste."

I glance down, and my eyes catch the open sessile; I stop for a second, my eyes flitting down the page's length, then back up to him just as the sound of breaking glass brings itself to my attention and my arm has something about it—his hand—and my yelp as my foot catches on the shelf's edge as he turns about it is drowned up in the immediate scream issuing to my side as Perei drops to the ground, bringing me with him and my arm lashes out to catch the carpet just as his hand flies to his shoulder.

"Shit, shit, *shit*—" he gasps out, and I can tell as I force him over onto his back and look him in his wide eyes that his prognosis isn't good— it's *poison*, I don't know what kind yes I do it's *barriered cardiopathic acid*, he's dead, he's—no, he's not dead yet. He's breathing and he's alive and he is *not* yet *dead*, and I take a quick, deep breath and force myself to *look*.

"*Áyenii myzh ysj áshentyra tyzh consenjs mávnyrii rug–lyn consenjs hédsuir,*" I say, the perfect words forcing themselves from my lungs in the time it takes for me to grab his shoulder—where his own arm is weakly reaching—and find then quite uncarefully rip a little barbed black shard from the blue and red overlay—it's in the veins, there's a chance—spread over his slow-breathing body, laid flat I hope-know more of his own volition than the poison's.

"How bad?" he says, and I only realise he's speaking because I see his voicebox, cyan against navy, contorting underneath his skin along with the redness spreading along his veins from the now-sealed incision in his shoulder as I reach to my hip and pull and the misericorde flips about in my hand between my fingers as its axle as I stab down into his chest right above his thoracic cavity with what I must say is a remarkable gentleness and make one of my own—twelve seconds, eleven—and my mouth moves so quick I can't quite understand what I'm saying but the tower does enough that the membrane is rephrased over and *through* his veins, brilliant shining white against pale blue, and the wound closes in on itself before my eyes and all I can do is watch.

The dark red moves down towards his beating heart; my flow estimate is correct. Three seconds. One.

The red stops at the white. He breathes and does not die.

I dismiss the subjective, and the gently pinkening white upon the blue turns in an instant to bloodied flesh.

"Ow," he says, taking a rather profound breath, "That really hurt."

I blink once or twice; I realise that my mouth is dry as it comes to my mind to respond. "I stabbed you in the chest," I say, massaging my sublingual gland with my tongue as I lick my lower lip. "Cardiopathic acid has a numbing effect. It'll wear off in an hour."

"That's nice to hear," he says, his voice containing the slightest tinge of an emotion I can't immediately identify as he tilts his head up, then lets it down quite abruptly with a slight groan. "Where did you say we were going?"

"Antamanaria," I say, the word rolling quite pleasantly off my tongue. "The Shattered Circus."

"You could've just told me to go on ahead," he says, his smile weak.

"What?" I swallow and breathe; I can't quite hear my own voice, and my vision is clouded. Stress.

"You know," he says, arm reaching over to his spotless forearm to cradle it. "When I was turning around. What with how the place is and all." He looks to the side, resting his cheek on the ground for a second, before he looks back up to me. "I guess you were right about the whole 'field experience' thing."

"Are you—" I say, taking another deep breath, "—are you trying to make me laugh? Were you going to make some other reference you thought would be amusing to me? A one-liner to lighten the mood?"

I stare at him as he stares at me.

We look into each other's eyes for a few seconds before I start laughing, a thin, breathy noise shifting down my throat into an unstoppable series of short, alternating squeals and breaths that I imagine is a mockery of real laughter, and I laugh and laugh so hard my head throbs and it feels as though as I'm not even laughing but I haven't really laughed in so long that I can't find it in myself to stop.

He joins me—I'm sure with some hint of nerve I can't quite detect—as footsteps begin to echo sharply down the hall.

eight
Crushing a Flower

Today I crushed a flower.
It was much smaller than me.
(There are people who would suggest this would be a given,
but the world is filled with so many they haven't seen.)

I looked at it for a minute or two.
Then I plucked it by its stem,
the violet-rimmed white
with seeds of green
I brought it into my hand and crushed it
between my fingers.

Its slime laid clear against my skin.
One of its seeds was caught between
my palm and my finger,
and I'd kept my finger against my palm,
as I dragged it up
and split it in half with my nail
then licked a bit off it.
It tasted as I expected.

I did not know its name,
and went on to do other things.

'*Flattening bread with hands covered in napellus*', *Genyivé aup-*
Purus
Three Hundred Poems on Death and Resistance
compiled by Andresrea qu'n'av dasnamr
published by the Aimelan Anthropological Society and approved
for limited academic distribution by the Administration for Media
Development under the continued grace of Khaliesrea das Sikharea eliyit
Tamarisrei, Administrator for the Arts
initial resale publication by Mitras Press Holdings

ZHANGHWAMPEYZH

Aysmanratyss pyr Aysmanrat' Aimelzh pyr Cysinscandyra Ocilentzhra.

9
N'shéneganyr
to change the unchangeable

There are three fundamental flaws with any 'fertile region' concept.

Firstly: barriers are profoundly disparate with membranes; both suffer profoundly diminishing returns. While a theoretical thirteen-square-kilometre bit of sung spawncloth and around two hundred drops of orator blood could cover the hundred-thirty-thousand square (round?) kilometres of land that comprise the Zhanghwazh Valley with a single barrier, the membrane would either collapse upon itself at the five-hundred point—assuming stable-tolerance—or have the membrane separate from its increasingly intolerant barrier and dissipate altogether, hence 'stable-tolerant'. Individual barriers would be outstandingly inefficient, and wouldn't be much of an improvement from the way things are done as it is—such barriers in fact already exist, facilitating the ongoing urban sprawl both in the Protectorates, the Twin Enclaves and, to a lesser extent, in the Valley itself.

Secondly: hydroponic farms require specialised environments profoundly hostile to civilised inhabitation and nutrient soil is expensive enough that its only purpose is gardening for people with more money than other people.

I'd say 'more money than sense', but soil-planted plants really are very pretty.

Thirdly, and far more fundamentally: barriers must reduce their threshold as they grow larger, and a threshold too low makes large-scale construction projects physically impossible as barriers within resonate with the city's; city-sized barriers are therefore invariably as big as they can be while still remaining tolerant of intolerance. Small pacifist communities in Andresrea's Plains keep—

—Ish-al-wyent`e!

    My digression is saved from itself as the prone figure besides me forces itself to bend its torso in an instant at an angle literally perpendicular to its legs; he stays like this for a full second, his fingers splayed out and chest arching a little back in what I can only assume is absolute agony before slumping a little with his hands and pressing themselves hard to his chest as he lets out a very low groan, sinking pitifully into the new saddle-bedding our kind former host handed us as we left.

    "You've made a fine recovery, I see," I say, glancing to him as I speak over his whimpering. "Self-perpetuating dilution membranes usually take days to work their way out. The anaesthetic effect should have suffi—"

    "Rivet yourself up the nose," he manages to let out, his voice shaking as a harsh breath tears itself from his lungs every other word. "Rivet yourself so hard your nose falls—*oh god this hurts so **much***—falls off your *goddamn*—"

    "Hold on," I say, tugging the glasswalker a little to the left; he winces as my leg brushes against his, and I reach over to his chest. It takes a few minutes of gentle whispering before his arms go slack, a relieved sigh that's almost a moan pressing against his throat as I draw away.

    "Your chest's nerves shouldn't be bothering your brain for a day or two," I continue, tugging myself back away.

    "Okay," he says, looking down at his chest with a peculiar sort of surprise. "Okay. Thanks."

    I nod and get back to thinking.

    The second flaw is simple to address—

    "So," he says, and I regret not drugging him instead for the moment it takes for my sense of medical ethics to reassert itself, "spell it out for me. Why'd we get out of that place? Wanted to test out the finest saddle I've ever laid my ass upon?"

    "Do you honestly think someone would have been able to get

into the courtyard without help?"

It doesn't take him more than a moment to make the connection; I suppose the thug life engenders a certain quickness of thought.

"You mean—"

"Yes."

"But w—"

"He really doesn't like Aimela."

He throws his hands up. "Hell. Sounds like a guy I'd wanna meet."

It takes me almost a minute—during which his stare grows increasingly suspicious—to come up with something in response.

"I didn't think you'd like to meet him, considering where he chose to accommodate you."

A similar clarity lights up upon his face within the next few seconds; unsettlingly, he doesn't look angry insofar as he is unhappy in a way his face wasn't built to convey.

"Oh," he says.

He's quiet long enough for me to think.

"So, they bulldozed one city."

I look from my sessile to him. "Along with two million people."

"So, they riveted some old folks' home."

I restrain myself from forcing him to his point. "Severing contact with the last authority in Central Aimela, effectively splintering the Aimelan Administration into two provincial governments, a de facto colonial military command and a series of city-states in common association until the Reserve Council is brought into contact, the Reserve Administrator for Parks and Public Recreation comes back from Carj or General Amensitrea das Vasksharei elects to assume reserve command."

He stares at me. "There's a Reserve Administrator for Parks and Public Recreation?"

"Telesrei das Teshkharea ermit Erindrea. Born 9 Septimus, 3828. Appointed Administrator for Parks and Public Recreation on 3 Primus,

3864. He declared his writ to be the Writ of Privilege, exempting public parks from obscenity regulations on speech. Retired 9 Septimus 3908 to spend time with his children. His daughter, Administrator for Parks and Public Recreation Erindrea das Cimcharei, resides or resided in Cimsas. She declared her writ to be the Writ of Exemption, making all parks, public or private, subject to administrative oversight. The Administrator for Parks and Public Recreation, and by extension his Reserve Administrator, is twenty-sixth in line to the succession to the office of the Provisionary Administrator."

His stare is past me by the time I'm finished; it seems to take a few seconds to register before he shakes his head and they refocus. "How the hell do you know that?"

"I like parks."

"Maybe I didn't say it right the first time," he says, his head shaking slowly. "How in Isha's loving name do you even come close to knowing *half* that?"

"I *really* like parks," I say, absentmindedly twiddling my thumbs. "What were you saying before I gave you your answer?"

"Uh, I—um—I thought you were gonna ask me what my point was."

"I'm not letting you fool the rule of three. Do go on."

He scratches at his neck and then goes down to his collar, shadows hidden from the sun as his fingers poke their ways under. "They, uh—they shot some muds?"

"Well," I say, shrugging, letting my head rest on my thigh-mounted fist as it carries the most affectedly apathetic smile I can possibly give, "I suppose I can't think of anything."

"Okay, okay, rivet it like an itsystrong—"

"That's a disturbing image."

"—out the kayay. Just think about it. We're busting our asses here picking shit up because some lady said we'd rivet a whole army doing it."

"I distinctly remember having a conversation of this sort before."

"Not just that. What the hell are we fighting? A bunch of assholes who got lucky? They can't get past a bunch of muds with bolts. We could just—I don't know what the hell we'd do, but the jings? What the hell do we need the jings for? It's not like there's more of them than us."

It takes me a moment with my memories to find my answer. "The administrator they're fighting for. If I'm understanding it right, he's the one who's manufactured their weapons and armour."

"We don't even know if the shithead's *alive*. How d'you know it isn't over already? How many people d'you think they even have? Twelve days, Ash. Give or take, we've been doing this shit for twelve days. *Twelve days* and we haven't seen *one* of those guys outside a city—don't you think they'd try and mess us up 'round the point we're *not* under everything they ever thought up that could keep us *not messed?*"

"They might be massing for an attack," I say, and realise as I speak that my posture's been stiffening throughout his monologue.

"Yeah, massing. Just like the muds down south, right? Fifty years and counting. Wonder how much mass they've got now."

I let his words take their time sinking in; I take a little more formulating my response.

"Let us suppose you're right," I say, looking to the horizon. "Let us suppose we're going about collecting priceless exodus caches for nothing. Suppose we decide to turn around at this moment, with an administrator' faith, an army behind us—whose eventual extinction doesn't quite preclude their immediate danger—and enough Concordance violations in our hands to have both of us hanged five times over if we don't hand them over right away for a pension the size of a moringa nut."

His mouth hangs a little open on his soft-featured skull as I turn to look to him.

"Say the administrator doesn't quite mind our dereliction. Say we don't get shot the moment we stay in one place. Say we aren't strung up the moment we show our hand. Say our nation crumbles and we are hung out to dry. What on earth would you like to do *then*? Requisition land in Ilgishnarea y Mitras and grow taraxacum in the yard? Perhaps I've been neglecting your agency here, and I'm sorry if I am, but *what exactly* do you propose we do instead?"

The expression of mild shock that's printed itself across his face takes half a minute to break against my similarly mild glare.

"Isha," he says, his lips coming back together at last, looking to his sides then back to me with his arms out—one with its tip to the front and the other to my back with the former lower than the latter, fingers splayed in questioning—as he speaks. "*Tell me* the next time it's your time of the month."

I consider apologising for my nerves; my sense of civility is caught for a moment in a deadlock with my sense of pride.

"Ash?" he says. and civility falls out the window.

"Yes?"

"Weren't we supposed to get to Antamanaria?"

"We're taking an indirect route. Why do you ask?"

He points past me, far to my right. "Because I'm pretty sure most people don't stand still on the way to Antamanaria in packs of twenty."

I look to his gesture—twenty discrete figures on glasswalkers, a blur against the day's heat. A kilometre away, give or take.

Nine hundred and ninety metres away.

Nine hundred and eighty.

"We're taking a detour," I say, and instruct our glasswalker to hurry up the littlest bit as Perei pulls Ayerei's sessile-arm from his back. "I was planning to tell you when we got there."

"God*damnit*, Ash, where're we getting ourselves killed now?"

> *Shenzhraszyera*
> *—Sunwind*
> *Shenzhraszyera, Yienfung Strip, Zhanghwampezyzh*
> *Demilitarised Free Trade Zone*
> *Description: Area colonised by United Aimelan Materials Concern (UAMC) on 3 Undecimus 3809 under the name Shenzhraszyera, 'Wind of the Sun'. Application cites vast mineral reserves. Site abandoned on 2 Primus 3910; accounts of the area report a vast area of exotic, soil-based vegetation ending at the very edge of its dysexaptic field. No visitors have returned, and the vegetation is reported to have various unusual and dangerous properties.*
> *Investigated 29 Undecimus 3910, SOP 391-3910*
> *29/1/3911: Division 392 has failed to return on schedule. Suggest reinforcements.*
> *9/2/3911: Approved. Backup operations authorised.*
> *9/3/3911: Division 958 has failed to return on schedule. Suggest exfiltration team.*
> *13/2/3911: Unconditionally denied.*

"There," I say, looking to the horizon. "Seven kilometres. I'm praising my foresight."

"Is this really happening *right now*? Is this 'cause I said this was dumb?" he asks, fiddling around with his rifle as he looks intermittently towards the now unmistakably familiar black-on-white armour of a group of people I don't particularly enjoy associating with. "I dunno if objectives can do that, but if this is a joke *I'm not laughing*."

"Six kilometres to Shenzhraszyera," I say; its Pari dunes have come into sight now, the slight glint of a membrane in the sun glinting over its edge. "They're closing. Get ready."

Something very bright and very loud—loud enough for its sound to travel unimpeded through our barrier—hits my ears and eyes.

"What the hell was that?"

I blink to see a very bright light—brighter than the sun, I realise, its shine past our membrane three times wider than the sun's disc—rising far above them; it takes me two more very loud sounds to come to a conclusion.

"Tutć vétirymj ánuyr," I begin, and feel a cool, heavy substance beginning to run past my throat. Perei squeals a little; I look closely at the light, rising as I rephrase my membrane gently through my alimentary canal's thinnest walls, delicately coating my internal organs. *"Ápyfrét létyjs."*

"Ántt vin'lekmétyr páræyr," I continue, and the light grows bright enough to blind and I *feel* the heat behind me—*hotter than the sun's corona*, I realise, the temporarily rent membrane resealing in an instant—as the sheer force sends me against my mount's mane.

"Brace yourself. *Ástt!*" I shout, and the glasswalker's hooves crack the glass beneath us as we go from two hundred kilometres an hour to zero in barely an instant; I am intimately aware that our organs should be lying crushed against our ribs, the membranes within us quite admirably doing what the laws of physics mandate them to.

"Son of a brother's broken cu—" Perei coughs out, just as another wave of pressure and heat pushes against us and I force us forwards once more, another burst making its presence known against the ceramic on my back.

"Two kilometres," I say, and it takes twenty seconds for my estimate to be a kilometre off as our mounts begin to scale the dune; a whistle fills the air for a split second, and I feel an acute force against my back as I realise my wing's barrier has absorbed the very slight burrow of something whose force I wish I wouldn't recall.

Perei leans back, bracing his firing arm against his walker's mane as he takes aim; we clear the dune before he has the chance to fire, and we face heaven just as a sound I've just learnt to dread fills my ears once more.

The first thing I notice past the brilliant blue on its opposing end—Tachiesrea's barrier may have been retrofitted, but it was unmistakably ancient in a way that this one avoids brilliantly—is an amount of greenery I might reasonably think impossible. The plants have grown against the barrier with an intelligence almost beyond nature, the absolutely enormous trees—not trees, I realise, but some utterly alien, semi-cyatheaceaean construct with its massively upscaled succulent leaves spitting in the square-cube law's metaphorical face—grown against the very surface of the barrier almost a kilometre high, the leaves wrapping it in a verdant cocoon that we're accelerating towards at about a hundred and eighty kilometres an hour.

"Tower—" I begin, and I'm blind for the second it takes for me to feel the fused silicon below me turn abruptly for a single step into a sort of powder—*ash*, I realise—before the slightly more familiar resistance of soil hits my mount's hooves. I force my eyes shut and then open, the flash-blindness fading quickly enough that the enormous, branch-like yellow-green stretch of succulent biomatter a metre from my face has a chance to make my heart palpitate before it slams into my head with enough force to excise it from my shoulders.

The thought—my head smashed against a branch, body riding onwards without it—rehearses itself through my mind as I sit perfectly still, looking straight forwards into nothing, alongside a man lying on his back with his hand on his chest breathing as slow as he could reasonably be.

We are in complete darkness. I don't know how the light has faded and I do not know when, but I know that it has.

"Collision-stop routine," I quite calmly say, and the words work themselves out just as an enormous gout of red and blue washes over us both, covering our membrane entirely in an impressively sustained flame that is quite decidedly not hotter than the sun's corona. "Barrier tolerance just enough to avoid resonance. I didn't think about the resonance. We're exceedingly lucky to be alive."

"Okay," Perei says, looking up to the fires engulfing us, "what the hell now?"

I imagine he might have stressed his sentence's end if he had the requisite motivational capital; as it is, his tone lies as flat as him.

"I suppose we could begin to move." I breathe in, then out.

"Maybe we could, uh—stay here for a while. The membrane's not going anywhere, right?"

"I suppose fire's better than darkness."

"Not sure that works so well when you're *in* the fire."

"Do you *want* to stay here?"

My question is rather graciously answered by the very polite sound a barrier makes when something that very hard, very sharp and very fast pierces it and presumably skewers the screaming man inside; a series of gunshots—barely a few hundred metres away from what I can hear past the particularly loud crackling and hissing above us—answers it before it all cuts out with a swiftness that doesn't quite seem entirely natural.

"Not really," he says, exhaustion preempting emotion. "How 'bout you?"

"I don't either."

The fires above us show no sign of waning; we lie quite still for a bit, and I wonder what to do.

"Okay," Perei says, snapping his fingers up before his face idly as he has in the silence, "what're we gonna do now?"

"We could turn around," I say, looking away from the patterns the swirling flames make on the membrane. "And quite possibly get ourselves killed by something we won't ever see coming."

"Could stay here too, I guess." He stops snapping his fingers, craning his neck over his glasswalker's saddle's edge to see the grassy mud below. "Can't see what's coming, maybe get ourselves killed. What the hell kind of fire is this, anyway?"

"Oxyhydrogen. I'm not sure how this place hasn't burnt to the ground."

"Not stopping these things. Where d'you think it's coming from, anyway? Prelacs aren't supposed to try and hurt you themselves, right?"

Doubtlessly on cue, the fire goes out; I recognise the sounds preceding it, a hail of simple gunfire, right as Perei flips half over in his saddle. The knee-stirrups hold him as he holds himself to his glasswalker's side with his left arm, the shortened barrel of his weapon pointed onwards.

"*Oy!*" a thickly-accented female voice yells, and Perei looks up from his weapon's sights—a dull bioluminescence clearly casting a light glow now across his face—before a lightly illuminated figure reaches from behind him and grabs him by the neck, weapon clearly visible upon her back as she spikes her hand underneath his trigger-finger and *pulls*, a scream echoing from his throat as a burst of gunfire issues right into our barrier's inside with a light flash; I unbind my restraints in an instant and bring my foot up to my mount's back before another pair of arms surround me and I force my wings' barriers to regenerate intolerantly right into where I suspect his to be and the resonance sends me quite bodily tumbling into the woman before me who has Perei's weapon within her grasp and I fumble about my belt for my misericorde for half a second as she yells and hits at me and she *could* kill me but she doesn't and I find it and grasp tightly onto her unwisely grown hair just as she grabs me by the thigh and throws with enough might to send her falling halfway to the ground, my momentum counteracted with a single flap as I force myself down over her, knee planting into moist silt along with the first centimetre of my blade as its edge lies tightly along her very smooth neck.

I take a breath. I cannot see her clearly in the barely perceptible light, but her eyes are a distinctly alien sort of green, clearly illuminated from within—I glance to the right and see a man laying right below one of the low-hanging trees in armour I've only seen in imprints, eaten-away fabric barely retaining the spiked insignia upon its shoulder.

"Sestiyari Armed Forces?" I say, and my voice comes out with less exhaustion than it ought to.

"Yeah," the woman below me grunts out, her eyes looking between me and the blade. "I never thought I'd see the military here. Very good show." Her exact tone—some member of Jarasmi—is clear against my ears.

"I'm not an member of the military," I say, and I catch my semi-lie too late to prevent its conveyance. "I'm—we're exodus hunters."

"Isha save my ass," Perei coughs out, his hand rubbing his throat and hand reaching to his firearm as he hangs down besides me.

"Right," she says; my blade slips a little closer to her carotid artery through the mud, and her nonchalance holds the slightest tinge of an emotion I can't quite identify beyond a faint negativity. "So should I take it for granted that you're not here to send us to jail?"

"Depends how much you'd get us," Perei says, and I praise his mindfulness in spirit as he unbinds his first stirrup with an œvjt-án'em and sends one leg down to the ground, manually snapping the other. "Two specials? Might be worth about *half a strangle*."

"It's a bloody infantry choke," she says, her head too still to look at him. "Grow some balls, brother."

He raises his pistol and fires, the sound filling my ears before I can blink; a gaping hole appears in the mud between her thighs, and the ground we're over bulges out the littlest bit.

"Grow your own, sweetheart," he says, and I repress the urge to jump up and murder him. The woman under me shudders a little, a sharp, strangled breath emerging from her throat.

The man on the ground past us—long since silent—begins to speak in a low, guttural tone. "Yskristari Skullcrusher, high-explosive magazine-fed handcannon-type pistol utilising the Saltic barriered ignition method. Produced by the Yskristara Liable Concern."

The woman turns her head a little in the mud in an effort to view her compatriot, thick smears of it trailing along her cheek; I make sure to tilt my knife to match. "*Fullmoon?* Fullmoon, you're okay?"

"Yes," he says, and stays almost completely unmoving. "I'm perfectly fine. The appendages on her back offer some sort of barrier protrusion."

Perei looks over his shoulder and then back to him, now keeping his weapon trained on what I presume to be his torso with his finger notably rested on the trigger guard. "Guessing you're the server? Hell're you doing snatching little girls?"

"You have read too many books, brother," she says, her accent very apparent. "There is no such thing as a 'server'. He is just—socially awkward."

"Yes," he says. "Very awkward indeed."

I look back down to my captive. "Do you have anyone else here with you?"

Her look is convincing. "No."

"Division 392's two people?"

Her face gains a peculiar character of fear, muffled a little by the part of it covered in slow-drying mud. "Division three-nine—bloody damn hell. You are with the Expeditionaries, aren't you?"

"Don't know what that is," Perei says, going to a knee with his weapon carefully pointed, "but I'm not—*wha*—"

I barely see the man's hand moving in as the world turns into a streak into the darkness as my hand is twisted back and the *pain* in my wrist, and I pull and scream and kick back up right into the segmented aramid-steel hard enough for the clang to reverberate through to my knees as I'm forced face-first into the mud and there's a moment of silence before I'm pulled up, mouth filled with a substance I'm caught in the process of spitting out too hurriedly to take a taste of.

"Now," she says, her right breast mushing up against my flattened wing as the armour remaining on her left keeps cold against me, hand under my armpit and around as she yanks me to my feet, "tell me what you know."

A light green tinge highlights the length of the dagger against my throat, and I can distinctly hear Perei yelling behind me as her arm goes down my cloak and seeks the seam, her breath warm against my neck.

"I'm not with the Expeditionary Branch," I say, trying my best not to bring my tongue into contact with the mud before my lips. "I'm a—"

Her hand reaches under my cloak and reaches under the pants below; her skin touches mine, and my larynx-shaped exhalation stops before I intended as she pulls a cold square of metal from my waistband.

"Ashrea das Cimcharei es-Aysinfitrit," she says, nodding to me. "Aysinfitrit? What a pretty name. I could have sworn you were not a day older than ninety-five."

"It's an honorary administrative status granted—"

"To nameless of exceptional merit," the man behind us says, and the yelling turns muffled. "Perhaps you have just decided to take your title with its regeneration at last, Peratirei?"

"Judging by her choice of companion," she says, slipping my permit back into its band, "You might be quite right."

I take a deep breath before I speak, her arm tightening around my chest as I do. "I don't know *anything*."

"Sure, sure," she says, quite bodily yanking up, a squeak issuing from my throat as my muddied feet emerge from the ground, legs hanging with her softness pushing against my weight for an instant before she lumps me onto my glasswalker's back and pulls the long stirrups up to tie me in somewhat uncomfortably over my rhomboideus, arm moving down over my body to tighten itself around my feet.

"We'll see. *Séytj sek-métyr pársec.*"

The ground begins to move under me, and I groan with a profoundly unjust rehearsedness.

It occurs to me, as it has perpetually for the last few minutes, that the forest is extremely dark. The few spots of luminescence seem to have faded, and my perspiration-slick arm is beginning to go numb—there isn't a barrier or a membrane between us and the atmosphere's dampness, and I'm beginning to itch in places I don't usually anticipate touching.

The humidity isn't a comfort, and my throat begins to burn against the moist air.

"I'm thirsty," I say, and my voice has a hollow quality about it that I haven't heard in years; the woman above me, her silhouette barely visible, seems to reach for her side before a much bulkier silhouette reaches to interdict her.

"Aimelan administrators have sessiles in their throats and necks," the man says, his Jarasmi—I'm not certain what kind—palpably better structured than his Aimelan. "Don't bother. She'll probably find a way to kill you with it."

A muffled noise issues from Perei's throat; I don't ask why exactly they haven't gagged *me* instead, and allow a light dry cough just light enough that it doesn't aggravate my thirst to slip past my throat and then my lips. "Please. I don't have any sessiles."

"Kill me with it?" the woman says, an expression of mild interest in her distinctly gold-spoken Arakeshi voice. "Do tell."

"One fellow, right—gha-ninety-seven, you know him?"

"You don't mean he—"

"Harvest op, back when the dems weren't throwing a shitfit. I handled the poor bastard over the sessy. He got three in the hole, all admin kids. He took one, jumped on his walker, cleared out. In and out in fifty minutes. Poor bastard didn't gag her, he said, because she was something like five years up. So twenty minutes in, she asks for some water. Now, he's a nice guy, so he gets the skin out, lets it drip. Five seconds later, he's got two ices through his goddamn neck and three through his eyes—that's what he's saying right before he stops saying— got his sessy in her hand and went 'hey, who's there?'"

"No shit? How the hell's Arakesh still around?"

"Not sure what happened to her after that, but nine-six saw her going five-to-ten at the Games about a year later. Guess she never told anyone. Think her name was Khali-something."

"Khalitendrei das Tachiesrea? Administrator for the Military, right? I always did hear he started out different."

"Eh, he's just a bit twisty. The op got done around Sikhas—I don't think she fixed her bits anyway."

She shrugs. "Don't know anybody but the Big Twelve."

"Me neither," he says, and for a moment I imagine I feel his own shrug in the almost slimy air. "I think we're almost there. You've got the clicker straight, right?"

It seems as if she's about to respond before a particularly uncomfortably ballistic sound rips through the air and against my eardrums. There's a jump and a moment of silence before the woman yells, my legs freeing and leaving me dangling by my torso; I let out my own, considerably more restrained yelp, leg hooking on as well as it can to the walker's mane.

"Seven-three?" the woman says. "Seven-three, are you *insane*?"

"Re-*lax*, Sunrise." A mild rustle emanates from above us along with a distinctly childish voice, and I catch a mild glint in the darkness for a moment before the canopied pseudo-clearing—I see it in the instant before I can't—explodes into light, the ensuing yell notably failing to pull itself from any of our lungs. "Who's the friends?"

"I can't believe they sent the spec-ops in here after us," the man grumbles. "One of these trees're gonna snap us up one day. I'm never getting used to you psychopaths."

My irises begin to desaturate as he finishes his sentence—the half-fallen canopy above us, noticeably moist branches weighed down by flaky brown seed-pods, sways with the unnatural weight of a boy looking to be about ten, his entire body clad in something approximating an outline of his physique dangling from it by a horrid metal thing evidently joining his spine at the tailbone; an almost pinpoint-bright light issues from its very tip, leaving his shadow in his wake.

"*Psy*-cho-paths?" he giggles, the appendage jutting from his back uncurling as he sends his arms up to grasp about the branch she's just vacated—something in her hands making a clear *shunk* in the instant before they let go, sending his noticeably bare feet down to the leaf-padded ground with a hard *crunch* before he begins to sink into the soil. "*I'm* not the one doing sweaty things with baby girls and little boys, am I?"

"She's an admin," the woman—Sunrise?—says. "Not a very impressive one, but—"

"—impressive enough to send you two to the dirt?" he grins, walking forward with a gait to which I try and fail to stop myself applying the description 'whimsical' to as he reaches up to swipe a flake of dried mud from her reactionarily twitching face. "I wonder what the one who *isn't* an admin did."

"Screw off, seven-three. We roped them anyway."

My grumble is parched as my throat. "Lucky you."

The man looks over his shoulder at me with a particular venom in his stare.

'Seven-three' turns to me, seeming to squint for a moment before he begins to speak in a language so closely packed I barely understand how I understand it. "The shores come down as if cut quicker than the water boils—"

"Too far, not like they said," I say, the words instantly familiar on my tongue. "And the sun shines over the lost waves—its rays caught by the glass sands—as he catches me and takes me home. Exodus Archive ninety-seven, datum nine-three-seven-six-nine."

I don't quite expect his response.

"Good show," he giggles, his excitement uncomfortably obvious. "Very strong. Close your eyes, kids!"

Sunrise frowns. "Seven-three, thi—"

I choose the moment in which I see him jump to comply.

The first *shunk* encourages me to keep them shut about a second before the second, and the crunch of weights against leaves issues from below me before they open. I stare straight ahead into the sky, and do not look down. A moment passes, and another, far lighter crunch hits my eardrums sharply enough to make me twitch.

"Hell—o? Anybody in there?"

A rather loud series of smacks fills the air.

"Aww, he's gone lights out. I guess it's the heat."

The crunches draw close to me, and I feel a slight tightening about my chest for the instant before I fall entirely, crushing through the dried layer into the shallow moistness; I wiggle my fingers a bit in the warm soil, the water elsewhere keeping away from the hydrophobia my robes express.

"Tower," I say, taking a deep breath. "You really killed them, didn't you?"

He flicks his wrist and rolls his eyes a little. "It's not like they were important anyway."

"Okay," I say, slowly pushing myself off the ground as little globs of mud slide past my wrists; I make sure to keep them low enough that they don't slide down to my armpits. "Okay—you killed them because—because I knew something everyone does?"

"Wasn't the original, silly—the N'avarais dialect of Canqant're Nisais's polysynthetic, *really* precise and it's got about twenty speakers, all of whom have a different word for 'glass' and no word for 'wave'. I was just guessing you'd have gotten the fàndyura first—it's standard procedure to think you have."

"Standard procedure? What on earth would you have done if I hadn't picked it first?"

He looks up, as if in thought, then looks back at me with a little giggle ending in a smile.

"Let's talk about nicer things!" he says, gesturing back over his shoulder. "Mind helping me get him up?"

"Okay," I say, and follow his thumb; Perei's form is still moving, chest rising in perfect rhythm, and I feel something cold upon my neck as I begin to walk towards him.

The groan that accompanies the splash carries a low, dry character. I stick my thumb under his lower lip, the sticky, mildly ulcerated mess that is its frenulum rendering as little resistance as the fabric over my forearms as I begin to water his gums, my motions methodically incompetent.

It takes about ten seconds before he lets off with a violent cough, and I retract my hands just in time to avoid his frenulum-scraping spasm; the heel of my boot pokes against what I considerately lie to myself to allow myself to believe isn't a man's armpit, and he takes in a few harsh breaths before his eyes come back into focus, arms grasping in what I imagine is an instinctive motion to the handles at the saddle's base before commencing a very slow, groaning slide off its side.

"I—sha," he moans, the sweat collecting along the edges of the ceramic fabric he's been left for a shirt, "what th—who the *hell* is that?"

"Don't mind me," Seven-three says, the little smile across his unnaturally prepubescent face particularly at odds with the corpse—a faintly sickening smell beginning to emerge from it and its companion, a light, unfamiliar buzzing clear against the otherwise tranquil day—he's kneeling down to. "I'm just your friendly neighborhood—what d'you guys call us? 'Subversive elements'?"

"Isha," he says, looking absentmindedly to his quite gently removed robes lying across his mount before looking back somewhat hesitantly to the bodies laying before it, "those're the assholes that netted us. The hell'd you do to them?"

"I killed them," he says, flicking his wrist at us as if it was the most natural thing in the world. "Just a little stem-push. They'd have ruined our fun!"

"Right," Perei says, chipping a flake of dried mud off his cheek. "Okay, thanks. What now?"

My brow twitches. "He told me. There's an exodus cache somewhere around this forest's centre. He knows how to reach it, but the trees—the trees would rip us apart."

"You're shitting me, right? The *trees?*"

Wordlessly, Seven-three pulls a remarkably shiny little device—and it is here I notice that the light illuminating our little clearing fills it entirely from every side, the yellowish luminescence somehow shining from everywhere at once—from his rather loose-fitting pants, pushing his finger through a little hoop protruding from its side before casually letting it fly towards what appears to be the body of one of the pseudo-clearing's trees.

It bounces off without much of an issue, and lies at the thing's roots; he quickly jerks his hand back, and I realise that the loop has a wire leading from it as it flies back into his waiting palm.

"Uh," Perei says, and the tree's body quite clearly contorts, the portion of its branches comprising one-fifth of the place's coverings twisting in place for a moment before a solid wall of instantly grown heartwood reaches down as if it were a limb and forces its way down past the leaves into the ground, the soil underneath my feet quite noticeably bulging upwards around my soles.

A wet silence hangs in the air for a second or two.

"Oh."

"The edges and center's way quicker—I've done loads of experiments!" He shakes his head in a sort of mournfulness that seems almost mawkish in character. "Poor Injul and Asha never had a chance."

"But they don't react to me," I say, "for reasons he won't disclose." My hands clench a little, and my fingers run over where I know the veins within it to be.

"State secret!" he titters, spinning in place on the mud in the most inappropriate manner I could imagine.

"Uh-huh. What d'you need me to do?"

"The trees merge around three hundred meters before we'll hit the center. I need you to be the bait!"

His smile would be disarming if it wasn't so clearly armed.

"Okay," Perei says, his own smile, as strained as a sprain, pushing itself across his face as he looks between his knee—now almost propped up against his chin, a centimetre or two separating them—and us. "So you want me to risk my life for a psycho midget who's literally got *four hits* on his hands?"

"I was kinda expecting a little hit at what I look at funny," he says, his finger pushing up against his cheek as he tilts it to the side, "but yeah, I might just be trying to get you down into the ground! I don't think life's any fun without a little suspense, do you?"

He seems to consider this for a bit longer than a normal person should before finally shaking his head rapidly to himself for a second, then looking straight at me. "Ash?"

"I trust him," I say, and my hand twitches the slightest bit in place; the little monkey-like boy stares up to me, his eyes wide in a disgusting mockery of childhood curiosity. "I trust him entirely."

The extremely perceptive person before me nods slowly. "You're sure?"

My jaw struggles against its heat-stricken muscles, the movement evidently seamless on the outside. "I'm sure."

It takes barely a second before he nods with a seriousness I genuinely wish is facetious.

"Sure."

Delightful.

I cannot see.

I could possibly try, but if I would I might die; the trees, Seven-three says, don't respond well to light. My arms are held out before me, arms brushing the mane, and though the field about us keeps the air cool, the moisture seeps from the ground and lies semi-stagnant in the air as we walk past. Perei's much larger frame is held over me, and his chin lies against my minutely barriered right wing.

"Ash?"

"Yeah?"

"Your pits smell like the devil's ballsack."

I force my wings' barrier intolerant for the slightest fragment of a twitch, and a yelp issues from behind me as the weight laid upon me shifts; the arms below my pectorals tighten, and the high whisper that issues from behind us both carries an uncharacteristically venomous character.

"*Stop*. If we move more than a meter or two behind you, the forest will crush us all. We're surrounded any place that isn't in front of us. The forest isn't parting. *Stop*, or I will make you die with me."

The air is empty of every sound but the light sloshing beneath our glasswalkers' feet.

"Sounds like you hit a line into him," Perei grumbles, and his choice of words inexplicably gladdens me. I am happy.

"We're almost there," Seven-three says, and I notice as his voice moves above his loud whisper that his accent has slipped from Cimsas Uytrimelan to a rather flat, generic Keshtari. "The reaction will take twenty seconds. You'll need to creep over, pierce one of the roots, then run back. They'll hit the ground before you."

This is a blatant contradiction. I do not move and do not speak. Perei should know this.

"Got it. How close?"

"My clicker's telling me that we're coming to a stop in about five se—*wh*—"

There is a quick rustling noise behind me, and I hear something so loud I do not realise it is a scream until his vocal chords creak amongst the sudden screeching cacophony of mechanical stress before us; I hold tight by instinct, and *I am free* and my body is bathed instantly in a gentle white light as we stroll into the newly crafted tree-orifice before us and stop two or three metres after.

I can think. I can speak. I look behind me and see Perei outlined in the dawn, rubbing his neck hard enough to rid himself of the skin. "Sestiyara is a wreck of a country," I say, and I can feel thoughts that I *could not think* coming back to me. "It is a miserable nation, having betrayed its fundamental precepts for the pursuit of supremacy in the face of a force infinitely its superior. Yes. *Oyjj*—" I can revel in my flaws and reach up to scratch the itch under my eye and *breathe* as a trickle of pure water begins to issue from my fingers, clotted blood from his face dissolving in it, and something is *different* in this place, something filled with life somewhere beyond the freedom I've just reattained—something else, filling me almost like a feeling. "Not dead. Thank you."

"Thanks," he says, wincing; I'm too happy for his courage to mind his pain. "Stupid idea. Shitty idea. *Worst goddamn idea I've ever had.* He could've had tritty arms or Libra—"

He closes his eyes for a second, taking one of the longest breaths I've ever heard before opening them and shaking his head.

"God, this place is pretty."

"It is," I say, and look up into the sky—the *sky*, the membrane lending it a light blue hue here in this land of grass and flowers surrounded by leaves glistening with the dawn's sunshine, and I realise in a single moment, as the gnarled, old 'trees' before us hundreds of metres high with their dried bark closes behind us, that the outer trees with their endless permutations are parasites over something *else*, a single great columnar over an invisible tree—a single being, living at once, each part connected under the soil and I don't know *how* I know this, my mind in a moment glimpsing the connections here spread beneath my feet into something greater than I know.

I sniff the living air for the first time through my nose, a long breath, and then shake my head. My lungs are *living*, living far more than anything else possibly could.

"How did you know?" I say, gently slipping my feet off the stirrups and quietly throwing myself off; I hover for a second over the water-dusted grass, the surface tension of the soft soil perceptible as my soles touch the ground but not worrying in the slightest. "*Tower*, this place—how am I still alive?"

"Figured you'd hit me—knew you were tied the whole time. Got a snatch on his lifeline." He holds up a thin, reddish-brown strip of wire; something small and hard is at its end, and I recognise it in an instant, moving off the ground a little to bow over the glasswalker and gently take it. "God, what *is* this?"

"Remote burning tether," I say, and I'm quite suddenly aware of its part; I reach to the back of my neck as I hang in the air, gently pulling the device off my neck with a gentle *schlick* and putting it into one of Perei's numerous pouches. "Sessile-mechanical, mechanical contact point. He could have burnt my c—"

"Meant the air."

I look once more at our life-walled paradise, the field clear from end to end with the invisible haze of something wonderful and natural all at once. It's something beyond a dream, vivid beyond imagination and yet still familiar enough to be given words: the world seems complete, here, and I cannot help but wonder about it the same way I wondered about the stars before I knew what they were.

"I don't know either."

I look down to the ground, and something appears to me in a way in which sight alone cannot allow. "It seems exodial," I continue, looking forwards as the soil beneath my feet—seeming so soft that I should stumble or fall through, but I do not—pushes back against them, a single cant confirming my hypothesis. "The focus is apparent—there is no oration here. It's not pre-Laceration, it's *exodial*."

"Shit." I can *feel* him move behind me, arm reaching for his weapon before he seems to realise the futility. "*Shit*."

"Not inherently bad," I say, the ground before me beginning to twist before my eyes without twisting, its essence moving as its body lies still. "Not inherently bad—"

The ground breaks, and I am full.

My arm moves. It is a part of me, but it's a part of another me. I am not its mind, the trillion trillion thoughts here barely on my consciousness' fringe; I am its soul and I am its mortal, stupid god, power without understanding incarnate as my other—*understanding, power, exodial not pre-Laceration*—I am here, myself, this whole world—

The forest is quiet. It does not sing, it does *not* sing nor even whisper. I am here, I am in myself and everywhere, and the thing I called me sings to the Tower forever and ever but I cannot hear it through these ears but just through those of the thing I called me, and a piece of me sings and I am here, I am now, arms and legs nothing to the world about me and within, a centillion things besides myself just below the touch and no, it is me, we are me, I am what I am in every different way and:

I am standing in a beautiful field, warm and bright, and my feet are on the ground.

The ground erupts in a realm beyond sight, and I do not worry. I am no wiser before as the world hums within me, its hundred billion hearts—*metaphor, I'm constructing metaphor to understand that which I cannot, I have been this whole time*—beating without beating.

The Tower is a kind god, I think, walking within my frame. It feeds. It nurtures. It destroys only by creation. It does not make things like the monstrosity that I now am.

This is not a creation of the Tower; it was created after, almost certainly, by something far beyond its grace with science so foreign it has no meaning I could glean from any book still on paper. The forest thinks with me, not in response but as the thought's own natural conclusion: this air is the world and is me.

The invisible eruption begins to take form in minute experiments of cellulose matter, resolving into a set of slowly flowering perennials that follow my step. Nothing has left; I am myself and yet a little more.

The wings upon my back are beyond myself, I realise, just as my veins are beyond myself within me with my intestines, and as the forest's every surface is my skin I cannot feel within myself except as I could before. It stops upon me, and it stops upon Perei, who—clearly having gotten over the mere novelty of whatever it is I now am—is staring at my body, the invisible ground sweeping the dirt from my pores of its own accord.

"The hell?"

"Looks like I'm an exodial," I say, and I cannot say that the forest is less me than myself, its hearts beating with the one I cannot control. "I've taken over it. I'm tempted to say that maybe it's taken over me, but I don't think that's the case."

"I'm gonna say it again," Perei says, stepping back a little—he's apparently gotten used to being within me. "The hell?"

"This forest," I say, and a tendril of wood surges from me below him, leaves surging from me to cushion his baggage and neck as I wrap in an instant around both his feet, the yell—*ish-al-wyent'e you piece of mother—goddamn*—audible through a trillion pores as his face is brought before me and my lips curl into a little smile.

"Ash," he says, his teeth gritted so harsh they look as if they might chip, "What the shit."

I'm about to respond when I feel something *inside* me, something foreign and yet inviting, and I see him standing here in the field of my soul, blood running down his brow. His hair has faded from its natural-seeming brown to a sickly yellow. Every bit of his face is still instantly recognisable but for the look in his eyes, a broken arm by his side.

He's been pretending to be insane, I realise, as he raises an arm that's already half gone and receding, eyes blankly staring at his arms for the moment that he has them as his body is shredded peacefully and efficiently by the wind, particulate matter gold in the light before it scurries through the air down to the ground past the bits and pieces of metal once within him.

A series of quick breaths follows the moment. "Did *you* do that? Oh, God, Ash—"

"No," I say.

Yes, a voice familiar as my dreams echoes, and something greater than myself prods at the edges of my—

It's gone.

I'm standing still in the middle of a beautiful field and it's gone. I'm gone.

My fingers contract, but there is no shock nor regret—I have tasted the fruit, and I do not mourn its passing. I breathe out, head tilting down at the perfect angle to stare at Perei as he lets out a low groan on the ground, leaves lying limp besides him.

I hear the voice just as I begin to reach down.

It very much was you.

I stop.

A cell in the system.

It's the same voice I've held in my mind since I wrote her down, and I arise and turn to see something wonderful, her dress too high for the ground.

"Missy?"

Who do you think I am?

I do not know how to begin to describe her beauty; the phrases I've already used feel cheap and stock to the perfection that her physical form conveys. Her mouth does not move as she begins to walk towards me with an immeasurable grace, her silhouette framed by the sheer whiteness darkening over her chest.

"Is that you?"

Her mouth moves for the first time, and a voice sweeter than bred phoenices issues both from within it and within me:

"In the flesh."

"No, you don't exist. I've written about you to myself." I am shaking a little; Perei says something behind me, but I do not hear. "Who are you? How did you know about Misatrea?"

"I've always been here, my girl."

Her arms reach out down towards me as she closes the distance between us, reaching down to my hands. They're as soft as I remember, and as we look within each other I see that her eyes in all their endless lustre hold depths further than the Tower's tip just as I have dreamt in countless dreams.

I am not insane.

I am not delusional.

An elaborate fantasy of mine is grabbing my hands.

"I haven't dreamt of you," I say, "not since I left. The horrors come and go too quick by the night for me to call for your solace."

"That's a little big for your pretty little tongue, isn't it?"

I let my tongue out a little past my teeth; it strikes me that this is the silliest, most frivolous thing I've allowed myself to do; I attempt to let out a 'you really think so?', the familiar words familiarly distorted, and my attempt fades out into a low giggle.

She laughs, and the moment the first perfect tone pulls itself from her lips, I am content.

"You hadn't written me in a while. I was getting worried."

"I lost your sessile," I say, hands almost shaking. "I lost your sessile, and I didn't keep any backups. All I have left is—"

"What's up here?"

She puts a finger to her perfect pitch hair right above her ear.

"Nature's own sessile," I begin, my heart fluttering as I anticipate her response.

"Perhaps a square decimetre altogether, worth five thousand more."

The haze my mind has fallen into dissipates, leaving not the slightest shadow of a remnant.

A straight rip from Kharbalis Sesirtkhari ar-Mirali—her quotes were only verbatim in the sessiles. I spoke with her in my mind only to mock them.

"Why are you here?"

"I need you to die, my girl."

I am immediately aware of my position. My legs are planted firmly to the ground. My knees, however, are unsteady; my heart is already palpitating—it already was. My arms are relaxed. Perei has said something behind me, but I pay no regard.

My eyes are lost in its facsimiles, and I stay *absolutely still*.

"Missy?"

Its arms move up mine, its bare hands caressing the ceramic fibre

I must not exaggerate nor go stiff as a little shudder goes down my spine. I can feel the force behind it—the muscles upon its breathing corpse are likely stronger than I can allow myself to think.

"*You're fighting for a war lost somewhere else. Thousands of people fight and die as we stand here to speak. You have to end it. We have to end it together.*"

"You're always right, Missy," I say, my voice as enraptured as I can force it to be. "You're always right."

"*That's the girl I remember.*"

"Can I just ask for one thing?" I say, expression reverent.

"*What?*"

Its voice has gained a light air of impatience. Missy was never impatient.

"May I have a hug?"

It does not hesitate in the light, slightly shocked manner she would. Its arms begin to creep gently and slowly over my shoulders and down my back.

I'm not sure if I don't think for the next second or I think too much to remember that I do.

Dorsiflexion on both feet. I fall four centimetres into the laxity of her arms. They tighten faster than I can estimate.

Too late.

Its fingers tighten too late to touch me and too late to stop my free wing curling and *pushing*, the barrier about the skin and bone extending and *forcing* its way through her lack of a barrier into her side—*it's not flesh*—and in that moment the only thought I might think I should have thought before doing this is that its movements do not take into account my wings as it lets go in an instant, its instincts still flesh, its pain still extant, its humanity still preserved in her nerves and mind, and in that instant I back up and try to step back as fast as I can and its eyes, its *eyes* are empty for as long as it takes for its arm to reach mine as my other begins to reach away and *oh Tower my ulna is fractured, it's fractured* and I can see the nothingness upon the skin stretched over its skull, and it's driven its arm a centimetre away from my side probably harder than a bullet and it's not in front of me and I hold my forearm—*immobilise, hold*—and through my tears of hurt I see a figure in a stained garment much like mine with his equipped arm pointed towards me, a very distinctly threatening shape outlined even past the haze.

The sound that follows is now almost familiar.

The pressure lets off my arm, and no pain follows as I fall into the grass, barriers upon my back letting me slide down the accommodating soil for a metre. In the corner of my eye, the light over my shoulder goes from cyan to green.

I look up just in time to see her—*it*—far above us, its bloodless frame completely visible for the second before it disappears past the barrier into the haze.

"Okay," Perei says, and I look down to see him, now, slinging his short-barreled weapon back over his back as he looks to the sky. "So—"

"Probably some kind of sessile-corpse—I just made that word up, didn't I?"

"No, I mean, so your *old friend*—"

"Was imaginary, yes." I raise a finger. "Don't say a word."

"I mean, y'know, that looked a lot like—"

I exhale sharply. "No, it didn't."

"I mean, I'm just sayi—"

"Shut up."

The silence that passes between us lasts for about a decasecond.

"So," he says, open palms to his sides, "Looks like you hit the ground. What's up with that?"

I'm too tired to give him any look at all, but I imagine my voice says enough. "Hit the ground?"

"Y'know. Level. Straight. Down. Fallen straight from the Tower's penthouse with an intolerant under your head." He pauses. "Come to think about it, how'd it send you up there in the first place?"

I go to the ground; the soil shapes itself to cushion my hand as I sink it deep in. The surface tension—perceptibly artificial—breaks, and I pull a fairly large fragment of still life right from the ground.

"I have absolutely no idea," I say, the substance writhing under its surface upon my palm, "but I intend to find out."

He looks at the clump of dirt in my hand.

"The hell're you gonna do *that*?"

I pull at one of the figuratively endless bags bound to Perei's front and unbind it with a word that sounds like a whistle.

"I have absolutely no clue," I say, and toss it in. "But I doubt we'll find out staying here. Let's move."

The leaves part before us, now almost servile in their evidently instinctive friendliness; I suppose a thousand men will be here days after the first one checks. I allow my membrane to grow carefully outwards, and the sun's rays carry a different hue as our we let our glasswalkers out onto the Sea.

"So, I was wondering."

"I'm certain you were."

"Your 'best friend'—"

I turn my head towards him, lying as I am on my back; the sun is hitting its lowest point, and the glasswalkers are moving with such a resolute steadiness that I feel a little as though my body has fused to the saddle.

"Stop wondering."

"Hey, I wasn't gonna judge or anything. I mean, like, was she a hundred percent—"

"Entirely borne of my own imagination. A mildly emergent sessile whose thoughts I carried into my dreams and from there gave it the soul that let it live within. I don't know how that thing knew about her. I want to know, but—"

"I thought you didn't believe in souls."

"I'm simplifying. Do you really want me to tell you the name we've given to the meat in which the soul resides?"

I count the seconds to his response:

One.

Two.

Three—

"Nah."

We don't speak as we ride.

nine
Avoid All Travel

"Do you see the thousand clouds burning above? Do you see the trillion grains laid before us? Do you see the beauty of God's own creation? In this moment, does the world seem beautiful to you as it is to me?"

"Yes, father. Yes, a thousand times yes."

"Very good," the man said, and fired.

The body laid for an hour on that tower's tip; his right canine survived the night, long enough for the agents to see, and was gone the morning after.

—Prashrei qu'n'av dasnamr

Claiming Bodies: The Story of Idhrakhrei Life Insurance, 3888-3889

Antamanaria has been undergoing a regime change since the 8th of Nonus 3883. Formerly an Uytrimelan city and archaeological site for Fransai research, the strip of land under Antamanarian sovereignty is considered *terra libra* as per the Concordance; as such, Aimelan extraterritoriality does not apply.

The internal security situation in Antamanaria has worsened considerably since 3886. Discriminatory attacks with financial motive (ranging from AR-3 to JM-1) are generally perceived to be the most common crimes against 'outsiders'. Indiscriminate attacks with sexual motive (ranging from ASA-3 to SM-1 and including K-5 to K-1) against feminine-presenting 'outsiders' remain commonplace regardless of perceived material gain. Almost no crimes against 'outsiders' are stigmatised in areas not specifically set aside for their use; the usage of the term 'outsider' is dubious at best, as the indigenous population has accepted a wide variety of variously collaborative and mutually hostile criminal and extremist elements since c. 3888, existing on an equal level with local self-legitimising elements.

Widespread barrierfountain sabotage has left large exposed sections of the city subject to miniature communal barriers, usually operated by criminal elements. Singing a personal membrane at all times is heavily advised; while non-perpetuating spawncloth is relatively cheap in all districts, local singers tend to have insufficient tessiture or education to sufficiently utilise it and the material tends to be used for disposable storage, as is the custom in most of the rest of the West. While self-conflicting barrier resonance could theoretically allow a cascade failure to arise, sabotage by extremist groups and low-level criminal elements are a far more pressing concern and occur at an unacceptably high rate.

The city's overlapping structure, reaching up to three kilometres high at parts, depends upon millions of structural barriers located at well-documented key points in the city's timeless steel superstructure. Though no attempts have been made to undermine these full-structure barriers, pre-3867 occurrences of the Ashlakrei-Khirisrea error could allow a resonance cascade to occur.

Line Raiders patrol the outskirts of the city at all times. Entrance to the city is usually done under heavy military escort or by trusted people-smugglers, both in and out. It is not advisable to pose as a Line Raider, as both Zhanghwazh and Aimelan military patrols kill bands straying out of the DMZ on sight. The former gates to the city are generally left open and kept secure and neutral by local consensus, despite its defensibility. The Insurmountable-mounted defences formerly employed by the Antamanarian government have been decommissioned, and are inoperable.

Important notice: Alasintrei das Tachiesrea, Administrator for Public Welfare as of 23 Primus, 3900, has declared his writ to be the Writ of Enforcement, abolishing all Line Raider categorisation or collaboration. All tagged Line Raiders will be shot on sight regardless of official affiliation.

Despite the social and physical pressure against 'outsiders', a significant expatriate community remains and is in fact continuing to grow, generally protected by the criminal elements whose services they most often patronise. This aggravates its Atrisrea-type urban sprawl, which is escalating slowly into a Khisratarei-type catastrophe; a rising expatriate demand for high-volume property and relative safety have left thousands homeless due to widespread eviction, and very little new housing is being built.

TIPS:

» Be armed at all times and have trusted companions who are also armed. Most Line Raider bands are unwilling to engage armed Aimelan bands of more than five travellers.

» The city is built vertically almost as much as it is horizontally. Watch out for attacks from above and below.

» 'Hotel-ambushers' have been known to barrier-climb through unsecured windows at night. Insist on a windowless room, have a trusted guard or weave intolerant barriers into your walls if the local tolerance permits it.

» Maintain a stable-tolerant Khamisret-Aparkisrea (dysexaptic) field at all times while in public, even while handling equipment. Remember: Antamanarian communal barriers are not standardised, and intolerant barriers may allow for severe resonant effects.

» If you must handle fine equipment, learn to shape your barrier appropriately.

» Be ready to rephrase at a moment's notice.

» Practise your rephrasals carefully. A mispronunciation can be fatal!

» Antamanarian subcultures are profoundly diverse. If you are visiting alone or with less than five companions, research the customs of a specific 'neutral' culture and casually mimic them, but do not blatantly pretend.

» Cults of war—the most prolific of which being the Irimentarists, the Hookfeet, the Sacred Band and the Soulknives—are known to kidnap and indoctrinate Aimelan citizens who prove especially adept at self-defence. Do not make a spectacle of yourself.

» Do not carry any non-essential valuables.

» Petty criminals greatly value permits for their aluminium content and travel potential.

» Do not patronise criminal elements.

» Failing this, do not patronise competing criminal elements.

» Do not go to Antamanaria.

SUMMARY — AVOID ALL TRAVEL

The Department of Transnational Affairs does not endorse any Aimelan presence in Antamanaria. If you wish to travel to or are currently in Antamanaria despite this advisory, your safety is your own responsibility. If you die while you are in Antamanaria, the Familial Administration will not retrieve your corpse.

Travel Advisory: Antamanaria, Primus 3920
promulgated by the Department of Transnational Affairs under the grace of Ilesintarei das Cimcharei ermit Arisarea, Administrator for Foreign Affairs, Alasintrei das Tachiesrea, Administrator for Public Welfare, Plisirea das Vasksharei, Administrator for International Law and Mishrea das Cimcharei eliyit Santanadrea, Administrator for Mortal Affairs

ANTAMANARIA
AYRISANVYSTIR RITYSYSSYA

10
Átymánysyr
to live on the other side of a mountain

I can feel.

"Get up."

Not very well, of course. The spikes are clearest; the pain is not dull. I lie upon a bed of spikes as the blood rushing from my back—withered, I recall, with age—

"Ash, get up."

—flows and the hypokalaemia keeps my eyes too weak to close *it hurts* as they stare up into something *it hurts* whose exact form *it hurts* is fading *it hurts* from my memory as they open wide into the blinding day and *it hurt so much and I can't take it it hurts*—

"Get up!"

My heart is beating so hard that I can hear it and I breathe so quickly that it's almost as though I can no longer breathe as a shouting voice pulses mildly against my thudding eardrums as I force myself entirely upright, spine twisting almost too slowly for my muscles as I narrowly miss someone's head, and I am alive.

"You look like hell," Perei says, still recoiling from his dodge, and I realise now that this time I've remembered the dream.

"I think I've just seen—"

I am interrupted by the unfortunately distinctive sound of a bullet tearing air, and I almost immediately throw myself back down onto the saddle's royal bedding; the fluff cradles my nose entirely, and I find myself breathing in the very pleasantly artificial scent of stoechas.

"Just in time." Out of the corner of my eye, I see Perei pull Ayerei's sessile-arm up from his back, turning it up against the sky and firing three times—

"*Shit,*" he says, and I somehow hear the word before I hear the bullet grazing past his arm, the ceramic fabric distorting just enough to avoid penetration. I can almost feel the bruise, and he takes cover behind his slowly walking steed. "Not buying it. Time for Plan B."

"Plan B?"

"Turn their faces into cherry pie."

"I get that reference," I stupidly, emptily say, just as he pulls the trigger.

The sound is immediate and familiar, and my nerves are as profoundly stable as my slightly shaking breath. Our glasswalkers are barely moving, and I cannot see what he is shooting, and in a moment I realise something:

If we die, I will have done nothing to stop it.

"*Létyjs ápyfrét av set'senmétyr,*" I begin; my wings flap once, and I begin to move.

My chest leaves first, and my arms follow without very much fuss. I barely notice the barrier transition, because I am further away than I thought I would be before it might have crossed my mind. My feet touch nothing; I am not moving, and I take far less time than I should pondering my stupidity before my eyes open to see my corner of the world. The membrane is already in place, clothes it up; the one I've left behind will be stable for at least another half an hour.

The sight before me is clear, though it takes some time to fully comprehend: the Insurmountables guide my eyes down to the earth, and before me are the very distinct figures of ten men in groups of two, one of each pair's short and the other long—just a little below, I realise, close enough to kill me—rushing in from a handful of kilometres, all of them just quickly enough to stay moving. Perei writhes below, clearly firing blindly into the distance as the incoming men reach twenty degrees and go for thirty; the men at the back look to me, pausing their aim, and I know in an instant what I must do.

"I am the pinnacle of idiocy. There is not a single person upon this yellowed earth possessed of less wisdom than I, and there will not be one ever again. What I am about to do is one of my stupidity's symptoms. *"Tutć vétirymj ánuyr,"* I begin, my arm where it should be and holding what it must.

I move.

I am there before I expect, but long after I am ready; my stomach moves without me, and I barely fear—*I am ready to die*—for the instant before it settles into its membrane-dictated space. The motion is effortless; the man, his face contorted in concentration and greed and *fear*, seems just human enough to die, and the barrier thrusts when I should.

Almost. It's off by two or three centimetres; his death will not be quick. I only notice by the time I've pulled. His friend—his face is relaxed, almost kind—has not noticed, and he sees his death as he feels it in his spine. I don't think he felt very strongly about it.

I saw a widow's tears for the first time when I was eight.

I don't know why the memory occurs now, but I cannot stop it as I yank the short, heavy weapon from his slackened palms, my slightly bloodied weapon held grip-to-grip. I recognise its design, though I don't know from where.

She wasn't normally a very kind woman, I think, just from her face.

I move again, turning mid-flight through the almost frictionless air to see my destination. This time, they know I'm there; I'm behind them before they can really make an effort to act upon the knowledge, and move in.

Her arms were streaked with scars; she cried so hard that I knew they weren't her husband's work.

I pull the trigger close enough to hear the breath of something I cannot attach anything but humanity to, the recoil throwing me over five metres back in a second and eliciting a yelp symptomatic of a feeling that might make me laugh in any other way.

She was far too young, and her hair was a brilliantly solid black rooted in a faint yellow. I didn't look closely enough at her eyes to ascertain their colour, obscured as they were by what was coming out of them. I don't suppose she was meant to be a widow.

I turn in place. The fear in the man's eyes does not register in mine until he no longer sees.

She certainly wasn't a widow then, was she, with her husband's heart empty and his brain flesh?

I don't know how many of them know I'm there. The membrane's isolation lets my clothes' song hum in my ears just long enough for me to catch the tune of my clothes' barrier—soulless and mechanically perfect.

The tears she shed before I told her were those of a wife.

This time, she—her hair is red, her eyes no longer visible past the blood—twitches enough to fire into the air. The other's eyes are wide upon his thin, rosy face, Shelflander in complexion—there is no surrender, he knows, there is nothing here that can save him because I cannot know that he wants to live, I can *save* him, I realise, and I stop, I say *wait*, and in that instant he fires.

I had made her a widow.

He's missed.

I blink, then hold the trigger down before I have time to react, the barrier resonance between my own and his shuddering through my bones. He looks at me, and *oh Tower it hurts* I grab onto one of his outstretched arms and swing down right around his front, my aching wings wilted over him with his gaping wound between us as his intact intestine paints my stomach, the weapon receding away from us in the sand.

I feel his tachycardiac heart beat against my own, and something heavy and warm drips from my left eye to roll down the side of my nose; I am in mortal danger, I'm aware, and though my life depends upon it, I do not move.

My wings ache. He is breathing erratically underneath me, and he is *dying* and I did it, I've killed a man—I've killed a man, something I can see truly in this moment to be a man and not simply a target, though he breathes and blinks and might be alive if he were already on the table.

No.

No, I'm too busy singing a rebind to say as I halt the walker with a single word, the table is wherever I am. Five syllables to rebind almost the entirety of the celiac artery, though I can barely see it; the surface area is small enough that even if it wasn't broken it wouldn't be worth it to check. I pull this grown man onto me, the bulk almost causing my spine to buckle before I scoot my backside backwards; a blood-choked gurgle echoes from the back of his throat and over my shoulder as I begin to rebind the gastric lining itself, the entirety of the membrane pulling itself back together as the contents spill within his abdominal cavity and over my robes.

My right claws for my instrument, the routine melody beginning to squeak from its bloodstained catgut, the other hand pulling the slick fragments of his bellyskin together by their hairs over the organs. It takes scarcely a minute for the fresh rebound skin to shine over his once semi-vacated abdomen.

Peritonitis is inevitable; he hasn't a drop of singing blood, and there is no preservation to save him. The pain must be unbearable.

"What's your name?" I whisper as I push him forwards onto his back and look into his shallow, chlorine-like eyes—the whistle of another shot becomes clear as it passes through the barrier, but I don't mind it one bit. The mathematics of a hit are unlikely at best. "What is your name? Where are you from? Can you swallow for me?"

"Alfred?" he croaks out through a mouthful of bloody vomit, barely looking at me past his tear-choked eyes. "Alfred, is that you? I wanted honey with my tea."

A Shelflander.

"*Gysétáwiyr pœmyiiratj,*" I say, and the sugared water begins to flow from my palm down to his tongue; his throat contorts to let it through. I'll have to purge his—

A hand lands on my back, and my heart skips.

"Isha throw me."

It settles, and I look to eyes that aren't looking at me.

"I'm trying to think of one thing I'm not getting socketed about right now."

"Socketed?"

He looks back to me, makes a poking motion towards his eyes sliding past his right zygomaticofrontal suture to the base of his skull, and then spurs his walker a little further onwards to look down at the man's paled face. "Isha. Isha, Isha, Isha. I didn't even *think* that'd be possible."

"I think I'd have done something like it sooner if it would have helped." My hands are crusted with blood and chyme, and I force myself not to care that it's not all my patient's. "No, I'm confused about what I should be lying about. I'm supposed to be lying about—I—barriers, hands, I—"

I begin to cry.

It's a very strange process, like a limb recovering from obdormition. The heaving within my chest makes itself known before I can stop it, and I look to our sides as I begin to attempt to swallow the rising tide, safeless glasswalkers long gone—I think, until I see one of them safetied, standing alone with its charges absent.

"I used the word patient," I say, the words almost a croak in my throat.

He looks down to me, stooping to come level with my face. "Ash? Ash, you're—oh, damn. Damn. Uh—"

"I used the word *patient!*" I shout out, and my fists slam down onto my—*his*—glasswalker's sides, pinkish-yellow chunks flying from my hands to splatter against the uncaring sand. "*I used the word patient, I used the word patient in my mind to talk about someone I*—oh, *Tower*, what have I done? What in the world have I done? How many people, I can't—I know how many, *why am I asking you?*"

The last word comes out in a scream, and I hold myself from hugging the nearest thing possible—this takes an enormous effort, and my heart palpitates in the emptiness—and instead let my hands dig into the saddle's sides as I rock a little in place. I contort a little against the posture I've confined myself to, twitches and little struggles as I take deep breaths to fuel the globus giving my contracting throat something to hiccup against.

"Ash—"

"*No,*" I say, my eyes closed against the sky. "Shut up. Shut *up.* Don't you dare. Don't you *dare* try to—"

"Thanks. You saved my life."

I look to him; my tears cloud my vision. The man below me breathes steadily.

"So," he says, "you've saved my life how many times now?"

"I like to think I'm not vulgar enough to keep track," I say, and as the words come out of my mouth I realise I'm completely sincere.

As we approach the twist in the Insurmountables that heralds its infinitely defensible body, the ground below us riddled with charred shapes I prefer not to identify, we see the milling thousands in their spilt-over dwellings and barely functioning barriers holding up spotty membranes in the far distance in the horizon—very reminiscent of imprints taken of Cimsas before the Permits.

"Isha," Perei says as I look back down to my patient, cleaning the miniature incision through which I've cleansed his abdominal cavity. The smell's begun to fade, and he's breathing well enough to allow me to take my mind off him. "I thought the Reservation was bad."

"The Reservation?" I say, looking somewhat nervously between the man and the distance—our clothes are a cynosure, and even in the distance I can already see the eyes jumping in our direction. "You've been there?"

"Yeah, I've been there. Ay took me, what, seven years ago, I think. Back when he was couriering. Shit's fucked. I don't think it's getting any better any time soon."

"You don't tend to use that word lightly, do you?" I say, tilting my head at him as I steer my mount closer; we're side to side, now, legs almost touching. "Not even for death or pain—unfairness, perhaps, helplessness, incapability, even zugzwang—are those the senses in which it bears meaning to you?"

He raises an eyebrow. "Are you high?"

"I had no choice, right? I had to kill those people, right?"

"Uh—"

I lean over and grab him by the shoulders.

"Is that how you'd use the word?" I've never said it before, and I decide not to start. "Was that what it was? Would you give me the honour of acknowledging that my situation left me no recourse but mass murder?"

"Ash, I thought we already—"

"No, we settled nothing. Tell me, and tell me honestly."

I seem to have forced him to think. He lets out a long sigh, looking down to his feet, and speaks. "Well, I dunno. You don't like killing people, huh? And you had to, I guess. But y'know, I wouldn't call it *fucked* if your only option was to save your own ass over someone else's."

I almost let my anger show, throwing it into a laugh that is edgy enough to keep him tense but not quite enough to make his sense of humour tingle.

"I never had a reason to believe that I'd have to kill someone, you know? I killed that girl, in the cache—that's worth the word, right?"

"Oh, yeah," he says, evidently relieved to be able to agree, "that was fucked."

"No, it wasn't. I don't actually feel bad about it. I never did. It's what you do, you know, when you have a nervous system wrapped in sessiles—it's what you do when you have a neurospinal weave too tight to dismiss on the spot. You break the nexus—you kill them, if necessary. You probably felt far worse about it than me: I felt, for a moment, that I might have made the wrong decision, but I forgot about it in *minutes*. So why haven't I *now?*" My face is stuck in a very grimacey sort of grin, and the glances he throws to my hands upon sides tell me he's not entirely comfortable.

He seems to think for about a second, then shrugs. "I guess you like killing kids a lot more than you like killing grown-ups."

"Not a trait we like in our men," an entirely different voice resounds, and I twist to its source too slow to see the origin of the fingers grabbing my face and filling my nose with a familiar *wake up I need to wake up I'm awake*

Anaesthetic is an extremely interesting substance.

On ethnic Aimelans, a 2-kilogramme-appropriate dose—the smallest one—will induce preservation for a period of about thirty minutes. It is impossible for an Aimelan to overdose on anaesthetic, and a non-emergency preservation cannot be prolonged for more than thirty minutes at a time.

On non-Aimelans, the awakeness reflex prevents anaesthetic awareness with a process so esoteric it might well be a placebo. The internal purge-membrane prevents residual curarisation, the rearticulation prevents shivering, and a hundred other little processes prevent a hundred other little problems.

These processes are entirely useless to someone in preservation.

They also can't be chemical, which makes it particularly

disturbing that non-Aimelan overdoses stop hearts.

There's a suggestion, thus, that preservation itself is a fairly recent mutation, and that anaesthetic was created for an evolutionary state between preservation and unconsciousness—Silpeslevesra's Garden does not make any references, and late Kanandrisra-era literature mentions the state only in passing, usually as a form of unconsciousness. Rarely is the rapidity of trauma-induced preservation (its most common form) commented upon specifically.

Only in the mid-Atfilgaentatresra era war memoirs are the differences between simple unconsciousness and preservation elaborated upon—there are many, and the fifth most important is perhaps the third most interesting: there is no recovery period, no withdrawal, no moment after the eyes begin to function once more that the conscious mind cannot assert its dominance over itself and its body in its entirety and I *force* my wings' barriers outwards and under my backwards-facing arms as I propel myself forwards with something cold pressing up against my buttocks—*my bare buttocks*—to which my arms are tied, the only thing before me a man looking at something on his wrist as my minute mass slams coincidentally into his coeliac plexus shoulder-first and as an awfully quiet scream empties itself from my lungs and out my hot, sticky mouth as I feel the bone slam against heart and nerve, wings awkwardly flapping against my armpits as I flip onwards into the steel before me, the chair—it can't be anything else—slamming by a leg into the wall and giving me a second of freefall before I clang down onto the ground, a sharp, cold ache filling my right (both my side and the wing) the moment the shock of the hit passes.

I take quick stock of my situation.

I'm cold, naked and strapped to a chair by something I can't see, several days' worth of pent-up, mud-streaked teenage body odour quite suddenly becoming quite recognisable to my unpickable nose in a room shaped in a mockery of late pre-Laceration architecture, a very big and likely extremely strong man lying right behind me.

Not the very best start, but I suppose I could be dead.

I look down to my uncannily pale body to ensure I'm not just imagining the invisible nature of my bindings—my serrati anterior strain in a particularly physical way, the fatty tissue about my upper arms quite clearly distorting around something that reflects nothing, not even the ungodly scent emanating in what I presume to be steaming gusts from my untamed underarms.

I choke a little and shake my head. I need a bath.

My hands are bound by a similar method, the fingers each tied individually—it will take me minutes to orate anything more complicated than a substance, and as I open my mouth to speak I realise that my tongue cannot move, my throat filled with something resembling a breathing tube.

I manage not to panic and choke as the instinctive tears begin to well up in my eyes.

The breath through the tube—I have no idea if it's physical or oratory—comes slow and steady. My wings let loose a pained flap as I attempt to right myself, dragging the chair and me along the stainless floor with a long, screeching cry for a second before I angle myself well enough to send me into the air, my weightless body stopping short enough of the low ceiling to avoid brain damage.

I shift about in place, here, the pained groans from the fur-clothed below me at least letting me know I haven't yet killed another man before it dawns on me—the slight door-shaped seam in the wall before me giving me a clue—that I might have to.

I carefully let myself down, wings scraping gently against the air as the chair's back legs scrape the ground. I manoeuvre the chair's upper-right leg right above the man's windpipe, careful to maintain my tilt.

I grunt, and his scrunched-up eyes open a little before opening wide. He seems to begin to try and reach for something on his belt before he realises his situation and his breaths turn laboured.

"Wait," he says in whatever gutter tongue he knows, his hands shaking in their sleeves. "No, wait, I'll let you out, please. Don't. I'm sorry for helping 'em nab you, please don't kill me—"

I nod.

He opens his mouth, and I put an ear close to listen with extreme care.

"*Œvjt-tut,*" he begins, "*curientarana l'khalim isetinir pashanti.*"

Poetry, I realise, as I feel the bonds around my fingers fade right before the ones about my chest do—the nonsense syllables are almost certainly a printempraesis pulled from a poem whose rhythm I instantly recall. The chair clatters down behind me, the back making a horrid clang against the ground, and I push myself down over him, straddling his soft furry side as I shove my fingers up against his nose, feeling about his waist for whatever it is his arms were reaching for.

"It will take me less than a second to kill you. Why am I here? Where's my friend?"

He seems to take a few seconds to process my words, and he doesn't seem to understand them all that well; he begins to squeal like a sowpig, his words coming through in an almost awe-inspiringly pathetic squeak above his enormous, oily beard.

"Me—me have not twelve i—"

"Speak in your language," I say, and I grasp onto what feels like the end of a pistol and pull, the thing coming up into my hand—it's much smaller than Perei's firearm, and I feel about its metallic veneer without pulling my eyes from his.

He takes a deep breath, the air against my fingers turning cold before being caught up in the disgusting, doubtlessly disease-ridden miasma he expulses.

"Just my job," he says, as I grab onto his shoulder-hanging steel-and-catgut instrument with my spare hand and coax it down his yielding arm, "saw you deal with those Liners an hour back. Just about shit myself hearing Ina wanted you with us."

"With you?"

"Working. Working for us, weaving you up and—"

"You wanted to *spine-weave me?*" I say, bringing his own weapon up against his chin as I throw the hand-sized harp's filthy leather strip over my neck. "And my friend? Is he okay?"

"He's okay—boys're dealing with him now, I guess. It's a he?" He looks at me, and I suddenly remember the status of my sartorial particulars.

I glance back down over the rest of my body and shudder with a deep, sick revulsion. "Tower save me, you saw me naked. A person saw me naked." I'd normally hold back, but some mixture of rage and mental fatigue has helped clear my inhibitions. "I want to cut your eyes open," I say, bringing my nail up close enough to almost scrape his cornea. "I want to cut your eyes wide open and watch the fluid drain from them and then open your skull up and suffocate your hippocampus until there's nothing left but dead tissue in a dying skull. You *saw me naked*, and I want to destroy every part of you that did—what made you think you had the right, you disgusting, snivelling—"

"Aimelans do take that sort of thing very seriously, don't they?"

I throw myself off the man and force my wing's barriers out with the mass before bothering to look around, wrapping myself in one as I look down at him from the ceiling; I see in an instant a very large, very large-nosed man in a black suit that reaches only to his knees, shaven legs *visible*; a slight tinge of revulsion fills me at the sight.

"Unarmed," he says, raising his empty arms; I sing a subjective in seconds, and the room's orations appear to me in enough detail—a series of disengaged sessile locks around the now-open door, what looks to be an imprint relay strong enough to consume the tessiture of twenty men fading into the distance—to let me know he isn't lying. "As you can no doubt see."

I realise I've forgotten about my newly-acquired weapon; I let my hand hang down with its pistol, pointing in his general direction, and he chuckles as the tackled man underneath scrambles to his fours and begins to scurry out the room past his lifted leg.

"I'm no Aimelan, dear," he says, and I look carefully at him—his arm clearly has quite recently been cut, the rebound skin dark brown. "Your friend's given us enou—'

"Where's my friend?" I aim the weapon a little better. "Don't lie to me."

He doesn't react. "He's with us. Safe. We're just here to throw you a simple offer—"

"You were going to *spine-weave* me."

"—a handful of chores—in exchange, we will guarantee the safe delivery of your friend. A simple deal, nothing more."

I take barely a second to think.

"Give me my sessile."

He smiles, evidently secure in himself, and gestures to the side; a rolled-up sessile lands in his palm and flares up in my subjective, and he rolls it down into the centre of the room. It's untrapped, the oratory signature completely benign, and I drop from the ceiling to grasp it, wing covering as much of myself as I can as I reach the ground.

"Alright," I say, "Where's my friend?"

"Not yet!" he tut-tuts. "Your chores. We were very impressed with your talents earlier."

I grit my teeth. "You wanted me to kill for you after you wove me, didn't you?"

"Now, now, let's not dwell on the past." He reaches behind the doorframe and fetches a miniature steel-backed sessile, throwing it at my feet; upon its surface, a man with red-coloured hair stares hatefully up at me, a curly bush practically enveloping his face. "I want you to kill for us *without* being woven."

I don't look back up—I can see the man's shadow upon the ground, the light behind him brighter than the one above, and keep my weapon straight. "Who's this?"

"Atarilsis Irinteli ar-Sesinkhatari. He's been clawing into Kasharyn's profits for a year now—"

"You want me to kill him."

His smile is wider than his face. "Forward! I like it."

"That was a question. You want me to kill him?"

"If you want to see your friend again, I suppose. He's a kind man—likes taking gifted children in for his silly little school. I'm sure someone like you would impress him very much."

"And what's my guarantee?"

"You don't have one, admin." He seems to have settled quite well back into his role as the superior, and turns about in place. "My people will dress you and help you on your way. Welcome to the Shattered Circus—hope you enjoy your stay."

My arms relax, and I fire.

The weapon's kick is almost nonexistent. He doesn't seem to realise he's been shot, the only clue the very precise hole in his scapula, and nothing moves until gravity chooses to assert himself upon his frame to pull a trickle of brown heme from his wound.

"No," I say, and nothing happens; I hear a murmur from the hallway, and walk casually onwards. The relief lets me realise my heart is beating so hard I can feel it in my throat, and I swallow. "Does anyone else have an offer for me?"

There is no response. I walk towards the door, left wing covering my privates, and the four men surrounding me—two on each side—do not kill me.

I look down and grab him by the hair, bringing the pistol to his head and tilting over to stare him in his very much conscious face.

"I recognise localised membrane circulation when I see it. You should have thrown some food colouring on the wound—your orators would be screaming to keep you alive if you had any on tap."

"We don't have the shithead," he grunts, his newfound accent quite exotically soft in its ugliness.

I press the thing harder against his temples. "I know it still hurts—you can scream if you want."

"Not lying. Freak cut my ass up out of preservation, hit and ran on the surgeons, shot the thing ten times and it didn't slow it down—no clue where it went."

I shift my weapon over to his right eye. "Did you weave him?"

"No, hell no, I'm sorry," he says, his melanin-deprived irises contracting as he stares into the barrel, and for a second I feel like a horrible person, what am I *doing*, "we were *gonna*—"

I tug on the trigger a little; it makes a very slight click on the pressure safety.

"*No!*" he screams, his legs shaking in place. "No, we didn't *do* anything. Thing woke up a few minutes ahead of schedule, before the doctors made the first cut, took its shit and left, we didn't do anything, Isha, get that thing away from my eye."

I look to the right, then to the left; past the legs of the still men around us, the hallways ending in bends towards stairways. We're in some kind of apartment, I realise, the sort reserved for fourth-tier citizens—the wall at the right's end marked with some sort of graffiti in one of the few languages I cannot read, the script some sort of perversion of Far Northern calligraphy.

"Perhaps you should start putting yourself back together," I say, unbuttoning his shirt. "We're going for a walk."

I'm proud of myself.

The clothing around me, as thick as it is, cannot protect me from the stench of the city below us; the enormous iron-laced clearglass walkway my mount's ironclad feet leave little scratches upon as he shuffles quickly onwards gives me a view of a world with a sphere of interest more vertical than the sky's. The building from which we've emerged appears to have grown from it like a tumour, haphazardly hugging the walkway's sessiles for support with a thousand concrete arms.

"Nice view, huh," I giggle, putting my mouth up against his ear, "daddy?"

"You're insane," he says, his upper-class pretence returned with his health.

Under a shroud of rug-like cloth, a muscle-propelled pistol leaves a round bruise on the side of the man's head, the recently released blood within him doubtlessly rushing to the hit; a cloud of dust casts itself from the wool over my shoulder.

"No, just purpose-driven. You're the one spine-weaving children."

"You're not a kid, you're an admin—" he says, his voice back to its natural rhythm. "Hey, you know what? I don't even know where the bastard's gone. You don't need me."

"That's why you know I won't hesitate to kill you. Play the part."

He looks to the side, onwards into the remarkably clear view about fifty metres to the building across from our platform. "How do you know I won't pull you straight back into another den?"

"Do you value your life more than you value your twisted sense of justice?"

He grunts. "You wouldn't know if I did."

"Cute," I say, tracing a circle around his ear with warm steel. "Game theory. I take it we'll get going?"

"Where the hell to?" he says—no, he *asks*, and I almost appreciate his sincerity.

The subjective in my vision has started to fade a little; I've long since learnt to filter unused subjectives from the realm of conscious thought, but they're now so persistent that I get a microfright every time I notice that they're still there. A third—

I've forgotten about something.

"*The man!*" I say, and I almost feel silly for remembering him before I've found the man I *need* to find, but I continue with my sentence in a minute spurt of logorrhoea. "The man with us. The Shelflander, the one with the pink cheeks, the—"

"The raidshit?" he grunts out, and I can almost imagine the distaste in the part of his face beyond my sight. "Threw him at the camp."

My eyes widen. "His insides were rebound."

"Doubt the retard had a problem. Friends probably tore his ass to shreds the moment he threw them the news. Asshole tried to fuck you up for your permits—hell, you *gutted* nine of the tittysprinkles. What the hell do you care?"

"Wait," I say, tilting my head the tiniest fraction of a degree; the syllables are certainly Aimelan, but they're so far removed from any context or meaning that I can scarcely imagine what they're meant to signify. "Tittysprinkles?"

"You know, tittysprinkles. The little—"

The thought on his part appears to be enough for the cache to learn it for me, and I almost gag. "No, that's enough," I say, and my attention turns back to the subjective—I suppose the Shelflander's fate is a matter more of pride than compassion, and there is no point in dwelling upon it further. "I take it you have absolutely no clue in which direction he went?"

"I've already *told* your little brown ass what I know."

"And he took the permits, did he?"

"Yeah, ran out clothed in bags, robes, blood and whatever the hell it had stuck on his spine. I guess it'd get picked up by the Slicerbacks."

"The *Slicerbacks?*"

"Well, yeah—nasty fuckers, seen them blowing up the kayays for kicks. Got a den about half a block from here. Usually leave you alone unless you look tough enough to get joined up."

"What do they *do?*"

"Eh, typical fleshers. Bunch of old ashy mercs sloughed off the present war, got screwed out of their papers after the permits kicked in, same old story—they go around picking kids off the street, sticking 'em on spikes off their backs, drink their blood, stuff like that."

"And what the hell are they going to do to him when they see him?" I shout, leaning in closer against his head; I almost forget that I'm holding a weapon, and he freezes up as the barrel grinds up against his temple with the force of a little girl's arm.

"das Cimcharei," he says, his voice so calm I can feel his fear,

"Lower your gun."

"What are they going to do?" I say, almost apologising; the demonym bears no personal significance, and so I don't realise the attempt at familiarisation until the words are out of my mouth.

"Eesh, they're not gonna kill it. Shove some spikes in its back, get it a few—"

I prod him. "Stop that."

"Stop what?"

"'It'. I'm aware he killed some of you monsters, but he's my friend. Stop it."

"That's not— oh, yeah, I forgot. Aimelans." He seems to suppress a chuckle. "Alright, alright, I'll check my privilege. *Now* are you gonna get that gun off my head?"

"No," I say, easing it up a centimetre or so, "but I won't make it fracture your skull. I won't bother asking you why you didn't tell me about them before—where are they?"

He turns his head back up to stare at me with his discoloured eyes with a look that screams disbelief, head brushing against the steel under my fingers; I suppose it would be easier to empathise with the child-abducting, spine-weaving excuse for a man entitled to rights if he weren't so *different* from me, and the thought gives me pause.

I shake my head of the thought and focus. "Should I be worried?"

"They're *soldiers*. Honest-to-the-Tower *soldiers*, about a hundred of them with so many guns counting the ammo would kill us with age— we're not getting in there. You kicked our shit in, I respect that, but we're just the hired help. This isn't Aimela, no matter how bad your hood was. They're a nation of their own."

A phrase strikes at me somewhere from memory—*self-legitimising elements*. "The hired help?"

"Ina Valksryn," he says, holding on gently to my left ankle; a greeting for children, and I don't take offence. "Colonel of the Three-Nine-Eight. We procure promising individuals such as yourselves and grant them fulfilling employment in the service of a number of worthy causes."

My curiosity suppresses my disgust. "Velkisrin? You're Tapkeki?"

"*Valksryn*. I'm Teptesryn."

"I've never heard of that ethnicity."

"Consider me a survivor," he says, "and consider yourself outwitted."

I look up, and realise that I'm stupider than I give myself credit for.

I can't see them, but I know they're there; I'm unsure whether the sound or the bone-breaking grasp on my ankle makes the fear real, but as my body moves without me, as I lose *control*, as nothing I could possibly do would help me—

I hit the ground with a relative lightness, my wings flapping reflexively right before the numbness strikes; my arms shudder so much as I try to push myself up that they slip in place, my thence-elevated chin resting upon my own blood as I look hazily up to see against the light a man with a grin wider than the sun.

"Lost a bit off that bar, huh? Wondered how your freak friend worked." My weapon lies upon the ground, a few metres from my arm; I entertain the thought of going for it just as he raises his steel boot and lands it gently down upon my neck. "Sent its ass all the way down to green."

"His," I swallow, and blood follows the saliva.

"Cute." He extends his arm to the side; a fairly familiar figure shrouded in the sun's light walks up alongside him, and he extends his arm to receive a thrown sessile-arm. I recognise the red stripes upon its chassis, and I begin to laugh.

He seems to appreciate my humour as he points the weapon's barrel in my body's general direction. "What's so funny?"

"You're—you're killing me," I say, every other syllable wracked with suppressed laughter, the pain in my bruised nose beginning to register. "You're killing me with the only thing he has to remember his old friend by. Isn't that a laugh?" I giggle, and the humour is genuine as the tears forming in my ducts. "It's practically—practically diabolical."

"Heh," he vocalises, and the sound that follows is the best I've failed to hear in my life.

I'd imagine my vision would be far more impressive if he was protected by anything rigid, but as it is his chest simply bursts open, the cloth around and over him too complete to really get an impression of the exact point the body ends as it jolts back; his circulating membrane appears to rupture irreversibly as it does, the blood flooding his skull right before he tips over as a thoroughly familiar shout echoes above it all.

"*Told you!*"

A quick burst of gunfire follows, and I close my eyes before I can see its result.

I don't know how long I lie still; logic tells me I should be standing up, running, flying, doing *anything*—but I'm still as it feels right to be, and the slapping of hooves on clearglass is surprisingly therapeutic. A set of feet follow, and as I open my eyes I catch the petite shadow of a short-cloaked man covering entirely over two dead bodies.

"Hey, Ash—you alright? Sorry for leaving you back there."

"I'm fine," I say, and as I do my voice trembles more than I expect it should. "That weapon—it wasn't yours, was it?"

"A thoroughly astute assumption, milady."

I steady myself against my right arm, blowing my nose—no new blood, now, Madeline's gift evidently working quite well—right before my eyes follow the hooves up to the man in his armour, weapon larger than me lying casually against his shoulder.

The titanium plates are shrouded partially in a single-shoulder cloak of gold-rimmed blue, and I stare for a second before I remember.

"Hanjat," I say, trying to find the appropriate words, "how?"

"Now is not the time, milady—I fear there may be more of the miscreants en route." He doesn't bother looking back. "A group of men with curved blades mounted upon their backs, arms presented, from which I rescued your charge. Arise."

I push myself up, ceramic-soled foot gripping the glass as I throw a handful of the fabric off myself to reveal my old clothing underneath. I note that a fleshcrawler has already began to squirrel in towards the corpse, no doubt led by the blood— I've never seen a burst circulation membrane before, and the sight is quite intriguing: every bit of his frame appears to be suffering from subcutaneous bleeding, the skin upon every uncovered part of his bloated corpse a wet brownish-red, loosened enough by the force to visibly bulge and then sag as the unclotted portion begins to ooze out of his split tension lines and begins to pool thickly on the clearglass below.

He apparently had good enough sense to keep his eyes unorated; the black-framed blue and whites are islands over the shattered brown bits of vein and stained ligament outlining his face that remain, the fluid draining into his now almost transparent jowls as they begin to harden through their contents and slump against his perfectly preserved skull.

The smell of rust has filled the air; I pinch my nose.

"I need a bath."

"Cleanse me," I say, and the sessile above me begins to flow.

There's a certain luxury in saying *khaslashkil-mi* instead of *oyjj pár tri-dis-kystyrii pyfrynét* and the hundred parameters that should come after. The stream that results—water, but not quite—is all the sweeter for the effortlessness with which it comes.

The parts of me that aren't immediately wettened and made warm turn to grime and sweat in my mind, and my wings twitch and flutter of their own volition. I touch them, and the shudder that goes through me is a symptom of one of the few true pleasures I've had for a while.

"If I may ask—"

I look to the door, wood framed in opulence; the sessile-lock is reinforced by a mechanical one of solid steel, 'MELAILI PRUDE LOCK *jen ren'tiklatis akh the INSIDE not out*' scrawled on it in red-inked Akashrak abiguda. The words themselves are some creole of Aimelan, and the realisation almost makes me giggle as the voices reverberate through the wall.

"Yeah, nah, no thanks."

I begin to lie back a little, the quickly pooling clear fluid edging up to my neck before a 'stop' issues from my lips.

"You knew what I was to say, then?"

I push my face under for a second, the faint buzz of rug-borne dust quickly dissipating under the surface, and my ears stay just enough above it to catch his reply.

"I'm not into guys."

I choke a little underneath, and quickly pull myself up to let the cleansing fluid dribble down my chin. The unclogging is slow, far slower than I've been accustomed to, and I barely feel my teeth being purged of the plaque until I scrape my newly pristine nails across them.

"That—that's not—"

"Just messing with you. What d'you need, Tinhead?"

"I was simply wondering what you really are. You do not wear a servant's seal, nor do you speak in the language of your mistress—"

"'Mistress'? How many shades've you got on you? I'm my own man."

"I've never heard of an administrator of such high standing travelling with only a mercenary for protection."

I relax just long enough for the burning to start.

"We're friends."

It strikes so fast that I don't bother looking before my wings flap by themselves hard enough to send half the fluid to the gold-and-silver-coloured ceramic floor, body forcing itself a metre up in the five-metre-high room in an instant.

"Friends?"

My feet, I realise, and pull one up in midair; I begin to spin a little as my centre of gravity shifts, and I push myself steady just as an appendage comes up to show me a perfectly pink sole, white, moist fragments of epidermis hanging from the edges of the lost skin.

"Yeah, friends. If I could see your ass through the metal, would I see it tight around the pole?"

I sigh.

"No! Absolutely not. I'm simply surprised."

"What, I don't look good enough for her?"

It takes me a few seconds to drift carefully down, dampened wings too wet to really do more than sway in the air; the idiot who sung the bath sessile must have tried to turn it into a substitute for a pedicure.

"I shall not deny my feelings on the matter, though I do not condemn."

The fluid has already begun to evaporate and then empty out into vacuum as it touches the ceiling, both in the tub and upon my face; the orator's evidently set the dissipation threshold at thirty degrees. The man-sized ceramic container is already half-empty.

"Sheesh. Jings."

I drift over to the clothesbar and dress in the silence; it takes barely a minute, the ceramic fabric's exotic lining soft against my skin.

"I share more with you than you know."

I undo the lock and open the door into a room almost black with darkness, two highlighted figures and a false flame the sole exceptions to the rule.

"What," Perei says, lying back in the pellet-filled red sack on the rug-covered floor, "you think you're normal 'cause your skin's normal? Don't act like you're not pink on the inside. Aren't you a knight or something?"

Hanjat's helm moves such that its ridge faces me, the titanium reflecting the light orange lighting of the false fireplace behind him. "Ah, milady. You've come just in time. Your—your friend has just raised a point I sought to explicate and in which you might be interested—excuse me, but *are you floating?*"

I look down at my hanging feet, the lowest point upon my robes barely grazing a stray fibre off the rug, and shrug. "Long story. Please go on."

"Right," he says, looking me up and down, "I've had my knighthood revoked."

"What?" I say, and realise as I do that Perei's followed.

"Apparently my blood is of insufficient prestige to sustain the honour. I bear no shame and my pension is intact, but I am in no mood to lay down and do nothing as the wheel of the world's fate turns. I have been in this city for a day, and a few coins buy the tightest lips—I knew of your arrival within an hour, and of your capture within minutes. I apologise for not being able to rescue you sooner."

"How did you know we would be coming to Antamanaria?"

"The library's surveillance systems, naturally."

Perei and I share a look.

My companion shrugs. "Ask a stupid question, get a stupid answer."

"So why follow us?" I ask, my right foot absently rubbing against the knuckle of my left's big toe.

"I know that you are doing something to halt the menace who put my life to tatters, and I certainly cannot do it myself—who else would I follow?"

I am looking at a man behind centimetres of metal; for all I know, a perfidious grin might well be spread across his features and an imprint oration could await my nation's betrayal.

I nod. "Fair enough. I suppose I've trusted worse."

"Now," he says, pointing at my groundless feet, "why are you flying?"

"It's a long story."

Unknown Cache KaTiETa
Sipyak Monument, Crescent City, Antamanaria
Description: Located by Tower energy exchange. Emits an intolerant barrier with a diameter of approximately five kilometres; no entrance is possible. Readings show entire superstructure filled with barrier signatures. Current hypothesis indicates a pre–Laceration minimal-resonance dual barrier resolution similar to OIKhaTa. Two–way information transfer suggests human or otherwise tessitura–gifted response.
Penetration is unlikely; study will continue.
Found 28 Primus 982, Great Expansion
2/7/3883: Abnormal energy exchange detected.
4/7/3883: Suggest energy exchange analysis.
5/8/3883: Analysis of current data confirms recurring two–way information transfer; entered into database as UC KaTiETa.

"And that's why we're here," I say, finishing just as the breath runs out.

The knight's entire frame shifts back in its seat; he's remained still throughout the speech, and its shift makes me jump a little on the inside. "The *Sipyak Monument?* Milady, you can't be serious."

Perei picks something from his teeth. "She's never *not* serious."

"You're not perturbed? It's impossible at *best*, and the fog—" He turns to me. "This Sestiyari document—how do we know it isn't a simple trap, milady? You've been almost slain countless times following its path, once by the Sestiyari themselves."

The man on the beanbag snickers. "Key word being 'almost'."

I say nothing, and he seems to ponder Perei's argument with the seriousness of a serious man before nodding.

"A fair point—nonetheless, how do you propose we breach the Monument's barrier?"

"She'll find a way. Hopefully without getting ourselves riveted up. Right, Ash?"

"And when shall we depart?"

"I suppose we'll go tomorrow, once we've all had some rest—I suppose we've been through enough for today."

The man nods. "If you suggest so, milady, I concur." He pushes himself to his feet, walking off to his own room with a surprising swiftness.

Perei's eyes follow the man out before he turns to look at me with a mightily smug countenance. "Please. I'm just getting started. I know you're the kind to get your feet burned off by novelty rinsewater, but did you *see* the roads? It's like another *world* out there. Cities tall as the Insurmountables, houses so *original* they could never be in the capital—saddlebackers as far as the eye can see."

"I don't want to know what that means," I say, scratching absently at the edges of my bareskinned soles, "and I would have been too busy burying my face into my rugs to notice if I did. Don't you think it's mildly dangerous for you to be going about on your own?"

"We could go down there *together*. Field trip. Don't you wish you could take a vacation every now and then?"

I have to choke back a laugh. "A holiday? In *Antamanaria*?"

"Ash, try and look out the window."

I look about; the room is absurdly ill-lit, but I note a straight, lighted crack along one of the enormous place's unforgiving walls. I put my finger to the corner of my eye and pull, staring at him through a blurred eye. "I suppose I look Bisheldi to you?"

He sighs, the words following his exhalation in a language I don't recognise. *"Azure sunrise one-six-two."*

Before I can question his pronunciation, the crack widens both ways along the ten-metre wall; the plaster upon the wall seems to crawl into nothingness, and I realise its nature just as the light swirls in from a thousand corners at once, spreading a perfect view of Antamanaria's endless metropolis before us: elaborate structures of crystal and stone rise about twenty metres below us to the superstructures above—clearly visible against the barrier-distorted greyish-brown backdrop, each a palm in the face of the Mitaranatarea law—separating the sett-paved setting of Avishenra mansions and full-bloom trees from which serrulata blossoms fall from the ramshackle piles of concrete and stonerise reaching up into the sky above us, countless men and women milling beyond the barriers above and below; the light shines through perfectly, filling the room in an instant with a whiteness so harsh it turns the red upon the walls pink.

"Thousands," I say, almost speechless as I approach the sessile.

"Thousands of people? Thousands of houses? Thousands of di—"

"Thousands of orators." My hand touches the completely flat wall, likely forged originally of steel, and the false glass retains no marks. "The beginning of the seamless transition itself must have taken six hundred tessiture-days—this room alone must have been worth over a thousand three-kilogramme strangles before the Reclamation. The sessile's complicated enough that I can't imagine the reflection being imperfect. The work is simple, yes, but it's beautiful."

"Huh. Real barrier-lover, huh?"

"It's as much of an art as a science. *Venytj áœyii myzh,*" I begin, and as I continue the sheer thickness of the nexuses before me leaves nothing but a tight-knit web of almost solid blue threads against each other, the view disappearing in my vision for one far more intricate.

The sound of a sessile-arm being tugged from its holster reaches my ears. "Uh, Ash—"

"Look here, for instance," I say, pointing at a Sundown junction, "The Sundown's normally used for stitching displays together, but they've obviated its obvious function by making the entire display unitary—they've stitched sessiles *within* the walls to—"

"Ash, you might want to get away from that *right now.*" I can hear his footsteps, and absentmindedly let myself float down to the ground; the feeling that my excoriated feet give me is immediately apparent, but I barely notice it past the excitement. *"Tinhead! Bring the big one, I think you might wanna see this!"*

"What?" I say, the floor below my nerve-burning feet—I realise around then that I can't take the pressure and swiftly move up a little to compensate—shaking slightly as the metal-clad man thunders past a door to my left. I look to him, the nexuses behind the supportive barriers and reflective sessiles filling his frame lights against lights, the sunlight glowing through them to create something both beautiful and awfully uninteresting.

"Step back," he says, and I note as I comply the object he's lugged along with his left, something he's beginning to pull up to mount against his chest.

"What's wrong?" I ask, mumbling out the words I must to repeal the subjective; as I begin, the people around me back further away from the solid work of art before us and I feel quite suddenly terrified that the beauty I've been presented might just be about to be lost.

I pull my sessile out and hold it before the wonder before me, and the nexus imprint completes just as the subjective pulls itself from my vision to reveal a vaguely man-shaped object clad entirely in something hard and pitch-black with his left arm somehow glued to the wall, a series of thick strings leading from his back to *something* I can't quite make out the shape of submerged in the sun's glow.

"The Cockroaches," Hanjat says, "this time in new clothes. Milady, shall I fire?"

I glance down to my sessile to reaffirm the imprint's composition.

"No," I say; the man pulls a cylinder the diameter of a child's arm's length from his back by its briefcase-like handle and, with what appears to be a moment of trepidation, shoves it hard against the wall, thick bolt-like appendages around its rim visible as he pumps down.

In my imagination the junctions within the wall-sessile stitch themselves to each other, instantly generated barriers resonating against each other outwards towards the force his device creates; the sessile goes dark in that spot to reveal the engraved wallpaper underneath, and through the rest that remains I see a man hanging limp from the wall by his arm, the other quite thoroughly missing along with his device.

"Induced barrier resonance utilising the reactive properties of the Sundown junction as a means to instantly counteract kinetic force," I say, stepping further back from the wall before us. "It creates a barrier around an assailant solely to force its resonance. Genius."

"I would have slain myself if I'd opened fire then," Hanjat says, the shiver in his voice betraying his heartbeat's rapidity. "The Emperor's dwellings have been using that method for decades—I must thank you, milady, for advising me."

"Decades?"

"Did you believe we've steeped ourselves in tradition so deeply that we've become numb to the dangers of the world beyond our wall, milady?" he says, and I can imagine the smugness under the titanium. "There is no part of the Imperial Palace older than a century. A state secret, to be sure, but I bear no debt to any master."

Perei lets a little *'pfft'* issue from his lips; the tension thus past, my heart begins to calm. "You'd think they'd shut you up before you could tell anyone."

"A revoked knight normally has his secrets indebted to the Emperor by a single penny bearing the seal of the Registry; the Marquis was desperate enough to strip me of my rank that he did not bother."

I nod, keeping a close eye on the strings dangling from the hanging man's back; they appear to be tightening even as they lower. "The Registry has no authority to issue currency, does it?"

"It does not," he says, and as the string goes taut I see its source.

Perei backs up, raising his weapon. "Uh, guys—"

"Get down!" I shout, and as I follow my own advice the sound rings in my ears past the bones in my hands as the world bursts open.

The gunfire comes just as I force my barrier intolerant, and the breath I take as the force washes over my floor-anchored body stops in its tracks as I *move*, the dysexaptic field replacing it letting me know of a single gout of flame brushing across its surface as I force myself towards the fire-spitting metal beast, its twin pincers poking through the thoroughly pulverised wall's wreckage.

"Milady, *what are you doing?*"

I hold tight upon the thing's shell as I slam into it, and I realise with a start that it *isn't* metal; the studded material feels like nothing I've ever laid my hands upon before, and as I look up I see the entire body of the insect-like thing I've forced myself upon, its abdomen slowly beginning to part to reveal something past the horizon it creates.

"Ash, you al—*Ash?*"

Three pairs of hands clad in the same armour as the arm-hung man grab on to the abdomen's edge, climbing in *my* direction.

One of their heads begins slowly to ascend, the crown of his armour becoming wholly visible.

"Fire!"

Most intolerant barriers aren't fully intolerant and not fully frictionless; they have to allow just enough movement to sustain life. *Neteléresynyr* is not the same word as *n'teléresynyr*, its nominally stable-tolerant counterpart; a mispronunciation is not usually fatal, though it tends to be thoroughly uncomfortable. Electrical activity does not cease, so the brain lives long enough to register its impending death when it is.

That is why I panic when the barrier-piercing round does not pierce his—*its, its heart is not beating*—hull-anchored barrier, and as it pulls its weapon fairly methodically over the edge every part of my brain lies convincingly enough '*netel*—' to my neocortex that what I choose to do seems intelligent as I push onwards and he *has* to lower his barrier to fire, '—*éresy*—' and it *does* and as he does '—*jt'* and for the moment in which the resonance hits me I do not think.

I'm in the air.

My organs and skeleton are still intact, certainly, which would be impressive to celebrate alone if not for the fact that I'm willing to celebrate the universe's continued existence in the face of the first formulation of the irresistible force paradox.

I'm going to hit something, I realise, and I sing a simple stable-tolerant pegged to my velocity as I look down at the rapidly receding object—a vehicle, isn't it?—below me, slowly beginning to force a deceleration as my wings flap against the relatively billowing wind.

I appear to have done something; a handful of black-covered figures flail in the sky, presumably lacking the tessitura to regenerate their barriers, and something in me makes my heart sink as I reverse my path.

I realise that it's beginning to close as I approach, the abdomen's halves pulling themselves back together over about three unmoving figures strapped into the fairly mechanical-looking chairs built into its sides, now turning back in towards the floating thing; I accelerate as fast as my gut tells me I should, and as I soar my target quickly grows quicker than my field of vision as I bounce harmlessly feet-first past the freshly closed flaps off the similarly exotic floor, pinging off the now-closed, light-lined ceiling before making a fairly solid landing *right* on my still-skinless feet, at which point I let loose a disbelieving yelp, throwing myself about a centimetre off the ground to let the air soothe the pain.

"Worked better than it did for Ayerei," I mumble, looking immediately to where I imagine the front must be. In my path is a fairly simple-looking Southern-style door with a simple-looking sessile-lock; I fumble about through my ceramic robes and find my misericorde where I last put it. Whatever's within isn't nearly as sophisticated as the armour without, and the dead men to my sides, limbs twisted at obscene angles that expose the white-stained-red fabric underneath, obviously aren't built for whatever it is they're wearing.

I walk towards the door, ready to break things, just as it bursts open itself; I instantly throw myself to the side, left slamming into the door, and I can hear my heartbeat as nothing comes through.

Nothing's before me, either; I am looking straight into the wreckage of the wall I've just looked through, the room's insides visible past the sessile-wall's still transparent remnants through which the giant insect-machine's pincers jut; Hanjat and Perei are clearly visible, both standing at the edges of the structural wound and—judging by the smaller man's face—arguing over something.

And then I realise that I've missed something far more crucial: a particularly ergonomic-looking chair bolted right onto the nothingness.

"*I surrender!*" a shout issues from beyond it in some dialect of Ajhyliyy, black-and-white gauntlets raising almost to the ceiling; I nearly scream in my shock, and contain my expression just as he tosses his sidearm to the ground and stands to look straight ahead in his helmetless uniform.

"Please," he says, his sickly-soft tongue arousing in me some sort of unconscious bile, the bulk of his neck-touching hair splitting along its height as he looks to the sky past the invisible walls. "I surrender myself to you."

"Do you understand the speech of the civilised man?" I ask, feeling very much like a siction's protagonist; something within makes me speak as I imagine I should, the thrill giving me a spell of slight air-headedness. "Kneel, savage, your arms above your head."

He does, and I walk forth onto what my body tells me is nothing just as my boot lands upon it and reports old-fashioned steel. "Is this of your own make?"

"The Administrator provides the materials. My cousin Anastasia is amongst those who build the machines. I am a pilot," he says, and here he gestures to subjectives beyond my eyes, "and I take our war to the skies."

"The skies—how, and at what speed?"

"Faster than I imagined was possible. I have gone half the way to the blast threshold in mere minutes." He pauses. "It is quite the sight. I can only assume God has put us in His hands."

I put my blade close enough to his back that he does not feel it. "Quite a lot of good that did for your friends."

He looks back at me with an expression to which I ascribe the compound adjective 'fearful contempt'; the longer he looks at me, the less fear seems to moderate him. "We have taken half the layers of Sikhas and the city Haroudesh is under our charge. Our troops march down the streets to the marketplace."

"'To the marketplace'—you've taken Vasksharei?"

He nods. "In a mere month, our Administrator shall bring our people the justice they deserve. That is his promise to us, and I do not doubt his words. I have surrendered, Pretender—I need volunteer nothing."

"I'm not beholden to the rules of war," I say, prodding the back of his neck. "And neither are you, outside the terms of the Concordance as you are. How did you find us? Where are you based?"

He seems to consider the question for a second, then lets out a rough *hah*. "I might have reaffirmed my stance, but this is a question too simple to answer—we hail from the Tower. We hail from the hand of God Himself, and it is more beautiful than anything infidels will ever see."

"Drugs?" I ask half to myself, tempted to interrupt my questioning to check.

"The sinner thinks miracles come only of sin." He chuckles in a manner unbefitting his stature. "Only the blessings of God. Remember, Aimelan—a month."

I nod. "And what if we put a halt to your advance?"

"A month—no more, no less. We are merely His feet; the Administrator is His curling fist, and when it falls no evil shall survive."

"Turn this thing so that we may step out onto the floor. Open the doors."

He stands, and I let myself drift off the ground to match his height with my blade as he sits back in his chair, pulling strips of some kind of webbed fabric in the shape of an 'x' over his chest, tapping upon the point where they meet. He taps at the air for a handful of seconds before holding down on nothing for several more; the invisible walls turn a translucent grey as the sides burst open, the transition between steel and the black material clear along the doorway's rim as the flaps slam down upon their own joints hanging in the air just as the blade in my hand slams against something with a remarkable swiftness, sending it flying back to clatter against the ground; I back up without thinking, and realise with a start that the chair is *missing*, along with the roof, and as I look up to the distant sky, past the blue-coloured barrier, I see a black spot quickly losing itself amongst the day's heat.

I realise as I back up to stare at the empty space—my companions looking quite thoroughly bewildered past it—that the subjectives that must have been before him have turned objective, red Fransai script in the air; I read it out loud, and the words become semantically clear to me as they issue from my mouth.

"Twenty-five seconds to self-reactive combustion. Cancel-write: 'eternal'."

The text quickly fades into a series of light blue objectives, mostly arrows and numbers; without thinking, I grab the sidearm—it doesn't give me the pain it should, for some reason, evidently being some sort of post-Laceration weapon, and a moment of hot relief washes over me like similes through the pens of hacks—and then my blade, tucking both into my robes.

"*N'teléresynjs ápyfrét av set'senmétyr s'indéziyra drimænyzh myzh, cærjánt an'mitmétyr syit-là,*" I say, just in case; my breath stops where it should, and I tap one of the arrows before me.

The very tip of my finger is bathed in fire, the barrier little enough under my skin for me to feel nothing of a few dead cells being incinerated.

My intolerant wears off into stable-tolerance just as I'm thrown head-first onwards towards the wall before me so quickly that I can barely see the two figures flashing in my peripherals before I slam into it, the slight give in the barrier's shape sending me flipping over onto my back with my wings splayed out under me as Perei throws himself down to his knees next to me.

Hanjat keeps a respectful distance.

"*Ash!*" he exclaims, hand so close to my face I almost want to smack it away, "The hell just happened? You alright?"

I match my eyes with his. "Perei."

"Please, Ash," he says, giving me a smile. "I thought I told you to call me Penny."

My lips curl faintly to mirror his.

"Perei qu'n'av dasnamr," I say, "Let's go on a field trip."

Crescent City stands a few kilometres to the north of our recently damaged dwellings, and the strangely well-tiled streets leading there under the sessile-illuminated concrete sky are blessed with a relative peace; my legs are unburdened entirely, the variety of women—curiously, very few men—in exotically repulsive clothing shuffling down the streets. A few men look at me in a suspicious manner, but as their gazes sweep over to Hanjat the immediate deflection is too obvious to be coincidental.

"And that bitch over there, ti—"

I stare at him in a manner I haven't quite before, my mouth slightly open to show my teeth as I furrow my brow to indicate my overwhelming, unrelenting disapproval. "No. Please stop."

"Hey," he says, clearly taken aback, "I thought you—"

"Thus far, you have managed to endear yourself to me via your relatively neonate, adolescent behaviour. The last ten minutes have convinced me that I would despise you if I were forced to come into contact with you throughout the course of my day-to-day interaction and has completely eliminated any lingering moral opposition I might have had to the permit system through my prior interactions with you in a dual-party environment."

He seems to comprehend, along with a briskly walking light-skinned man in a bright red bedlah who appears to have found his destination right as I finish, and in that moment I despise the Exodus cache within him for allowing him to do anything other than let his ignorance preclude a serious conversation.

"Sheesh, Ash, lighten the hell up. Aren't you *twelve*?"

"Yes, and I'm clearly older than you."

He snickers. "Yeah, you're right. I oughta get an *imaginary friend* too."

"I don't pretend to be the impressions of masculinity a child might gather from its failures."

"You don't get out much, do you?" he says, almost sputtering as he tries to compensate for his lack of wit.

I stare at him, and it seems to take him over half a decasecond to discover the nature of his offence.

"I'm sorry, Ash."

"Don't mention it."

He seems to pirouette mentally around the indignity of the apology in an instant, almost as if he does not feel it at all, and puts his hand to his chin. "So, the guy you were talking about—the hell did he even say 'fore he shot himself out the roof?"

"Vasksharei is theirs. We have a month, apparently."

"They went all the way down to the marketplace in a *week*?"

"They're everywhere, if he's to be believed. Peshkharea is under siege; he didn't mention Tachiesrea."

Out of the corner of my eye, a woman in a croissant vest missing its webbing over her left breast catches my attention by the motion she makes as she evidently hears us, immediately throwing her arm up such that her hand catches her opened mouth; I can't help but find myself wishing that she'd cover her chest instead.

"Everywhere, huh? What about the South?"

"He didn't mention the South either."

"Damn. Was hoping for some *good* news for once. Maybe the muds've ran them over themselves."

"The Purus?" I say, sneering; my foot brushes against a drunken man's bare shoulder as I do, disrupting my concentrated condescension for a fragment of a second. "They keep women in kennels."

"You don't really believe that Joulette-tier bullshit, do you? That's like *one* tribe."

"I'm sure the ones that kill all the Aimelans they find are exemplars of tolerance and equality. Why, I'm certain they're *so equal* the women may impregnate the men and the men bear for the women."

"Hell, could you blame them if they're all like you?" he huffs, upwards-facing hands almost perpendicular to his arms. "You know what I don't get? You say I can't call them muds, and *you're* the one that want them gone off the map. What's your problem?"

"Milady!" Hanjat says, thankfully rescuing me from the

conversation, "We're arriving at Crescent City within minutes—I don't doubt your capabilities, but it would be disgraceful of me not to restate my hesitance, even if only with our path. Perhaps we should seek an alternate route."

I raise an eyebrow. "We've already tread through an urban environment shadowed by a thousand windows. How much more dangerous could more of the same be?"

"I'm certain the affairs of the Shattered Circus have never found a reason to concern you 'til now, milady—perhaps it would be best for you to view the City for yourself."

I look back forwards, and am promptly greeted by a fog so thick it looks like candyfloss beginning right past a gap in the architecture; I realise as I look to the sides that the streets have come deserted by now, the shops boarded up and what look to be the stairwells to the residences reaching to the superstructure above shuttered with steel.

"I haven't the slightest clue—I only saw it this morning, only hours before I was alerted to your presence. The sessile reflections upon my helm cannot penetrate their fog. It would be beyond most men's souls to venture within."

Perei grumbles as I begin to strum a little at the instrument upon my neck, the practised words a whisper. "And you didn't tell us earlier?"

"I'm certain that I spoke of it," he says, the fog slowly turning into nothing.

Nothing, not darkness nor light; my field of view does not *include* the area which the fog covers, the material composition of the buildings that do not surround it and do not have a relative position to it because it *does not exist* highlighting subjectively in my retinae. It takes me a second to close my eyes and another to look away; I shake my head as I stare at the solid ground, refocusing as well as I can.

"Ash? Hey, the hell happened?"

I keep my eyes angled down to my saddle as I centre my head. "We're *not* going through that fog."

"Why not?"

"It's not a fog," I say, noting the unusual cellulose content in the leather below right before the numbers and letters fade. "It isn't a *thing*. I'm not going in there."

"Right, Tinhead, what's the other way through?"

Hanjat's tone seems apologetic as it issues from his sessiles.

"I'm not certain there is one. I was merely raising a concern."

"Well, I'm not wading through—" and here I pause to think up a name so grand it deserves its propriety, "—the *Voidmist*."

"The Voidmist."

"Yes, the Voidmist. I suppose you think you could come up with a better name?"

"Not really. It's just a cloud on the ground. A *groundcloud*."

"No."

"No?"

"No."

"Who the hell made you the—"

"*Milady!*" Hanjat's voice echoes from within his helm, upon which I look back to see him dismounting with a sessile-arm pointed up to a window about ten storeys up, arms aligned perfectly even in midair before his feet slam down; I pull my sidearm as my stable-tolerant slides against itself, barely rephrasing into an ovoidal configuration with an œvjj as my hands tighten around the carbon grip.

"Hi, hi, calm yourselves!"

I sight a man in the window past the light with his hands raised in what I presume to be surrender just as he speaks, rifle longer than his arm in his left; his face is a bright pink-and-white, a visage framed by a strange front-pinched black hat with an upwards-curved little brim, and I can barely recognise his foreign features but something about him tells me he's—

"Isha's hooks," Perei says, interrupting my self-delaying train of thought, "it's the shelfie you fixed up."

"This man is an acquaintance of yours, milady?"

He leans over the windowsill and lets out a cough—I half-expect his intestines to follow the air. "I shan't deny our prior meetings, as inglorious as the circumstances that preceded us they may be. I must say—"

I yank the pistol from my waistband; the grey architecture around him is barely visible in the light of his coloured visage, and as a target he excels. "I'm not partial against destroying my work. What do you want?"

"You misunderstand. I was merely an observer—"

"With a gun," Perei says, drawing his own weapon.

The Shelflander blushes, pulling on his—his *tie?* He's wearing an outfit that requires a *tie.* "Who did take aim upon your own sacred person and did pull upon the trigger—not the actions of a gentlemen, I admit, but purely out of the weakness my humanity grants me. I am but an adventurer, a noble from the Caelestian court, a man of many names and few presumptions; I am here to—"

Perei throws an em-dash into the man's dialogue and terminates it with a sigh that is almost worth calling a yell, shuddering as he lets it out. "Hot damn, and I thought Tinhead was bad. What are you, related?"

"I gather you refer to the charming fellow here, no doubt of an esteemed Zhanghwazh court. The people of Caelestis, though purer of blood, are indeed—"

I raise my left arm, right still armed. "This isn't getting us anywhere. I'm asking you again—*what do you want?*"

"Merely to grant you compensation for your efforts in the preservation of my body. I presume you wish to observe the only artefact upon which Mitreshielantielra could not plant his standard, now obscured past the Withering Mists."

"Withering Mists?" Perei says, evidently impressed. "Hey, Ash. Withering Mists."

I ignore him. "And why do you think you can help us past an inexplicable phenomenon with no precedent?"

"Mere illusion! Our race has dealt with this menace threefold!" he says, and as he does he pulls something that looks to be a multi-pronged steel hook from his back with his free hand, spinning it by some sort of black rope before throwing it upwards over our heads such that it curls around a protruding lamp-post. Hanjat's sessile-arm tracks it for an instant before its muzzle snaps back to his head. "I shall guide you to the Sipyak Monument, thus paying the fee that the doctor hath decreed."

"Your internal organs shouldn't yet be well-acquainted with your body. Are you certain you—"

He throws himself out the window.

I scarcely think; my body throws itself forth, the wings upon my back leaving a gust behind me as my spread arms wrap around him at the point my mind tells me I will meet him, ceramic fabric letting the fine leather vest that lies over his chest. My grip tightens, my whole body contorted to handle his girth; we slam into the wall, his gritted yellow teeth spreading their bacteria onto my left cheek as I whiplash into them. We begin to slide slowly down the side of the structure, and I try my best to keep afloat long enough to check if he's alright; the only thing pinning us in place are my wings.

The man blinks as he seems to realise where he is; his legs kick a little, the fight dying down just as he interprets the sequence of light before him well enough to prospognate me, and as I look up I realise that the line running from his hook leads to a series of straps upon his back that my hands have given me notice of and decide that I'm less mentally competent than I give myself credit for.

His arms wriggle a bit, and I realise as he does that he's still holding his rifle. "Though I appreciate the motivations behind your noble gesture, I really must—"

"Quiet," I say, and kick at the wall; the winding mechanism on his back, no doubt requiring so much tessiture that it must be a treasure in his homeland, seems to pull itself into its harness (into the harness itself?) as we descend backwards, the opposing wall rushing towards us. I let go, now, though every old instinct within me tells me not to, and let myself down without losing my blood's grip on the air.

I land with the utmost grace, toes first; my heavenly descent is punctuated by a nearby *clunk*, and I look to its direction to see the pink man sweeping the dust off his knee-exposing garments as the hook—its prongs evidently folded back into its form by some means—winds back down towards whatever it is that's upon his back to hold it quicker than gravity can throw it to the ground. He smoothly raps his rifle's barrel upon the ground like a walking-stick, the seamless metal tube splitting lengthwise. The whole thing ripples like a liquid before collapsing into the receiver and leaving what looks to be a respectably large pistol.

"An exodus cache," I say, walking to my mount as I stare; my companions seem to share my expression. "Almost certainly pre-Laceration."

Perei's rather dashingly long eyelashes descend the slightest bit, his eyes sheltered from my field of vision by the rest of his head. "How the hell did you keep that shit from your buddies?"

"A hit a little too hard," he says, winking and pulling something resembling black, solidified resin from one of his vest's pockets. "Come, then! Off to adventure we shall ride."

We stay still as he strides confidently onwards into the unyielding fog—the noticeably hook-missing sheet of metal on his back shining in the light—his silhouette disappearing on its second step. "Follow the sound of my voice!"

Perei coughs into his balled-up fist. "Anybody else think this isn't such a hot idea?"

Hanjat's head turns such that his viewing sessiles align with my eyes.

He says nothing.

I roll my eyes and tug on my glasswalker's reins.

"What happened to all the *people* here?" Perei says. "We must've been in here for hours."

"They yet slumber," the Shelflander says, voice carrying a lighthouse-like quality through the opaque fog. "The Withering Mists, when they first emerge, put to slumber those within; they do not wake until they are removed from the Mists, or until the Mists flee from them. The air nourishes their bodies as their souls are away."

A heavily muffled voice echoes into what I presume is metal somewhere behind me, and I shudder a little, stomach giving me an unidentifiable sort of ache I've been chalking up to nerves. My arms are shadows before me, and I'm seriously starting to reconsider my suitability for decision-making. "I'm certain we should have tripped over something by now," I say, my wings twitching a little.

"The young lady would be surprised by what a few ventures upon this boundless sea of ours will grant the determined. The device that rests before my sight shows all as it is—a small present from those who came before."

"I suppose I shouldn't be complaining about the Concordance violation," I say, just as something thick, heavy and cold touches my exposed hand; I clench my jaw to avoid the scream, jerking in place.

It's Hanjat, I tell myself, and am deeply relieved long enough not to panic when I turn to see his vague form slumped against his glasswalker's mane, arm reaching out to grasp weakly at my leg. His cloak dangles all the way down, presumably dragging along the befogged ground.

"Alfred," I say, grabbing Hanjat's palm. The four-centimetre titanium plates over his fingers are one-sided, leaving them just light enough that I only strain a little lifting it up into my lap. "Is that your name?"

"*That* is the name of my manservant, the one—"

"Yes, yes, that's perfectly excellent and remarkable, but my companion, the one in the armour—"

"Oh, dear. Oh, dear, I forgot to mention—oration within the Mists does not function," he says, and I immediately draw my pistol and pray that it isn't a sessile-arm. "Was his armour orated?"

"Wait," Perei says, "what the hell's happening? Singing doesn't work in here?"

"Hanjat," I say, the same barely perceptible voice muffled by the centimetres-thick titanium coffin around him; I bring him closer, tugging the rein from which his hand no doubt just fell. "Are you alright? Can you breathe?"

Another rumble emerges from the metal; we've been in the fog for quite a length of time, I recall immediately, and the knowledge that he would already be dead if he couldn't gives me a relief so immense that it almost drowns out the fact that one of the pillars of modern science and one of my basic biological processes have both been rendered nonfunctional.

"Okay, wait, you mean my gun wouldn't have its shit spewing if I held it down? How're we fixing ourselves up? *How's this place still standing?* Ish-al-*wyent'e*, is that even possible? Ash, tell me that's not possible. How're these goddamn walkers even walking?"

"I apologise with the utmost sincerity. It slipped my mind the extent to which the people of the Tower depend upon its blessings."

As he speaks, I reach over to the base of Hanjat's helm with my left and begin to tug; he raises his arm and lands it. It takes me about half a second to ascertain its new position, at which point I yank it up, throwing it against my chest to comfort the bruise that's formed upon it.

"There's non-verbal methods of communication that don't include attempted dismemberment," I grumble, taking care not to pull the trigger as I rub before looking back in his voice's direction. "How far are we from the Monument?"

"We've closed in to about five hundred metres."

"Right," I say, looking closely at my weapon. A little blue light, formerly unnoticeable in the sun, shines from its grip—whatever the light's coming from, it's not the Tower. "You're aware that I cannot heal myself, you're aware that most of our armament has been rendered ineffective, you're aware that we will not be taken by preservation, and so I trust that you're intelligent enough to be aware this would be the perfect place to stage an ambush."

He doesn't pause before he speaks. "It would."

"Men on the other side of this fog, if there is one, with sessile-arms. We wouldn't survive."

Perei's tone is the pinnacle of a particularly jocular variety of cognitive neurasthenia as he speaks. "Hey, hey, Ash, don't give the guy any ideas."

"But I suppose you wouldn't do such a thing, would you?" I say, prompting my glasswalker to go just a little quicker; it seems to delay its response a little, its movement growing a little sluggish.

He doesn't respond. My stomach is beginning to hurt.

"If I'm replied to by a hail of gunfire," I say, "I will be very, very disappointed."

The mist vanishes, and the sunlight blinds me for a long instant as the pain fades; I don't stop to ponder why.

"Ápyfrét létyjs," I say, the form of a very finely dressed pink man with his eyes obscured by coloured resin standing in the sun amongst a handful of men and women rousing from their slumbers upon the delicately paved ground in the piercing sun becoming apparent as the rhodopsin trickles away from my photoreceptors.

"My *eyes*," Perei yells, and my immediate instinct is to thank the man in charge of the barrierfountain for placing it underground.

"I have a confession to make," he says, thrusting his fist towards the ground; the black liquid in his hand surges forth, a series of tiny tubes forming right before the gaps between them are bridged to compose a weapon. "I have had the means to rid ourselves of this disgraceful mess for quite a while."

The groan emanating from my left seems almost practised. "Oh, come the fuck on."

I nod, respectfully levelling my weapon at his face. "Why now?"

"Yes, William Solaris. Why now?"

The voice is Aimelari, and I look immediately over my shoulder in time to hear the sound of burning air.

Parakheirei das Vasksharei es-Maurenia, a coat so long it looks like a dishdasha hanging upon his measly frame, wasn't aiming for me. Besides me, the cloth and flesh upon Perei's back bursts open like a ripe mangifera fruit, his scream punctuated by the objective on his back very prominently turning a bright, shining red as a woman I cannot see yells in what I hope is sympathy.

I don't bother with surprise, looking immediately between him and my compatriot; Perei writhes upon his saddle, arms reaching to his blood clotting—not streaming, thank the Tower—upon his back as he contorts forwards to assuage the phantom pain of a wound long since gone.

"I hope you're aware that this isn't really a weapon," he says, looking down at his weapon.

I suppose the one-liner he hopes will herald my death is coming, and I do not hesitate.

The trigger clicks against my finger.

He claps, the saggy fabric along his arms smacking against each other with his hands. "*This* is the backup line. An egg hidden in the bushes for the curious. Wouldn't you like to know the first one?"

"You are a despicable human being," I say. "You'd be one even without a despicable cause. There is nothing about you that is worth redemption; your evil works are in service of your monstrous affiliation, but without it you would be an awful person all the same."

"Go on," he says, the enjoyment palpable from his expression. "Say what I expect you to."

"If that isn't a weapon, what is?"

"Not recommended for ages twenty-three and below."

Something very long and very dark intrudes upon my field of view just in time for him to say 'below', and I decide that this is a battle I can afford to avoid.

"Ádrakyts-là áćéyshyr," I shout, making the motions I need to in the air like a demented sort of puppet. *"Ántt!"*

The kinetic beacon hits the ground behind me right as we go, and it takes me a while for me to realise that it isn't a kinetic beacon.

The first clue I have is that my eardrums are still intact.

The second is that my saddle lacks a glasswalker and that I'm about three hundred metres from the ground.

Easy estimate: fifteen seconds.

I almost slow myself down—*fourteen*—in that—*thirteen*—instant, and I throw—*twelve*—myself to the side—*eleven*—as the first morsel of thought—*ten*—comes to the plate within: *Perei.*

He's not there—*nine*—and the saddle—*eight*—is all that remains.

Hanjat.

I can infer where he is—*seven*—and throw myself blindly—*six*—at a chunk of titanium descending at around seven-tenths terminal velocity.

I miss but not too much, and my barrier resonates against one of the many barriered parts of his armour, the structure of its nexuses redundant enough that the non-serial nature of their reoration doesn't seem to have spoilt its usefulness in any way; the resonance barely moves me, as reinforced as my tessiture has made it, but the man in a tonne of armour is thrown very suddenly and violently up, and my count stops about a hundred metres from the possibility of his grave.

The artificial lighting does not shine in the same way the hole through which we have fallen—a monstrous, jagged thing, deeper than it is wide and thank the *Tower* it hasn't dropped anyone but us—has, and I'm almost blind as I elegantly throw myself into the darkest spot, quietly hoping his neck hasn't snapped.

My flesh meets metal, and our velocities are close enough that I hardly have to feel the weight before I begin to throw ourselves sideways, the multispectral faults in my vision clearing with the fifth blink.

The semi-unique Mihakilian architecture right below Crescent City, its beautifully chipping brick-built ceiling-scrapers so dependent on oration—curving almost into spirals around each other, connected at points like base pairs between strands—that just a whiff of the withering mists would probably give them cause to crumble within seconds, rushes towards us in a way I cannot see as I frantically sing a membrane into my organs; I feel the cold, heavy substance penetrating me through every end I can make it, and I hope his armour is shockproof as we slam past something doubtlessly breakable and my head moves independently of my torso for just a second before the barrier covering it slams straight into his once more. The kinesis the breach generates sends me spiraling back onto the floor, the blissfully soft substance lining the floor allowing me to keep my spine intact.

I lie still for a little while, breathing in the longest gasps my body will let me, before I choose to speak.

"Have we killed anyone?" I ask, staring straight at the pink ceiling. A muffled thump issues from before me, and the ground shakes a little.

"No," an unfamiliar voice says, and I struggle to identify what accent she has until she continues. "It would have been nice if you had, though. The policy on my wife would cover this five times over."

Ipletinari, without a doubt. I snicker, the attempt at an expression of amusement coming out in a series of pained gasps. "I'll pay. Hanjat, are you alright?"

"I'm alive, milady," he says, "but I can't feel my legs."

I stand to look down upon him; as I do, I hear water streaming into a cup.

"Would you two like some tea?"

I raise an eyebrow, looking suspiciously at the steaming cup below her spout.

"What's tea?"

I let out a low moan as the warm, bitter fluid streams down my throat, glancing once more to the man-shaped displacement in the brick wall to our side; the place seems bare of the symptoms of human living, and I quietly feel the disturbance to be an improvement. "I apologise for the damage."

The pale woman, her eyes seeming half-closed upon a complexion holding the oiliness characteristic of her ethnicity, shrugs. "Oh, don't worry about it. Nissy's not the best bricklayer, but she can burn bricks better than anyone I know. All we need to pay for is the clay—and it's not as if we don't still have another window."

"Nissy?" I ask, taking another sip. "That doesn't sound Northern."

"Nisantanasendrea das Pelentrea," she says, chuckling. "Aimelan, but more Northern than I'll ever be. I suppose she saw me in the throes of squinty fever and thought herself lucky to find one who knew how to take a bath."

"Pelentrea? She's of one of the twenty? What's she doing in Antamanaria?"

"One of the twenty-five by now. Quite a few new citizenships being carved out up there—which reminds me, is it true?"

I rub a spot of fluid from the side of my lip. "What is?"

"Cimsas."

"I'm from there," I say, looking somewhat absentmindedly to the resting form of my companion—whose condition, as far as my subjectives can tell, is entirely psychosomatic. "I saw the Tower crumble."

"Ahh," she says, her muscles tightening in a way that seems involuntary. "I figured they'd do anything to sell the sessiles, especially in a place as free as this little Saltic happens to be. I'm sorry for your loss—I don't suppose it's part of the reason a Zhanghwazh knight and you have smashed your way into my living room?"

"A small part of the reason. I don't think you'd be interested."

"And the wings, of course—I don't suppose public transit was good enough for you."

"A symptom of importance." I pour myself some more of the leafy water evidently called 'tea'. "Honestly, I'm not very sure why I'm still here. It's likely that the thing that's tried to kill me by dissolving the ground before my feet is about to try and kill me the same way."

She doesn't seem particularly surprised, pouring a tiny bit of sucrose into my drink. "Dissolving the ground below your feet, you say? Why not you?"

"I'd imagine they can't harm me directly, for various reasons."

"Ahh," she nods, the smile on her mildly aged features pulling on the wrinkles attached to her lips. "I suppose I'd wish that constraint applied for every feud, but I can't imagine having Purus cheese for a home."

She appears thoughtful for a moment.

"I'd certainly want wings. Wings would improve *every* conflict."

"I should be out looking for my friend," I say, sipping. "Or at the very least looking for his remains upon the pavement below. I hope I haven't actually died and been thrown into a surrealist masterpiece."

"I'm sure you'll have time to—"

The sound of shattering glass meets my ears as I speak, and I don't even bother looking behind me; I instead elect to lower my forehead down to the fine wooden table and groan.

"I absolutely must render my apologies if I've caused you any distress whatsoever," a disgustingly familiar voice says in a distinctly Shelflander tone, and as it does I reconsider my vote and pull my pistol from its holster, turning to see a brilliantly sung suit of titanium holding the pink bastard to the ground as Perei groans next to him.

I immediately pull myself over to Perei's lying form; he's breathing, as far as I can tell from his gasping profanities, but the acrid scent emanating from below his cloak makes half my diagnosis for me.

"Can you move your legs?" I ask, and the barely coherent babbling—*al-akhband-il-as-sakhv*—*holy fucking shit*—*al-il-al-izameen-at-tamayeen*—that greets me between the question and the answer (*fuck you*—*al-akarin-al-akazeen*—*does it look like I can*) makes the other.

"Please unhand me," William says from under the weight of a man whose memories of confinement are presumably quite fresh, "for I swear upon all I am that I am not an evil man."

I presume that Madeline's gift is planning upon fixing Perei up when it can, and pat his head as calmingly as I can as I turn to the man to my side. "I'm not going to ask you why we should trust you, because I already know why I shouldn't. What do you have to offer us?"

"Information."

"What?"

"The heuristics that modify the configuration parameters that determine the allocation of energy *ex implanta* have almost certainly called for a moratorium on contact."

Perei kicks out, his spine evidently healed as the light on his back goes out entirely, and my ears adjust to the ensuing cheers as he throws himself off the ground and throws himself into a very pungent sort of animalistic celebratory outburst before I continue. "I guess you'll tell me what that means."

He winces a little as he tries to twitch against Hanjat's completely still form. "Have you ever inquired, dear lady, as to the causes for your longevity in the face of the Tower's own power?"

"I was too busy enjoying it," I lie.

He smiles, the sweat off his reddish brow highlighting the contortions the motion puts his face through. "They may never visit harm upon you in this way again—Parakhirei did not know this when he pulled the trigger twice a centimetre from your head, and he lost an arm for it. Every attempt eliminates an opportunity on their part. I've just helped you eliminate two—the withering mists and the dissolution beacons."

"I've been shot multiple times by sessile-ar—"

"Those aren't weapons."

I narrow my eyes at him, and his smile—more of a smirk, really—widens; the gesture might carry more gravitas if Perei weren't practically singing in relief a few metres away.

"And how do you know this?"

"There live people in this world older than you can imagine, Ashrea." He looks away from me for a bit, the man upon him restricting him just enough to let him look to the hole he's made. "Could you unhand me, please? I must give you something that will help."

Hanjat looks to me, and I nod; the living restraint rises from his prone form, and he pushes himself up in much the same way, rubbing at his joints as he reaches his standing position and runs his arm down into his pocket, pulling what looks to be a small sessile-tab out. I grasp it gingerly, looking closely at it.

"Just a few additions to your sessile," he says, putting his head on its side. "I understand the numerous causes you have not to lend me your trust, but if you ever find in your life the time to audit it, you might find its contents interesting enough to observe."

"*What in the Tower's own name are you people doing in my house? Pekka, why haven't you* shot *them?*"

I look up to see a very angry, very Northern woman with her short-cropped hair a solid, natural pink; she seems to be switching her stares rapidly between us, the now-still Perei and the remnants of her shattered windows, her hand over her mouth.

"Oh, Nissy, hush—they're not locals. You've always wanted to be in a siction." The Ipletinari woman turns to us, "Don't worry about her. She wants me to shoot *everything*."

She seems to want to say something before she evidently notices the smell emanating from Perei's robes, cringing in what I can only presume is utter repulsion; she seems to deflate so consistently the process seems almost mechanical, pulling a bag of spawncloth from her belt as she slides down the frame of the doorway and grabs a handful of something apparently edible.

"Go on, then. Defile our home. We shall watch."

"Oh, Nissy," she says, as I look back to William to see him standing at the wall's fresh apertures, "the drama's far deeper than that. Look—he's going to have to disappear, next."

"I'm afraid I'll have to disappear for a while," he says, the metal on his back contorting like a fluid towards his hand through the air, trailed by a thick black fog whose particles flood into a solid mass as the metal touches his flesh and shapes itself into something extremely sharp and extremely metallic. "I wish you the best of luck."

"But—"

"I don't know anything more," he says, spinning the hook by its congealed miasma; more particles flow from nonexistence to compose more rope, and he flings it in a perfectly straight line matching his hand's angle towards something we can't see. "The only things I can offer are in your hands."

"Hey," Perei says, absentmindedly pulling at his waistband, "thanks for saving my life."

His arm remains in the position it was, and the rope forms from the cloud at his fingertip; the final length of rope forms and pulls taut against his chest, and as he turns towards him the rope loses its coherence for a second to stay in place and reforms with a strangely reassuring consistency upon his back.

"Please replace your pants," he says, and falls quite gracefully backwards out the window's remnants.

I lean a little forwards over the safety bar and pull my sweat-stained hood back; the metal is cold under my exposed fingers.

"So," I say, taking a breath to remember, "There it is."

"An amazing sight, milady, is it not?"

The mass before me is so amorphous as to defy any description that doesn't include the word 'amorphous'; thousands of pitch-black platelets scream from the Insurmountables, the barrier's rim demarcated by the millennia of rapid sub-saepological erosion that's left it and the dark grey stone to which its barrier is anchored standing out a clear twelve metres from the ocean of tawny behind it. Some vague semblance of order seems to have been thrown upon it to the west, stretches of the thing's near-flat building blocks congealing to forge what looks to be a platform of some kind providing the base from what would be a quintessentially fat classical tower, angles and monochromy and sheen, if it wasn't for the fact that it's burst open from head to toe, its fragments suspended in mid-air; one of the cuboid tendrils poking from its surface reaches onwards to an enormous, almost totally solid column extending down to sands probably older than the Tower, its own tendrils reaching out to fail to touch around seven five-hundred-metre, vaguely dodecahedral, horizontally elongated frusta at their midpoints. Four enormous demihexagonal platforms reaching out to taper flatly and then angle back down towards the superstructure jut out from each frustum at a half-right-angle to the tendrils, some fragmented and some whole, all of them lying below blunted, bezeled rectangles mounted upon each frustum's surface.

"Probably more amazed we're here to see it," Perei says, his soles slowly clinking on the marble from behind us, each sound louder than the last. "Asshole who runs this place wants a word."

"Several words, in fact!" a Shelflander whines, the length of his nose already visible in his silhouette. "I've lived here far too long to be harassed by you eater thugs—"

"'Eater?'"

"Please *do* stay calm, Mister Childerman," Hanjat says, what I can only presume to be perfect Shelfspeak. "We're simply working through some technical difficulties."

"Every single day! Every single cycle of the sun I receive your epithets in my box and now you've presented yourself here upon my very own balcony, free for the world to see!"

"It's not *my* fault you were the only man with a penthouse gullible enough to open the door," I grumble, barely audible.

"Look," Perei says, "we'll just take a little while. Don't make this hard on yourself."

"Right," I say, "I'll be taking Perei to the barrier—"

"I refuse! I *refuse* to be tr—"

I pull my pistol from its sheath and fire into the air; the sound itself is imperceptible, but the ringing that ensues in my ears would seem to justify the screech and back-fall that ensues on his part; he begins to scoot away before he seems to remember that the pool's barely a metre behind him and gets up, quietly and efficiently plodding away to the side into the doorway that decorates the faux-wood façade below the deep blue clay mansard that adorns it.

"Might not've been the best thing to do, Ash."

I turn back to the Monument. "I'll carry Perei to the barrier— Hanjat, you'll shoot anything that it looks like I'll dislike. Does this seem reasonable?"

"*Carry?*" Perei says as I step back; he seems to freeze as I firmly interlock my fingers with his, powering past the uneasiness the calluses induce as I bind my right arm to his with a four-word, non-printempraeic acapella; it's not as if he's going to sing himself free anyway.

"Very reasonable. How do you plan on getting past the barrier, milady?" Hanjat says, barely shifting a centimetre.

"Ash," Perei says, weakly tugging at my hand as I catch and bind the other, "we're not—"

"I've done it before."

He seems to have completely frozen at this point, his knuckles barely shifting. "Ash, we're not ma—"

"Maybe it's because I've been awake for longer than I should sleep, Perei qu'n'av dasnamr," I say, stepping back so that my right foot lies between his, "but I don't care."

I take a step forwards as quick as I ever have, and my next step misses the ground as my wings burst forth from my back, the muscles parting to let metres of bone and sinew surge onwards from nothing and weigh nothing.

The thin, wooden crenellations before us come closer for a second as an involuntary flap so strong it's enough to affect my course signals its recession past the lower bounds of my vision. Perei's chest rumbles against my back, but I can no longer hear him past the wind; I can already feel his weight beginning to moderate my ascent.

I'm not sure how fast I can go—which, in retrospect, is likely the fifth worst oversight I've ever made—and my wings fold forcefully around the pile of meat upon my back as I burst past the barrier facing the Monument's and my lips *hurt* so much blood from the cracks within them begging to evaporate as I say the single word I need to:

"Vétirymj."

My head feels for a second as though it's going to pop, the pressure around my entire body so complete that for the slightest moment I wonder if I've finally overstepped my luck and it's gone, totally gone, and I don't need to let the rest of the song leave my lips to feel them stitching themselves back together as we hurtle onwards through the membrane that appears to have replaced the barrier towards one of the enormous demihexagonal platforms, the dark grooves in its pitch surface quickly resolving into channels probably thicker than men and from there *definitely* thicker than men; I breathe and force myself slower, wings unravelling from my breathing load and receding a little into my back as I push against my own inertia, the near-blinding glare off the platform making me avert my eyes as I yell out the song's remainder.

My organs stage a brief revolt as we slam right into one of the channels, bouncing a little before landing hard enough for the semi-tolerant barrier to shatter, the resonance leaving us to land along the smooth surface, skidding finally to a halt a few metres from the wall before us.

I breathe and thank the Tower it doesn't hurt.

"Hot damn," an unfortunately familiar voice notes, his voice echoing a little, "what a rush."

I throw myself off the ground, the dramatic gesture beset by the fluttering of my now-tiny wings as my feet fail to hit the ground; some kind of metal-like substance I can't be bothered to sing to greets me, and as I look up I note that I'm in a crevasse at least three metres deep. "You're not going to lambast me for putting you in terrible danger?"

"Nah. I figure life's too long to get too pissy about getting myself burned alive."

I touch the metal with my sleeve, then move to slide my nail against it.

I shield myself instinctively from the rush of motion that ensues, and the horrifically uniform shards of metal that ensue splatter against my arm, the cold liquid they form crawling down my arm and cheek; the slurry *crawls* down my arm and face into my clothes, and I screech the air a millimetre from my skin intolerant for about a second.

As the apnea subsides, the living liquid now pooled at my feet scurries back into the wall to dissolve right under the series of cables—red, blue, green and yellow glowing against black stripes—spilling forth.

I'm not entirely sure what possesses me to touch one of the cables, and I'm absolutely uncertain as to why I choose to touch the red one. As my finger makes contact, the walls about us quite suddenly begin to look somewhat not *right*; the unease sets in just in time for them to dissipate with a sudden violence, the droplets of now-liquid metal thrusting themselves into the ground to let the sun blind me for an instant as I feel the watery substance wrap itself about my feet and harden the moment it touches.

It's too late to sing a barrier without losing my legs, now; in the grip of steel (and here my pedantry interferes to tell me that this as much steel as iron is oxygen) and death, my mind turns inexplicably towards birth and motherhood.

"Oh my God," Perei says, and as it washes over my mouth, leaving a cavity for my respiratory system so that my lips can still move well enough to make me conclude that I'm not *really* about to die, I decide that I don't really want children.

His voice is muffled, but reverberates past us as the cavity before me climbs with the metal well enough—the light still shining down past the near-matte material—that I almost understand his vaguely vulgar speech. I try to tell him to calm down just as a jet of decidedly stale air fills my mouth, the light fading slightly as the thing dissolves as quickly as it appears; I go to my knees, then, as the support disappears, Perei's suddenly tapered shout echoing about the air around me.

I make sure not to look up before I mentally establish what my eyes have just whipped past—one of the enormous rectangular entrances, of which only the bezel remains—and analyse the strange metallic strands that catch the light within, each dangling perpendicular to dozens of slightly thicker strands running across the chamber's rim (walkways, I realise, each at least fifty metres long); the walls are curved the slightest bit, but the effect is barely perceptible over the four hundred metres that reach from its top to its bottom.

It isn't until Perei—his deep breathing alerting me to his presence—turns to me do I recognise the importance of a set of individually simple facts:

     —firstly, that the closest walkway and by extension the most likely entrance is approximately a hundred metres away from us, giving way to a two hundred metre climb,

     —secondly, that my feet lie about a metre above the ground,

     —and thirdly, that his do not.

"I hate you," he says, evidently having come to the same realisation, and we go on our way.

"I hate you," he says, his hands making a rather pleasant pitter-patter upon the pitch metal bars. Nothing my singing can tell me tells me anything about the substance reasserting its strength every other second upon his palms, and to the Tower's eyes he climbs upon mounds of very spotty patches of vacuum.

"Your muscles can't strain," I say, manoeuvring quietly through the pleasantly stagnant air to face him, matching his uneven ascent with my measured glide. "The damage's repaired too quickly for you to have to mind the pain."

He pauses for a second, and I halt just quickly enough—momentum and whimsy sending my legs gently drifting up above my head as my hands go to my jaw, as though I were some kind of scarred pixie—to have my face level with his.

"Still hurts like a bitch."

"I guessed."

"Get riveted."

He continues rising, and so do I, moving out of the way to preemptively avoid the platform that cradles the shut Madeline-reminiscent aperture I've determined to be our destination, jutting only halfway up the chamber's wall, and it suddenly occurs to me that it's almost unjust that I've let the cavity masquerade within my mind as a 'chamber', a purposeful space, solely by virtue of its human birth: if it ever was a chamber of some sort, austerity and desuetude have divorced the signifier from its sign.

I shake myself out of my semiotic trance as he pushes himself up and over the walkway, ready to catch him should the presumably granular material allow him to pass through—he lands without incident, however, and I drift alongside the safety rails corralling him as we approach the hexagonal doorframe before us. As we draw closer, it becomes apparent that they aren't quite the same as the ones in Madeline's doors, interlocking, irregular plates stuck in configurations impossible to untangle mechanically. I slide with a newfound grace between the catwalk and the bar above, settling a little closer to him.

"For Isha's sakes," he says, his footsteps heavy with petulance; my theatrics appear to have made his bitterness intensify. "At least walk with me."

"I don't think I can."

"Why the hell not?"

I almost ponder the possibility giving him a serious response in the tones of the fatigue that compose my being as the most labio-hypothermic words I've ever failed to contemplate flow unbidden. "The ground seems bitter now that I have tasted flight."

"Kill yourself."

The plates that compose the sealed aperture before us begin to work to invalidate the latest adjective I've applied to their set in response to either his frustration or proximity, grey things sliding through themselves to reach the rim, each plate in the way of another splitting in two to allow their deeper kin to pass. They expose the subject they guard as they slide into the walls: an oblong room, its scale so diminutive against everything about us that for a moment I mistake it for an alcove.

I look to Perei; he shrugs, and as he steps forth I drift to join him. The room, about three metres in diameter at its widest, appears to be padded—squishy-looking, white rounded rectangles lie along the light grey walls. The impacts Perei's feet make upon the ground turn resonant as we come face-to-face with a thick, translucent substance blocking off what looks to be the beginning of a corridor, our faces reflected slightly in its shimmer.

—*SAPI link protocol established. Welcome to Macarena, sysadmin_1@legacy. This facility is currently under lockdown.*

The voice against my skull comes with an unfortunate sense of familiarity; the language is assuredly different, but I'm not terribly confident in its delivery method. "We can't get in?" I ask, carefully avoiding the yell of astonishment the speech should induce. To my right, Perei's own little yelp hands me a petite quaintness.

—*Lockdown override accepted. Lockdown information will be*

provided upon entry. Your SAPI integration is under-developed. The Treaty of Barcelona dictates that it be reconfigured to comply with SU standard AEGIS-23. Please stand by.

The thick, presumably congealed mess before me begins to dissolve with a perceptible slowness—some kind of acid clearly making it shrivel and chip down to the ground, where it dissolves instantly into a liquid that dissipates from its shallowest points. I glance to Perei, who stares at me with some measure of horror; his gaze leads me to a tendril of angularly particulate metal reaching from the ground to the beginning of my spine, and I resist the urge to send myself careening into the ceiling as I look back to him to behold the mass of *stuff* rushing from the ground to wrap itself around his back. I reach out and grab him by the hand, his rough digits grasping at mine as I make contact.

"*N'teléresynjs ápyfrétiira.*"

A bright purple shimmer surrounds the grey slurry against the cold white light; it moves with the mass as it seeps through the impossibly dense ceramic fibre, itself thrown outwards by the unyielding force. The segmented lights upon his back fizzle the slightest bit before they reform amongst themselves, the gaps thinner and more numerous by far, and as the barrier fades the cloak rustles a bit as it settles back down upon his now bare skin.

Whatever it was, I realise, it was part of us the moment it touched us.

—*We're sorry, but your biotype is incompatible with SAPI AEGIS-23 and has been submitted to 1//31//415=415AMSTRADSURLABAIE per distance for further review. The MISSE-019i3401.2 integration has been introduced in its stead. Please report to the base's medical officer.*

I look to Perei in exhaustion, my fingers still touching his; he looks to me with an uncanny sort of awakeness, and as the voice finishes a thick strip of bright green light rolls along the ground down the newly-exposed corridor to complement the almost inexistent shade of blue that seems to wrap vaguely around Perei's figure.

« *You seeing this, Ash?* »

« *You're not speaking,* » I say, the words failing to leave my mouth, and I decide that this is a wonderful time to panic. Perei's own emotional reservoir appears to have run thin, and he just stares at me.

Right, I say, and I can feel the little spike of panic fading too quickly to be natural. « *Shout—not to me. Anything, just—* »

My eardrums are quickly resonate with a tone I'd rather not ever hear, and I quickly solve a mystery thoroughly peripheral to my areas of concern. « *Coherently!* »

"I really like pickled onions!" he shouts, and I stare.

« *Pickled onions?* »

« *You said anything.* »

« *Right,* » I say, pulling my fingers from between his, «Harmless.» "Easy to control. It's certainly not exodial, whatever it is."

"You've said that before," he says, leaning forwards a bit as he peers into the now-open passageway, the unyieldingly bright shine at its end too powerful to discern past, "Exodial, I mean."

I let out a little breath, staring absentmindedly at the entrance to what is no doubt another excitingly regretful adventure, and I realise that the stress of the violation I've just endured only magnifies the lethargy that's been coursing through me the past two hours. "The Laceration's afterbirth—pieces of simple machines we can't understand well enough to use. The only pieces of an archaeological dig that can kill you."

"Don't think Madeline was postlac," he says, interrupting my half-conscious train of external thought. He doesn't seem particularly inclined to continue on either, and the frequency of his tear-eliciting nictitation betrays the impression the uprightness of his stance seems intent on expressing.

"Come on," I say, shaking my head a little. "Let's get this over with before we faint."

We walk forth into the blinding light.

As the spots clear from my vision, it becomes clear that the radiance isn't about to fade. The voluminous room feels suffocatingly tiny, both by its relatively diminutive size and by the enormous glow every surface reflects. The white-gold balustrade-rimmed terrace upon whose thick guardrail I lean as my feet touch the marbled ground has the glare off of its balusters provides the creases along the light-streaked tawny hands upon them into sharp contrast, and I realise that there's only one light source for the entire empty fifty-metre room before and under me, its roof two men's heights above me.

« *Jeez, Ash, I think you might be crashing.* »

"Please stop doing that," I say, the thoughts prodding at the rim of my besieged consciousness. The strip of light glows persistently upon the ground to my right, leading down one of the two curving slopes that reach their terminus upon the ground.

"What're you talking about? Feels the same either way. Probably feels better."

"I know. Shut up."

« Come to think of it, I'm taking this brain-talking thing a little too easy. »

"I hypothesise that pre-Laceration technology renders itself intuitive and overrides user concern through some kind of neuro—"

"Turning the tables, huh? Shouldn't you be trying to figure out how this whole thing works?"

The beginning of a fatigue-induced headache signals itself with a light pulsating almost-pain across my forehead. "I'll do it when death stops seeming rational."

"Isha, you can't be **that** tired."

"I can and I will be," I say, sidestepping a little with a resolute thump before taking to the air a few centimetres above the smoothened stone, following the path laid out before us down the slopes at a pace within reason. Miniature subjectives—I'm not certain how I know they're subjectives, but I take the assumption as surely as I take my sight—form as I walk, the numbers and letters upon them giving me perfectly comprehensible quantities of incomprehensible things.

"Date of departure: NaN. Nan? The hell does that mean?"

I glance at the scribbles around us, Fransai script etched into thick air; more and more pop up alongside us as we move, but the ones I haven't read—whatever the sessile here's doing, it knows where my eyes are pointed—follow me as I continue to walk. "Non-numerical quantity. Perhaps you'd be better off asking yourself how you're reading what you are."

"I stopped asking myself things a long time ago. This stuff mean anything to you?"

The rhythm of ceramic on marble punctuates my digestion of the information I've gathered off the screens that flit past the edges of my field of vision, the fragmented words giving me a vague understanding of something I shouldn't.

"We're here," I say, my finger drifting up to the numbers laid out before me to the upper right of my vision in a layered series of matrices turned almost solid by the sheer density of the numbers, arranged in a sort of facsimile of the structure that sits around us; its inaccuracy becomes immediately clear, eight frusta manifestant in place of seven. "I'm guessing that these numbers are a spectrometry measured in volume counting the percentage of some sort of cubic unit non-architectural objects occupy—", and here I lean in close enough to discern each figure, "—we're occupying a little under one percent of this block, so I'm guessing the unit's around ten thousand cubic metres."

"Sounds like info I'd save for the second date."

I run my hand against the subjective, fingers grazing the numbers; they react somewhat violently to my touch in an uncomfortably comfortable way, the dense cloud pushing the rest of the subjectives away to encase me in a translucent shell of royal blue. "I'm seeing a block of 100%s extruding from one of the tendrils."

"Walls?"

"I don't think walls move," I say, glancing with a nervousness I thought I was too inured to have affect me as the hundred-block pushes itself into the space behind us, "it's entered our frustum, whatever it is."

—*bshcmd: sudo*

"Did you hear that?" Perei asks, evidently straining to listen to the whisper that surrounds us.

—*chmodx 000*

I listen closely to the tune in the air, the tune barely a whisper; as unlikely as it might be, its origin seems almost human: a man with a tenor. "Some kind of song. The numbers are Fransai, but—"

——*R --preserve-root*

"But?"

—*Hangar06-ISOCOM.xsh*

"I haven't an idea of what it's meant to do."

—*enter*

Perhaps the most interesting about the puncture wound that forms in the wall the moment the final syllable resounds is what happens to the platelets around it; they lie suspended in midair around the thick

tendril of sharp-angled vegetation that conceals the wound it has made,
catching and redirecting the rays of the artificial light that enclose it.
Its mouth, a moist thing surrounded by a series of light green, obtuse
arrow-cut triangles split down the middle and angled against each other
at about a hundred-thirty degrees that would look to be the composite
element of its skin if not for the bright white flesh revealed by the ripples
that presumably indicate its breaths.

"Oh, come **on**."

I pull the sidearm from my waistband, leaning forwards the
littlest bit. Perei mirrors the motion in his own way, rifle level with the
lightly wriggling appendage. The matrix tells me it's taking up 93.2%
of the imaginary cube at the very entrance, its mass bleeding into the
surrounding ones. I reach to the figure again with my left, sending the
matrices collapsing into their allotted place in the series of subjectives
that have seen fit to give my sidearm their attention, a thin, light red
cylindrical line extending onwards from the thing's barrel surrounded by
information I understand well enough to know I cannot understand it.
The rest of the subjective settles behind me, and as my hand shakes the
littlest bit I note that the sphere that surrounds me, hole centred centred
on the line, moves according to my arm's dictates, receding as I lean
forwards.

"Think it's friendly?"

—*bshcmd: sudo vi enter*

The sound, now that the barrier between us has broken, would
be aetherial if it wasn't loud enough to hurt. The tenor is so deep that
it should shake the metal beneath my feet; it does not, and my feet
are steady upon the ground as a miniature scrawl appears in front of
me, the Proto-Fransai incomprehensible to my contemporary eyes: *un
commandement d'Anastasie.b.Ali.Uma.dAube@macarena peut t'affecter:
laissez-la être exécuté ? (select, sysadmin_1@legacy macarena=(ALL:ALL)
ALL, delete, enter)*, two words below it impossible for me to read before
the monstrous thing surges forth, metal surrounding it shattering like
glass. Perei fires, then, and the membrane surrounding it bursts open on
the first impact, its contents forming a thin film upon cracking plate-
leaf—I can barely analyse the wound before the thing surges past and
between us, the sound of Perei's weapon hissing through an atmosphere
far too tranquil for the violence.

The fire turns muffled; the creature stays still for a moment
before it throws itself up, its end thrashing about a few metres from me
to gain momentum as though it were upon a trampoline before it bursts

out of the ceiling, the metre-thick roof shattering into kilolitres of air-suspended fragments; the sun's rays fills the lit, reflective space, leaving an unfittingly beautiful pattern of shadow and light smeared across the scene. The tendril wiggles about without any aim that I can discern before throwing itself out of my sight.

I'm so braced for Perei's input, putting my weapon back where it belongs and binding it with a word, that it takes me just a second for the shock to set in when it doesn't come.

« *Perei, where are you?* »

A moment passes, and my beating heart is all I can hear.

« *Isha, it smells like dead fleshcrawlers in here.* »

« *Are you alright?* » I say, and it occurs to me to look to the blue subjectives to my right—the mass is gone entirely from the matrix but for an enormous space in an enormous building about two kilometres away. « *Can you ascertain your current heading?* »

« *Looks like we've stopped. One sec.* »

A very loud sound echoes from somewhere far away.

« *Yeah, we've sto—fuck.* »

I see something moving above me and I reflexively put my feet down upon the ground before I jump without falling, my view of the world expanding to its limit in a second as the enormous thing slams down into the structure now behind me. The subjectives around me change as I do, receding as a mirror of the world behind me—sessile-quality, a patent impossibility—projects itself a little above my head across the width of my vision in a thin strip. The vigour discontent has given me makes my eyes seek with an alacrity I oughtn't have expected from them.

Or perhaps I'm giving them too much credit for finding a creature the size of a frontier settlement about ten metres behind me, standing deathly still amidst a field of white and silver. If the still-standing shards before me have caused it any damage, it's invisible past the hard, leaflike shards that coat its body.

« *I think I've found you,* » I say, and as I throw myself to the side—I don't precogitate anything in particular, just that being stationary is a *terrible* idea—the thing moves quicker than anything its size has a right to, the newly formed membrane across its skin visibly stretching and then bursting open as the fibrous strands that evidently compose it decide to enforce the lacuna of its rights and split open with an impressive violence, revealing an enormous puncture in its side along with Perei's flailing form, pistol in hand.

I accelerate towards him, and he reaches out to me as I match my velocity with his, decelerating at an even rate as I go past his hand to hook my arms under his armpits. I can feel the muscles that control the ligaments which tug upon my back flex to allow the Tower to supply the matter that floods the space behind me, fresh white wings moderating our descent right as I push forwards. Gravity compels them to shear the wind as I manoeuvre towards one of the platforms about thirty metres to our left, singing myself stuck to the man at my fingertips before turning the eye that guides my tongue towards allowing us not to die on impact.

"*Pàrpyrpàr pàr ansec pàr dis'métyr téléresynjs ápyfrétiira.*"

I hear my words echo in the confines of my mind as the barrier forms before and around us almost intolerant as the platform approaches, and I'm certain we'll land unharmed just as the tendril comes down between us.

I barely feel the urge to curse myself as the echo proves to have been beyond my mind and the resonance strikes; I can feel my arms snap before the preservation takes me and I feel no more.

END BOOK ONE

appendix a
Placenames
and the Compass

Though the de facto end of the Zhanghwazh Empire has long since left living memory, its two major cultural contributions to modern Aimela have been cartographic: placenames and compass points.

Placenames

An Imperial place-name, called a 'placename', is a name bestowed upon it by the Emperor. Though out of general use, placenames are used colloquially and poetically. The Emperor personally continues to ascribe placenames to new cities, but only pre-30th-century placenames tend to be in common use.

Once used extensively in commerce under penalty of death as per Tarmandasilra's 1872 Fraud Edict, most cities once referred to solely by their placenames have either subordinated the name to their endonymous names, such as Antamanaria, the Shattered Circus (see obverse), or eliminated it entirely in official contexts. Tachiesrea, the Velvet Citadel, is notable for being the oldest city in Central Aimela to never have had its placename bear legal standing.

Placenames are decided solely by the Emperor, and do not necessarily reflect reality as it stands. They customarily follow the definitive-adjective-noun snowclone template, and apply solely to a single city or settlement—a handful, however, such what is currently known as the Oiesya Confederacy, 'That Land Where the Children Live to Sing', do not adhere to this convention. Antamanaria was ascribed its placename, 'the Shattered Circus', due to the treachery of its exodial superstructure and the appearance of Sipyak Monument. Cimsas was given its placename, 'the Shimmering Tribunal', by Khalamarisdantara the Cynical to christen it as the seat of the Imperial judiciary; it lost this seat in 2298 for the seat of the Zhanghwazh legislature, and lost it again in 2799 for the seat of the Aimelan Administration.

It is important to note that placenames are always initially drafted in Angzhwen; Meizhehwa, the Emperor's spoken language, does not have any legal status in Zhanghwazh legal documentation.

ANTAMANARIA
AYRISANVYSTIR RITYSYSSYA

Antamanaria's placename has been written subordinate to its endonymous name since 2894. The text along the seal's rim reads 'Discovered 28 Primus 982 by Mitreshielan-tielra' and 'Chartered 17 Septimus 2281 by the Saltic Syndicate'. The seal is written in the Hollowvoice style and uses its antiquated method of dating: '982' is written 'nine-eight-two', while '2281' is written 'two hundred eighty-one'.

The Compass

Perhaps simpler is the Zhanghwazh compass; standardised some time around 900 by Francisca Her-Life-Was-Full-and-Joyous, jester to Khandmisra the Well-Prepared, it designates North to be 'towards the lands where the sun begins its skyward ascent'. All Aimelan endonymous place-names are based off of the Zhanghwazh compass, and most maps are oriented to the North. The classic image of the compass is incorporated into the design of each one of the Aimelan Administration's sub-national symbols.

However, in scientific use, north is defined as the Westwards-pointing lodestone. This is reflected in modern maps, with the Angzhwen or classical script symbol used for 'East' and the Zhanghwazh symbol used for 'North'.

The Memory of Navigation
The Cultural Memories of the Zhanghwazh Kingdom in Relation to the early Aimelan Confederacy
Aremis Talembi ar-Khalsandim
published by the Sestiyari Institute of Sociological and Historical Research and approved for private distribution under the Sixth Decree by Administrator Atfilgaentatresra dar Sinter under the continued grace of the Aimelan Administration

"To the North, the tamed; to the South, the barbarous; and in-between, where the sun reaches its peak and shines upon all the lands mankind has touched, stand the civilised."
—*Melisan Harissanin Her-Spirit-Was-Unbroken*
"Where The Lands Do Lie", 1092

appendix b
Syntactics

Abstract

Though adaptive and perpetual applicability are both verifiable on a quantum (q-cantata) level, they are mutually exclusive due to the existence of βR-d type quanta. We propose that βR-d, αP-a and γP-a quanta are in fact saepologically identical manifestations of an *ex implanta* form of printempraesis as per the third ar-Sundash principle.

Body

No valid theory currently exists unifying adaptive and perpetual applicability[1] due to the contradiction inherent in the existence of several irregular saepological quanta of saeposyntactic system A1 exhibiting non-zero Rp_1, currently classified 'βR'. This results in the irreconciliation paradox between adaptive and perpetual applicability and makes the current standard model self-contradictory. Despite sharing crucial characteristics with α-type pained cantate (αP), namely finite Rp_2 and immutable *tRpA*, the deviated quanta of βR q-cantata (βR-d) are never consistent with P-type conjugation patterns[2] and are capable of including *idiomatic* quanta, such as in the third-person reflexive preterite of *dégajyr* (see fig. 1).

Nonetheless, βR-d cantata share weak P-exclusivity (*wPex*) with αP and γP actional quanta (αP-a/γP-a) and not the strong P-exclusivity (*sPex*) of the βP cantata[3], suggesting that βP and αP/γP cantata are entirely separate genres and that, as all βP cantata share indefinite *tRpA*, *wPex* is not a variation on *sPex* but is rather an extension of printempraesis as per the ar-Sundash principle.

fig. 1. illustrative list of saepological quanta from αR, βR and αP q-cantata, non-zero Rp1 quanta bolded

C.	A1	Ex78	Rp1	Rp2	tRpA
αR-a	*vésjj*	go_JJ	0	sit.	ind.
αR-a	*vésjt*	go_JT	0	sit.	ind.
αR-a	*vésss*	go_SS	0	sit.	ind.
αR-c	*vésssya*	go_SS.PAST	0	0	0
αR-a	*vésttjgul*	go_TT.FHAB	0	sit.	ind.
βR-a	*dégajjj*	disengage_JJ	0	sit.	ind.
βR-a	*dégajjt*	disengage_JT	0	sit.	ind.

βR-a	*dégajss*	disengage_{SS}	0	*sit.*	*ind.*
βR-d	***dégajssya***	**disengage_{SS.PAST}**	**1**	**1**	**1**
βR-a	*dégajssjgul*	disengage_{SS.FHAB}	0	*sit.*	*ind.*
αP-a	*rétyjj*	rebind_{JJ}	7896	13829	3
αP-a	*rétyjt*	rebind_{JT}	235	7896	37
αP-a	*rétyss*	rebind_{SS}	235	7896	37
αP-c	*rétyssya*	rebind_{SS.PAST}	0	0	0
αP-a	*rétyssjgul*	rebind_{SS.FHAB}	0	*sit.*	*ind.*

The non-indefinite *tRpA* apparent in αP-a, γP-a and βR-d cantata and the loss of these limitations at the adaptive level suggests a printempraeic origin, as opposed to the immutable perpetuity inherent in all quanta of all βP q-cantata[4]. If the third ar-Sundash principle is applied equally to all forms of printempraesis, βR-d, αP-a and γP-a quanta can be said to be a single class in a theoretical extracantatal model (see fig 2. and fig. 3).

fig. 2. current model
P-type q-cantata

αP-a   βP-a   γP-a
αP-c   βP-c   γP-c

R-type q-cantata

αR-a   βR-a
αR-c   βR-c
           βR-d

fig. 3. proposed model

Adaptive quanta   Perpetual quanta

αR-a   βR-a   βR-a
αR-c   βR-c   βP-c
αP-c   γP-c

Printempraeses *ex implanta*

αP-a
γP-a
βR-d

REFERENCES

[1] Aritandrei d.C, L. Lan, Iritesantandrea d.C, Kharedis T. a.K., Khalasarea d.C. Khariesmarei d.P, T. Sak, C. Bakerson and Q. al-Bazaine a.T., "Review of currently proposed integral models", Aimelan Journal of Saepological Linguistics, pg. 8-21 (3918)

[2] Iritesantandrea d.C., Anantandarei d.V., P. Fungpyingzh and C. Tsaozyingzh, "Characteristics of βR q-cantata", Saeposyntatics, pg. 13-48 (3872)

[3] Aritandrei d.C., "Comparative analysis of the βR-d quanta in relation to P-type q-cantata", Whispers, pg. 231-275 (3879)

[4] Q. al-Bazaine a.T., Iritesantandrea d.C. and P. Jangtan, "Singing in pain: an investigation into the characteristics of P-type q-cantata", Our Tessiture, pg. 189-359 (3873)

[5] P. Fungpyingzh, "Responding to Baron Zhangfung the Third of Nangcheng: implications of βP q-cantata regarding perpetual applicability on an adaptive scale", Noble Inquiries, pg. 2-9 (Primus 3901)

REVIEW

Aritandrei das Cimcharei: Concise and promising hypothesis unifying adaptive and perpetual applicability valid in the light of current experimental evidence. Suggest publication as a probable hypothesis.

Lakchang Lan: I concur.

Iritesantandrea das Cimcharei: I've got the unspeakable urge to reject this paper for its length alone, but I might just be too old to appreciate the genius of brevity. I concur.

Khalasarea das Cimcharei: It is worth noting that the qualitative semantic nature of most βR-d quanta is in support of this hypothesis; the vast majority of βR-d quanta are believed to have been of significant cultural relevance to pre-Laceration culture Fa1, judging by what Angzhwen literature we have (see Asharisra d.O., "Academic ventures through the 78th Exodus Archive," Administrative Archives, Secundus 3227—esp. pg. 4923-5829). I concur.

Christopher Bakerson: I concur.

Kharedis Talani ar-Karamasim: This is perhaps the only piercing insight this journal has had in living memory. I am proud to concur.

Qassim al-Bazaine at-Talib: While I can't say I approve of the furor this will cause, I must concur.

Khariesmarei das Peshkharea: I suppose I should elucidate my intentions should someone decide to ruin the first full approval this committee intends to give this decade solely out of spite, but I refuse to incriminate myself. I concur.

Teknam Sak: I concur.

Hypothetical solution for the lack of a valid integral model in saepology: ex implanta printempraesis as an explanation for contradictions between adaptive and perpetual applicability
Aurissanis Purani ar-Milradinisan and Andrisandrea qu'n'av dasnamr
Review of currently proposed integral models, Aimelan Journal of Saepological Linguistics, 3919 issue
published by the Aimelan Saepological Society and approved for private distribution under the Sixth Decree by Administrator Atfilgaentatresra dar Sinter under the continued grace of the Aimelan Administration

appendix c
Silpeslevesra's Dilemmata

Silpeslevesra stood upon the steps to greet the new dawn. They heard something, and turned to listen.

The seminal work of both Old Aimelan literature, *Silpeslevesra's Dilemmata* stands as a profound testament to human dedication, intergenerational social stratification and dumb luck.

Beginning only months after Kanandrisra's consolidation of the Aimelan Confederacy, the merchant and genius Chalysandysra dar Idran wrote his magnum opus over the period of a decade in his desire to give the 'classless' Old Aimelan language—then called Odrysra—its own place in literary society. Chalysandysra, however, could not speak Odrysra, and began his work with the word-by-word advice of five renowned human dictionaries: Arisandra dar Oder, Marisindra dar Oder, Lissindrint Her-Soul-In-Her-Final-Moments-Held-Itself-Back-With-Joy, Mieshel Khasandaris dar Mandos and Clasadin dar Parsquisant.

Relating the words he wished to convey in Angzhwen and writing down the consensus that would emerge from amongst them, he relied entirely on the output these five men gave him—while four of them were blessed with an extraordinary knowledge of Old Aimelan's almost entirely oral vocabulary, he asked no more of their vast faculties. Two, Lissindrint and Mieshel, grew senile one quarter into the book. While it is likely that these instances of senility, likely some sort of early-onset dementia, grew entirely out of a congenital predisposition, Marisindra and Arisandra feared the same fate for themselves should their drudgery continue and quit, eventually becoming famed sessile writers in their own right; the classics on which they collaborated include *Maltandin who Lived upon the Sea*, *These Men Are Fit to Die* and *He cried when it happened.*

This left him with Clasadin, who could not speak Odrysra and who Chalysandysra had included in his panel solely to increase his readership amongst the Parsquisi. An expert Angzhwen grammarian, Clasadin simply responded with Angzhwen words modified sufficiently in phonology and inflection to sound Odrysrazh; this greatly increased the speed of his work and its comprehensibility, and the remaining three quarters of the book were finished within three years, clocking in at a total of three million, seven hundred and fifty thousand, nine hundred and twenty-six words.

Once his work was finally written, Chalysandyra invested in a sessile-press—a novel technology at the time, and the third one in commercial production—and took fifty copies of the manuscript across the Confederacy, giving it to publishers, priests, poets, scholars, artists, labour leaders and his mother.

The Musical Revolution's nascent period, awash with bloodthirsty nationalism, working-class solidarity, upper-class notions of cultural supremacy and the savoury anticipation of complete, irrecoverable change, was in Chalysandysra's mind the perfect environment for his painstakingly detailed catalogue of witty vignettes set in the perfect lives of a diverse group of quirky, unemployed petit bourgeois men and women plagued solely by their neuroses in an essentially static world, presented in a language completely unintelligible to eight-tenths of the population and utterly abhorrent to the remainder.

> "Surely they've finally come to appreciate the power of my art."
> "Half of them aren't intelligent enough to understand it, and the rest are intelligent enough not to."
> —Dialogue the Thirty-Nine-Thousand-Two-Hundred-and-Seventy-Fifth: Standing in Silpeslevesra's garden, Prakisandra the Pedantic speaks in the presence of Misselins the Wry

He was wrong, and it appealed to no one. Famously, the grammarian Maritandra dar Oder returned his own copy a day after its receipt in a pail of red ink.

It is likely that Silpeslevesra's Dilemmata would have remained a remarkable historical curiosity and a decorator at the dinner-tables of the post-ironic if not for the unearthing of the ninety-seventh Exodus Archive in 2800. Known as the Archive of the Old World's Soul, the ninety-seventh Archive contained an enormous archive of pre-Laceration literature. While persistent authors like Sheksprei—existing then only in oral tradition—were well-represented, thousands of threads left extinct were found in the ruins.

Silpeslevesra's Dilemmata was found there on a pedestal standing in a room of its own, transcribed fully into a sessile folded as though it were a book. Kanandrisra, upon seeing a vague approximation of Odrysra reveal itself upon its surface, was convinced that the Tower's mandate for an Aimelan nation had been made clear. He immediately ordered the text 'modernised' by a panel of thirty of his camp's literates and then copied onto every data-bearing sessile his army produced, including the twenty thousand sessiles designated for sale to the Confederacy's civilians.

> "Trust that history always judges the truth. Know that you will never have to be ashamed of what I have done. Never be one of those who mock but never mend, for they are hypocrites: weak, worthless people who will never have the power to turn their beliefs to action. Be strong. Be strong and know that life is wonderful. Be strong and know that good always wins."
>
> "Get away from those ropes before you get yourself hanged, you dumb bastard. Why on Earth did Silpy even put those things here?"
>
> "I assume it was to remind us of the sacrifices the martyrs make even today in the service of humanity."
>
> "I assume it was to remind you to martyr yourself."
>
> —Dialogue the Twenty-Six-Thousand-Nine-Hundred-and-Thirty-Ninth: Standing in Silpeslevesra's garden, Herelita the Brave speaks as she stands upon the platform below the gallows in the presence of Iresandra the Tired

News of the event reached the homeland after about three months, and the formerly obscure Chalysandysra became a national hero, much to the disgust of his nation's intellectuals. The manuscript itself remains a topic of intense study, but almost all modern translations are based off of Kanandrisra's initial modernisation. Kanandrisra, to his credit, did not distort the text in any way; comparative translations show that his group's modernisation has made very little progress, though the semi-incomprehensibility of much of the original text makes it impossible to ascertain the purity of his conveyed intent. Abridged forms of his magnum opus have become part of both public and private curricula, and the most egregiously unidiomatic instances of his idiom have become arteries in the heart of the Central Aimelan language.

Silpeslevesra themself speaks a single sentence throughout, their entire character subtly sketched out in the shadow of their passivity. While few people have ever read the entire book, almost every child within our borders knows its final words:

"It's alright—I think I'll just get back to bed."

SANDISANDREA DAS CIMCHAREI HAS BEEN AN EDITOR WITH STANDING STILL FOR TWELVE YEARS. SHE HAS WRITTEN, EDITED AND PUBLISHED OVER TWO HUNDRED ESSAYS ON AND REINTERPRETATIONS OF POST-LACERATION LITERATURE, INCLUDING THE EPIC 'DEAR SILPY' AND THE POETIC ANTHOLOGY 'SONGS THAT TAKE LONGER THAN THE LOVES OF WHICH THEY SING', AND IS RENOWNED AS ONE OF THE FINEST LITERARY HISTORIANS ALIVE.

A stroll through Silpeslevesra's garden
Sandisandrea das Cimcharei
Editorials, Standing Still, 3879 issue
published by the Aimelan Historical Society and approved for private distribution under the Sixth Decree by Administrator Atfilgaentatresra dar Sinter under the continued grace of the Aimelan Administration

appendix d
The Concordance

Like most of the things humanity has granted itself, every aspect of the Ocilentran Concordance is as subjective a thing as the distinction between the colours blue and green.

In a **historical** context, as luck would have it, not even its declension remains untainted, and that is the context in which most people know it today. When we refer to 'an' Ocilentran Concordance, we are typically referring to one of the text's ten major revisions, comprising 27 articles; each major revision has been named by the Judicial Administration, and are valid terms of art. They are considered to have been 'signed and ratified' after the last article they comprise.

» The **first**, or the **First Concordance**, documents the accedence of its contracting parties to *'the complete, unassailable and sempiternal sovereignty of the Aimelan Confederacy and its potential successor states over the region of Aimela, heretofore defined as the perimeter of the New East as defined by the Edict of Mitreshielantielra excluding the Old Territories as defined by the Emperor's Court in* Adielstriara v. the Throne Ascendant in Crystal Bismuth (2113) *as of 5 Octavius 2838 and also excluding the city limits of the city of Sipshirea as of 1 Primus 2838'.* Other crucial provisions include the elimination of emigratory restrictions within the Empire, international contract law reform, the supremacy clause, the disclosure requirements and the protection of Imperial emigrants. This was signed and ratified 29 Octavius 2838 by Kanandrisra dar Oder representing the Aimelan Confederacy and Emperor Fei Guangzheng representing the Zhanghwazh Empire. Historically, this marks the end of the War of Aimelan Independence.

» The **second,** or the **Assimilation Compromise,** codifies *'the inviolable and unique cultural and economic heritage of the Uytrimelari nation'*, mandates the establishment of *'a protective symbiosis between the Uytrimelari and Aimelan people and cultures in the form of the organisation of the lands formerly sovereign under the Saltic Syndicate into what shall be known as the Uytrimelari Special Administrative Region'*, promises that *'no action undertaken by any government may unfairly affect the situation of this Region without their consent, as determined by a neutral party agreed to by the Siancestys, who shall determine the unfairness of any Aimelan action by the commissioning of an impartial body subject to the approval of the Representative to the Region'*, that *'the current form of subnational government in the Region, though subject to complete Aimelan sovereignty in matters not under the purview of this Concordance, shall not change until 1 Primus 3800'* and that *'the Uytrimelan people shall be sempieternally exempt from all Aimelan regulations on economic activity as defined by an impartial body determined by the Siancestys with the agreement of the Aimelan government in their ancestral homelands as defined by an impartial body determined by the Siancestys with the agreement of the Aimelan government and of the Aimelan Anthropological Association'*. Other crucial provisions include the uniform implementation of Aimelan judicial principles to Aimelan citizens living within the confines of the borders of the contracting parties, the creation of an army funded by the Syndicate, the Uytrimelan system of privileges, and the independence of the Deremistilan Republic and Sovereign Uytrimela. The Second Ocilentran Concordance was signed and ratified 12 Decimus 2838 by all prior contracting parties and by Syndic Kaelis Metrelan and Syndic Cedric Audrenalis representing the Saltic Syndicate, Mayor Cyslils Àkharelsafis representing the Deremistilan Republic and Syndic Aldralis Palaounée representing the cities of Mandralis, Kharalmandana, Chalandis and

Parquantis. Historically, this marks the end of the failed Subjugation of Uytrimela.

»   The **third,** or the **Vasksharei Document,** redefines the Concordance to be *'the singular instrument of trans-national law; that is to say, an international document, unbound by sovereignty'* and establishes *'the independence of the High Contracting Parties, with the exception of the Uytrimelari Special Administrative Region'.* Other crucial provisions include the renaming of the Aimelan Confederacy to the Aimelan Administration, a set of rules of war known as the *Mariesi Declaration* and a body of individual and national rights that restrict the conduct of governments with regard to their own citizens and deal with contract law. The Third Aimelan Concordance was signed and ratified 1 Primus 3000 by all prior contracting parties and by Ambassador Rindalis Masharkhati ar-Mirali representing the States of the Boot. Historically, this marks the introduction of the Atfilgaentatresra Doctrine, and each of its components were signed in different places on the same date with the coordination of the relay sessile, the then-novel technology that eventually allowed for the Landrush. It is the longest Concordance.

»   The **fourth,** or the **Arbitration Principle,** affirms *'the role of the Aimelan government as arbitrator in any dispute between the High Contracting Parties, with the exception of the terms set down by the Assimilation Compromise'* and *'the right of the Aimelan government to make war to enforce the principles of this Concordance'.* Other crucial provisions include the exclusion of all non-signatories from all prior agreements with signatories and the annulment of all treaties with future non-signatories. The Fourth Ocilentran Concordance was signed and ratified 21 Septimus 3111 by all prior contracting parties, with the exception of the States of the Boot. Historically, this marks the beginning of the Aimelan Landrush.

»   The **fifth,** or the **Sovereignty Amendment,**

affirms that *'all land claimed by the Aimelan Administration shall be considered integral and inviolable territories belonging to the Aimelan state in perpetuity'*. Other crucial provisions include the affirmation that the Ocilentran Concordance, the Assimilation Compromise, the Universality Principle and the Arbitration Principle are sections in a single document named the Ocilentran Concordance. The Fifth Aimelan Concordance was signed and ratified 1 Primus 3129 by all prior contracting parties and by Ambassador Kyllasii Aissikainen representing the Pilisyari Republics, Ambassador Tim Goodman representing the Pilisyari Union and Ambassador Matthew Hardfield representing 'all the states of the Shelf'. Historically, this marks the end of the Aimelan Landrush.

» The **sixth**, or the **Structure Amendment**, affirms *'the nature of this Concordance as a law specific in the plainness of its text'* and prohibits *'the creation of clauses in any further amendment to the Concordance that obscure the nature of the text by structuring it such that an unnatural amount of context is necessary for its understanding'*, sets out a style guide for future amendments and provides a structure for practical legal notation without altering the text of the Concordance itself. The Sixth Ocilentran Concordance was signed and ratified 1 Primus 3594 by all prior contracting parties. This amendment has no historical significance, though it is arguably symptomatic of the Quiet Times.

» The **seventh**, or the **Oiesya Convention**, recognises *'the status of the Oiesya as a complex and independent people and a race separate from civilised man'*, establishes *'the responsibility of the Aimelan government for the preservation of Oiesya culture'* and mandates that *'any tribe of Oiesyan people may at any time choose to immigrate to the Aimelan Administration under certain rules to be determined by the Aimelan government'* and that *'the members of tribes not given leave to immigrate be shot on sight should they* *exit their internationally recognised territory without special permission from the Aimelan government'.* The Seventh Ocilentran Concordance was signed and ratified 1 Primus 3828 by all prior contracting parties. Historically, this marks the end of the Oiesya Subjugation.

» The **eighth,** or the **Freedom Amendment,** affirms *'the eternal and fundamental right to free commerce unburdened by tariffs or other transnational restrictions to trade'.* Other crucial provisions include the establishment of the Twin Condominiums, sales tax equity and the right to sessile-derived goods. The Eighth Ocilentran Concordance was signed and ratified 7 Septimus 3828 by all prior contracting parties and signed and ratified 1 Primus 3865 by Ambassador Kharalinis Sesirtkhari ar-Mirali representing the Sestiyari Republic. Historically, its initial signing codifies the most aggressively enforced point of the Atfilgaentatresra Doctrine and its second marks the end of the Tariff Wars.

» The **ninth,** or the **Protection Mandate,** mandates *'the protection of the states newly made independent to the South'* and affirms that *'all land more than 10° to the geographic west of the meridian not under the sovereignty of one of the High Contracting Parties is heretofore part of the territory of the Aimelan Administration'.* The Ninth Ocilentran Concordance was signed and ratified 1 Primus 3866 by all prior contracting parties and by Ambassador Joulette bin Forestiye al-Sikhi al-Nistiri ebu Khalisa aš-Šhanri representing *'all those states to the South that wish to parlay with the Administration'.* Historically, this marks the beginning of the Present War. It is the shortest Concordance.

» The **tenth,** or the **Justice Amendment,** reaffirms *'the complete, unassailable and sempiternal sovereignty of the Aimelan Administration and its potential successor states over the region of Aimela',* mandates *'the free and unrestricted passage of Aimelan citizens onto Zhanghwazh soil'* and *'the subordination of all* *placenames to terms of common reference as determined by the Aimelan Anthropological Association in transnational affairs as determined by the Aimelan government'* and recognises *'the existence of certain states, such as Antamanaria, that are not obliged to recognise the extraterritoriality of the Aimelan people nor any of the provisions of this Concordance'.* The Tenth Ocilentran Concordance was signed and ratified 1 Primus 3885 by all prior contracting parties. Other crucial provisions include the subordination of the placename to the term of common reference in the seal of Marapistanir, the right of appeal for Zhanghwazh citizens, the renaming of the Zhanghwazh Empire as the Zhanghwazh Kingdom and the invalidation of the 'integral land' precedents set in *Jiptang Xin v. the Throne Ascendant in Lustrous Nephrite (3727)* in the Emperor's Court, *United Aimelan Materials Concern v. Kitlang Jin (3729)* in the Court of Affairs and *Mintang Yui v. the Throne Ascendant in Crystal Bismuth (3730)* in the Grand Court. Historically, this marks the end of the Enforced Return.

That is, of course, a purely historical view, and if all this book gave you was history I would have been put out of work a very long time ago. The remainder of this book will focus on the **legal** context of the Ocilentran Concordance as a single document and its relevance to the modern judiciary, and an overview of *that* will take a lot more than a bulleted list.

Introduction: The Ocilentran Concordance
An Overview of Transnational and International Law,
Aritinsanfrea das Cimcharei
published by the Department of Education and approved for private distribution by the Administration for Media Development under the grace of Khaliesrea das Sikharea eliyit Tamarisrei, Administrator for the Arts

appendix d
The Wards of the Tower

Their churches and convents dot the landscape of today's cities, moreso than any prostration or hermitage, yet they have a tenth of the followers. Their members' prayers never go unanswered, nor their secular pleas. They have no lay members. If you live in Cimsas, the object they worship glints at you perpetually in the corner of your eye. If you live at all, it is because of it. They do not proselytise and they do not ask for your belief; after all, your faith does not affect them, and it is theirs that may see you living or dead when next the sun rises.

One might think that this church, half-religion and half-university, found its root along Shenzhpulra's rim or the ancient medical colleges that populate the Syndicate or the beautiful, sprawling religious metropolises in the South, but the reality of the matter is far more interesting: its origins lie in the humble North, far from the tumultuous forces that tend to produce these institutions.

Founded 9 Primus 1128 by Tailirsif, seventh Paprinse of the Monarchy Withering in the Mist[1], the Order of the Wards of the Tower was originally a government healthcare agency of whose original name we possess no record. The people of the Monarchy held the belief that a 'thick mist' had 'descended upon the lands to block out the sun' and made oration impossible within what is now known as the Shelf[2]. The Order

---

[1] This name, a gloss of *Kinslad Aurarinmis*, was ascribed to the state by the Pilisyari historian Bobbil Jax in *The Fall of the Monarchy Withering in the Mist* and is unlikely to have been endonymous. No internal records containing its name survive the Monarchy, though literature exported from the region is stamped with a bookplate reading *'produced under the auspices of the Paprinse _____ in the lands beyond the pale mist'* and the testimony of contemporary Wards use similar terminology. No foreigners were allowed within a hundred kilometres of what the Monarchy's residents claimed was the mist, and Jax himself, who relied on eyewitness accounts, is unlikely to have had a full view of the affair. The first non-fictional records of the region originate from the mid 1300s, by which time the Monarchy had long since ceased to exist.

[2] Modern saepologists believe that this 'mist' was likely some kind of barrier produced with some form of crude saepological experimentation, possibly utilising a type of gas that may have obscured the sun; the highly technical nature of many Ward orations seem to support this, and Pa's assertion regarding the Mists' non-orated nature suggests an

opened its hospital in the city of Met in what is now the northernmost part of the Pilisyari Union, and according to the historian Jon Man served over twenty thousand people a year, carting dozens of men in by the day on men-driven carts across what was likely an extremely advanced road system made possible by the 'Mist'. Their techniques were grounded in both exodial printempraeic and technical orations to compensate for their members' relative lack of tessiture, along with a series of purely physical techniques allowing for the stabilisation of a patient in the absence of oration. These were not recorded in great detail, and have since been lost to time[3].

The collapse of the 'mist' occurred around 11 Septimus 1301[4], extinguishing the Monarchy in its entirety. The Wards and a handful of patients were all that remained after, and the hospital became a monument to the vanquished civilisation; the survivors set about mourning, and, unsure of their fates or futures, began to fall into abject despair. This state of affairs persisted for over three months before the arrival of Pa Gudman, a Ward who had traversed four hundred kilometres from the ruins of his city with his paramour Jak Parmans by his side; he had subsisted solely upon what the Tower could give him. He ascended the podium in the hospital's hall, drawing an enormous audience, and began his speech with the words that serve as a motto for the Wards today:

These men are fit to die.

Pa, having firsthand seen the devastation wrought by the dissipation of the mists, had come to the decision that anything not originating from the Tower—by then in the North a semi-mythological but no less physical notion—was of an infernal nature, inherently impermanent, and argued that the Tower alone was responsible for all 'true' things. A charismatic voice amongst despair, he reorganised the Wards' hospital into a religious order dedicated to the worship of the Tower and its gifts, amongst which he included humanity.

The Wards and their patients, numbering about two hundred

---

origin ancient enough that it predates saepological redundancy. This is likely what led to its sudden and genocidal collapse.

[3] Quite a few of these techniques have been reconstructed and some are still discussed hypothetically by more advanced hospitallers within the Order, but they have not been tested for fear of causing unnecessary death.

[4] This date is uncertain. It is said that the collapse of the 'mist' could be seen on this date from Met, though the horizon would have been far too close for such a thing to be possible. It is far more likely that this was the date that the last cart arrived.

and three hundred respectively, were organised into two separate orders: the hospitaller order, for the Wards, which would treat patients and train new Wards, and the misericordial order, which would clean, take care of financial matters and retrieve patients. The former would be headed by Pa, whereas the latter would be headed by Jak.

Wardship cut a swathe south towards the Tower over the next eight hundred years in a strange, slow pilgrimage. Its strict academic prerequisites never let it grow above five hundred thousand members, mostly recruiting from orphans and patients with quick wits and few other prospects. Its greatest expansion happened during the Musical Revolution, in which almost all Wards abandoned their posts over a period of ten years to head south to the site of the discovery, allying themselves with Kanandrisra's camp and ensuring their place as a fixture in Aimelan society. What growth the Order had was first dedicated mostly to the misericordial order, then diverted into a host of newly formed orders; amongst these are the amanuensic order, which would conduct research into the Tower's machinations, the doctrinal order, which would focus upon the technical saepological education of lay people, and the custodial order, which took the responsibilities of cleaning and disposing of bodies from the misericordial order. Though a Grandfather, the head of the Order, is elected by its various abbots and abbesses once every ten years, he or she[5] has little actual control over the doctrines as written, and is only permitted to make a single substantial change for each term he or she serves. In practice, there is no authority greater than an individual bishop, who exercises control over a city's ministries and has the power to 'excommunicate' those who fail to follow orders.

Though not a particularly popular faith in the North, losing out to the far more ancient Tapatars faith, they and their medical expertise and education are welcomed wherever they go. Their cultural impact is undeniable; the Tower has the name 'Hem of Goed' in Pilyaspek and 'Godspike' in Shelfspeak. In the Zhanghwazh Empire, the Hospitallers are the only medical personnel in the retinues of most noblemen[6], and in most of the South they are the only doctors available.

---

[5] The title is gender-neutral.

[6] As part of Grandfather Maritandrea's Doctrine of Preemption, Wards of the Tower must minimise the impact of war by supporting the side closest to victory at all times; they must not heal losing combatants if it may allow them to rejoin combat. The Hospitallers currently in service to the Zhanghwazh militaries are thus of the understanding that they are not protected by the terms of the Third Concordance, even though they personally do not usually carry arms.

While certain forms of surgery remain almost entirely dependent on tessitura, Ward medicinal techniques have been combined with early Arisirimisatari oration to create a simultaneously tessitura-driven and specificity-controlled form of medical oration. This method allows people with any level of tessitura to perform lifesaving procedures and treatments, and is taught in almost all secular colleges today.

JIM MASKLMEN IS THE FIRST ETHNICALLY PILISYARI CONTRIBUTOR TO STANDING STILL MAGAZINE, AND IS ONE OF THE THIRTY-SEVEN FIRST-TIER CITIZENS AMONGST HIS PEOPLE. WITH THE AID OF THE COMMISSION FOR HABILITATION, HE HAS EDITED AND PUBLISHED SEVEN THOUSAND POEMS AND THIRTY BOOKS ON VARIOUS ASPECTS OF PILISYARI HISTORY BOTH IN CENTRAL AIMELAN AND IN TEPTESRYN-RANTETALK, HIS NATIVE LANGUAGE.

The Wards: Where did they come from and what do they want?
Jim Masklmen
Opposing Editorials, Standing Still, 3379 issue
published by the Aimelan Historical Society and approved for private distribution under the Sixth Decree by Administrator Atfilgaentatresra dar Sinter under the continued grace of the Aimelan Administration

appendix e
Marriages

The day made beautiful by the burning light of the stars above, the barrier tainting the light blue, coloured the scene over the ceremony. The dependant stood before the bride before the flat of hardwood that they could afford. There were about four in attendance before them excluding the dependant's parents, who stood by her side.

The dependant stepped up upon the flat and bowed her head. Her parents stepped back, then, and turned their backs to the two.

"Where have you been," the bride said, her silken hair held gentle by the ground as though it would be a raven leaf upon a tree in the breeze of the land before, "all my life?"

Her lips heavy with the silence of love, she put her head down to the dust before the bride's feet and worshipped the soil blessed by her touch.

Her bride looked down, and bent at the waist as her downwards-facing head arose, and kissed her upon the crown of her skull.

She looked up, then, her eyes with her bride's, and smiled with the lightheartedness of the beloved, and spoke her name and shared their first true kiss as the quivering of her heart greeted the lovers' dawn.

An account of a marriage between two Aimelans under the dependency system witnessed confidentally by a trusted associate of theirs who is Sestiyari

(A Night Bespeckled: A True Romance in the Centre, 3914)

"You have been with my soul, but not my body. You have drifted upon the edges of my dreams to touch upon my mind and pulled away when I needed you most.

You have deserted me countless times upon the break of day like a creature whose home is the night, though the radiance of your body can no longer let your soul's darkness hide as it does amongst the light.

And even now—you have lied, and lied again, and the charges before you are grave. As you stand before me, arrogant in mind as well in stature, a being made of shadow and illusion, unknown to me as she stands before me, what truth untainted by falsehood could you give me that could fill what your lies have left?"

The woman grabbed him by the shoulders, and by the back of the neck, and kissed him as though he were the last man alive, and pulled back.

"I love you," she said, and spoke her name to her husband as he, in a shock rehearsed to perfection, did the same to his bride.

In this way, the two citizens were bound both by the laws of man and of their inner gods.

An account of the marriage of Alantandrea das Cimcharei and Khalisrei das Vasksharei es-Maurenia under the trial system witnessed by the Andityan elector Mirachandra d'Kalleint accientr'Aurkhadra

(Customs of the Aimelans, 3849)

Of all the experiences I had with the Central Aimelans, perhaps none were so remarkable as the ones I had at the breakfast on the 15th of Jan *[nb: 15 Octavius]*.

Breakfast was as usual for this day: spring onions, mint tossed into the brew. I have mentioned earlier that I was lucky to have decided to settle in a place where paste would take more effort to sing than it would for food to grow, but I have not yet mentioned the sheer mind-numbing horror of the cuisine that resulted: while paste would often be flavoured

with varying degrees of piquancy and sweetness
and other pleasant things, and textured with a
fair bit of success, the natural food these men
had become inured to had a habit of making me
violently sick.

But I digress.

Khaladrei y Kambaris had been
sharing a little faux-wood house with Alarissa
Malitandrin for twelve years, then; the colonial
life was hard when they met, and so were they in
equal measure, both for themselves and for the
other.

I understand that the reader has a
certain disposition towards the suspicion that the
journalist exaggerates the facts of each matter he
covers for a story that his poor pressman can sell;
he surely must ask for a fact that ascertains this
woman's prowess.

In my memory, I saw in the corner of
my eye Alarissa's severed breasts in a transparent
jug of saveflesh upon the quaint wooden shelves;
the blood having been drained from them, all
that was left was the pale yellowish fat shrouded
in a shard of pale tawny skin. I had asked her
once why she had done it, and she looked at me
as though I was developmentally retarded before
she spoke:

They were slowing me down.

I asked her, then, why she would put
them in a jug, and I sensed that her childrearing
patience had turned into outright contempt:

I like tits.

That was that, then.

In any case, I would never have thought
that anyone would dare speak the words
Khaladrei did that day, bold as if he were asking
for a bolt:

"Ever thought about getting married?"

Alarissa looked sideways at the man
next to her.

"You're asking me in front of Pip?"

"Pip doesn't give a damn. Do you, Pip?"

I looked up from my soup—so badly

seasoned, mind, I hesitate to call it soup—
solely to shake my head. I wasn't sure it would
have mattered if I did; I had become such an
ornament to them by then that they would likely
have confessed to murder without taking note of
my presence.

"In that case—yeah, sure."

"You've got a real name, right?"

"Pssh. Rivet you, my family's been here
before your paternal granddaddy got his ass
pounded full of your mom and your mommy
ploughed her full of you. I've got more names
than you've got balls."

"Rivet you too, dicktits. I take you to be
my bride."

"I take you to be my husband."

"We shall speak our names and thence
be bound."

So they were.

An account of a union between two
Aimelans under the vow system witnessed by the
Tapkeki journalist Pip Spekrman
(Bauxite's Toil, 3820)

How do foreigners witness our various marital customs?
Andresrea qu'n'av dasnamr
Perspectives, The Songs Our Souls Sing, Octavius 3873 issue
published by the Aimelan Anthropological Society and approved
for private distribution under the Sixth Decree by Administrator
Atfilgaentatresra dar Sinter under the continued grace of the Aimelan
Administration

appendix f
Law

COMBINED STATUTORY ACTIONS; féscrytgyluss cynbinuss faityr, per the law Common, codified & recent: the action, variance, procedure, contraindications, benefits and jurisdictions thereof

In the metropolitan common law, a combined statutory action (known colloquially as a chargesuit) is the term for an ancient form of prosecution in which a person against whose soul, body, name or property an offence has been allegedly committed has the right to petition that the barrister in charge of the prosecution seek restitution against a defendant in the form of a civil suit integrated with the criminal proceedings and subject to the rules of said criminal proceedings sharing a single disposition. The denial of such a petition is generally understood to be subject to judicial review[1].

VARIANCE

The procedure for the combined statutory action, both having existed for over a millennium, (first established almost in its whole by the ruling in *the Throne Ascendant in Adamantine Malachite (Aralielra dar Oder) v. Marantiene dar Parquisant* (2549) Ps. 3 Zhan 2. §24) and being codified in the Vasksharei Document[2] as an optional provision, is fairly consistent across the metropolitan region. Like the rest of the Fifteen Fundamentals, the Vasksharei Document provides that Zhanghwazh rulings on the action bear special significance subject to Aimelan approval. No matters related directly to its practice have ever come into contest in any non-Zhanghwazh appellate court, and none there since 3409. As such, the procedure has remained completely unchanged for over five hundred years.

The motion to combine is used widely in Central Aimela, where most jurisdictions expand the usage of the combined statutory action to almost all cases due to the popularity of singing-hours as a form of debt labour for indigent tortfeasors. The motion is generally avoided by both

---

[1] Oc. Art. 15 §16.
[2] Oc. Art. 15 §13.

Siancestys and private prosecutors in Uytrimela, as the introduction of a civil component to the case allows for the defence to insist that the prosecutor be held liable for their expenses in the event of acquittal as per the Saltic payment rule. Zhanghwazh prosecutors are freer in using it in spite of the classic payment rule, because they are generally compensated by the government.

Procedure

Generally, the prospective tortfeasee, the executors of their will, their next of kin or their well-attested friends, in order of their successive right, approach the prosecutor in the controversy and request that a combined statutory action be initiated on their behalf. Most judicial and executive authorities will provide information on this opportunity to prospective tortfeasees, but access to this information is not currently considered a right by the office of the Executor. If the prosecutor dissents, a formal notice of denial must be provided in the same session, either in the form of a sessile datum or yellowsheet; this may be brought to the local judicial authority and filed with the clerk, elder, assistant or other receiver of documents so that a hearing may be scheduled to determine the merits of such an action. Such an action will only be permitted if the prosecutor dissents if it is not against the interests of the tortfeasee for a motion to combine to be granted.

The prospective tortfeasee may make a special appearance in the action and dissent to a motion to combine so as to preserve the civil case, but not their heirs, even if their heirs would inherit the right to initiate civil action; in cases where the prospective tortfeasee's heirs do not seek to pursue a case or do not exist, the prosecution may push forward in their name regardless, provided the judgement has a place to which it could be reasonably applied. For example, a young victim of an offence against the soul may have their judgement be applied to a trust to their benefit, or in the case of the tortfeasee's death, a fund for youth in similar circumstances.

The motion to combine itself is generally forwarded during the cause hearing for the case in which the prosecutor intends to apply it. Motions tend to be transmitted by sessile before the trial, although verbal motions are generally accepted by the court. At this stage, the onus is on the defence to provide an acceptable reason for any refusal, such as a civil case concluded (under the aegis of judgement completed) or in progress (in awe of judgement awaiting); there are almost no other reasons to refuse an order to combine. However, it is generally in the best interest of the defence to allow the motion to be granted without contest. Notable exceptions exist in the case of indigent tortfeasors, who may be compelled to debt labour regardless of ability to pay depending on jurisdiction.

The court will issue a writ of combination and amend the caption of the case to designate the real party in interest, either by indicating their name and the nature of their interest in the descriptive title to the overarching motion (in Central Aimela) or by indicating that the 'real party in interest' on the prosecutor's part is the person who claims liability in tort on the defendant's part (elsewhere). The case then proceeds as normal.

In Central Aimela, the actual jurisdictional action remains unchanged: the motion hearing proceeds as part of the court's criminal action.

In some trial courts, such as the Court for the First Instance of Determination in Pentelis, a losing defendant will be named the 'defendant-tortfeasor' in the opinion and the real claimant in interest the tortfeasee, mirroring the practice of tortfeasor designation present in all metropolitan law without having the effect of actually designating the defendant a tortfeasor.

The civil component of a combined statutory action may not be adjudicated in the context of a non-judicial proceeding, such as incarceration incident to arrest, corporal punishment administered in immediacy to the offence and other purely executive actions; for example, a petition for a writ of rendition may not be pursued as part of a prosecution for illegal arrest, and must instead form its own petition[3]. While purely equitable relief against a private defendant may be possible, such relief is generally rendered moot either by executive action or as part of sentencing; this makes sense on occasion, however, such as in cases where a victim of domestic abuse seeks exclusive title to their criminal spouse's property, or when a person seeks rescission of a contract as a remedy for criminal fraud in the inducement.

CONTRAINDICATIONS

It is important to understand that a combined statutory action may not necessarily produce a more favourable result for the injured party than a separate civil suit.

Firstly, while the record of a conviction for the same issue may be admitted as evidence of the defendant's fault or misconduct regardless of

---

[3] *The Throne Ascendant in Adamantine Cassiterite (Maliensantra dar Oder) v. Tarasintiene dar Parquisant* (2794) Pr. 4 Zhan 1. §29.

the facts of the case and may trigger an automatic statutory judgement for the value of the identical or substantially similar tort, the pecuniary award to the tortfeasee in the case of a combined statutory action is adjudicated on the facts of the case, which allows the compensation awarded by the civil suit's ruling to be subject to sentencing guidelines depending on the jurisdiction's local rules.

Secondly, an element of civil liability must be proven at the same time as criminal liability, which may in some cases endanger the overall case against the defendant; moreover, certain defences, such as the questioning of judicial notice, are available to criminal defendants that are precluded from civil suits. However, this also provides an incentive for the prosecutor to fulfil their ethical duty of zealous advocacy.

Thirdly, rulings not in the favour of the real petitioner, plaintiff or claimant in interest, whether the defendant is judged guilty or not guilty, may not be appealed due to the rule against successive prosecution[4]. Any attempts to re-file the action are estopped by the same rule.

Fourthly, the compensation awarded as a result of a combined statutory action is subject to the usual rules of collection and enforcement for civil suits, and no special assistance is awarded to the real petitioner, plaintiff or claimant in interest in collecting this judgement. Still, the judgement will necessarily be consistent internally and incorporate orders to facilitate the enforcement of its civil portion.

Fifthly, the defendant is entitled to all the rights available to them as a criminal defendant, which may sometimes include free legal representation. A separate suit allows for a victim of greater intelligence or means to pursue his claim far more effectively against an indigent tortfeasor, even if the criminal case against the tortfeasor is dismissed or he is acquitted.

Sixthly, even upon conviction, the status of tortfeasor will not generally attach to the defendant due to the action's failure to provide the self-financing requirements of tortfeasor designation. This does not apply in the case that the prosecution is self-funded.

Finally and most crucially, the defendant's guilt in a combined statutory action must be proven beyond a reasonable doubt as in any criminal action[5] and not to the median of reason, as in the prosecution

---

[4] *The Throne Ascendant in Luxurious Amber (Lauyung Jin) v. Roussard bin Laurentine d'Aumer* (2810) Pr. 1 Zhou 4. §19.
[5] Oc. Art. 15 §15.

of most civil causes of action, nor to the precipice of doubt, as in actions for punitive damages. As such, a claim that may hold merit in a pure tort action may be thrown out entirely and the defendant shall be under the aegis of judgement completed.

BENEFITS

Firstly, the real petitioner, plaintiff or claimant in interest may not be held liable in tort for vexatious litigation or malicious prosecution in the case of an adverse verdict, nor may they be held liable for any kind of fees for legal representation or other expenses on the part of the prosecution (assuming a public prosecution) or defence unless their initial complaint is proven to have been made maliciously. This holds true even under the Saltic payment rule, in which case the prosecution will pay all fees.

Secondly, due to the inability of the defendant to make a counterclaim, the prospective tortfeasee does not bear any chance of being designated a tortfeasor or having any other sanctions taken against them[6]. This allows a person to make a case for restitution against a person without exposing themselves personally to retaliation nor any expense on their part, this being its initial purpose.

Thirdly, it may be difficult to enforce a civil order originating from a separate suit when it comes into conflict with the stipulations of a criminal judgement. For example, lacking the specialized orders requested and issued in the case of a combined statutory action, a careless tortfeasee—perhaps appearing in their own person—may have to wait for an incarcerated person to serve their entire sentence before debt labour may be enforced. In extreme cases, a combined statutory action may actually be necessary: for example, a person sentenced to death will not have that penalty stayed to enforce a separate civil judgment, whereas executive authorities acting on an order deciding both criminal and civil matters will generally execute multiple sentences in order of severity[7].

Fourthly, the process of discovery is greatly accelerated: depositions are enforced by writ, not requested. This allows for the speedy disposition of cases that may otherwise take months to, in Cimsas and

---

[6] *In re counterclaim of Taofung Ling* (2992). Pr. 5 Tan. 1. §34.

[7] *The Throne Ascendant in Vitreous Hessonite (Arasaine dar Oder) v. Matrielra dar Oder* (2939). Pr. 2 Man 1. §3. See also *Motion to compel the Administration to whip, execute and hold liable in tort Ilamkatandra dar Oder, a soldier of the Aimelan Guard under the ID b11-dapmaa, for raping and murdering Melissa Waterman, a resident of the village Chifflerton subject to the Principate of Solaris*, cs. 14-213-3130; aka 'the Tortious Murderer Ilamkatandra', *In re Satlang Tan on Execution* (2949). 49 Admin. 2d Rptr. 209.

several Saltic cities, years.

Finally, the combined civil action is especially convenient for non-citizens who may not have the legal right to hire an advocate to litigate against a citizen depending on their immigration status, or lower-tier citizens in Aimela who may otherwise be held in contempt of administration for pursuing a potentially illegitimate civil action against an administrator. This consideration is not present elsewhere in the metropolitan region.

As such, the motion to combine or petition for writ of combination is a risky procedure and should only be sought if the civil elements of an action can in fact be proven beyond a reasonable doubt.

OTHER JURISDICTIONS
The combined statutory action is generally not conducted nor allowed in signatory states nor pseudostates outside of the metropolitan region, with the exception of some courts that allow it on a case-by-case basis amongst the Shelf Dynasties. 'Restitution' is sometimes available, usually as part of sentencing or as a separate, minor hearing.

> *Fundamentals of Motion Practice: the Combined Statutory Action*
> Aritinsanfrea das Cimcharei
> *Criminal Procedural Law*
> published by the Department of Education and approved for private distribution by the Administration for Media Development under the continued grace of Khaliesrea das Sikharea eliyit Tamarisrei, Administrator for the Arts

Amitabho Chattopadhyay was born in Singapore.
She began writing Central Aimela
in 2011 and finished it in 2015.

Special thanks to Nahuel Méndez Diodati,
without whose enthusiasm and expertise this
work would not bear the medical verisimilitude
it now does.